"If it's all ~~~~ **it a night."**

"Not yet." Chase reached up and brushed her cheek with his thumb. "I'd give anything to know why you were crying."

Kate froze. The touch of his thumb on her cheek and the warmth of his hand surrounding hers sent a rush of heat all the way through her body and out to the very tips of her ears and toes.

She tugged at the hand held tight in his.

He refused to let go. "Tell me what made you sad. Please." His rich baritone wrapped around her like a lush, sexy blanket, warming her in the chill night air.

Her gaze shifted from his eyes to his lips and a new fire burned from the inside. Chase Marsden was a good-looking man with full, sensuous lips that begged to be kissed.

"Let me help you."

"I'm supposed to be here to help you," she whispered, feeling herself fall into the man's eyes.

CLANDESTINE CHRISTMAS

ELLE JAMES

Published in Great Britain 2015
by Mills & Boon, an imprint of Harlequin (UK) Limited,
Eton House, 18-24 Paradise Road, Richmond, Surrey, TW9 1SR

© 2015 Mary Jernigan

ISBN: 978-0-263-25324-5

46-1115

Harlequin (UK) Limited's policy is to use papers that are natural, renewable and recyclable products and made from wood grown in sustainable forests. The logging and manufacturing processes conform to the legal environmental regulations of the country of origin.

Printed an
by CPI, B

Elle James, a *New York Times* bestselling author, started writing when her sister challenged her to write a romance novel. She has managed a full-time job and raised three wonderful children, and she and her husband even tried ranching exotic birds (ostriches, emus and rheas). Ask her, and she'll tell you what it's like to go toe-to-toe with an angry three-hundred and fifty-pound bird! Elle loves to hear from fans at ellejames@earthlink.net or www.ellejames.com.

This book is dedicated to all my readers.
You make it possible for me to follow my dreams.
I love you all!

Chapter One

Chase sat back in his chair at the Lucky Lady Saloon in Fool's Fortune, Colorado, letting the three-hundred-dollar-a-bottle whiskey and the lilting sound of Sadie Lovely's voice wash over him.

Today marked the anniversary of his obligation to his grandfather's will. In order to inherit all of what his grandfather left him, he had to agree to live at the Lucky Lady Ranch for two entire years without leaving for more than one month out of each year.

Finally, he was free to choose wherever he wanted to go, whatever he wanted to do and whomever he wanted to do it with.

But he wasn't really. In the past two weeks, he'd gone from anticipating leaving the ranch to his overseer to promising to stay until things settled down with Sadie.

Fifteen years older than him, she was a friend from his former playboy life, really an acquaintance who'd saved him from being mugged by thugs and drowning in a gutter when he'd been too drunk and stupid to help himself.

Tough as nails, with a heart of gold, Sadie had held off the thugs with a .40-caliber pistol she kept strapped to her thigh beneath her evening dress. She'd dragged him into her home, sobered him up and asked for nothing in return.

He'd offered her his friendship, and even got to know her grandson, Jake, a cute little boy with curious green eyes. He wasn't sure what had happened to cause Jake's mother to crash her car, hadn't asked and Sadie hadn't volunteered the information. It was clear she was raising the boy to the best of her ability.

When she'd come to him two weeks ago, scared and in need of his help, he'd opened his doors to her, set her up with a job at one of the businesses he'd inherited from his grandfather and helped her move her and her grandson into his big empty house on the Lucky Lady Ranch until she could get set up in a place of her own.

Sadie ended her song and descended from the stage to sit in the chair opposite Chase. In her late forties, she was still an attractive woman, with smooth curves and a sultry smile. "I'm glad you came."

Chase sat forward, the mild buzz from the alcohol clearing as he leaned forward. "I came as soon as I got your message. I must say I'm surprised you agreed to perform tonight."

She shrugged. "I never know when a threat is real or just a threat. All I know is that I can't live my life like this. I have to work to support my grandson. Speaking of which." She bit her lip, the lines around her eyes more pronounced than usual. "I want to make sure you're still good for my backup should anything happen to me where Jake's concerned."

"I'm his godfather now. I'd do anything for the kid."

She reached across the table and touched his arm. "Even raise him as your own?" Sadie held his gaze.

Chase's chest tightened. "That won't be an issue. He's got you."

"I'm serious. I have a bad feeling."

"We moved you from Leadville to give you a new start. Hopefully, whoever burned down your house won't follow you here. You should be okay."

She smiled. "I have a limited number of skills. Changing my name and hair color hardly constitutes going incognito when all I'm qualified to do is sing and…"

Chase covered her hand. "Look, Sadie, you're done with that other life. You don't have to go back to entertaining men. You have a good job here, where all you have to do is sing for a living." Though he subsidized her earnings, he wasn't telling her. He owed her his life.

She nodded. "Thanks to you. I'm just afraid my past is catching up to me."

"Why? What has you scared?"

"I had another empty message on my voice mail. On my new cell phone." She bit her bottom lip.

"It was a computer-generated sales call gone bad." Chase shook his head. "What else do you have?"

"I feel like someone is following me. Watching me." She turned her head and stared out at the practically empty barroom. "Especially today. Every time I turned around I saw nothing, yet I can swear someone is there. Waiting. Watching."

"Sweetheart, after having a stalker following you around for the past few weeks, you have a right to feel paranoid."

She pulled her hand away from his. "It's more than that. When I left my dressing room earlier, I locked the door behind me. I went back because I forgot my throat spray. The door was open. I know I locked it."

"Perhaps the janitor?"

"He doesn't come on until after midnight."

Chase's anger simmered just beneath the surface.

Sadie was his friend and he hated seeing her so distraught. "I placed a call to a man I know of who provides specialized, undercover bodyguards. I asked specifically for a woman to blend in with you and the saloon."

Tears welled in Sadie's eyes. "A bodyguard?" Then she shook her head. "I can't pay you back. Not yet."

"No need. I don't like the idea of you and Jake in danger. At least you'll be safe at the ranch until you find a place of your own. And hopefully, we'll discover who's stalking you and nail the jerk before you move back to town into your own place."

She smiled. "In the meantime, I need to know that you'll be there for Jake, if anything happens to me. You're the only one he trusts besides me and the Quaids." She leaned closer to him. "Chase?"

"Yes, Sadie?"

"If anything should happen to me, I want you to have this." She pressed something cold and hard into his palm and curled his fingers around it.

"What is it?" He could tell by the shape, it was a key, but to what?

"It's the key to my safe-deposit box at the First Colorado Bank in Denver. You, me and my attorney are the only ones who have access to the box. He has authority to turn it over to the police should you and I disappear."

"Which you aren't, and I'm not," he assured her.

Sadie took a deep breath. "I'm sorry I haven't told you everything about me. The safe-deposit box has information in it that would explain a lot. I can't say that I've lived a perfect life. Far from it. Basically, it's a compilation of my secrets and Melissa's, Jake's mother."

Chase snorted. "As if I would be the one to judge."

Sadie gave him one of her gentle smiles. "You've changed in the past two years, Chase." Her forehead crinkled. "I'm glad you're not drinking as heavily, but I think you've lost some of your fire."

It was his turn to smile at her. "The last time you gave me advice, I slowed down. Are you telling me I slowed down too much?"

"You did the right thing. You were on a suicidal path. Your grandfather's will was just the ticket to get you back on track, not me."

"I wouldn't have come back to Fool's Fortune if it hadn't been for you."

Her mouth twisted. "Sure you would have, if for nothing else but to spit on your grandfather's grave for the way he disinherited your mother."

"My parents might still be here if he hadn't been so hard on my mother."

Sadie clucked her tongue. "You don't know that."

"Well, they wouldn't have been living in New York City. My mother never liked living anywhere else but Colorado."

"That's the past. As a wise man once said to me, you have to let go of your past to live in the present or you will have no future."

Chase sat across the table from Sadie, the woman who, despite her former trade, reminded him of the mother he'd lost six years ago. He pocketed the key, determined to guard Sadie's secrets. "Thanks, Sadie. Rest assured. I'll take care of Jake if anything happens to you."

She nodded. "That's all I ask."

"Now let me take you home."

"I drove my car here. I can drive it home." She pushed to her feet, a tired smile curving her lips. "I should be okay."

Chase shook his head. "I won't take no for an answer."

He, too, rose from his seat. "Besides, I'd like the company on the drive back to the ranch."

"Are you sure you don't mind that Jake and I are staying with you at the ranch?"

"The house is too big for just me and the Quaids." With a smile, Chase added, "Jake should be sound asleep by now. Knowing Frances, she's plied him with homemade cookies and read him several books by now. Probably let him stay up late, despite his nine o'clock bedtime."

Sadie's lips twisted. "I'd be angry at her, but she's so good with Jake and he adores her. The poor boy needs a mother."

"He's got you."

"And I love him with all my heart. Too bad Melissa didn't live to watch him grow into a man. Hard to believe she's been dead almost six months."

"Still hurts, doesn't it?" Chase slipped an arm around the older woman and hugged her to him as they walked to the little room behind the stage where Sadie had left her faux fur jacket hanging on a coat rack.

Sadie stopped in front of the coat rack and waited for Chase to gather her coat and hold it out to her. As she slipped her arms into the sleeves, she said, "A mother should never have to bury her own child."

Jake let his hands rest on Sadie's shoulders for just a moment. "You never told me what happened to Melissa."

"She ran her car over the side of a cliff. The police ruled it an accident, but the people who knew her said she'd been acting funny, almost paranoid."

Jake shrugged into his coat, his eyes narrowing. "Do you think she committed suicide?"

"I wouldn't put it past her. But then, she exacerbated her problems by continuing to put herself front and center of trouble." Sadie's shoulders sagged, making her appear every bit of her forty-something years. "I should have spent more time with her when she was a teen."

"If she was like every other teen, she wouldn't have wanted you around."

"You don't have any kids scattered across the country, do you?" Sadie pinned him with her stare. "You were the wild one for a while there."

"No, I was sure to protect the women I'd been with… and any child that might have resulted, from getting a father he couldn't count on." Fishing his keys from his pocket he held the door for Sadie.

She touched his cheek as she stepped through the door. "You would make a good father."

"I don't know why you think that. My father was never home. He and my mother never settled for long."

Sadie smiled. "I know because I can see what a good man you are."

Chase led the way out the back door and around the side of the building onto Main Street. The wind had picked up, sending a chilling blast from the snowcapped peaks surrounding them down to the streets. Bowing his shoulders, Chase did his best to block the wind from Sadie as they crossed Main Street, their feet making sharp clicking sounds on the icy pavement.

"When are you going to find yourself a woman to share your life with?" Sadie asked.

"Again, my parents weren't the best advertisement for marriage. I'm not the least in a hurry to find a woman to settle down with. I like my solitude and I'm beginning to like the seclusion of the Lucky Lady Ranch."

At the middle of the street headlights shined in Chase's eyes. He lifted his hand to block the brilliant glare blinding him. "We'd better hurry." Chase gripped

Sadie's arm and guided her toward the other side of the street.

Before they reached the sidewalk, tires squealed and the vehicle sped up, aiming directly for them.

"Run!" Chase shouted, shoving Sadie toward the sidewalk, then he turned to face the oncoming vehicle.

KATHERINE RIVERS BLINKED tired eyes as she entered the outskirts of Fool's Fortune, the quaint Colorado town in the middle of the Rockies. It was well past eleven o'clock, Texas time, and she'd been on the road since four that morning.

All she wanted was to get to the Lucky Lady Saloon, find a bed to crawl into and save the introductions to her new assignment, Chase Marsden, until after she'd had a decent night's sleep. She wasn't even due in until tomorrow. Surely a good night's sleep would boost her spirits and set her on the right path with this new job and her first CCI assignment.

The streets, cheerfully decorated in bright Christmas lights, were pretty much deserted with the occasional car passing. Small town life would suit her fine after the insanity of Houston traffic and crime.

Her GPS indicated she was two blocks from the saloon on Main Street. She could see the neon lights of a building ahead and presumed it was her destination. Two shadowy figures emerged from the entrance and started across the street. Good. Maybe the place would be empty and she wouldn't have to speak to anyone but the desk clerk.

Her back ached and the scar on her belly twinged at the enforced inactivity of driving across Texas and New Mexico all day. She needed to move, to perform the stretching exercises the physical therapist had armed her with after her surgery.

She snorted. A broken-down Texas Ranger, medically retired after a shoot-out gone wrong. Some bodyguard she'd be.

Faced with finding a job sitting behind a desk, Kate had been more than happy to accept Hank Derringer's offer of employment in his supersecret organization, Covert Cowboys, Inc. Although, being female, she wasn't sure how that worked. Technically, she was a cow*girl*, born and raised in the panhandle of Texas on a four-thousand-acre ranch.

She knew her way around horses, cattle and a barnyard. The fourth daughter of a rancher, she had never felt she was a disappointment to her father, who would probably have preferred sons to carry on the Rivers name.

Her father treated her like any other ranch hand, only with a whole lot of love and care. She could ride as well or better than any man on the ranch and she'd done her share of roping, branding and castrating steers. Her sisters had preferred to work in the house, but knew how to ride and feed the animals.

Her father boasted she was as good or better than any son he might have had and he wouldn't have changed a thing. When she left the ranch to join the Texas Rangers, Kate Rivers wasn't afraid of anything.

All that had changed in one night, one fateful shoot-out.

Resisting the urge to floor her accelerator and finish this trip, Kate pushed away thoughts of that night eight months ago and maintained her speed, her goal in sight.

A dark SUV darted out in front of her from a side street.

Kate slammed her foot on the brake pedal and skidded to a halt.

The SUV's tires spun, screeching against the pavement, and then it sped toward the saloon.

Kate fired off a round of curses and hit the accelerator, her adrenaline pumping, angry at the idiot's disregard for other traffic on the road.

As quickly as her heart leaped, it came to an abrupt halt when she noticed the two people who'd left the saloon running toward the other side of the street.

The SUV driver seemed to head straight for them, increasing his speed instead of slowing to allow them to make it to the other side.

No.

Kate punched the gas pedal, a gasp lodged in her throat as she watched the scene unfold, unable to stop it.

One figure pushed the other toward the sidewalk and then turned to face the oncoming vehicle.

"Fool!" Kate yelled inside the confines of her truck cab. She slammed her hand onto the horn. "Get out of the way!" she screamed.

The SUV swerved at the last minute, ran up onto the sidewalk, clipped the man in the side and hit the other figure head-on.

"Oh my God!" Kate's stomach lurched.

Thrown by the impact, the figure landed hard on the concrete and rolled to a stop against the front of a brick hardware store.

The SUV bumped back onto the pavement and sped away, disappearing out the other end of town.

Heart rampaging inside her chest, Kate skidded to a halt, grabbed her cell phone and jumped down from her truck.

Dialing 9-1-1, she ran toward the two people on the ground, reliving a nightmare she'd hoped never to experience again.

A dispatcher answered on the first ring.

"We have a hit-and-run on Main Street in front of the Lucky Lady Saloon. Two people down, send an ambulance ASAP!" Kate barked into the phone. Without waiting for a response, she shoved the phone into her pocket and bent to check the first person she came to in the middle of the street.

A ruggedly handsome young man pushed to a sitting position. "Don't waste your time on me, for God's sake, check Sadie," he said, his voice raspy.

Altering her direction, she pushed on, leaping up onto the sidewalk.

An older woman, possibly in her forties, wearing a long faux-fur coat, lay tragically still at an odd angle against the side of a building.

Kate dropped to her knees, swallowing hard on the lump lodged in her throat, her eyes blurring. The last time she'd hurried toward a body, it had been her partner's.

For a moment, she froze, paralyzed by her memories. She'd thought the nightmares would have stopped by now. But she was awake and she was seeing Mac's face, his eyes open, his expression slack in death.

Kate closed her eyes for a second and forced herself back to the present and the woman lying in front of her. When she opened her eyes, she reached out and touched her fingers to the base of the victim's throat. For a long moment, she felt nothing, and her heart sank into the pit of her damaged belly.

Then a slight pulse bumped against her fingertips and a hand reached up to grasp her wrist.

Kate flinched and would have pulled back, but the woman's eyes opened and she stared up at her. "Jake."

The man who'd been hit stumbled to his hands and

knees and crawled to Kate's side. "Sadie?" He knelt beside her and took her other hand. "I'm sorry. I should have seen that coming."

Sadie gave an almost imperceptible shake of her head. "Not…your…fault." Her fingers tightened on Kate's hand. "Jake."

"He'll be okay," the stranger stroked the older woman's hand. "I'll make sure he's safe while you're getting better."

Sadie shook her head, closing her eyes. "Take care of Jake. He needs a family…to love him." The last words came out in a rush on nothing but air. Kate had to lean down to hear. The words made a sob rise up in her throat, which she choked back, determined to be strong.

Sirens sounded in the distance.

Kate felt again for the pulse in the woman's throat, praying for even the slightest tap against her fingertips. "Sadie, hang in there. The ambulance is on its way."

The woman's grip on her wrist slackened and her hand fell to the hard, cold concrete.

"Damn it!" Kate eased the woman flat on her back and ripped open the fur coat. Trying to remember all the times she'd trained on CPR, she laced her fingers together, and pressed the heel of her palm against Sadie's chest, chanting in her head with each compression.

You will live. You will live.

The man kneeling beside her checked Sadie's pulse and shook his head. "Let me take over."

"No," Kate snarled, continuing the compressions as the blaring sirens grew closer.

A sheriff's SUV arrived first, the deputy leaping out of the driver's seat. "What happened?" he said as he dropped to the ground beside Kate.

Kate jerked her head to the injured man. "You tell him." She continued applying compressions, refusing to give up. She'd be damned if someone else died on her shift. Not on her first day on the job.

The next vehicle to arrive was the ambulance.

A sliver of relief washed over Kate, but she wouldn't give up on the compressions until the EMTs were out of the vehicle, with their equipment and ready to take over.

"We've got it," a uniformed man bagged Sadie and another nudged her arm.

Kate couldn't stop, afraid that if she did, Sadie wouldn't live.

"Ma'am, you need to let us take over." The EMT took her hands and forcibly removed them from Sadie.

More hands locked on her shoulders and dragged her to her feet. "Let them do their jobs," a man said near her ear, his breath warm on her chilled cheek.

Kate stood on wobbly legs. Her back ached and her arms felt like limp noodles. She couldn't take her focus off Sadie, afraid that if she did, the woman would die.

The man who'd been hit by the SUV, slipped an arm around her waist. "Lean against me. The medical techs will take good care of Sadie."

"I have a pulse," said the EMT forcing air into Sadie's lungs.

"Thank God." The one providing the chest compressions eased off. "Let's get her loaded into the ambulance."

They eased Sadie onto a backboard, braced her neck and got her onto a gurney.

The man Kate had been leaning on left her side to follow the procession to the ambulance.

Kate wrapped her arms around her middle, for the first time since she'd leaped out of her truck aware of the biting cold and her lack of a warm jacket. She shivered, but didn't make a move toward her truck, her attention glued to the woman being carried away.

As the EMTs approached the open end of the ambulance, the woman gasped, sucking in a deep breath. "Chase!"

"I'm here, Sadie." Her companion ran to her side and clasped her hand.

Opening her eyes for only a moment, Sadie said, "Where's Jake?"

"At the ranch. Don't worry, I'll take care of him," the man named Chase said. "You concentrate on getting better. Jake loves his grandma."

Kate stood to the side, her focus on the woman, heart hurting for her, and the grandson that stood a good chance of losing his grandmother.

When the doors closed on the ambulance, the sheriff's deputy touched Chase's arm. "You should ride with her to the emergency room and have the doctors check you over, too."

"I can't." The man shook off the deputy's concern. "I have to get back to the ranch."

"Do you want someone to drive you there?" the EMT asked.

"No. I can get there myself." He turned to face Kate, his face pale and haggard for such a young and vibrant man. "Thank you for doing what you did for Sadie."

Her body trembling from the cold, Kate forced a casual shrug, ruined by the full-body tremor that shook her to the core. "I'd have done it for anyone."

"That's good to know. If you hadn't come along when you did, no telling what the driver of that SUV might have done next." He held out his hand. "Anyway. Thank you for saving Sadie. She's a good friend."

When Kate clasped the man's hand an electrical charge zipped up her arms and into her chest. "I'm just glad I decided to push on, rather than stopping back in Albuquerque."

"Where are you headed?"

She nodded toward the Lucky Lady Saloon, stomping her feet to keep warm. "I'm hoping to find a room at the Lucky Lady tonight. I have a reservation for tomorrow night, but, like I said, I decided to drive through instead of stopping."

The man's brows dipped. "Are you here on vacation?"

She glanced around at the Christmas lights and decorations on the buildings and streetlamps. "Though it's a pretty little town, from what I can see in the dark, I'm here on business."

"Meeting anyone I might know?"

She shrugged, not sure she wanted to share information with him. Kate figured she'd better jump into her role, the sooner the better. "I'm auditioning for a singing position on the stage at the Lucky Lady Saloon." Her hand still warmly clasped in his could feel the instant tightening of his fingers.

"Auditioning for who?"

Never having sung on stage in her life, she figured, performers had to be personable and outgoing to attract a crowd. She forced a friendly smile when she'd rather be on her way to her room, a warm blanket and a recharging night of sleep. "I'm meeting with the owner, a Mr. Marsden. Do you know him?"

"I do." The man's hand squeezed hers once and he let go, his face grim, his lips pressed tightly together. "What's your name?"

"Kate Rivers," she answered.

"Is your talent agent Hank Derringer?"

She nodded, her brows furrowing. How many people in Fool's Fortune knew she was coming and that Hank

Derringer had sent her? Immediately on guard, she sized up the man in front of her. He was tall, darkly handsome, with a face that could have been on the silver screen. "As a matter of fact, Hank is my agent." Or rather, she was Hank's secret agent. "Your name is Chase. It wouldn't be—"

"Chase Marsden." The man's lip curled upward on one side, his blue eyes dancing with the reflection of the streetlights. "Pleasure to meet you, Ms. Rivers."

"Oh, dear." Her heart fluttered and butterfly wings beat against the insides of her belly. She glanced around as the sheriff's deputy jotted notes on an electronic pad. Kate lowered her voice. "I guess you needed…a singer more than I realized."

"I wasn't the one I was hiring you for. I wanted you to provide backup to Sadie. She's the star."

Kate's eyes widened. "Sadie, the woman on her way to the hospital as we speak?"

He nodded.

"I take it the situation has gotten a lot more dangerous than you'd originally let on." She glanced around. "Looks as though I'm a day late."

Chapter Two

Chase had asked for Hank's help in finding a woman who could blend in with Sadie's everyday life.

The brown-haired, green-eyed woman standing in front of him was not what he had in mind for blending in with Sadie's world. Her hair was pulled back in a low, no-nonsense ponytail at the nape of her neck and she wore little, if any, makeup around her brilliant green eyes fringed by thick, naturally dark lashes.

This woman intrigued him. What woman was gutsy enough to take on the job of bodyguard? Especially one who looked as if she could chew nails with her teeth and still have enough warmth in her heart to help a wounded animal. Kate was attractive in a girl-next-door way, not the typical female type Chase usually went for. But then, he'd never dated a woman longer than a month and usually was the one to break it off, finding them boring with only enough ambition to find the next great fashion statement to wear.

Chase tore his gaze away and asked, "Can you even sing?"

Her spine stiffened and she drew herself up to her full five feet eight inches. "I sing in the shower all the time."

Chase glanced at the saloon and thought better of it. He wanted to get back to the ranch and check on Jake.

"Skip the saloon. I know of a place you can stay and not put up with the noise of the bar." He hooked her arm and started back across the street, sure to look for any oncoming, insane drivers before he took one stop off the sidewalk.

Kate dug her heels into the ground. "If it's all the same to you, I don't know you. You say you're Chase Marsden, but for all I know, you're someone else."

Chase dug his wallet out of his back pocket, wincing at the sting of road burn on his palms. He flipped open the bifold and held up his driver's license.

Kate leaned closer to read the printed name. "Okay, so you are Chase Marsden, the man Hank sent me to meet."

"I'd take you back into the saloon and fill you in on everything that's happened, but I really need to get back to the ranch and check on Jake."

"Jake? That's the name Sadie called out several times."

"Jake is Sadie's grandson. He's with my housekeeper right now and I want to make sure whoever hit Sadie doesn't head out to the ranch for Jake."

"You think someone is targeting Sadie and the child?" Kate asked.

"I moved Sadie and Jake to Fool's Fortune a couple weeks ago after their house burned down. They narrowly escaped."

"Accident?"

Chase shook his head. "The fire chief of Leadville said it was arson. They didn't have anywhere else to go, so I brought them to Fool's Fortune."

"Why would someone target Sadie and her grandson?"

"I wish I knew. Then I might have a clue as to who was doing it."

"All right, we'll have to do some digging to find out who might be targeting them. In the meantime, let's get out to the ranch and check on the boy," Kate said. "We can go in my truck, since it's right here and you look a little worse for the wear, having been run over by a speeding SUV."

Chase glanced at the big black truck. "That's your truck?"

Kate shrugged. "Comes with the job when you go to work for Hank."

"I don't mind letting you drive." He rubbed a hand through his hair and winced. "I must have hit my head harder than I thought."

Kate tilted her head toward the truck. "Get in."

Chase climbed into the passenger seat while Kate slid behind the wheel. "The roads can be tricky at night in the Rockies."

"Then you'll have to stay awake long enough to guide me." She shifted into Drive and pulled away from the curb. "Which way?"

Chase got her going on the correct highway. He dug his cell phone out of his pocket and dialed the hospital before they got completely out of town and lost cell phone service.

Sadie had arrived at the county hospital and the doctor was working with her. So far she was holding on, but she hadn't woken up since she'd last spoken with Chase. Because of sketchy vital signs and possible internal injuries, they'd intubated her and placed her in a medically induced coma.

With the connection crackling in his ear, Chase thanked the informative nurse and rang off.

"How is Sadie?" Kate asked.

His jaw tightened and he stared straight ahead. "They've intubated her and she's in a coma."

"I'm sorry to hear that." Kate glanced his way. "Are you related to Sadie?"

"No, why do you ask?"

"Most hospitals won't give out that much detailed information about a patient unless it's to a close relative."

Chase shrugged. He'd donated a considerable amount of the fortune he'd inherited from his grandfather to the little hospital to give the locals a place they could trust for their medical needs. Everyone in the hospital knew that. "Sadie gave the hospital and her primary care physician a medical power of attorney for me to inquire about her medical conditions and needs. I'm the only family she has."

"Everybody needs somebody," Kate muttered.

"What did you say?" Chase asked, sure he'd heard her, but giving her a chance to expand.

"Nothing."

"Hank told me he was sending a former Texas Ranger to help out."

"And he did." Kate's gaze never left the road in front of her. She wasn't offering much in the way of information. If he wanted to learn more, he'd have to drag it out of her.

Chase had the advantage, sitting in the passenger seat. "Why did you give up the Texas Rangers?"

"It wasn't my choice," she said, her voice flat, unemotional.

"Were you fired?"

She shook her head. "No."

"Then what happened? Surely they aren't downsizing like so many corporations in America."

"No." She let out a long breath. "I was medically retired from injuries received on the job."

Chase nodded. He'd noticed a little hesitation when she'd risen from Sadie's side, but had attributed it to the situation.

Having been in several car wrecks during his younger, more daredevil days, he knew the pain of old injuries.

Kate shot a narrow-eyed glance his way. "If you're worried I can't handle the job, don't. In hand-to-hand combat, I can still take down a man twice my size and I fired expert on Hank's range using the .45, nine millimeter and .40-caliber handguns."

His lips quirked and he couldn't contain his smile. "That's all good to know. Have you ever worked undercover?"

She didn't answer at first. "No, but I've worked on SWAT-type ops several times, infiltrating and neutralizing several large meth labs." Her fingers gripped the steering wheel so tightly, her knuckles turned white.

"Is that where you were injured? On one of those missions?" he asked softly.

For a long time, she didn't answer, but the tightness of her lips gave her away.

"In another mile you'll turn off the main highway onto a small road. There will be two big stone columns with a sign arched over them in wrought iron."

Kate slowed the car, turning in at the gate to the Lucky Lady Ranch.

For a gate that had stood for almost one hundred and fifty years, it was still in good shape with a coat of black paint applied every other year to the ironwork. The only change had been the addition of an automated gate opener with a keypad.

Had Chase thought ahead, he'd have grabbed his remote control from his truck before they'd headed to the ranch. He gave Kate the code, trusting her from the moment she'd thrown herself into saving Sadie's life.

After she punched the number in, Kate waited for the gate to swing open. "To answer your previous question, yes. The last meth lab sting was also my last mission as a Texas Ranger."

The drive up to the ranch house was completed in silence. As they cleared the twisting mountain road and emerged on the hilltop, the moon overhead shone down on the mansion his great-great-grandmother had built from the proceeds of the Lucky Lady Gold Mine before it had run dry.

The huge structure loomed three stories above them with its colonial-style verandas and double layered porches wrapped around the entire house. The only concession to the deep snow and frigid winters of the high country in Colorado was the steep roofline. Though the original roof had been of split shingles made of hardened hickory, the new roof his grandfather had installed consisted of highly polished aluminum. The snow never stuck, simply sliding off.

Frances Quaid opened the front door and Barkley bounded out. The giant black-and-tan Saint Bernard raced across the ground to the truck.

Kate remained in the driver's seat, the door closed. "Yours?" she asked.

"That's Barkley. He's friendly as long as you don't try to attack me, the Quaids or Jake." He climbed down from the truck and braced himself.

Barkley reared up on his hind feet, standing nearly as tall as Chase and weighing almost as much. He planted his paws on Chase's shoulders and gave him a big sloppy kiss.

"Okay, okay, you've said your hellos. Behave yourself now, or you'll scare Ms. Rivers away."

Kate stepped down from the truck and rounded the front.

Barkley dropped to all fours and loped over to sit at her feet, his big tongue lolling out the side of his mouth. He barked once, the sound deep and booming. Then he nudged her hand with his nose. At first stiff, Kate reached out a hand, allowing the dog to sniff. When Barkley nudged her again, she ruffled his ears, a small smile curling her lips.

Chase watched in amazement as her expression transformed. From tense, almost pinched features, her entire face lit up as she smiled down at the dog.

Seeing her happy for the first time, tugged at Chase and made him look at her in a different light. Not as an agent sent by Hank, but as a beautiful woman who stirred his blood and made him want more than he should from a bodyguard.

"He's not shy, is he?" she asked.

"Not in the least. And he knows what he wants, which is more than I can say about most people."

Kate bent to run her fingers through the dog's long coat and to scratch his head. "Not much of a watchdog, are you?"

"On the contrary, Barkley would lick any intruder to death before they could get to the front door."

The big dog proved Chase's point by laying a long wet tongue along the side of Kate's cheek.

"Ugh." Kate straightened and scrubbed the dog slobber from her skin.

"Consider yourself initiated into the family." Chase dragged his gaze away from Kate and glanced up at the porch where Mrs. Quaid stood.

"Mr. Marsden, Jake refused to go to sleep until you got home. Will you come in and tuck him in so that he can finally close his eyes?"

Chase nodded. "I'll be right in. Seems Jake will be staying with us longer than we first thought."

Mrs. Quaid frowned. "Is everything all right?"

"No. But we'll discuss it after Jake goes to sleep." Chase hooked Kate's elbow and leaned close. "I'd rather no one but you and I knew why you're really here. I'd like to initiate the undercover op now."

Kate ground to a halt. "What do you mean?"

"Go along with what I say." He tugged her arm, escorting her up the stairs. "Mrs. Quaid, I'd like you to meet someone special."

The older woman turned a welcoming smile on Kate.

Chase performed the introductions. "Mrs. Quaid is my housekeeper, and in charge of keeping me sane. Her husband is my foreman-overseer and my right hand when it comes to all things to do with the ranch. I inherited the Quaids when I inherited the Lucky Lady Ranch from my grandfather. And believe me, they were the best part of my inheritance. Without them, I would probably have sold the Lucky Lady."

Mrs. Quaid's cheeks pinkened. "Oh, go on, Mr. Marsden."

"I really wish you'd call me Chase. You're more like family than just a housekeeper." Chase faced Kate. "Speaking of family... Mrs. Quaid, this is Kate Rivers... my fiancée."

KATE NEARLY TRIPPED on the step she had been climbing when Chase announced her as his fiancée. Chase had invoked the undercover op, but playing the part with his own employees seemed to be overkill. Kate struggled for something to say when her tongue was tied with the surprise of her engagement. "Mrs. Quaid, happy to meet you."

The older woman gripped both of her hands in her own and grinned. "Oh, my. And I didn't know Mr. Marsden even had a girlfriend. How did you keep this from us over the past two years?"

Chase smiled and circled Kate's waist with an arm, cinching her snugly to his side. "You know all those monthly trips I took to Denver?" He tipped his head toward Kate. "Let's just say, I wasn't alone."

What the hell was he trying to prove? If these people were as close as family, he'd just lied to them.

"What a surprise. I can't believe our own Mr. Marsden is engaged."

Mrs. Quaid pressed her hands to her cheeks. "When did you arrive in town?"

Kate leveled her gaze on Chase. "I came over from Denver today for the first time and bam. I'm just as surprised as you." Which wasn't far from the truth. Mrs. Quaid seemed like a nice lady, but Chase must have his reasons for lying to his housekeeper.

"I'm so happy for you both." Mrs. Quaid touched Chase's arm. "But you better check in on Jake. He's missing his grandma. I'll put on a kettle for tea. When's Ms. Sadie coming home?"

"She's been in an accident. She's in the hospital."

Mrs. Quaid pressed a hand to her chest. "Oh, dear. Is she going to be all right?"

"I hope so." Chase touched her arm. "Jake only needs to know she's staying in town for a few days."

The older woman nodded. "Understood. If there's anything I can do for her…"

"There's not much any of us can do for her. She'll

have to get well on her own." Chase glanced around. "Where's Mr. Quaid?"

"He's checking on the horses. He thought he heard something. He should be back by the time you tuck in Jake."

"Good. I need to talk to you two about some issues that have arisen." He grabbed Kate's hand. "Come on, there's someone I'd like you to meet."

Her heart thundered in her chest and her belly clenched, the scar tissue seeming to tighten around a wound that would never heal. "No, really, I can wait in the kitchen with Mrs. Quaid."

"It will only take a minute and it will be worth it. I promise."

The big warm hand holding hers, tugged her toward the staircase.

Once out of earshot of Mrs. Quaid, Kate asked, "Was it necessary to introduce me as your fiancée?"

He didn't let go of her hand as he climbed the stairs. "I thought it might make it easier for you stay here and be seen with me and not generate more questions."

Kate trudged up the steps, her breathing abnormally fast for the little amount of exertion. She had already worked back up to her usual three-mile jog every day. A few stairs shouldn't have had a debilitating effect on her lungs. As much as she'd like to blame it on the stairs, she knew it was the thought of tucking a little boy into bed that had her breaking into a cold sweat and struggling against the desire to run right out the front door and all the way back to Texas.

She thought she was ready to face the world. But she really wasn't. Sure she could fire expert, shoot a perp and perform physical training all day long, but being around a child was beyond her endurance.

At the top of the staircase, Chase made a left turn and hurried down the hallway to the second door on the right. He pushed the door open and peered into the shadowy interior. "Jake?" he whispered softly. "Are you asleep?"

Chase let go of her hand and opened the door wider, allowing a beam of light to cross the bedroom floor to the full-size bed in the middle.

"No, I'm awake," a small voice called out. "I was waiting for you and Grandma."

"You gotta stop doing that. Young bodies need sleep to help them grow." Chase entered the room and settled on the side of the bed. He brushed his hand across the boy's forehead, pushing back a swath of dark brown hair, almost the same color as Kate's.

Kate fingered the long ponytail over her shoulder, her heart gripped in her chest. She didn't want to move into the room, afraid the walls might close in around her.

Barkley the Saint Bernard pushed past her and sprawled on the floor at the end of the bed.

"Where's Grandma?" Jake leaned up on his elbow and stared straight at Kate. "Who are you?"

Ignoring his first question, Chase answered the second. He held out his hand to Kate, an invitation to step into the room. Somehow, she managed to move one foot in front of the other until she stood beside the bed and glanced down at a little boy with green eyes, who looked entirely too small to sleep in such a big bed by himself. "Hi," she said.

Chase clasped her hand and drew her closer. "This is Kate Rivers. She's coming to stay with us for a little while."

Jake smiled and settled back against the pillow, a huge yawn splitting his little face. "Are you staying for Christmas?" he asked, his eyelids drifting closed.

Kate shook her head, but the boy didn't see her through his closed eyes. She shifted her gaze to Chase, trying not to stare at Jake, his little body buried beneath the sheets and a thick goose down quilt.

Despite being a tomboy from the moment she could strut around in her own cowboy boots, Kate had pictured herself with a big family of her own, she'd wanted half a dozen boys for her dad who'd gotten stuck with three froufrou girls and a tomboy.

The day the meth lab sting went down, she'd lost not only her partner, but she'd been shot in the gut, the bullet damaging both her uterus and ovaries. Having been a Texas Ranger from the time she'd graduated college with a degree in criminology, she'd hardly slowed down long enough to consider what she wanted next in life. In the back of her mind, she'd always known she eventually wanted kids.

After her last botched mission with the Texas Rangers, Kate's injuries had cut off any chances of her ever having children. Those kids she'd pictured having would never be.

"Miss Kate will be here through Christmas," Chase assured the boy. He let go of Kate's hand, pulling her back to the present, and brushed the hair out of Jake's face once more, then stood.

Jake's eyes opened. "Grandma always kisses me good-night. Where is she?"

"She had to stay in town for a few nights." Chase leaned over the child and pressed his lips to the boy's forehead. "There, that will have to do for now."

He blinked his eyes open again, his gaze shifting from Chase to Kate. "Can't Miss Kate kiss me, too?"

Chase turned to Kate, his brows raised. "It's totally up to Miss Kate."

Kate took a step backward, ready to make a run for the door.

Jake captured Kate's gaze with his own green-eyed one. "Please."

Frozen to the spot, she couldn't leave. Not with that trusting gaze gluing her to the floor. She wanted to run, but couldn't. Her feet carried her forward to the bed, where she leaned over the little boy.

He closed his eyes, a smile curling his sweet lips.

Her pulse pounding in her ears, Kate had to follow through. She brushed his forehead lightly with her lips.

"You're pretty, Miss Kate," Jake said on a sigh.

Kate straightened, the warmth of the little boy's skin seemingly imprinted on her lips. How could one little boy have so much impact on her?

She opened her mouth to tell Jake good-night, but a lump the size of her fist lodged in her throat and her eyes blurred.

Chase shot a glance her way.

Kate turned, hoping he didn't see her moment of weakness.

"Good night, little buddy." Chase tousled the child's hair and reached over to switch off the lamp on the night-stand.

Glad for the darkness, Kate gulped to force the lump back down her throat. She nearly stepped on a teddy bear lying on the floor. With a sob rising up in her chest, she bent, retrieved the bear, crushed it to her chest and ran for the door.

What was wrong with her? She hadn't cried when she'd bent over her partner's inert body, performing CPR while she bled from her own wounds. Nor had she cried when the doctor entered her hospital room after they'd performed surgery on her, only to tell her Mac had died on the operating table in the room next to her, despite all his efforts. She hadn't cried when the doctor told her she'd never have children.

In the shadowy room, her eyes swimming in unshed tears, she didn't see Chase until she crashed into the solid wall of muscles.

His arms came up around her and he steadied her. Glancing over her shoulder at the boy, he hooked an arm around her waist and guided her through the door.

Barkley lumbered to his feet and started to follow them out of the boy's room.

"Stay," Chase said, his voice gentle, but firm.

The dog dropped to his belly on a rug, laying his chin between his two front paws.

Chase closed the door halfway. Without saying a word, he led Kate down the staircase, grabbed their jackets and ushered her out the back door onto a wide, wooden porch.

Outside, she broke free of his grasp and walked to the steps leading down, wondering if she could make it to her truck without being stopped.

"What's wrong?" Chase asked, his voice so close, he had to be standing behind her.

She shook her head and brushed a hand across her eyes, realizing she still held the worn teddy bear in her other hand. Swallowing hard, she pushed the lump in her throat back and half turned, shoving the toy toward Chase. "Could you take this to Jake? He might be missing it." Her voice sounded gravelly to her own ears. She hated that she was showing emotion when she was sent to be a bodyguard, not a basket case. Kate should have known it was too soon after all that had happened.

"He was half-asleep before we left the room. I'll take it to him later." Chase reached for her empty hand

and held it. "Do you want to talk about what happened in there?"

"No." Kate turned her back to him, staring out into the darkness. "Look, Mr. Marsden—"

"Call me Chase."

"Chase," she said. "I can't work for you."

"Why?"

Kate shook her head. "I'm not the right person for this job." Hank had assured her she was ready, and that she could handle the assignment. He'd been wrong. Had he told her a child would be involved…then what? Kate wouldn't have thought she'd react so strongly to Jake's request for a kiss. But it hit her like a punch to the chest.

Kate would never have children of her own to hug and kiss good-night.

She dug her cell phone out of her back pocket and stepped down off the porch. Swiping at more tears forming in her eyes, she punched Hank's number and walked toward the barn.

As was typical of Hank Derringer, he answered as if they were continuing a conversation. "Oh, good, you made it there."

"Hank, my body to guard is in the hospital."

"What happened?" he asked.

She filled him in on the details and added, "Marsden wants me to stay on, even though Sadie is in the hospital."

"I think you should. Perhaps you can figure out what's going on."

"That's just it." She screwed up the courage to back out of her first assignment. "I don't think I'm the right person for this job."

"Kate, darlin', I wouldn't have sent you if I didn't think you could handle it. You're the best shot, and you know how to defend others as well as yourself."

"You recruited me and sent me here because I'm female," she stated, her tone flat. "Don't you have someone else who could take my spot? I'd rather chase down drug cartel members or serial killers."

"I'm limited on female agents right now. Maybe if you tell me what's wrong about the job, I can help you figure out a way to handle it."

Her hand shook as she held the phone, trying to think of the words to describe all that was wrong with this assignment. None of the words she came up with sounded nearly convincing enough in her head. She stared down at the teddy bear she still held in her other hand. "I just can't."

"Well, do me a favor and stay on the job for at least a couple days while I see who I can pull to take your place."

She wanted to wail and gnash her teeth. A couple of days might as well be a lifetime. The more she was around these people, the more she'd be reminded of what she no longer could have.

"Kate, I'm counting on you," Hank said softly. "And so are they. Do this for me until I come up with a plan."

Her shoulders sagged. Short of quitting her job working with Covert Cowboys, Inc. she had to do as asked. "Okay. I'll do what needs to be done." She sucked in a breath and let it out. "But only until you find a replacement."

"Tell him to send someone to guard Sadie," Chase said from behind her.

"I heard," Hank acknowledge. "I can get one of the cowboys up there tomorrow, but getting a female to take your place will be trickier."

"Do what you can." Kate ended the call and stared

out at the snowcapped mountains and clamped her teeth together.

Chase placed his hands on her shoulders and turned her toward him. He stared into her eyes, the starlight reflected in his blue eyes. "Are you leaving us?"

Kate sighed and faced the man. Though her first instinct was to run as far and as fast as she could, she had to say, "I'm staying. For now." She had no choice, other than to quit. And Chuck Rivers didn't raise a quitter.

Hank's offer had been the only one she'd gotten in the past six months. Who else wanted to hire a broken former Texas Ranger?

Chase let out an abrupt sigh. "Good. With Sadie in the hospital, I could use all the help I can get. Jake lost his mother not long ago. He needs to know he has people who aren't going to leave him."

Guilt settled like sour milk in the pit of her belly. "I said I'm staying," she snapped, angrier at herself for her desire to leave Chase and the boy behind.

"Thanks." Chase tugged her hand, bringing her closer.

Kate staggered forward frowning. "If it's all the same to you, I'll call it a night."

"Not yet." Chase reached up and brushed her cheek with his thumb. "I'd give anything to know why you were crying."

She froze. The touch of his thumb on her cheek and the warmth of his hand surrounding hers sent a rush of heat all the way through her body and out to the very tips of her ears and toes.

His cool blue eyes seemed to burn a hole through the wall she'd so carefully constructed around her emotions. The same wall that had taken a direct hit when a little boy asked her to kiss him good-night. A moan rose up her throat and out her parted lips before she could stop it. She tugged at the hand held tight in his.

He refused to let go. "Tell me. What made you sad, please." His rich baritone wrapped around her like a lush, sexy blanket warming her in the chill night air.

Her gaze shifted from his eyes to his lips and a new fire burned from the inside. Chase Marsden was a good-looking man with full, sensuous lips that begged to be kissed.

"Let me help you."

"I'm supposed to be here to help *you*," she whispered, feeling herself fall into the man's eyes.

He bent and lightly swept his lips across hers, the touch so soft, at first Kate thought she'd imagined it. Then he crushed her to him, his arms clamping around her waist pressing her body against his, his mouth coming down over hers.

The second time his lips touched hers, she had no doubt she was being kissed.

When his tongue slipped between her lips, she opened to him, allowing him to delve into her mouth and caress her in a long, warm, wet glide.

Kate leaned into him, her knees suddenly too weak to hold her steady. Her arms rose to lace behind his neck as the hard evidence of his desire nudged her belly.

For a moment she lost herself in a kiss that should never have happened.

Eventually, they surfaced to breathe. At that point, a rush of awareness slammed her feet back to the cold hard earth and she tugged against his grip. "I can't do this."

"Do what?" he breathed against her mouth and traced her lips with his tongue.

She wavered, her body swaying toward him. "I can't.

Do. This." Finally, she planted the teddy bear against his chest and pushed back. "This is wrong."

He let her step back, but retained his hold on her wrists. "Please. Don't go. I promise not to ask you to do anything you're not comfortable with. All I ask is that you stay and help protect my friends. They need you." His gaze burned into hers and she could feel herself melting.

"I told you I'd stay." She finally pulled free of his hold, and pressed the teddy bear to her chest, holding it like a shield to guard her from a man who had heartbreak written all over his face. "Now, if you have a blanket, I can sleep on the couch."

"As far as my housekeeper and foreman are concerned, you're my fiancée and my guest. I have plenty of bedrooms. You can sleep in one of them. I'll have Mrs. Quaid prepare one for you. Shall we step inside before we freeze out here?"

Feeling the cold for the first time since she stepped outside, Kate preceded Chase into the house. His hand rested on the small of her back, reminding her of how dangerous it would be to like this man. He was a job, nothing more.

Even if his touch sent tingles across her skin and filled her chest with a sense of anticipation.

Chapter Three

Chase rose before dawn, a terrible habit he'd picked up when he'd moved to the Lucky Lady Ranch. This far out in the mountains, when the sun went down, there wasn't much to do but sleep.

All the years of late-night partying with beautiful women and staying up until dawn had taken their toll. The thought of going back to that lifestyle held no appeal to him. After a year on the ranch, he'd become accustomed to the slower pace and the clean, fresh air. After two years breathing clean mountain air, smoky bars would kill him.

He'd started getting up early when William sprained his ankle jumping down from the loft in the barn. He'd been forced to either take over the farm chores or hire out the work. Since he valued his privacy at home, he chose to take over some of the chores, rather than hiring additional ranch hands. Chase discovered a love of working with the animals. Even mucking horse stalls was a balm to his wayward soul.

For the two years he'd been forced to stay at the ranch his grandfather left him, he'd focused on the end of that time frame, thinking he'd leave when he'd served his sentence. Now he knew he couldn't leave. He loved the place. William and Frances had become family to him and he couldn't imagine living anywhere else.

As he crawled out of bed, he could feel every bruise and strained muscle he'd suffered from the bump he'd endured by the runaway vehicle the night before. He'd called the hospital before he'd gone to bed and learned Sadie was holding her own, but that she was still unconscious in the chemically induced coma.

How he'd break it to Jake that his only living relative was laid up in the hospital and they didn't know when she'd come home, he wasn't sure. First he had to help William take care of the animals.

Pulling on an old pair of jeans and his cowboy boots, he dressed in a chambray shirt and a sweatshirt, shoving a hand through his hair. He was long overdue for a haircut, but he hadn't made a special trip to Fool's Fortune during the day to take care of it. At the ranch, no one cared if his hair grew long. Reporters didn't follow him around here. In fact his paparazzi days seemed to be over, for which he was eternally grateful. There was something to be said for becoming a hermit and guarding his anonymity.

He paused as he passed the room across the hall from his.

No sounds came from inside. Kate was probably still asleep, dressed in her oversize T-shirt and gym shorts. How a woman could make sloppy clothes look that sexy was a mystery to him. One he would love to explore, inch by incredible inch of her body.

He'd caught a glimpse of her crossing the hallway from the guest bathroom. The sight of her long, beautifully defined legs was enough to keep him awake until midnight, imagining what those legs would feel like wrapped around his waist.

Chase's initial impression of Kate had been one of a take-charge woman who lived, worked and breathed her job as a protector and bodyguard.

He hadn't been prepared to see her nearly break down when Jake had asked her to kiss him good-night. The tough-girl facade crumbled in that moment, and he saw the real Kate between the cracks in her wall. A soft, caring, heartbroken Kate. He wondered what had caused her so much pain that a child's plea would carve a huge chink in her armor?

At the top of the stairs, he heard the faint sounds of pots and pans clanking and dishes being stacked as well as the murmur of voices.

Frances always rose with William and cooked the men a hardy breakfast.

As he descended the stairs and headed to the back of the house to the kitchen, Chase was surprised to see Kate gathering flatware while Frances cracked eggs into a skillet. William sat at the roomy kitchen table, pulling on his boots.

Frances turned with a spatula in her hand and a smile on her face. "There you are. Grab yourself a cup of coffee, the eggs will be done in a minute." She returned her attention to the skillet and the bubbling eggs. "We were just getting to know Kate. She says she grew up on a ranch in the Texas panhandle and she learned how to ride practically before she could walk. She'll get along fine around here."

Chase frowned. Frances already knew more about Kate than he did. "She's a woman with many talents." And secrets. His gaze met hers as he passed the table to reach the coffeepot.

Frances cast a smile over her shoulder at Chase. "Now

that you're here, tell me how you two met. I'm sure it was purely romantic."

Chase's hand froze on the handle of the coffeepot. When he'd come up with the idea of Kate going undercover, he hadn't completely thought through the entire story, and that he'd have to play it out with his most trusted employees and friends.

He knew how much Frances liked to gossip with the quilting ladies in Fool's Fortune and word would get out quickly that way, cementing Kate's story.

"Well?" Frances shot another glance over her shoulder and then flipped the eggs in the skillet.

Kate's cheeks reddened. "I'll let Chase tell the story. He's so much better at it." Her brows rose in challenge, her gaze pinning his.

Chase took his time pouring his coffee, while he scrambled to come up with a plausible story. "We met outside a bar."

"A bar?" Frances grimaced. "Was it at least a swanky bar?"

Chase shrugged. "It was nice enough."

"What did you do to get her attention?"

Chase chuckled and took a seat at the table, wrapping his hand around the coffee mug. "She barely even acknowledged my existence at first. She was busy helping someone else."

"What was your first indication she might be the one for you?" Frances asked.

William frowned. "Frances, the kids might not like answering all your questions."

"Oh, shush, William. I live vicariously through Chase. He's had a much more interesting life than we have." She scraped scrambled eggs onto several plates and set the skillet aside. Grabbing two of the plates loaded with eggs, toast and bacon, she carried them to the table. "Go on, Chase."

"Well, you could say I fell for her the first time we met." Chase caught Kate's attention. "How could I not? I mean look at her. She's beautiful, confident and capable of just about anything."

"What about you, Kate?" Frances persisted.

Kate had pulled a chair back, a smile tugging at her lips over his responses when Frances hit her with the question. Chase fought the urge to laugh out loud at the way her smile faded when Frances addressed her and she grappled with an answer.

She looked up, her brows puckering. "I wasn't sure what to think about him. He kind of bowls a woman over."

"He does, doesn't he?" Frances gave Chase an affectionate smile and returned to the counter for the other two plates. "Guess that's why he could have had any girl he wanted." She turned a grin at Kate and carried the plates to the table. "I'm glad he picked you. You seem so much nicer than the women he had all those pictures with in the tabloids. He was quite the ladies' man before he came to live at the Lucky Lady Ranch, weren't you, Chase?"

Kate's brows rose again, questioningly. "He does have a way of making me do things I wouldn't normally do."

"Tell me about the proposal." Frances pulled up a chair and sat next to her husband.

"Now, that's enough. We need to eat and get outside to tend the animals," William said. "Save some of the stories for the evening when we sit in front of the fireplace."

Frances pouted good-naturedly. "Spoilsport." Then

she waved at Chase and Kate. "Please, eat. We can chat later."

Chase spent the next few minutes shoveling his food down his throat. The sooner he got outside, the better. He and Kate needed to get their stories straight if this ruse was going to work. He debated telling Frances and William the truth about their engagement, or lack thereof, but he knew Frances. She couldn't keep a secret to save her life. And he didn't want to burden her with the responsibility.

In record time he polished off the eggs, bacon and toast, pushed his chair back and stood. "Take your time, William. I can get started."

"I'll help." Kate had finished as well, eating heartily, unlike the women Chase had dated who picked at their food and wasted more than they ate, claiming they were always on a diet. Kate didn't have a spare ounce of flesh on her bones, probably from working out.

"No need for you to get all dirty," William said, pushing his half-eaten plate away. "Chase and I can do this."

"I know my way around a barn, and Chase can tell me who gets what. Besides, I'd like to get to know the place." She touched the older man's shoulder. "Finish eating. Chase and I can handle this."

William frowned. "Don't seem right. You're a guest."

Frances chuckled. "Let the two young folks take care of the animals. Can't you see? They'd like some time alone."

The older man's eyes widened and he harrumphed. "Well, then, I guess I could have that extra piece of toast." He reached for the stack of bread in the middle of the table. "I feel like I'm playing hooky from school," he said, shaking his head.

"You do more than your share around here," Chase

assured him. "It won't hurt for you to take your time eating breakfast." He grabbed a heavy jacket hanging from a hook near the back door and handed it to Kate. "Frances, do you mind if Kate wears your jacket until I can get her one she can work in?"

"I have my own coat," Kate protested. "It will only take me a minute to get it."

"No, honey," Frances interjected. "Wear mine and save yours. No use getting it all dirty. And wear my mud boots. It gets pretty sloppy around the barn when it snows."

"Thank you." Kate pulled on the boots Frances indicated and shrugged into the jacket Chase held out to her. He handed her a knit cap and a scarf, pulled on his own coat, and they left through a mudroom off the kitchen.

Clouds choked the sky, hovering low enough to smother the mountains from view and it smelled like snow. The first snows had already melted and Christmas was just around the corner. Ski resorts were hurting—the owners, ski instructors and lodge workers all prayed for snow. Chase liked it when fresh snow covered the ground and made everything look clean and new.

The only time he didn't like snow was when they still had cattle scattered in the upper pastures. Fortunately, they had herded them to the lower pastures before the first snows fell. Even the few stragglers had found their way down the mountainside in time.

Chase was thankful his animals were all accounted for. With the attack on Sadie last night, he had other concerns more pressing.

Once outside, Kate pulled the collar up on her jacket and adjusted her scarf around her neck.

"It's a little colder in the high country than in Texas," Chase noted.

She nodded, stuffing her hands into her pockets.

"Why did you feel it necessary for me to do this job undercover? Especially around your employees?"

Chase expected the question and answered with, "I love Frances and William, but I don't want to burden them with secrets I don't want the rest of the town to know."

"And why do we need to keep it from the rest of the town that I'm here to protect you, Sadie and Jake? For that matter, who am I protecting? If it's Sadie, I should be at the hospital."

"They have a security staff at the hospital. I'm certain no one will be able to get to her in the ICU." Chase reached for the handle on the barn door and opened it, holding it for Kate to enter.

She paused on the threshold, face-to-face with Chase. "People have ways around loose security."

Chase's heart thumped hard against his chest at her nearness and he struggled for a moment to focus on her words. "We don't know if last night's incident was related to Sadie's suspicions. Once we've taken care of the animals, we'll go into town and check on Sadie. It should be visiting hours by then."

Kate entered the barn and glanced around the dark interior. "Did Sadie say who she thought might be following her or why?"

"No. But she did tell me that she was afraid someone was watching her." Flipping the light switch next to the door, Chase followed Kate inside and grabbed a bucket hanging on the wall. "I moved Sadie and Jake here when their house burned to the ground in Leadville. She and Jake didn't have anywhere else to go." He handed the bucket to Kate and pointed to a bin against the wall. "Half a bucket per stall."

Kate nodded, her brows drawing together as she bent

to fill the bucket with grain. "Her house burned. You said the fire department ruled it arson?" She crossed to the first stall and opened it to a sorrel mare. The animal whinnied, tossed her head and stamped her hooves, as Kate dumped the feed into the horse's trough.

Kate reached up and stroked the horse's neck, neither affected by the size and strength of the animal, nor the attitude the mare gave her.

Chase grinned. "Penance isn't usually so easy to get along with."

Her brow rising, Kate glanced back at the horse. "That's the best you could do for a name for this poor creature?" She ran her hand along the mare's neck and across her back as the animal munched on her feed. "No wonder she's full of spit and vinegar."

"She's always been a bit high-strung. But she has a comfortable gait and she's good at herding and cutting."

Kate studied the horse. "Her confirmation is good and she seems sturdy enough for a work animal on hilly and rocky terrain."

"I'm glad you like her. She's yours to ride while you're here."

Her hand stilled on the mare's neck. "Thanks, but I doubt I'll be here long enough to take advantage of the offer."

"I told you, I need you here. I want you to stay until well after Christmas, if Hank can spare you that long."

Kate returned to the feed bin and scooped another bucketful of sweet feed, her gaze on the task. "Even if we resolve the issues sooner?"

"Yes. At this point, the less upheaval in Jake and Sadie's lives, the better."

"So what was the cause of Sadie's fire?"

"Her house burned because of a gas leak. Fortunately,

Sadie and Jake weren't inside the house when it happened because they were late getting home. Had they been on time, they would have been caught in the middle of a terrible explosion."

"Where is Jake's mother?"

"Died in a car wreck six months ago."

"Any connection to last night's attack?"

"Not that I could tell." Chase led a horse out of the second stall and tied it to the opposite wall. He reached for a pitchfork and entered the vacated stall. "You were behind the car that hit us last night. What did you see?" He scooped soiled hay from the floor of the stall and deposited it into a wheelbarrow.

"I would have gotten a license plate number if I'd known the vehicle was going to plow into the two of you." Kate straightened from the feed bin, the full bucket dangling from her hand. "It happened so fast. One minute I was headed to the saloon to get a room for the night, the next, the SUV whipped out in front of me and then went all kamikaze. I thought the driver would swerve away from you at the last minute—instead he turned toward you as if aiming to hit you."

Chase stabbed the pitchfork into the ground, his body aching with the residual effects of the hit. "Was the driver aiming for me or for Sadie?"

Kate shrugged. "I would think whoever was hurt the most was the target, if the driver was in fact sober."

Chase returned to cleaning the stall and Kate went about distributing feed to the rest of the horses in their individual stalls.

"I'd like for you to go to the hospital with me today to check on Sadie."

"Should someone keep an eye on things around here?" Kate asked.

"I'll have William and Frances keep a close eye on the boy. I want you to go with me. Two heads are better than one and I might make a trip into Denver after the hospital."

"Why Denver?"

Before he could answer, the dog let out a string of deep-throated woofs alerting Chase to the arrival of visitors to the ranch.

Chase leaned his pitchfork against the stall, wiped his hands down the front of his old blue jeans and stepped out of the barn into the gray light of morning.

"Expecting guests?" Kate asked, following him out of the barn.

"No." After all that had happened the night before, he hurried around the house, determined to head off anyone who might be there to hurt the Quaids or Jake.

Kate kept pace, half walking, half jogging beside him.

Barkley had beat them to the front of the house where a truck pulled up in the driveway and parked. A man wearing a cowboy hat eased out of the driver's seat and limped to the back door of the four-door truck. Barkley stopped barking and ran to greet the visitor, bumping his nose against the man's leg.

No sooner had the man opened the rear door then a tiny pair of jean-clad legs appeared below the open door and a little boy dropped to the ground. He rounded the side of the truck, a huge grin on his face.

"Mr. Marsden, we came to play with Jake. Mrs. Quaid said it would be all right." The little boy ran to Chase.

Chase dropped to his haunches and almost fell back when the boy flung himself into his arms. "Hey, there, Tad." He chuckled. "You're in good spirits."

"Mom said I could stay all day if you'd let me. Angus is going to stay, too."

Chase rose with Tad in his arms, his gaze meeting the cowboy's. He held out his hand. "Good to see you, Angus."

The cowboy took it in a firm grip. "Had word from a mutual friend you could use a little temporary help on the ranch." His gaze shifted to Kate and he stuck out his hand. "Name's Angus Ketchum."

Kate took his hand. "Kate Rivers."

"My fiancée," Chase added.

Angus nodded toward Chase, the corners of his mouth lifting. "Congratulations. Reggie will be excited to know there will be another female close by." To Kate he said, "Welcome to the high country. It has a way of growing on you."

"That mutual friend you mentioned wouldn't happen to be a guy by the name of Hank?" Chase asked.

Kate's held out her hand. "Hank mentioned you. It's good to have another CCI agent out here."

Angus nodded. "I agree. But I'm only here to help for the short term. I have to be back at the Last Chance this evening. Reggie's got me meeting with her and the contractor rebuilding her house since the fire."

"You know you're welcome to stay here until the house is complete."

"Thanks, but Reggie and I don't want to be a bother to anyone. The folks of Gold Rush Tavern have been good to us during this whole ordeal and we'll be moving into a rental house in town just before Christmas. We'll be all right there until the construction is complete."

"The offer's open if your plans fall through."

Angus tipped his head. "In the meantime, Tad's been champing at the bit to get together with Jake since he heard someone his age moved in nearby."

Chase's lips curled. "News travels fast around here."

Angus grinned. "I'm sure your engagement has hit the grapevine by now."

The boy in Chase's arms squirmed. "Can I go play?"

"Of course. I'll bet Jake's awake and eating breakfast. If he isn't, wake him up. He'll be happy to have someone to hang out with."

"Can I pet the bear?" Tad asked.

"Sure." Chase set Tad on the ground and he was off like a shot.

Once the boy entered the house, Chase faced Angus. "Thanks for coming. I didn't like the idea of leaving Jake. The Quaids don't know that Kate is a bodyguard. I fed them the line that she's my fiancée. I love them and trust them, but Mrs. Quaid has a hard time keeping secrets. I didn't want to put her in the position to keep any more than she has to."

"Understood." Angus turned to Kate. "Hank wants you two to send any information you can find on the vehicle that hit Sadie and any clues big or small that come up. He'll get his computer guy, Brandon, to dig into anything and everything he can. He already has him looking into Sadie's and her daughter Melissa's background to see if anything pops up."

"Good." Chase let out a long, slow breath. "In the meantime, Kate and I will be paying a visit to Sadie in the hospital. From there, we might take a drive up to Denver. I have something I need to check on."

"I understand Sadie's house burned down." Angus snorted. "Seems like too much of that going around."

"I only got involved in this when Sadie called in a favor. We got confirmation from the Leadville fire chief that they'd ruled the cause of the fire to be arson." Chase's lips thinned. "Had I suspected it was more than an accidental fire, I'd have called Hank sooner."

Kate weighed in, "The sooner we figure out who started the fire and tried to make roadkill out of Sadie, the sooner Sadie and her grandson will be safe."

Chase nodded. "You're right."

"I can help with the chores if you want to get to the hospital," Angus offered.

"Thanks. We got a start, but there are more horses needing to be fed. William can help."

"We'll take care of it and I'll keep an eye out for Jake and Tad," Angus said.

Chase led Angus to the barn and showed him the chores needing finished.

William joined them. "We've got it covered. You two go check on Sadie. Frances is worried about her."

"Thanks." Chase met Kate's gaze. "Ready to clean up and head to the hospital and then Denver? There's something there I want to check on as well."

She nodded.

He grabbed Kate's hand and left the barn. She'd been quiet through it all. When they were alone between the house and the barn, she pulled her hand free.

"If Hank has Angus here, there's no need for me to be around."

"You heard Angus—he's only temporary to help us out while we do some digging of our own."

She hesitated. "Okay, but I just don't think I'm the right person for this job."

When she started for the house, Chase stepped in front of her. "Why do you think that? You were fine with it until we kissed Jake good-night. What happened in there?"

"It's nothing." Kate tried to step around him, but he refused to let her past.

"How can it be nothing when you want to run as fast

and far away from here as you can? What is it that has you wound up tighter than a rattlesnake with a new button on his tail?"

"I'm not running and I'm not wound up," she said, her voice rising. "We're wasting time." She turned away, her body shaking.

He gripped her shoulders and forced her to face him again. "It's not a waste of time if I can get to the bottom of what's eating at you. Maybe I can help."

"You can't," she said, her shoulders sagging. "Nobody can." Her eyes filled with tears. "Please leave me alone," she whispered.

"At least tell me what it is." He cupped her chin, brushing his thumb across her cheek. When her bottom lip trembled, it was all he could do not to lean forward and capture it between his teeth.

"It's none of your business." A single tear slipped from the corner of her eye. "It doesn't matter, anyway."

He pressed his lips together, fighting the urge to pull her into his arms. When the tear reached his thumb, he caught it. "Let me be the judge."

"I don't like to be around kids." She jerked her chin away from his hand. "There. Satisfied?"

Chase shook his head. She wasn't telling him something important and he refused to let go of her until she gave him the whole truth. Even if he had to kiss it out of her.

Chapter Four

Kate wanted to run, to hide from the truth. If she just told him, she'd be done with it, but she couldn't. Because saying it out loud made it too permanent, too real.

She shrugged, trying to shake loose from Chase's grip, but he wasn't letting go. Short of taking him down like a perp, she was stuck with him.

"Why?" he persisted. "Did Jake say something that upset you? Hell, Kate, he's just a kid. Kids say stuff they don't even know might hurt someone."

"It's not Jake. He's a great kid. It's all children. I don't like being around children because I will never have one of my own." She pushed her arms up through the middle of his, knocking them away. Free of his grip, she darted around him, heading for her truck.

"Hank was wrong," she muttered. She had to leave. Now. If she lost her job with Covert Cowboys, Inc., so be it.

Footsteps pounded behind her. "Wrong about what?" Chase grabbed her arm and jerked her to a halt. "What was Hank wrong about?"

"That I was ready to handle a case. Obviously, I'm not. I need to get my head on straight."

"When did it go crooked?"

"When I was shot in the gut and my whole world fell

apart." She stared up into his face. "Can't you just let me go? I'm no good to you."

"Not the way you're acting now, you aren't. But you're here. You're my fiancée as far as everyone is concerned, and I'm not letting you wimp out on me. Do you understand?"

Kate wanted to spit in his face and tell him where he could go with his demands, but she couldn't. For a long moment, she breathed in and out through her nose. Then she let go of the tension. "You're right."

"Damn right, I am. And I'm counting on you." His grip tightened. "I need you to focus on finding the people responsible for putting my friend in the hospital." He glared down at her. "Jake isn't going anywhere, and it's up to you and me to keep him and Sadie safe." He shook his head and blew out a sharp breath. "Damn it, don't look at me like that."

She sniffed. "Like what?"

"Like someone just kicked your puppy."

"I can't help the way I look at you—"

Chase's mouth crashed down over hers, cutting off her words.

Shocked at first, she opened her mouth on a gasp. His tongue slipped past her teeth and grazed the length of hers.

The stiffness melted out of her and she leaned into him, absorbing the warmth of his body pressed to hers.

Chase's hands smoothed down her arms and circled her waist, drawing her closer, his mouth plundering hers.

Whatever they'd been arguing about flew from her mind. Never before had she been kissed so thoroughly, and she didn't want it to stop.

When Chase finally lifted his head, Kate dragged in a

deep steadying breath, her tears had dried on her cheeks and she stared up into Chase's angry face. "Okay."

"Okay, you're staying? Or okay, you're waiting for me to let go so you can run like a scared rabbit?"

"Okay, I'll stay." She hated to admit that his tirade was exactly what she needed to snap her out of the funk she'd fallen into the night before. But that kiss. Wow. It had completely befuddled her mind. "I'll stay on one condition."

"What condition?" Chase said, his hands still spread across her back, his hips snug against hers.

Kate tipped her chin upward, pressing her throbbing lips into a straight line. "You don't kiss me again."

A slow, incredibly sexy smile spread across his face and his blue eyes twinkled. "I promise not to kiss you again." He held up a finger. "Unless you want me to."

"That won't be a problem." Kate stepped back, out of his embrace. "I won't want you to kiss me."

"Even to carry off the fiancée cover?"

"Even then. Holding hands will be sufficient. You can tell everyone I'm not into PDA."

"PDA?" he asked.

"Public displays of affection."

Chase's boom of laughter cut through the lump of anxiety that had settled in her chest and belly from the night before and she relaxed. Still, she refused to let him know that. "Are we going to the hospital or not?"

Chuckling, he gripped her hand and pulled it through the crook of his arm. "We're going."

The gesture of endearment kept her close to his side all the way back to the house. When he entered the back door, he was still grinning at her expense, which made her frown deepen.

"Smile," he said. "You're supposed to be in love."

In love? With him? Hardly. But she was a professional and if she was supposed to be undercover as his fiancée, she'd better start acting like it and stop wallowing in self-pity over something she had no control over.

Jake and Tad sat at the kitchen table. Each child had a bowl of cereal in front of him and a glass of milk. Kate swallowed the ready lump in her throat prepared to breeze past them on Chase's arm.

The man stopped and ruffled Jake's hair. "You two stay close to the house unless Angus is with you, do you understand?"

Jake and Tad replied in unison, "Yes, sir."

"And don't knock the bear over. He could crush both of you."

They giggled, their little eyes alight with mischief.

"You have a bear?" Kate asked.

Chase nodded. "In the living room."

Kate cocked her brows. "Live?"

With a grin, Chase shook his head. "Stuffed. I inherited him from my grandfather, along with the Lucky Lady Ranch, Mine and Saloon."

He guided her into the hallway, away from the children in the kitchen.

The tightness in Kate's chest immediately abated. "I take it your grandfather assimilated a great deal of wealth in his lifetime."

Chase snorted. "Hardly. He inherited it from *his* grandmother, Lady Jones, a famous madam. She had quite the business acumen, unlike my grandfather. He did nothing to increase her wealth, preferring to live off the interest of her vast holdings and raise horses."

"And now you own it all. Are you following in your grandfather's footsteps and living off the interest?"

"Not exactly. I've been here for a little more than

two years as a stipulation of my grandfather's and Lady Jones's wills. All inheriting descendants must live at the Lucky Lady Ranch for two years before the estate passes into their hands. At that point I can choose to sell it if I wish."

"And do you wish?"

He hesitated a moment, staring at a black-and-white photo of a young man.

Kate studied the photo. It could have been Chase eighty years ago with the same dark hair and light-colored eyes. She guessed it was his grandfather as a young man.

"At first I counted the days, hoping they'd pass quickly. Soon, the weekends I spent away from the ranch dragged. The activities I used to enjoy, like gambling, clubbing and driving fast cars didn't hold my interest. I found myself wanting to get back to the ranch."

"And now?"

He shrugged. "I prefer the ranch to the fast lane I used to ride in. Now I limit my gambling to the stock exchange, day trading. I find it more profitable and easy to do from the comfort of home. I guess I've become a hermit. Never in my wildest dreams did I envision myself enjoying the merits of mucking horse manure from a stall."

Kate's heart warmed. She'd grown up on a ranch, beginning her career in caring for the animals at the ripe old age of four. She knew the value of manual labor and the satisfaction one got from a job well done, no matter how menial. "Hard work builds character."

"I'm not sure about that, but it definitely builds calluses." He paused in front of the room she'd used the night before. "I'll be ready in ten minutes. How much time do you need?"

"The same," she said.

"That's all? Most women take thirty minutes to an hour to shower, do their hair and makeup."

She crossed her arms. "I'm not most women." Her normal routine usually took about fifteen minutes, and that included sipping on a cup of coffee while she brushed her hair and put on her clothes. She'd had her coffee for breakfast. "Ten minutes."

Kate entered the bedroom, letting the door close behind her. With efficient movements, she unzipped her duffel bag, gathered fresh underwear, jeans and a long-sleeve flannel shirt.

When she stepped out into the hall, Chase had disappeared. Breathing a sigh, she crossed to the bathroom, entered and locked the door behind her. She spent five minutes in the shower, two to brush her hair and one to dress and she was back in the hallway, headed for her room to find clean socks and her boots.

She left the bedroom door open.

The click of boot heels against wood flooring alerted her to Chase's approach. Jamming her foot into her boots, she pulled them on and stood as the man filled her doorway.

His gaze swept her from head to toe, causing an electric tingle to spread from her core outward.

"I'm impressed. I didn't think you could do it."

Ignoring the heat building inside, she straightened. "Don't underestimate me, Mr. Marsden."

"Chase." He leaned in the doorway, his mouth twisting, his blue eyes dancing. "Remember, we are engaged to be married, we should at least be on a first-name basis."

She grabbed a small over-the-shoulder purse and a warm corduroy blazer and stepped past the man in the doorway. "Let's go check on Sadie."

Fortunately, the ride to town was conducted in silence. Kate had spilled more of her life story to this stranger than to most people, including her parents. The only other person she'd ever opened up to was her partner.

And he'd taken her secrets to his grave in that last operation.

Chase drove faster than Kate liked when she wasn't in control of the vehicle. Fortunately, he seemed to know the roads and the speed the truck could handle taking the sharp, hairpin curves of the Rocky Mountains.

By the time they reached the Fool's Fortune hospital, Kate had relaxed against the leather seat, going over the mental images of the SUV attack from the night before and the information about Sadie's house having burned due to a gas leak. If the two events had a common thread, it was Sadie. Not Chase and not Jake.

Chase strode past the information desk and straight to the elevator. Kate stepped into the car with him. When they arrived at the floor, the elevator door opened to what appeared to be an emergency.

A nurse pushed a crash cart past them, headed for a room farther down the hallway. The nurses' station was empty but for one nurse on the telephone, a worried frown pressing her brows together as her gaze followed the crash cart down the hallway. "The patient in room 326 went code blue. We need a doctor here stat."

"Damn. That's Sadie's room." Chase took off after the nurse with the crash cart.

"Sir!" the nurse at the station shouted. "You can't go down there."

Chase ignored her. Kate followed suit, racing after him, her heart thudding against her ribs.

The door was propped open, the room filled with six

nurses, all gathered around the hospital bed. One ripped open the front of Sadie's nightgown, while another prepared the defibrillator. Others checked the tubes and electronic devices connected to the woman.

"What happened?" Chase demanded.

A nurse stepped back, blocking his entry. "Sir, stay back and let us do our jobs."

The nurse from the station grabbed his arm. "Sir, please go to the waiting room. If you're a relative of Ms. Lovely's the doctor will let you know what's going on when he's had a chance to evaluate her condition."

"But she was holding her own last night when I called."

"I'm sorry, sir. A few minutes ago, she stopped breathing. We're doing all we can. You can help by staying out of the way."

Kate touched his shoulder, her heart going out to him and the woman the nurses worked over. "Come on. We need to let them do their jobs."

"Damn it!" Chase slammed his palm against the wall. "Sadie trusted me to take care of her. Jake is counting on me to bring her home. Alive."

"Some things are out of our control. Please. We're only in the way." Kate took his hand and led Chase down the hall to the waiting room.

Once inside, Chase let go of her and paced the length of the small room.

Kate stood near the doorway. The scent of antiseptic cleaners, coffee dregs and desperation made her want to run out of the hospital. The last time she'd smelled that particular blend of scents, she'd been flat on her back in a hospital bed after having her female reproductive organs removed. Her parents hadn't come to Houston for the surgery. Her younger sister was in the hospital in Lubbock having her second baby and they'd been so tied up with her good news, Kate told them her injuries were minor, not to bother coming.

Chase passed her, looking like a man ready to tear the walls down.

Pushing aside her own morose memories, Kate reached out and touched him on one of his passes. "Tell me about Sadie."

"What can I say?" He shoved a hand through his dark hair, the movement frustrated and sexy at the same time. "She saved my life."

"How?" Kate forced Chase to stop pacing and focus on her.

The intensity of his blue gaze made her chest clench. "I was on a one-way trip to hell. She jerked me out of a gutter and back into life."

By his tailored slacks, button-down shirt and classic wool coat, the man had enough money to buy only the best. She couldn't picture him lying in a gutter. "A one-way trip?"

"I gambled and drank too much, drove too fast and bedded too many—" He focused on her as if noticing her for the first time. "I was on a downward spiral into ruining my life. I got into a fight outside the club she worked in Leadville. Before I knew it, I was outnumbered and lying in the gutter behind the bar. If Sadie hadn't come along when she did, I'd have probably died of exposure. Frankly, I deserved it."

Kate shook her head. "No one deserves to die alone in a gutter."

"That's what Sadie said as she half dragged me into her vehicle and took me to the hospital. I spent the next week laid up in a bed in her house, where she fed me soup and a heavy dose of her wisdom." His lips twisted into a smile. "She got me back on track."

"She sounds like an amazing woman."

"Sadie's the best."

"What about your family? Why didn't they help you?"

"I'm the only one left. Otherwise I'm sure my grandfather wouldn't have left anything to me in his will."

"Your parents?"

"Died in a car wreck while I was out conquering the world one whiskey bottle at a time." He slouched into a chair.

Kate sat across from him. "What about Jake?"

"What about him?"

"He's Sadie's grandson. Does Jake have any other family?"

Chase pinched the bridge of his nose. "Melissa was living in Denver when she got pregnant with Jake. She quit her job as an executive assistant at the capitol building and moved back to Leadville to work as a bookkeeper at the club where Sadie sang."

"Tough life for a single mother. Especially when she's going through the pregnancy alone." In her work with the Texas Rangers, she'd seen the seedier side of life, filled with destitute women who didn't practice safe sex or were forced to have sex, got knocked up and had to raise the babies on their own, on what little money they made. "She was fortunate her mother took her in."

"Sadie loved her daughter and was so proud of Melissa when she'd gone on to college and went to work at the capitol."

"And Jake?"

"She thinks the sun rises on the boy. Since Melissa was killed in an auto accident, he's all she has left."

Kate's throat constricted. She knew what it felt like to be alone in the world. She'd distanced herself from her own family, too angry at life's injustices to go home. She'd lost so much and couldn't stand being around her family's home with all her sisters living within ten miles of her parents. They came together once a month for Sunday dinner and shared their joys, their children's accomplishments and personal successes.

What did Kate have to share? Not a damn thing. She didn't want to bring the rest of her family down and she didn't want to sound resentful of their happiness. So she'd been alone through her recovery, her physical therapy and her pathetic attempt at job hunting.

"Who will take care of Jake if Sadie can't do it?" Kate asked.

Chase glanced up, his lips thinning. "I will. I promised Sadie that Jake would always have a home."

As protective as Chase was toward a boy that wasn't his, Kate wondered how he'd be with a woman he cherished. Warmth rippled across Kate's skin at the fierceness of Chase's expression and she remembered how safe she felt in his arms when he'd held her. The man meant what he said. "What about Jake's father? Does he have a say in this?"

"As far as I know, Melissa never revealed the name of the father of her baby. Sadie said she didn't even know who he was, but that Melissa claimed he would never be a part of Jake's life."

Kate shook her head and glanced toward the hallway in time to see a police officer pass by. She rose. "Why are the police here?"

"WHAT THE HELL?" Chase leaped to his feet, his pulse racing.

Together, he and Kate burst through the doorway in time to see the police officer talking with a man in a white jacket and several of the nurses.

"What's going on?" Chase demanded.

One of the nurses spoke. "These are the folks who came to visit Ms. Lovely."

The doctor glanced past the police officer, raising his hand. "Are you members of Ms. Lovely's family?"

Kate and Chase replied as one. "Yes."

"We were able to revive Ms. Lovely and her vital signs are improving. Thankfully, we got to her in time and there doesn't seem to be any change to her brain activity. However, she's still in a coma and will be monitored closely."

The police officer turned to Chase and nodded. "Mr. Marsden."

"Burt." Chase held out his hand. "Good to see you."

"I wish it was under better circumstances," Burt said.

"Me, too."

"I understand Ms. Lovely is a friend of yours and that you two were involved in a hit-and-run last night. The officer who responded to the 9-1-1 call said it could have been an accident. I'm not so sure." Burt held a pen poised over a notepad. "Do you know of anyone who would want to hurt her? An ex-husband, boyfriend, jealous woman?"

Chase frowned. "I don't. She's a nice person. As far as I know, she'd never hurt anyone. Are you here because of the accident last night?"

"I wasn't at first." Burt tilted his head toward one of the nurses who stood with a tissue pressed to her lips, her mascara running down her cheeks. "I got a call from Miss Shaw, one of the nurses on duty when Ms. Lovely went into cardiac arrest. She was first into Ms. Lovely's room when the alarms started going off." He paused, his brows drawing together. "She found a pillow over her face and the oxygen tube yanked out of the wall."

"Damn." Chase's heart sank into his belly. "Last night, before the vehicle hit us, Sadie mentioned she felt like someone had been following her, but that every time she turned around she didn't see anyone."

He explained the reason for Sadie's move to Fool's Fortune and about her house burning to the ground due to arson and how he already had the Leadville police investigating the incident. He'd called Hank before the fire chief's ruling of arson, not leaving anything to chance.

"I'll get the chief involved and call in the state police investigations team. I'll see what I can do to get a man stationed outside of her room, 24/7 until we get a handle on what's happening. I think this case just got bigger than a hit-and-run."

"Anything that needs to be done, you have my full cooperation. An agent is coming from a security firm I know to stay with her. He should be here today."

"Good. We don't have a lot of manpower, but I can get someone in for the short term."

"Thanks." Chase glanced around the hallway, his gaze going to the ceiling corners. He turned to the nurse in charge. "Are those security cameras?"

She nodded.

"Where are the video feeds stored?" Burt asked. "We'll need to review them."

"As far as I know, in the security room in the basement of the hospital." She touched his arm. "We'll take good care of Ms. Lovely. You have my word."

"Do you mind if we join you?" Chase's gaze connected with the officer's. "Sadie's like family."

The officer's eyes narrowed. "Okay, but I can't have you interfering with the investigation." Burt headed for the elevator.

Chase followed, Kate at his side.

The three of them took the elevator to the basement, following the directional signs to Security.

The door to the room stood open, a man in a blue security guard uniform sat slumped over a computer keyboard, a soda can tipped over on its side, spilling sticky drink over the desktop and the floor at his feet.

When Chase touched the man's back, his chair swung around and he tipped over. Burt and Chase rushed forward and grabbed him before he crashed to the ground.

They eased him to the dry part of the floor.

Kate squat on her haunches and checked the man for a pulse. As she did, he groaned and his eyes blinked open, glassy, his pupils dilated.

Kate stood, pulled a tissue from a box on the desk, wrapped it around the phone and lifted it to her ear, pressing the zero for the operator. "We have an emergency in the basement security office. Send medical staff and a stretcher ASAP."

Chase glanced at the array of monitors on the desk. Every one of them had a bullet hole in the middle, the screen shattered. His gaze followed the cables to the actual computer beneath the desk. The case was ripped to shreds by what appeared to be the effects of bullets fired at close range.

Chase knelt beside the security guard. Reading the name on his tag, Chase said, "Mr. Martinez, what happened here?"

The man groaned again.

"He's not in any condition to answer," Kate said.

"Whoever did this didn't want us to see the recording," Burt said.

"I think he accomplished his purpose. That box is fried," Chase said.

A staff of emergency personnel converged on the security room and loaded Martinez onto a stretcher.

Burt herded Chase and Kate out of the way. "I'll have the state crime lab go over this mess. The less we disturb things, the better."

Damn. Chase's fists clenched and his back teeth ground together. Whoever tried to kill Sadie was smart and covered his tracks. But they'd find him. He had to have left some sort of trail and Chase would find him and take him out.

There wasn't much they could do with the computer ruined. Chase grabbed Kate's hand and took the stairwell up to the main floor. Still maintaining a tight grip on her hand, he led her outside to his truck in the parking lot. Even before they reached it, he clicked the remote entry, unlocking the doors.

Kate climbed in the passenger seat and turned toward him as he slid in behind the wheel. "Where to?" she asked.

"We're going to check out Sadie's safe-deposit box in Denver."

Chapter Five

Kate grabbed her cell phone from her pocket as soon as they pulled out on Main Street. "I'm calling Hank."

"Good. If you weren't, I was going to. We need backup on Sadie until we figure out who's responsible and stop them."

As usual, Hank answered on the first ring. "Kate, what's going on?"

"We just left the hospital. Someone tried to smother Sadie."

Hank cursed. "Did Angus make it over to the Lucky Lady this morning?"

"He did, and he's keeping an eye on Jake while Chase and I are away."

Hank shouted to someone on the other end, "Get Bolton on the phone. We need someone up in Colorado today." Kate couldn't make out the muted response before Hank was back. "I'll have my pilot fly a man up to Fool's Fortune today. If you think you need more, let me know before the plane takes off in the next hour."

"I think we'll be okay with the three of us."

"Damn shame about Ms. Lovely. Brandon's been hacking into her accounts, phone records, and anything he can find. The woman was a who's-who in the news twenty years ago. She was Denver's most famous madam."

"Interesting." Kate's brows rose and she glanced at Chase, wondering if he knew.

Hank went on. "Brandon just started in on her daughter's background. I'll have more later."

"Thanks, Hank. Anything will help. Right now, we're flying blind. We're headed to Denver to investigate Sadie's safe-deposit box."

"Let me know what you find," Hank said. "It might help Brandon's online search."

"Will do." When Kate ended the call, she glanced at Chase.

"What did Hank say?"

"He's sending someone up today in his private plane to guard Sadie."

"Good. Not that I don't trust the police, but I know the Fool's Fortune PD, and they really don't have the staff to provide security detail on individual victims."

Kate's gaze didn't waver from Chase. She drew in a breath and asked, "What do you know about Sadie's past?"

Chase's lips curled in a warm smile that set Kate's insides humming. "Enough to know she's a good person."

Pushing aside the effects of his smile, she continued, "Is that all?"

"She did mention she had a past." Chase's mouth firmed. "None of that mattered when she pulled me up out of the gutter."

Kate snorted softly. "It might matter now."

Chase shot a glance to her and then returned his attention to the road. "What do you mean?"

"Apparently, Sadie used to be a madam in Denver." Kate waited for Chase to assimilate.

He nodded. "That's what she meant by her past catching up to her."

"She said that?"

"She mentioned it right before the hit-and-run. That's when she gave me the key to her safe-deposit box at a bank in Denver. She had me added to the list of those who could access it in case she was injured or killed."

"Do you think she kept a record of all her...clients?"

"If she did, I'd bet my last dollar it's in that box."

"Wow. What a legacy to carry around with you."

"Sadie said she'd lived in her house in Leadville for fifteen years. Melissa would have been thirteen, old enough to figure out something was funny about her mother's chosen profession."

Kate could imagine the impact on Melissa if she or any of her friends discovered what her mother did for a living. Thirteen-year-old girls had enough drama in their lives. "She might have quit the profession when she moved to Leadville so that her daughter could lead a fairly normal life."

"Unless she continued with those clients who came to her at the club." Chase shook his head, the smile returning to his lips. "Sadie can be as tight-lipped as the best of them."

"It's too bad she didn't open up more about her client list. If someone has a lot to lose should it be discovered he was having an affair with a madam, he might be willing to get rid of the evidence, namely, the madam. Any major events taking place? Huge corporate takeovers, political campaigns?"

"The senatorial race has just begun in Colorado."

"Who's running?"

Chase's eyes narrowed. "John Michaels is the incumbent and a young candidate is running against him. Michaels's opponent is the son of the late Thomas Garner."

That name tickled a memory in Kate's mind, an image

of a national news report. "The late Senator Thomas Garner? Didn't he die in office a couple of years back?"

Chase nodded. "He was mugged in DC coming out of a restaurant. Stabbed on his way to his car. They took his wallet and left him to die in the cold."

Kate chewed her bottom lip, trying to decide whether the senator's death had anything to do with the attack on Sadie. "You think the two events are connected?"

"Hard to say. He was murdered in DC. Crime is high there. And that was over two years ago."

"It will be interesting to see if his name is in Sadie's little black book."

"Benson Garner is the candidate running against Michaels. He's been in the news recently. They've been showing footage of his campaign tour as he travels around the state. He's supposed to be giving a speech in Fool's Fortune at the end of this week for the annual Christmas tree lighting ceremony." Chase shook his head. "He's too young to have been one of Sadie's clients and he's not married. It could be a strike against him." Chase tapped his fingers on the steering wheel. "But John Michaels, now, that's a man with an agenda."

"What do you mean?" Kate asked.

"His time in office as the governor of Colorado had its ups and downs. He's running for the Senate on shaky ground. If he has any skeletons in his closet that hadn't already been aired, he might be desperate enough to try to eliminate them before they come out to haunt him."

Kate chewed on that. "Won't you feel strange going through Sadie's belongings?"

Chase's jaw tightened. "I can't wait around for her to die before I look in the box. Whatever is in there could have a bearing on the attacks. And, for the record, she *will* recover. She has to. Jake needs her. He's lost enough already."

"Are you afraid you'll be stuck raising Jake?"

"Not at all. He's a great kid and I'd be lucky to have him as my son. Now, whether or not I'll make a good father..." He sighed. "I'll do my best."

Warmth filled Kate's chest at Chase's declaration. "I never considered raising another woman's child. I guess I always thought I'd have kids of my own," she said, her voice low. Kate didn't expect a response and as soon as she spoke the words, she wished she hadn't. They exposed too much of her that she hadn't planned on sharing.

"We all have plans, but when those plans change, we have to regroup and choose different plans." Chase didn't glance her way, instead looking at the highway before him. It was as if he were speaking to himself, offering his own advice for consideration.

Somehow the fact that he hadn't been directing the statement at her gave her the freedom to accept it or reject it without judgment.

He was right.

Kate couldn't cling to her disappointment and the sad knowledge that she'd never have children of her own. As the nurse in the hospital had tried to tell her, there were plenty of orphaned children in need of a mother. Why cry over the inability to bring another baby into the world when there were so many children in need of forever homes? Children like Jake.

They entered Denver around noon when it seemed everyone who could leave their office went out to lunch. Traffic was thick and moving slowly all the way into the heart of the city, where Sadie's bank was located.

They found a space in a parking garage and hiked two

blocks to the high-rise building. The downtown streets were crowded despite the cold wind blasting down from the north. People wrapped in winter coats, scarves and hats hurried along the sidewalks.

As Kate and Chase neared the bank, a large man hunched over in a long black coat, his collar raised against the frigid wind, bumped into Kate. "'Scuse me," he muttered, and moved on.

"Let's get inside." Chase pushed through the door into the elegant lobby of one the largest banks in Colorado. Heat enveloped them immediately and Kate's tremors dissipated.

Chase strode to an information desk and asked to be escorted into the room where they kept the safe-deposit boxes. The receptionist put in a call to someone in another part of the bank and then asked Chase and Kate to take a seat.

Rather than sit, Chase paced the length of the reception area and back. As he came to a halt in front of her, Kate reached out and snagged his hand. "Sit."

"I'm terrible at waiting," he said, but complied, dropping into the chair beside her.

Kate chuckled. "I've noticed."

"Mr. Marsden?" A thin man, probably in his midforties, wearing a tailored suit and an identification badge pinned to his lapel, stopped in front of him.

"I'm Marsden," Chase said.

"Taylor Smythe, nice to meet you." He turned to Kate. "And you are?" He held out his hand for her to take.

Kate took his bony hand and gave it a firm shake, afraid she might break his brittle bones. The man had no grip and it was like shaking a cool, bony and dead fish. "Kate Rivers."

The small man smiled. "It is a pleasure to meet you."

"Miss Rivers is my fiancée. Will we be able to access Sadie Lovely's box today?" He gave the bank employee the box number.

Mr. Smythe slowly released Kate's hand. "Once I've had a chance to verify your identification. Do you have the key with you?"

Chase stepped between Smythe and Kate.

Kate hid a smile. If she was a betting woman, she'd have bet Chase didn't like how long Smythe held her hand. The thought warmed her insides. Chase pulled the key from his pocket and showed it to the banker. Then he tucked Kate's hand in the crook of his arm. "Ready, darlin'?"

A tingle of awareness traveled through Kate at Chase's endearment. No matter that it was nothing but a pretense in front of Smythe, it still left her feeling strangely tingly and feminine. For a former Texas Ranger, that was a feat unto itself. Since her teens, she'd considered herself tough and tomboyish. Never feminine. "I'm ready."

"Come with me." Smythe led them through a maze of hallways into the rear of the building. They were stopped by an armed security guard who checked their IDs. Passing through a metal detector, they were finally led into a vault with many boxes lining the wall. A plain metal table stood in the middle of the room.

Smythe walked to the correct box number and inserted his key into the one of two locks on the box. "Now you insert yours."

Chase pushed the key into the lock and turned it.

Smythe pocketed his key and backed toward the door. "If you need anything, I will be outside the vault."

The man left them alone.

Aware of a camera in the corner, Kate waited while

Chase pulled a long metal box from its mooring in the wall.

Chase leaned over the contents.

Kate hesitated. "Sadie gave *you* the key to her box. Not me. Are you sure she'd be okay with me being in here with you?"

"I'm sure she would. You're here to protect her. Hank sent you with a glowing recommendation. I'm sure her secrets will be safe with you."

Kate rubbed her arms, the chill of the vault seeping through to her bones. "I would never share any of her secrets."

"Good, because you're a smart woman, and I could use someone with good detective skills to help me figure out who is after her."

Kate peered into the box, finding it difficult to concentrate with Chase so close. His shoulder brushed against hers, temporarily paralyzing her with a shock of electricity. What was it about this man that had her insides tied in knots? She'd been around handsome men before. Some of the Texas Rangers were really nice to look at, but they weren't like Chase.

The owner of the Lucky Lady Ranch exuded the self-confidence of a man completely comfortable in his own skin and answerable to no one.

And he smelled wonderful. A heady combination of aftershave and the outdoors, evoking images of the Rocky Mountains, snow and blue skies so clean you felt you were breathing pure heaven.

He glanced her way, his blue eyes darkening. "Are you all right?"

She shook herself out of the trance he unwittingly held her in and focused on the items in the box. "I'm fine." Her attention zeroed in on the little black book nestled at the bottom of the box with several velvet-covered jewel cases. "I thought little black books were a myth." Kate lifted the book from the container and held it for a long moment, staring at the black leather cover with a scrolling *S* embossed in the center.

With all the care of someone entrusted with an infamous woman's secrets, Kate opened the book and stared at the even lettering of the words written across its pages.

There were dates, names and hours scrawled in the book. "This will take time to go through," Kate whispered.

"We can bring it back with us."

Reluctantly, Kate closed the book and returned her attention to the box. A stack of letters were tied together with a pink ribbon. Addressed to Melissa Smith, they were smooth, flat and wrinkle-free. "I wonder who wrote letters to Sadie's daughter."

"I don't know. Bring them. We might gain some insight into Melissa and perhaps her admirer."

The rest of the box contained stock certificates and a list of all of Sadie's accounts. Chase pocketed the accounts list and closed the box, leaving the stock certificates inside.

"Let's go. I'd like to go through this at the ranch where I'm not under video surveillance." He tipped his head toward the camera in the corner.

"Right." Kate tucked the little black book in her palm and held it against her belly, letting her jacket hide it as much as possible. If the black book was what made someone want to kill Sadie, it would make anyone carrying it a brand-new target.

Chase placed the box in the slot, shoved it home and twisted the key to lock it. Taking Kate's arm, he led her to the vault door and knocked once.

The door opened immediately and Smythe held it wide. "I trust your visit was satisfactory?"

"Yes, thank you." Chase moved past the banker, stepped through the metal detector and nodded at the guard as he marched Kate back to the bank lobby.

Outside, the wind had picked up. As they hurried toward the parking garage, snow began to fall.

Kate's hair blew across her face, temporarily blinding her. She slowed to shove the strands back behind her ear. People passed on the sidewalk, hurrying toward buildings or vehicles, anxious to get out of the biting wind and snow. Chase still held Kate's arm as they turned the corner and entered the darker interior of the parking garage.

A shadow detached itself from the stairwell and rushed toward them.

Before Kate could react, a man dressed all in black with a dark ski mask covering his face lunged for Chase, knocking him to the ground. Since Chase was holding on to Kate's arm, he half dragged her down with him. She stumbled and threw out her hands to break her fall, landing on her hands and knees.

The black book launched from her grip, sliding to a halt near the back tire of a car.

After scrambling up off Chase's inert form, the man in black dove for the book.

Kate swept her foot out to the side, catching his leg, and sent him crashing into the car, headfirst. Then, scrambling across the ground on her hands and knees, Kate snatched the book and rolled to the side, attempting to get out of reach of the man who'd attacked them.

She wasn't fast enough. He grabbed her ankle and yanked her toward him, his arm cocked, ready to swing.

With her gun locked in the truck for safekeeping
while they'd entered the bank, Kate had no other choice
but to throw her arms over her face and brace for the
blow.

Chapter Six

Fear and rage pushed Chase to his feet. Acting on pure instinct, Chase cocked his leg and powered his booted foot into the face of the man about to hit Kate.

The attacker's head jerked back and he slammed into a concrete beam, loosening his grip on Kate's ankle.

She crab-walked backward, clutching the book in her hand.

Chase dragged the man up by the collar of his jacket and slugged him in the gut.

The attacker doubled over and then surprised Chase by ramming into him like a football player tackling the quarterback.

Chase fell backward, smacking into the ground so hard it knocked the breath out of him. He absorbed the brunt of the other guy's fall as the big man bounced on top of him. Even without oxygen in his lungs, Chase rolled and, taking the man with him, shoved him off his chest.

Their attacker lay stunned for a moment, then scrambled up onto his hands and knees and stood. He walked toward Chase still lying on the ground.

"Don't even think about it!" Kate shouted as she leaped onto the man's back and locked her arm around his throat.

Winded and dizzy, Chase shook his head to clear it. What the hell was Kate doing? The man outweighed her by at least a hundred pounds. Still gasping for breath, Chase staggered to his feet, praying he'd be in time to keep Kate from being injured by the perpetrator. "Let him go, Kate!"

"No way," Kate said, her voice strained. "He has a few questions to answer."

The man in the black ski mask grabbed her arm, ducked low and flipped her over his head.

She fell hard on the ground, rolled to her feet but was too late.

Their attacker dove for the exit. Ducking out of the garage, he ran out into the thickening snow.

Kate ran after him. By the time she reached the exit, she slowed to a stop, snow blowing into her face from outside the garage. "Damn."

Chase raced up beside her. "Are you okay?"

"I'm fine. But that bastard got away."

"I don't give a damn about him. I'm just glad he didn't hurt you." Chase gripped her shoulders and turned her to face him, his fingers rising to cup her cheeks. "I thought he was going to kill you."

"I'm okay." She smiled. "And I saved the black book."

Chase stared down into her face as snowflakes dusted her hair and eyelashes. When the attacker had leveled him on the parking deck, he'd been helpless to protect Kate as the bad guy turned on her. He couldn't move fast enough.

Now she looked up at him, smiling, happy to have saved the black book. Never mind that she could have been seriously injured. Her lips curved and her green eyes sparkled in the dim light from the snowstorm as she blew out a cloud of steam with every breath.

"I'm just glad you're okay." He bent to touch his lips to hers, the light caress barely enough to satisfy his growing need. Her lips were cool, soft and pliable beneath his. When she leaned into him and opened to his mouth, he crushed her to his chest and pushed his tongue past her teeth to slide the length of hers.

For a moment in time, they were alone in a snowstorm. One man, one woman and no others.

A movement to his right made Chase jerk back and into a fighting stance. A woman clutching her trench coat around her hurried past to her vehicle.

Chase stepped away from Kate, his heart still hammering against his ribs. "I'm sorry. Now is not the time or place for kissing you."

Kate touched her bottom lip with her fingertips. "You're right. The attacker could return at any minute."

Chase slipped an arm around her waist and hurried her toward the truck, handing her up into the passenger seat before he rounded to slide behind the wheel. Without hesitating, he cranked the engine and backed out of the space.

"Well, we know one thing for certain," Kate said.

"Someone is after the black book." Chase eased out into the traffic, glancing all around in case someone followed them. With the snow falling in earnest, he couldn't see past the next street corner and stoplight. "We need to get back to the ranch."

"The storm's getting worse. Can you drive in this?" She leaned toward the window, her breath fogging the glass. "I can't see ten feet in front of the truck."

"Let's see how far we can get before we have to call it," Chase said. "I'm worried about Jake." Chase leaned forward, not that it helped visibility when the weather approached whiteout conditions.

Kate clutched the armrest as a car skidded through a red light on their right. "The good news is that if we can't get back to the ranch, no one else can," Kate said.

"Unless they're already there," Chase said, his chest tight, his knuckles turning white as brake lights flashed in front of him. He slammed his foot to the brake pedal and skidded to a stop just short of hitting the car.

"This isn't looking good," Kate said.

"No, it isn't," Chase agreed. "We might have to find a place to ride out the storm."

"I'll check in at the ranch and see if Angus can stay longer." Kate dialed the number for the Lucky Lady Ranch and punched the speaker button so that Chase could hear.

Mrs. Quaid answered on the third ring. "Lucky Lady Ranch."

"Frances, it's Kate."

"I'm so glad you called," the older woman said.

Chase leaned closer to the phone, his attention locked on the road ahead. "Is everything okay?"

"Everything's fine here. I was worried about you two. The weatherman is recommending everyone get off the roads and stay home. The system moved in faster than they expected and stalled out. We're supposed to get two to three feet of snow tonight. If you're still in Denver, stay there until the storm clears and the road crews have had time to clear the roads and passes."

"We were about to do just that. As long as you, William and Jake are okay."

"Angus called Reggie and let her know he'd be staying here until you return."

"Good." The relief was instant. "Have William crank up the generator and let it run for a few minutes. You might need it if the power goes off."

"He's already done that and he stocked up enough wood to last all winter for the fireplace. Don't you worry about us. We're as snug as bugs in a rug. We'll see you tomorrow when the roads are clear."

Kate ended the call and stared at the road ahead. "We have to find a place to stay. Traffic is going to get snarled and we don't want to be stuck on the road in a pileup overnight."

"You have a point. See anything?" He peered through the window, barely able to see the taillights in front of him much less the signs on the buildings as they passed by. They hadn't even left downtown Denver and it was already so bad, they might not get much farther.

Kate punched buttons on her phone and brought up the map. "There's a hotel two blocks up on the right."

Chase eased into the right lane and inched his way through the traffic to make the turn. He almost missed the signs for parking garage below the high-rise hotel.

When they made it into the garage, he loosened his grip on the steering wheel and let go of the breath he'd been holding.

"Thank God," Kate breathed beside him. "I didn't think we'd make it this far."

Chase snorted. "We might not make it much farther than this."

There was a line of cars in front of them all looking for a place to park. For ten minutes, Chase circled the parking area at a crawl, for a space large enough for his truck.

"This place is full." Kate craned her neck, searching row after row for any place they could pull in.

Chase finally gave up and parked in an area marked with yellow diagonal lines. "This will have to do."

"It doesn't bode well. If the garage is this full, will they have rooms available?" Kate glanced across at him.

Chase's lips twisted. "Only one way to find out." He pushed open his door and dropped to the ground. Kate followed suit.

Together, they entered the elevator that took them to the lobby. People lined up at the registration desk and milled around the lobby, cell phones pressed to their ears.

Chase found the end of the line and waited with Kate at his side.

Several times he overheard clerks at the desk struggling to accommodate the guests. "I'm sorry, sir, all we have left are rooms with king-size beds. No, we're out of cots."

By the time Chase reached a clerk, the uniformed customer service representative was shaking his head and clicking his fingers over the keyboard, a harried look on his face.

Chase slapped his credit card on the counter. "We'd like a suite. Money is no object."

The young man laughed. "I'd love to give you that suite, but I can't. I just sold our last room to the man ahead of you."

"Do you have any reserved rooms?"

"I have one left, but I can't give it away until six o'clock."

"Whoever reserved it will not be making it here in that storm."

"I'm sorry, I can't let you have it until six. I have to follow the rules. If by some miracle the guy shows up, I have to have a room for him. Until six. In the meantime, there are more people wandering in off the streets.

Do you want me to put you on the waiting list for that room?"

Kate spoke up. "Yes, please." She touched Chase's arm. "We can wait in the restaurant. Neither of us had lunch and it's getting close to dinner."

Chase nodded to the clerk. "I want that room. If you have to charge me now for it, do it. We're here for the night, even if we have to sleep in the lobby."

The clerk snorted. "You wouldn't be alone." He nodded toward the door where more people entered, shaking the snow out of their hair and clothes. "I won't be going home tonight, either."

Chase allowed Kate to lead him into the restaurant where they ordered steaks and salads.

"Should we look at the book and the letters now?" Kate asked while they waited for their meals.

"Let's wait until we're alone in our room. I don't want to risk someone swiping it off the table when we're not looking."

The tables were full and the staff was overloaded, making for a long wait. But the food was good and by the time Chase paid the bill, it was after six o'clock.

Back at the desk, the clerk smiled and handed Chase two room keys. "Thank you for understanding. The man who had reserved the room called a few minutes ago from the Chicago airport to let us know his flight was canceled. The room is yours for the night." He handed Chase a plastic razor, two wrapped toothbrushes and a travel-size tube of toothpaste. "I figured since you didn't have luggage, you were casualties of the storm. Enjoy your stay, Mr. and Mrs. Marsden."

Kate shook her head. "We're not—"

"—choosy about the size of the room or the flavor of the toothpaste," Chase finished for her. "Are we, darlin'?" He slipped his arm around Kate's waist and kissed her temple before throwing over his shoulder. "Thank you for getting us in." Then he whisked Kate to the elevator.

Once inside, Kate chuckled. "You were right. It didn't matter what the clerk thought. We have a room for the night and won't have to sleep in the truck freezing to death, or share the lobby with a hundred other homeless people for the night."

"Exactly."

The elevator stopped on the ninth floor and they exited.

Chase slid the key card in the door lock and the green light flashed on. He pushed the door open and held it for Kate.

The room was small with one king-size bed in the middle and a bathroom just inside the door.

As the door closed behind him, his groin tightened. He'd be alone with Kate for a whole night.

She stood with her back to him, looking toward the big bed with multiple pillows stacked against the headboard. She spun to face him. "I can sleep in the chair."

"That will not be necessary. The bed is big enough we could both sleep in it and never actually bump into each other."

Kate frowned, her gaze slipping to the bed again. "I don't know."

"If you're worried, we can build a pillow barricade between us so that we don't accidentally make contact in the night while we're sleeping."

"I really don't mind sleeping in the chair. It's still better than sleeping in the truck when the outside temperature dips below zero."

"Tell you what. You can have the shower first and

we can discuss it while we fight over what to watch on television."

She nodded. "Fair enough. But that chair is mine." Kate darted past him into the shower and closed the door behind her.

ONCE THE DOOR CLOSED, Kate leaned against it, her heart racing, heat rising from low in her belly all the way out to her extremities. Alone in a bedroom with Chase. Why did she ever think that was a good idea?

After what had happened in the parking garage, Kate didn't trust herself to lie in a bed with Chase.

That one simple kiss had rocked her world so much, the sight of the bed sent her mind spinning in all the wrong directions.

Pull yourself together, girl.

Her father's words echoed in her mind. A memory she'd thought long forgotten surfaced. She'd been sitting in the auditorium beside her father, waiting her turn to give a speech on patriotism. Her stomach had been knotted and she was on the verge of throwing up in an all-out panic attack.

Just when she thought she'd embarrass herself, her family and her entire school, her father laid a hand over hers and calmly whispered in his gravelly way, *Pull yourself together, girl.*

She'd glanced up at him and he'd nodded. Not a smile, not another word. But he'd shown her that he trusted she could do anything if she pulled herself together.

Straightening away from the bathroom door, Kate switched on the shower and looped a towel over the curtain rod. Then she stripped out of her clothes. The mirror over the sink caught her attention and she stared at her body. The six-inch scar on her belly was a mottled purple and pink, the skin pinched around it. They'd removed her appendix and one of her ovaries. Thankfully her kidney had been spared.

She should be grateful she was alive, even if she couldn't have children and even if she'd never look good in a bikini on the beach. It wasn't as if she'd ever worn one, preferring a body-hugging one-piece when she swam. So? She had an ugly scar. She'd lived through a sting operation gone terribly wrong where others on her team had not.

Her body was a testament to everything she'd lost that day. What man would want to see her body naked? Her gaze drifted to the door and her skin heated. That place low in her belly ached for something that was not going to happen. Not tonight. Not with Chase. For all the reasons she'd recited in her head.

Oh, and add the fact he was her client. Surely Hank had a rule about not falling in bed with the client.

Rather than discouraging her from even thinking about getting in bed with Chase, the thought of the handsome former playboy standing on the other side of the door made her body tremble with need.

"Oh, hell," she muttered and flung the shower curtain to the side.

"Did you say something?" Chase asked, his voice strong, despite the door between them, which meant he must be standing close. Close enough that if she opened the door, he'd see her and all her scarred nakedness.

"No," Kate choked out and stepped into the shower, letting the massaging showerhead pelt her skin with heavy drops.

Instead of soothing her and making her relax under the spray, it ignited her pilot light, making the heat build and spread. She grabbed for the shampoo and went through the motions of washing her hair and rinsing it with conditioner. Then she unwrapped the bar of soap and worked up a lather. As she spread the suds over her body she closed her eyes and her imagination took off. Though they were *her* hands slipping over her skin, it was *his* eyes watching as she slid her hand lower to the tuft of curls at the apex of her thighs.

A moan rose up her throat and escaped through her lips. This was not happening. How could she be so aroused by a man she'd only just met?

She buried her head under the water raining down on her, hoping the sound drowned out her own moans. Why did Chase have to be so sexy? And why did he have to hold her when she'd been shaken by the effort to revive Sadie? Why had he held her and kissed her on the porch at the ranch when she'd run out of Jake's room and after she'd been attacked in the garage? And why did the touch of her hands on her body remind her of his hands holding her?

The shower curtain yanked back, jerking Kate out of the rising wave of desire and back to the cool porcelain of the bathtub. She blinked water out of her eyes and squealed. "Chase! What the hell are you doing in here?"

"I heard moaning. I called your name twice, and you didn't respond. I thought you were hurt worse than you let on by that bastard." His gaze swept over her body.

Kate's hand rose to cover herself, the shower's spray running over her shoulders and down her back. She couldn't move, frozen in place by the hunger flaring in Chase's eyes.

"Don't," he said, pulling her hand away from where she held it over her belly.

"It's ugly."

"No, it's a part of you. That brave part that I'm learning is a force to be reckoned with."

She lowered her hand. "You shouldn't be in here."

"I was worried." He had removed his jacket and shirt and his boots. All he wore were the blue jeans he'd put on after his morning shower. "I was afraid he'd hurt you." Chase brushed her shoulder with his fingertips. "Did you see this?"

Kate sucked in a breath at the electric shock his hand set off when he touched her skin. She glanced down at the light purple evidence of a bruise slowly making an appearance under her skin. The bruise didn't make nearly as big an impact on her senses as standing completely naked in front of Chase. "It doesn't hurt."

It could. If she let her guard down and allowed him into her heart.

She stood for a long moment, staring at his broad, muscular chest, her tongue tied in a knot, her thoughts whirling. Then she glanced down at his jeans. "If you're going to get in, you might want to remove those first."

Her heart hammered, pumping blood through her veins like pistons feeding gasoline to the engine of a race car. For a horrifying moment, she held her breath, afraid she'd read too much into that kiss, or into his gaze devouring her body. If he didn't join her, she'd be completely mortified.

Chase let go of the curtain and it fell back in place, thankfully blocking his view of her humiliation.

Kate ducked her face beneath the spray, salty tears mixing with the water. Who was she kidding? A man like Chase would never be attracted to a scarred tomboy of a woman who could outshoot most men, and didn't have a clue about makeup or hairstyles.

She strained to hear the sound of the door closing behind him, but couldn't over the pounding of her own blood in the veins beneath her eardrums. She closed her eyes and prayed he'd leave before she fell completely apart.

Then warm hands circled her waist and pulled her back against a rock-hard body.

She gasped, her eyes flying open, the beat of her heart thudding as his fingers slid upward, cupping her breasts.

She moaned and leaned back, her skin connecting with his, the hard evidence of his arousal pressing against her backside. "This is wrong." But, God, it felt right.

"It might be a little late to ask, but are you married?"

"No," she said on a gasp as he tweaked the tip of her nipples.

He nuzzled the side of her neck, nibbling at her earlobe. "Do you have a boyfriend back in Texas?"

She leaned her head to the side, allowing him better access to the long line of her throat. "No."

"Then why is it wrong when I've wanted to hold you since I saw you fighting to save the life of my friend? Why is it wrong when every time I touch you I feel you quiver beneath my fingers?"

"You're the client."

"Is that all that's got you worried?" He kissed the skin where her throat curved into her shoulder. "You're fired."

A shaky chuckle rose up her throat. "No. I'm on fire." She pressed her hands to the backs of his and then turned in his arms. "And you can't fire me. We have to help Sadie. And when we solve the mystery and stop the madman, then what?"

"We take it a day at a time. We've only known each other a day. I'm not asking you for commitment."

"Isn't that what the woman usually says?" She shook her head. "I've never been good at this kind of thing." She spread her hands across his chest, liking how soft his skin was, encasing the rock-solid muscles beneath. "How does a wealthy playboy come off having muscles like this?"

He flexed his chest muscle, making it even harder. "Lifting hay bales and shoveling horse manure."

"Mmm, now you're just talking sexy." She pressed her lips to one of those muscles, loving the taste of his skin. "Promise me this won't make it awkward with us working together."

"I promise this won't make it awkward."

She trailed her lips lower and nipped the little brown nipple. "Liar."

"Okay, I promise to do my best not to make it awkward." His hands slid down her back to cup her bottom. "If you want to stop, just say so and it ends here."

She blinked up at him. If she were smart, she'd step out of the shower, dry off and sleep in the uncomfortable chair, secure in the knowledge she'd done the right thing.

But she couldn't. Not with Chase standing naked in the shower with her, him with an erection, while her body was on fire, ready to prove to herself she was still a woman capable of making a man burn with desire. Even if only for one night.

Chase's hands moved to the back of her thighs and he lifted her, wrapping her legs around his waist as he backed her up against the cool, smooth tiles.

Then he froze. His fingers digging into her skin, his staff poised at her entrance.

Kate ached to feel him inside her. She tried to sink down over him, but he held her off.

"What's wrong?" she asked, pressing her breasts against him. "Why are you stopping?" A moment of panic assailed her.

He'd changed his mind.

"Protection."

"I'm clean, if that's what you're worried about. And I'm incapable of getting pregnant."

"I'm clean, too. Are you sure?" He leaned back to stare into her eyes.

"Yes." This time when she eased down, he let her, sliding into her slick channel, stretching her, filling her until she'd taken all of him inside.

Kate closed her eyes and drew in a deep, shaky breath. "That feels so good."

"Sweetheart, we've only just begun." He moved in and out of her, starting slow, building up speed with each thrust.

"Harder," she moaned, her head tipping back against the tile, her hands digging into his shoulders. Just when she reached the peak, he lifted her off him and set her on her feet.

She held on to him until her legs stopped shaking. "Why did you stop?"

"I want to get you there, preferably in a bed, for our first time." He slapped her bottom and moved her beneath the shower's spray.

"But I was almost there," she whined, her insides quivering, her hands shaking with the intensity of her desire.

"Then we'd better hurry through the shower." He lathered his hands with soap and handed the bar to her. With careful precision, he slipped the suds over her body, not missing a single inch of skin in his ministrations.

Taking his lead, Kate worked up a sudsy lather and slid her hands over his chest, around to his back and down his front to the jutting staff, still hard as steel encased in velvety skin. Her fingers curled around him, sliding up and down, loving the feel of him in her palms and how hard he was because of her.

Chase grabbed her wrists and spun her under the water, rinsing the soap, first from her body and then his. He shut off the water, jerked the shower curtain aside and wrapped a towel around Kate, drying her from head to toe. By the time she'd dried him, she was even hotter and ready.

Chase tossed the towels to the side, scooped her up into his arms and carried her into the bedroom.

"What happened to going through Sadie's little black book?"

"Somehow, I believe she'd approve of this little detour," Chase said and laid her on the sheets, climbing into the bed beside her. "Still want to sleep in the chair?"

Kate stretched, loving the feel of the sheets against her naked back and the hungry expression on Chase's face. "Hell no."

Chapter Seven

Sun streamed through the narrow gap between the blackout curtains on the window.

Kate blinked and opened her eyes, reaching out for the man beside her, only to find an empty space. She turned her head and had a brief thought that perhaps she'd imagined what had occurred the night before.

She ran her hands over her naked body, pausing at her tender nipples. Leaning up, she recognized the redness of beard burn around her breasts, and she couldn't deny the ache between her legs.

"Chase?" she called out, getting no response. Doors opened and closed outside in the hallway, but Chase had left the room.

Kate pulled the sheet and comforter up over herself to guard against a sudden chill that had nothing to do with the temperature in the room. A white sheet of paper slipped from its position propped against the electric alarm clock, to lie flat on the surface of the nightstand. Kate reached for it and held it up to the sliver of light filtering through the curtains. Bold letters scrawled across the white expanse. "Gone for food and coffee."

Warmth filled her and made her tingle all over. Kate pressed the paper to her chest and snuggled deeper under the blankets, determined to keep them warm for when

Chase returned. Maybe then he'd be tempted to pick up where they'd left off the night before.

Something clicked on the door to the room.

Kate's pulse pounded in anticipation, the sheet sliding across her skin reminding her of her nakedness. Heat rose up her chest and into her cheeks. Was she expecting too much? Maybe she should grab clothes and dress before the door opened.

Too late, the handle turned and the door eased open, the light from the hallway casting the man in the doorway in shadows.

"Did you find coffee?" she asked, dragging the sheet up to her chin, a tentative smile curling her lips.

Without responding, he glanced back over his shoulder, the light revealing the fact he was wearing a ski mask.

For half a second, Kate froze, her body stiffened and her heart crashed to a halt, then slammed into high gear, pushing adrenaline through her veins.

The intruder entered the room, letting the door close behind him. The metal-on-metal sound of the latch being moved, sent a chill through Kate. If Chase returned, he wouldn't be able to get inside, even with the door key. And her gun was in the pocket of her jacket, hanging in the closet.

Kate rolled off the bed to the other side. "Get out of this room or I'll scream," she warned, grasping for something to use as a weapon. The lights were sconces on the wall. The phone was on the other side of the bed. Other than pillows and an alarm clock, she had nothing.

Footsteps pounded across the floor.

Kate screamed as loud as she could. She grabbed the black book and shoved it under the bed. Then she fumbled for the alarm clock and yanked it off the nightstand, ripping the cord out of the wall.

Crouched naked and vulnerable on the other side of the bed, she waited for him to round the corner. She'd be ready.

CHASE HAD WOKEN before Kate and lain for a long time staring at her in the gray light fighting its way through the curtain. Her rich brown hair fanned across the pillow, a dark contrast to the white sheets. Her lips were swollen from all his kisses and she had a little bit of a smile on her face.

His heart swelled along with other parts of his body, but he refused to wake her when she was sleeping so soundly. They'd been up half the night, exploring each other's bodies, learning what the other liked.

He respected her reluctance to mix business with pleasure, but he'd been happy she'd given in to her desires. She'd been a willing and exhilarating partner in bed. Chase feared with the morning light, she'd regret the night's passion.

Chase had slipped out of bed and checked the weather on his phone. The front had pushed through the night before with only lingering chances of light snow flurries for the day. A quick glance out the window revealed the snow removal crews had been at work through the night. The street in front of the hotel had been cleared and traffic moved steadily along in downtown Denver.

Reluctant to wake Kate, he dressed in the bathroom and left the room in search of food to replace the energy they'd spent, and coffee to get them going for the trip back to Fool's Fortune. He opened the door carefully and eased it closed behind him, hurrying to the elevator.

It hadn't taken long to find coffee and cinnamon rolls.

Chase was on his way back up in the elevator within less than fifteen minutes, balancing two cups of coffee and a bag of sweet rolls. As the elevator door opened, he heard a muffled scream.

Dropping the coffees and bag, he raced for their room, certain the sound had emanated from within. His heart pounded and he couldn't pull the room key card out of his pocket fast enough.

Sliding it in the slot, he twisted the handle and shoved the door hard. It bounced back in his face, the latch near the top of the door, barring his entrance. "Kate!"

The sound of something cracking, then thumping on the floor was followed by deep cursing. Footsteps thumped toward him and the door was shoved closed, the latch thrown and then the door jerked open to a naked Kate.

"Look out!" she cried as the man dressed all in black plowed into her back, sending her flying through the door into Chase, knocking him flat on his back.

The attacker leaped over the two on the floor and raced to the end of the hallway to the stairwell.

Kate rolled off Chase and would have gone after him, but Chase caught her arm, shoved his key card into her hand and said, "Get dressed. I'll take care of this."

"But I'm the bodyguard," she cried.

"And you're naked," he shouted over his shoulder, already halfway down the hall. "Get inside and lock the damn door."

Two times in as many days that bastard had attacked them. Chase refused to let him get away with it this time.

The pounding of boots on the stairs signaled the man was several flights below him. Chase took the stairs down two at a time, leaping the last four of each to the landing on the next floor. By the time he reached the bottom, his target had exited through the lobby level door.

Chase shoved through and raced for the exit, passing a bellboy pushing a cart full of luggage. "Did you see a man in black running?"

The bellboy pointed to the hotel entrance. "Just left. Should I call Security?"

Chase didn't slow to respond, slamming through the glass entrance door out into the frigid cold. A flash of black rounded the corner at the end of the building. Chase ran after him. Though the sidewalk had been cleared of snow, it was slippery. He took the corner a little faster than he should have, slid and steadied himself.

The man who'd attacked Kate was a good fifty yards ahead.

Glad he'd stayed in shape working on the ranch and jogging on his treadmill during the winter, Chase gave it all he had, shortening the distance between them.

When he was only ten feet behind the man, the guy looked over his shoulder, saw Chase and didn't look back in time as he ran out into a busy street.

Tires squealed as a delivery truck driver slammed on his brakes. With a thin layer of snow and ice still coating the road, the vehicle didn't stop, hitting the man full-on.

He crashed to the ground, his head bouncing hard on the pavement, and lay still.

Chase slid to a stop as the driver leaped out of the truck. "I didn't see him until it was too late."

A passerby bent over the man. "I'm a nurse." She pulled off her gloves and pressed her fingers to the base of his neck. "I'm not getting a pulse." She eased him onto his back and ripped open his jacket.

Chase knelt beside the man and yanked off his ski mask. He didn't recognize the guy, but he pulled his phone from his pocket to call 9-1-1. As he held the phone, he snapped a picture of the man. If Hank was as good as Angus and Kate said he was, he'd have some face recognition software. They might be able to match this man.

He placed the call to 9-1-1 and waited, shivering in the cold, for the first time realizing he didn't have on a jacket.

"Here, take this." A woman held out a blanket to him and he draped it over the figure lying on the ground, though it went against every nerve to help the man who'd tried to kill Kate, not once but twice just to get his hands on Sadie Lovely's little black book.

Chase felt in the man's pockets for identification.

"Find anything?" the nurse asked. "Anyone know who this man is?"

The same woman with the first blanket appeared again with another, wrapping it around his shoulders. She gave him a smile. "My husband makes me carry emergency items in my trunk. For once I'm glad he does."

He thanked her and stood by while the nurse tried to save the man.

Minutes later, a police car arrived, an ambulance right behind. The nurse was relieved by the EMTs and they loaded the man in the ambulance.

Chase gave a statement to the officer about the man breaking and entering his hotel room and the subsequent chase that led to the attacker running out into the road where he was hit.

The officer took notes and Chase's phone number, promising him he'd be by the hotel shortly.

Chase handed the blanket back to the nice lady who'd loaned it to him and hurried back to the high-rise, already gone much longer than he felt comfortable with.

What if there was more than one person after the little black book? Kate might still be in danger.

When he entered the lobby, Kate stood by the registration desk fielding questions from a police officer.

Chase let go of the breath he'd been holding and hurried to her side.

When she saw him, she broke away from the officers and melted into his arms. Her body was warm against his, driving away the chill from standing out in the cold for so long.

"Thank God, you're okay," she said, looking up into his face. "When you didn't come back right away, I thought…"

"I'm okay. Which is more than I can say for the guy who attacked you."

"What happened?"

He gave her the short version, his lips thinning as he finished. "He won't be bothering you anymore."

Kate buried her face against his chest and her body trembled. When she stopped shaking, she pushed to arm's length. "I have something that belongs to you." She turned to the registration desk to retrieve his jacket and held it while he slipped his arms into the sleeves. Anxious to get back to the ranch, Chase answered a few questions for the police, gave them his phone number and told them to call if they needed more information. Otherwise, he'd be headed home before another storm kept him in Denver.

With his arm around her waist, he pulled Kate close. "Let's go home."

KATE SAT IN the seat beside Chase, the black book open to the first page of entries. She held her cell phone over the pages, snapping photographs of them, one by one.

"Hank can have Brandon do a search on these names. Maybe some of them will pop up in the news."

"As long as he knows how important it is to safeguard this information," Chase warned.

"From what I've learned of Hank, you can trust him with anything, including your life. He's gone out of his way to rescue strangers and members of his own team, putting his own life on the line. As rich as he is, he doesn't have to put himself in harm's way."

"Good to know. What about the man he'll have searching the net?"

"Brandon is a straight shooter. He's tighter than Fort Knox when it comes to keeping secrets." Kate finished photographing the pages and sent them directly to Hank's private number.

Shoving her phone back in her jacket pocket, she returned her attention to the book, thankful Chase hadn't mentioned finding her naked in the hallway when she'd been attacked. Nor had he spoken a word about their mattress gymnastics the night before.

Determined to play it cool when she really wanted to ask him if the night before meant anything to him, she focused on the names and dates in the book, afraid of his answer. "I'm not familiar with any of these people. Perhaps they're more significant here in Colorado."

"I've kept tabs on the state, even when I was traveling around the world. Shoot some at me. I'll stop you if I recognize one."

She slid her finger down the list. "Brent Kitchens, Frank Young, Stephen Kuntz, Morris Longtree—"

"Longtree," Chase cut in, his brows pressing into a V. "Longtree. Might be the owner of the Mother Lode Mine in Idaho Springs. Remember that one."

Kate nodded and continued. "Raymond Hollings-worth—"

"Hollingsworth was the state attorney general eight or so years ago."

"Fenton Yates."

"Fenton Yates of Yates, Taylor and Michaels." Chase glanced at Kate for the first time in the past thirty minutes.

Kate met his gaze for a second, returning her attention to the black book, her cheeks heating. "John Michaels is the next name on the list."

"Of the same law firm."

"Wasn't he the governor of Colorado?"

"Yup. Michaels still has an interest in the law firm even though he quit his practice when he went into politics."

Kate's lips curled. "I wonder if the partners at the law firm shared interest in Sadie as well as their firm."

Chase didn't respond.

When Kate stole a glance his way, he was staring at her, his attention shifting back and forth from the snowy road to her. "Are we going to ignore what happened last night?" he asked.

Kate bit her lip and stared straight ahead with a shrug. "We probably should," she said for a lack of anything intelligent to say.

He chuckled. "What does that mean?"

Kate turned away, staring out the passenger window, afraid her face would reveal more than she was ready to reveal. Unfortunately, her reflection stared back at her and Chase's behind her.

"I wouldn't have left you alone had I known that man would be breaking into the room."

"Don't worry about it." She traced a finger along the edge of the book's binding.

"You were sleeping so peacefully. I hated to wake you."

"I'm all right. I don't expect you to rescue me."

"I should have been there for you."

"What happened between us doesn't mean you have any obligations toward me. I went into it with no expectations. We have nothing to discuss."

"Damn it, Kate." Chase slammed his palm against the steering wheel and the truck swerved on the slippery road. "Last night was more than just a roll in the sheets."

"Why?" She finally faced him, forcing all expression from her face. If ever there was a time for a poker face, now was it. "Why does last night have to mean anything? Lust doesn't last."

A frown settled on Chase's brow. "In my case, it damn sure does." He dragged in a deep breath. "Are you telling me you're done? You have no desire for a repeat performance?"

Kate's hands trembled and she gripped Sadie's book tighter to keep them from visibly shaking. She glanced away from Chase's intense gaze. "I don't see the need."

"Don't see the need?" Chase stared ahead for the next mile, a muscle twitching in his clenched jaw.

Kate's chest hurt with the effort it took to keep from taking back every word she'd said. She was lying to him and herself. What had happened the night before had been nothing short of magical. Did she want it to happen again?

Yes, oh, yes!

But she wasn't confident in her ability to walk away at the end of this assignment with her heart unscathed. Chase was handsome, charming and fantastic in bed.

He cared about children and a woman who wasn't even related to him.

He was the kind of man a girl could easily fall in love with. The drawback—based on the old news articles about him—he was a notorious playboy, used to loving and leaving every woman he'd ever dated. Just because he'd moved to the Lucky Lady Ranch two years ago didn't mean he had broken his old habits completely.

Besides, when this job was done, she'd leave and go back to Texas or wherever Hank sent her next. She would have no reason to stay in Colorado or visit the Lucky Lady Ranch, even if he wanted her to. And she couldn't imagine Chase going out of his way to come see her. Not when he could have any woman he wanted with nothing but a crook of his finger.

"We'll table this conversation for now. But we're not done." He shot her a narrowed glare. "With the conversation, or what's happening between us."

Chapter Eight

Chase made the hospital their first stop in Fool's Fortune to check on Sadie. Still in a coma, she was in ICU. As they reached her room he noted there wasn't a police officer outside her door.

His pulse leaped and he hurried into the room. A television mounted in the corner was on with a football game, the sound muted. A large man sat in a chair beside Sadie's hospital bed. As Chase entered the man sprang to his feet, his hands out front. "Tell me you're Chase Marsden or turn around and leave. This room is off-limits to visitors."

Kate pushed past Chase and grinned at the man. "Chuck." She wrapped her arms around the man's neck and hugged him.

Chase took a step forward, his fists clenching, wanting to break up the little reunion, but he didn't have any say over who Kate hugged. They'd only met a couple days ago and had sex the night before. That didn't count as a forever kind of a relationship. She was free to hug whomever she pleased.

That fact didn't make Chase any less angry.

Finally Kate turned to him with a smile. "Chase, meet Chuck Bolton, another member of Hank's Covert Cowboys, Inc. team. He's one of the first agents I met when I started with Hank." She smiled at Chuck again, making Chase's teeth grind. "He and his wife have the cutest little baby girl and one on the way."

Chuck grinned. "Charlie's running circles around PJ now."

"I'll bet PJ's exhausted," Kate sympathized. "It won't be long before that baby comes."

Chuck laughed. "PJ just wants to see her feet again." The love in the big man's voice and expression could not be misconstrued.

Drawing in a deep breath, Chase let it out slowly and extended his hand. "Nice to meet you," he said and meant it. Chase stepped around him and glanced down at Sadie. "How long will you be able to stay?"

Chuck joined Chase at Sadie's bedside. "As long as you need me. Or as long as PJ doesn't go into labor. She's got another month to go, so hopefully, I'll be okay here for a while."

"We can check with the Fool's Fortune police department to get you some relief."

"The nurses have been wonderful bringing me food. I'm good for the night. Although, I could use a shower in the morning and a change of clothes, either that, or they'll throw me out."

"We'll make sure you get that break." Chase leaned over Sadie and pressed a kiss to her forehead. "Hey, pretty lady. Hurry back. Jake misses his grandma Sadie."

Sadie looked so helpless and vulnerable.

Chase's heart pinched in his chest. He straightened and nodded to Chuck. "Take care of her."

Kate hugged Chuck again and stepped out of the ICU room. Chase followed. "Let's head back to the ranch."

In the truck, Kate sat silent in the passenger seat, her gaze following the curves of the road.

Chase glanced her way, wondering what was going on in her head. Was she thinking about Sadie? About the black book, or the man who'd attacked them and now lay in a morgue somewhere in Denver? Or was she actually thinking about making love with him?

His groin tightened, images of her lying beneath him, her hips rocking, her legs locked around his waist, still fresh on his mind.

Thankfully he knew the way to the ranch so well, he could get there practically with his eyes closed. He needed that rote memory, because all his thoughts were on Kate and what the night ahead might hold in store for them.

He opened his mouth to ask her what she was thinking.

Metal crashed against metal, the truck lurched forward violently and then skidded sideways toward the edge of the road.

"What the hell?" Chase held on to the steering wheel, his knuckles white as they slid toward the guardrail. He braced himself for impact and possibly plowing through the barrier. If the rail didn't stop them, they would plunge over the side of a steep hill and crash into boulders and trees at the bottom.

Praying for a miracle, Chase eased the steering wheel around and gently tapped the accelerator. At the last second, before grinding into the metal guardrail, he righted the truck and sprang forward.

Kate clutched the armrest and held on to the handle above the door. "What was that?"

His gaze shot to the rearview mirror where a dark SUV raced toward them. "Someone ran into us. Hold on, he's going to hit us ag—"

"Look out!" Kate cried as the SUV broadsided the spinning truck, hitting Chase's side.

Thrown sideways, Chase clung to the steering wheel, his seat belt tightening, pinning him to his seat. No matter how hard he struggled to right the vehicle, it continued sliding down the road sideways, the attacking vehicle pushing them like a bulldozer.

Kate dug in her jacket pocket and pulled out her handgun.

"He's got to stop," she said. "Lean back!"

Chase flattened himself against his seat as Kate pulled the trigger on a small pistol. The bullet ripped through the side window and slammed into the SUV's front windshield slightly left of the driver. The vehicle backed off, giving Chase the opportunity to hit the accelerator and turn the vehicle back onto the right side of the road in time to take the next hairpin curve. Another vehicle passed, coming from the opposite direction, hugging the centerline.

Had Chase not gotten the truck back in his lane, the other vehicle would have hit Kate's side. With the oncoming vehicle and the one that had attacked them, the truck would have been crushed between them.

Chase drove as fast as he safely could on the curvy roads, putting as much distance between his truck and the dark SUV.

Kate held her gun in her hand, sitting half-turned in her seat. "Either he turned around, or he's slowed down so much I can't see him anymore." She settled back, facing forward, every so often peering into the side mirror.

Cold air filtered through the hole in the window.

"You say you fire expert?" Chase rubbed the side of his cheek.

"Every time I'm at the range," she confirmed, a smile quirking her lips. "Afraid I was going to hit you?"

"Not as afraid as I was of being broadsided again as

we neared that turn." He chuckled. "I'm glad you take your weapons training seriously."

"I told you." Kate crossed her arms. "I'm good at what I do."

"Even when you're at an extreme disadvantage."

"Like being buck naked in the hallway of a busy hotel?" Her cheeks reddened. "I don't suppose you'd go so far as to forget about that incident?"

"I couldn't, even if I wanted to." Chase grinned, the image of Kate's beautiful body indelibly etched in his memory. "You were like an avenging, naked angel flying through the door of our room. I don't know what hit me harder, your body or the fact that you didn't have on a stitch of clothing."

"Please," she said, her cheeks bright red. "What gets me is how did he know how to find us? We couldn't see two feet in front of us getting to the hotel. He couldn't have followed us."

"And how did he know exactly where to find us on the road back to Fool's Fortune?"

Kate frowned and dumped her small purse out on her lap, sifting through every item.

Chase glanced her way. "What are you looking for?"

"A tracking device." She examined her purse thoroughly before placing each item back inside. Then she patted the pockets on her jeans, slipping her hands in the front ones, then the back ones. Finally she patted her jacket and stuffed her hands in the pockets. Her brow furrowed as she pulled her hand out with a little shiny object. "Damn. I was bugged."

Chase glanced at the small metal device. "It was in your coat pocket?"

"Yes. Although *when* he put it there, I don't know. We were too busy trading hits in the garage. It had to have been in my pocket when we went to the hotel where we stayed the night or he wouldn't have found us so quickly."

At the next juncture in the road, Chase pulled into a small gas station and stopped.

"What are you doing?" Kate asked, swiveling in her seat to gain a better view of the highway behind them.

"Hopefully throwing our tail off course." He got out of the truck and walked to another truck with an amber light affixed to the top and a sign on the side indicating it was a rural mail carrier.

Chase dropped the tracking device into the bed of the vehicle and returned to his banged-up truck. He was sad to see how much damage it had sustained, but knew it could have been much worse. At least they'd had the heavy truck frame protecting them from being crushed.

Back in the warmth of the cab, Chase grinned at Kate. "Hopefully that will throw them off for a little while. At least until we get back to the ranch."

"If they know exactly who we are, they'll find us there soon enough." She worried her lip, making Chase want to lean across and kiss her.

He lifted her hand and brought it to his lips. "We'll be ready when, or if, they do."

Kate stared at her hand clasped in his. "We might be ready, but what about the others?"

Chase didn't want to think of the danger to every member of the household or how they'd minimize it.

With a vigilant eye on his rearview mirror, Chase pulled through the gate at the Lucky Lady Ranch. The snow that had fallen overnight blanketed the hills surrounding the house, softening the jagged rocks, giving it a beautiful and pure innocence.

As a child his parents had left him with his grandfather on several occasions when they wanted to travel without the burden of a little one at Christmastime. He loved the snow, found an old sled in the barn and spent hours coasting down the hill in back of the barn. At night he'd fall asleep before his head hit the pillow.

Chase pulled into the five-car garage beside the house and hurried around to help Kate out. By the time he'd rounded the front of the truck, she was on the ground, reaching in for the little black book and the stack of letters. "We haven't even had an opportunity to go through the letters."

"Tonight. As soon as the rest of the house is asleep, we can meet in the office," Chase suggested. "I want to do some web surfing with a few of the names in that book."

"Hank's computer guru really is good at digging up interesting facts that have helped contribute to solving cases."

"I get that, but I don't like sitting around waiting for someone else to figure out who's trying to kill me, you or Sadie."

"Neither do I. Later, then."

When they entered the foyer, Frances came running in from the kitchen. "Thank God you two are here."

Chase tensed. "What's wrong?"

"It's Jake."

Kate stepped forward. "Is he hurt?"

"I don't know. Angus just came up from the barn. He can't find Jake." Frances wrung her hands, tears filling her eyes. "It's cold outside and the sun is setting."

Chase gripped her shoulders. "Where's Angus now?"

"Out by the barn looking for Jake. He wanted me to call you and let you know, but now that you're here—"

Chase didn't give Frances a chance to finish her thought. He was already out the door.

KATE'S HEART SQUEEZED TIGHT. The little boy could very easily get lost in the woods and not find his way out. "Don't worry, Mrs. Quaid, we'll find him," she said and pushed past her, running for the back door to catch up to Chase, praying she was right. As soon as they emerged onto the snowy white expanse between the barn and the house, she spied Angus and William near the rear of the barn at the base of a hill, calling out for Jake.

Her gaze panning the area, Kate hurried toward the two men.

Angus saw them first and met them halfway.

"When was the last time you saw Jake?" Kate blurted.

"Thirty minutes ago." Angus's brows were knit and he looked past Kate and Chase at the woods above the little hill. "We were sledding on the hill. I ran back to the barn for a length of rope to help drag the sled up the hill and when I returned, he was gone. Two minutes!" He spun, his gaze raking the hillside. "Where could he have gone in just two minutes?"

William Quaid joined them. "I was in the barn cranking up the generator. I didn't see or hear him, the noise was loud." The older man shook his head. "We've been calling for him since, and he hasn't responded. Poor little guy. If it gets much darker we won't be able to find him."

Barkley bounded over to them and nuzzled Chase's hand.

Chase knelt and rubbed the dog's head. "Where's Jake, Barkley?"

Barkley leaned against Chase.

Chase straightened. "I see we need to train you for search and rescue if we're going to have kids around here." He patted the dog's head absently, looking around the area. "Let's split up." He nodded toward the hill and the tree line. "Angus and I will check from the back of the barn up into the wooded area. If he's gone farther into the forest, we should be able to pick up a trail."

"If he's in the trees, he should be able to hear us calling," Angus reasoned.

"Unless he fell and got hurt." Kate moved forward, ready to follow the men.

"William, circle the house." Chase waved toward the massive house and parking garages. "Frances is checking all the rooms in case he went in without telling anyone."

"On it," William trotted toward the house and turned, making a wide girth around it.

"Kate," Chase faced her. "Check the barn."

"We looked through the barn, calling out. Never heard or saw him," Angus said.

"Check again, just in case. Like you said, he could have fallen and hurt himself. Go," Chase ordered.

Rather than stand around and argue, Kate entered the barn. "Jake!" she called out, the sound of the generator's engine all she could hear. "Jake!" Frustrated by the noise, she found the source and switched it off. As the engine chugged to a stop, the barn fell into silence.

Kate listened, straining her ears for any sound.

A soft meow sounded at her feet and she glanced down at a calico cat. The animal leaned into her leg, rubbing the length of her body against Kate's boots.

Kate shooed the cat away and ducked into the tack room, finding nothing but saddles, bridles, girths and brushes neatly stacked on saddletrees or shelves. She even checked behind a wooden workbench. No Jake.

One by one, she entered each stall, hoping to find

the little boy and yet not. If he'd wandered into a stall with a horse, he could have been kicked and be lying unconscious.

Her heart in her throat, she reached the last one and still hadn't found Jake. At least he hadn't been trampled by a horse many times heavier than he was.

The cat followed her every step of the way, weaving herself between Kate's feet.

"Shoo!" Kate nudged her away and continued her search. "Jake!" she called out, her hope of finding the child in the barn waning.

Kate worked her way around a stand of barrels, each containing feed. She peeled the lids off and looked inside in case Jake had been playing hide-and-seek and got stuck in one. She figured it was unlikely, but she refused to leave one lid unturned.

After searching the entire floor of the barn, she looked up. In Texas, they used pole barns to store hay. But this barn was as old as the house and had a massive loft, full of hay. She'd seen a steep wooden staircase at one end of the barn. Headed for it, she shook her head when the cat beat her to it and leaped up the steps to the top.

Kate followed.

The calico stopped at the top and watched as Kate hurried up after her. Then with her tail held high, the cat trotted toward a stack of hay bales and disappeared.

"Jake!" Kate called out. Had he climbed up in the hay and fallen between the stacks? Or had the bales tumbled over and crushed him beneath? Kate's pulse ratcheted up and she rushed toward the bails afraid to climb them in case some had fallen on top of Jake. She'd only make it worse by crushing him even more.

As she ran her gaze over the towering stacks, the barn

cat emerged from a crevice and meowed, turning, her tail high, she disappeared again.

Kate frowned and followed. As she neared the crevice between the stacks of hay she could hear the soft mewling of kittens.

The gap between the haystacks was big enough for the cat, but was it big enough for a small boy?

Kate squatted and peered into the gap. The mewling increased in intensity, probably as the mother cat settled in with her babies.

Kate couldn't see very far into the stack, the limited lighting in the barn didn't extend into the hay cave the cat had made for her kittens. What she needed was a flashlight.

She yanked her smartphone from her pocket, set it on the flashlight application and shined the beam into the narrow gap.

Cat eyes gleamed red at her and Kate could make out the small squirming forms of kittens nuzzling up to their mama for a meal.

About to give up and move on, she shifted the light and it bounced off something dark, but shiny. Nothing like the blinking red glare of cat eyes.

Kate's heart beat faster as she directed the light toward the dark shiny object. This time she could make out a child's shiny winter jacket. "Jake!" she shouted.

The sound of a small gasp made Kate almost collapse with relief. The shiny material jerked and a little face appeared in the gap between the hay.

"Uncle Angus?" Jake called out.

"Oh, Jake, baby," Kate cried. "We've been looking all over for you."

"Miss Kate!" he cried out and then sniffed. "I'm stuck. I can't get out."

"Don't worry, baby, we'll get you out." She pulled her cell phone from her pocket and dialed Chase's number. Nothing happened. She checked the phone. *No service.* Kate started to move away, anxious to find Chase and the other men and let them know she'd found Jake.

"Miss Kate!" Jake yelled. "Don't leave me. I'm scared."

Her heart ached for the little guy. "I have to get Uncle Chase. He'll help me get you out of there. I promise I'll be right back." She laid her phone in between the hay bales. "I'll leave the light shining for you. It won't take me a minute to get back. I promise."

"Please hurry," he said, his voice weak, little sobs wrenching Kate's heart.

Kate ran for the stairs and started down, leaping the last five to land on the ground. Then she tore through the barn to the door, bursting through. "I found him! I found Jake!"

Chase and Angus emerged from the tree line running. William ran from the direction of the house.

"He's in the haystacks in the barn." Kate didn't wait for them to reach her. She'd promised Jake she'd be right back. As scared as he was, she couldn't leave him for long.

Back up the stairs, she followed the glow of her cell phone. "Jake, I'm back."

"Please, get me out of here."

"We will. Uncle Chase, Angus and William are on their way." The barn door hinges creaked below and Kate let out the breath she'd been holding. "We're in the loft," she called out.

"I want my grandma Sadie," Jake whimpered.

"She's still sick, but Uncle Chase and I are here for you, Jake. You'll be okay."

Footsteps pounded up the steep stairs.

Kate turned as the three hulking men arrived in the loft.

"He's stuck in between the stacks of bales," Kate said from her position kneeling on the floor.

"It's okay," Chase said. "We'll have you out in two shakes of a lamb's tail."

"Hurry," Jake said.

Chase climbed to the top of the stack and handed bales down to Angus and William. The men at the bottom created a new stack against another wall, moving the wall of hay one bale at a time.

From Kate's position on her knees, it seemed to take forever. They worked their way down until the stack was only four bales tall.

"Almost there, buddy," Chase said. He lifted a bale and chuckled. "There you are."

Kate straightened, her body stiff from being hunched over for so long. All her stiffness melted away as Chase lifted Jake out of the middle and hugged him to his chest.

Jake clung to Chase. "I was scared."

"You had all of us scared." Chase held the boy close, his arms wrapped around him as he sat on the hay. When he finally loosened his hold, he glanced down. "What have we got here?"

Jake looked down, too. "Kittens." He looked around, his gaze meeting Angus's. "I'm sorry I didn't stay at the sled. I followed you into the barn. I didn't think you'd mind. Then I saw Fancy carrying a little kitten and I followed her all the way up here."

Chase ruffled his head. "I probably would have, too. Kittens are hard to resist. How many does she have?"

"Five," Jake said, his voice getting stronger, now that

he was safe and out of the hay. "She let me hold them and didn't even scratch me."

Kate retrieved her cell phone crawled up on the hay and shined her light down at the cat nursing her kittens as if it was every day her little cave was invaded by humans. Just as Jake said, five little kittens whose eyes were just beginning to open lay snuggled up to their mama, massaging her belly with their little kitten paws.

Kate almost laughed with her relief. The cat had followed her all through the barn as if trying to tell her she knew where Jake was.

Jake leaned away from Chase.

Before Kate knew it, he'd latched on to her and wrapped his arms around her neck. "Thanks for finding me." He buried his little face against her neck and didn't let go, even when she moved to climb down from the hay.

Chase beat her to the ground and reached up for her and the boy. His hands closed around her waist and he lifted her and Jake to the floor, pulling them into a tight hug. "We're glad you're safe, Jake."

"No kidding." Angus patted the boy's back. "You nearly gave me a heart attack."

"I'm sorry," he said. "Are you mad at me?"

Angus chuckled. "No. I would have gone hunting for the kittens, too, if I had seen the cat carrying one. But why didn't you answer when we called out?"

"I didn't hear you." He looked up. "I must have fallen asleep." He rubbed his fist into his eyes.

The salty tracks of dried tears lined his face.

Kate's arms tightened around the little boy, wanting to make him feel safe and secure.

"Want me to take him down the steps?" Chase held out his hands.

Jake's arms locked around Kate's neck and he buried his face against her, refusing to let go.

Her heart pinching tightly in her chest, Kate shook her head. "I've got him."

Angus and William hurried down ahead of them.

Chase went next, descending backward. He moved slowly to help Kate balance on the steep risers, his hand on her arm, providing support and reassurance.

Once on the ground, Kate breathed a sigh. Tragedy averted, everything could get back to normal.

Only she seriously doubted after the previous night of making love with Chase that anything would ever be normal again. And normal had never felt so warm and loving as a child clinging to you, completely dependent on you for his safety and emotional well-being.

Kate knew she wouldn't emerge from this assignment with her heart unscathed.

Chapter Nine

Chase shook hands with Angus in the foyer of the big house. "Thank you for staying with Jake yesterday and today. Knowing you were here with him let us do what we had to do with a whole lot less worry."

"I'm sorry to hear it was pretty rough in Denver and on your way back. I'll keep my eyes open for trouble and do some asking around. When do you need me back?"

"We'll let you know."

Angus twirled his cowboy hat in his hands. "Look, I'm sorry about losing the boy."

Chase's lips curled upward. "I'd be more worried had he gotten lost in the forest. He did what he was told and stayed close to you...with a little distraction of kittens."

His lips firming into a straight line, Angus nodded. "He's a good kid."

"Yeah, and his grandmother is the best." Chase breathed in and let it out slowly. "Neither one of them deserves to be hurt."

"Yeah, well, I'll be here whenever you need me."

"Go home and spend time with your family. It's nearly Christmas, surely you've got holiday plans."

Angus grinned. "If I don't, Reggie will have them for me. She's a one-woman dynamo. I don't know where she gets all that energy to run a ranch and be a terrific mother to Tad."

"I hope it wasn't too much keeping track of Jake."

"Are you kidding? I caught up on my ball games while the boys entertained each other yesterday afternoon. They spent all day in a tent made of sheets set up in the living room. Tad didn't want to go home when Reggie came by to pick him up. And your bear probably has a worn spot or two where they petted it at least a hundred times."

Chase chuckled. "I keep meaning to get rid of that bear. I don't know why my grandfather thought it was a good idea to keep his trophy bear in the living room. I might donate it to a natural history museum."

Angus shook his head. "You can't get rid of it. If nothing else, the kids love it."

The two men shook hands and Angus left, promising to be on call should they need him any time, day or night. Chase went in search of Kate. By now, she should be ready for a break from Jake. Being with the child was probably torture for her, knowing she'd never have any of her own.

Though Kate had been self-conscious about the scar on her stomach, Chase loved it. The scar was a reminder of who she was. In a way it defined Kate as the self-sacrificing cop she used to be. Tough, but sensitive enough to hold a frightened boy, even though it tore her apart.

Chase found Kate and Jake in the kitchen sitting side by side at the table, eating the fried chicken and mashed potatoes Mrs. Quaid had made for dinner.

William and Frances sat on the other side of the table, smiling at something Jake had said as Chase walked in.

Frances spotted Chase and half rose from her seat. "I can set the table in the dining room in just a second."

Chase held up his hand. "I prefer to eat my fried chicken in the kitchen." He winked at Jake. "It's warmer and smells better." When Frances straightened, he shook his head. "No need to get up. I can serve myself."

Frances sank into her seat. "Jake was just telling us Fancy had kittens in the barn."

Jake bounced in his chair. "Can I have one of the kittens? Please, Uncle Chase?"

"They have to get a little older. Their eyes barely even opened yet."

"When they're old enough, can I have one?" he persisted.

"You'll have to get permission from your grandma. You two are supposed to move into your own house next month."

"But I don't want to move again." Jake frowned. "I like living here."

Chase had been thinking about that, as well. Sadie had been there for him when he'd needed a friend. His house was so big, with ten bedrooms spread out on the first, second and third floors, she and Jake could have several of them all to themselves and it would be no trouble. "We'll see," he said. "First your grandma has to get well. We can talk then."

Jake turned to Kate. "I want the one with the black patch over his eye. I'll call him Pirate." The boy yawned and blinked.

Kate smiled at him and nodded to his plate. "Finish up, you still have to get a bath before bed."

"Will you read me a story, Miss Kate?"

Kate hesitated only a moment before replying softly. "Of course."

Jake set the drumstick he'd been gnawing on back on his plate. "I'm full." He yawned again.

"I'm done, too. Come on, squirt. I'll get your bath ready." Frances took her plate and Jake's to the sink and then followed the boy out of the kitchen.

William sopped up his gravy with the last of his dinner roll, shoved it in his mouth and carried his plate to the sink. "I'm going to check on the animals one last time before I call it a night." He exited through the back door, leaving Kate and Chase to finish their meal alone.

Kate concentrated on her plate, pushing the leftover potatoes and gravy around.

"About last night," Chase started.

She set her fork on her plate. "Let's not discuss it. What happened...happened. Let's not have a repeat performance."

His belly tightened and his chest felt hollow, as though the air he breathed wasn't doing enough to supply his body with oxygen.

If he thought she hadn't felt anything the night before, he'd let her go and not press for more. But she'd been as passionate as he'd been, and he couldn't forget about making love to her that easily.

For now, though, she was running scared. He'd have to play it easy, give her space, until he figured out the real reason. "If that's the way you want it."

She glanced up, her eyes narrowing. "It's the right thing to do."

"If you're worried about the client-bodyguard relationship, I'm not."

She pushed her chair back and rose. "What I'm worried about doesn't matter. It's not happening again." She collected her plate and utensils and carried them to the sink.

Chase picked at his food, eating a little and pausing, wanting to say something, anything that would change her mind. More than he realized, he wanted her back in his bed, her body beneath him, the warmth of her skin pressed to his. His groin tightened and he bit down hard on his tongue to keep from telling Kate he wanted her.

Clearly, she wasn't ready to jump into a relationship. But when she was, he'd be there. If she stuck around long enough.

He ate a few more bites of the delicious food Mrs. Quaid had prepared, to keep up his strength for whatever challenge might come their way. Then he gathered his plate, fork, knife and glass and carried them across the room.

Kate had filled the sink with soapy water and washed the dishes.

"Mrs. Quaid usually takes care of the kitchen," Chase reminded her.

"Mrs. Quaid doesn't usually have a little boy in the house, does she?"

"No." He slipped his plate into the water and grabbed a dry dish towel.

As Kate washed, he dried, reaching around her to place the plates in the cabinet to her left.

Every time he brushed against her, her body quivered.

Despite his decision to give her space, he found more reasons to brush against her with every dish he dried and put away. Finally, she slopped the washcloth into the water and turned just as he was reaching around her to put a coffee mug in the cabinet over her head.

When she faced him, his lips were mere inches from hers.

"Do you have to bump into me every time you put something away?" she cried, her voice breathy, her chest rising and falling, her breathing labored.

"I don't know what you're talking about." Chase

swallowed the smile that threatened to explode across his face. He placed the mug he held on the top shelf, requiring him to lean closer to her, his chest rubbing against hers. "I'm just helping." When he brought his arm down, he didn't back away, instead placing his hands on the counter on either side of her. "I didn't mean to bother you." His gaze captured hers, daring her to move.

"You don't bother me," she whispered, her green eyes flaring.

He nearly came apart when she slipped her tongue across her lower lip. Chase's body heated and his jeans grew decidedly tighter. Instead of sealing her mouth with a kiss, he leaned close enough he could feel her breath warming his lips. "I'm glad I'm not bothering you." Then he closed the cabinet behind her and stepped away. "I believe Jake wanted you to read a book to him. I can finish up here if you'd like to get started." Chase turned away and looped the dish towel through a drawer handle.

A soft snort behind him did not prepare him for the wet washcloth hitting him square in the back.

He spun to find Kate with her eyes wide a hand pressed to her lips. "Oops. I'm sorry. It must have slipped." She bent to pick up the washcloth and straightened in front of him, pressing her breasts to his chest. "I'm not bothered by you, Chase Marsden." Then she tossed the cloth into the sink and spun on her heals, and left the kitchen.

Chase laughed out loud and reached behind his back to pluck the wet fabric of his shirt from the middle of his back. Like hell she wasn't bothered by him. She'd been as turned on as he was.

KATE WALKED OUT of the kitchen when she really wanted to run. But she wouldn't give Chase the satisfaction. She'd be damned if she let him think he was getting to her by brushing his body against hers the entire time they'd been washing and drying dishes.

If she was being truthful with herself, she'd admit he'd more than gotten to her. He'd set her body on fire with every light brush, every intentional bump of his hips against hers and every time his chest rubbed against her back. When the front placard of his jeans nudged her bottom she'd practically come unglued. The man had her so tied in knots, she couldn't think straight. A cold shower might help her focus on why she was there.

She'd been hired to solve a crime, take down the person responsible and return to Texas where she belonged.

Kate climbed the sweeping staircase to the second floor, gathered her toiletries, a clean T-shirt and flannel pajama bottoms and headed for the bathroom.

Voices drifted from Jake's room as Mrs. Quaid prepared him for bed.

When Jake had asked her to read a bedtime story, her first reaction was to hope he'd fall asleep before she was forced to sit on the side of his bed and read from the pages of a children's book. But hearing him talk in his little boy voice to Mrs. Quaid, Kate found herself hurrying through her own cold shower, anxious to keep her promise, while hoping her focus on the boy would offset her desire for the man downstairs.

When she emerged from the bathroom, clean, her wet hair combed straight back from her forehead, she paused to listen for Jake's voice.

The hallway was silent. Disappointment tugged at her heart. She ditched her things in her room and hurried to Jake's.

She eased the door open and peeked inside.

The overhead light had been turned off, but the lamp on the nightstand glowed softly, illuminating the bed where Jake lay against the pillow, his body barely making a lump beneath the quilted comforter.

"Jake?" Kate whispered softly. "Are you still awake?"

"Uh-huh." His eyes blinked open and he yawned. "I stayed awake just for you."

Her heart melted and she stepped into the room. "What book would you like me to read?"

Jake turned toward the nightstand. "This one." He lifted a thin book with a picture of Santa Claus in his sleigh flying over a rooftop. '*Twas the Night before Christmas* was written in bright red letters across the top.

Kate's hand shook as she took the book from Jake. She remembered her father reading her this story every night in December before Christmas when she was a little girl. With that memory came a flood of homesickness. It had been a long time since she'd been home. "Did you pick this one because Christmas is just a few days away?"

"No." Jake scooted over so Kate could sit on the bed with him. "I like it because it has a mom and dad in it."

The boy's words twisted in her heart and made Kate's throat swell to the point she couldn't start reading.

Several times, she swallowed hard to dislodge the lump in her throat. Jake wanted what other kids had. He wanted a father and mother. A normal life to come home to. The boy didn't know how lucky he was to have a loving grandmother who cared about him, and a godfather who would do anything to make sure the boy was well and happy.

Kate sat on the edge of the bed and leaned against the headboard. Jake waited until she'd settled, then lay his head in her lap. Again, Kate had to fight a wad of emotion threatening to choke the air from her throat.

"Aren't you going to read to me?" he asked sleepily.

"Yes," Kate choked out. "Of course." She cleared her throat and began. "'Twas the night before Christmas…"

A stuttering start smoothed into the rhythm of the poem and her memories. Kate made it to the very end of the story and closed the book, her heart full.

Jake lay across her lap, his hand curled over her thigh, fast asleep.

Kate stared down at the little boy, wishing with all her heart that she had just such a son. Jake was polite, intelligent and curious enough to explore his surroundings, to the point he got stuck in a tight space with five kittens and a mama cat.

She'd been like that as a kid, following her father around the ranch, falling into the pigpen chasing after a baby piglet. Her mother laughed and hosed her down outside when she'd come back to the house covered in mud from head to toe. Her sisters had laughed at her hoyden ways, but she didn't care. She'd loved being outside. It meant she'd had her father all to herself.

Kate sat for several more minutes after the story ended, smoothing her hand over the child's silky dark brown hair so much like her own.

A noise at the door made her glance up, her gaze connecting with Chase's. His hair was fresh-from-the-shower wet and he wore only a pair of sweatpants, his chest and feet bare. He hadn't shaved and a dark shadow of stubble gave him a sensuous appeal that made Kate catch her breath. When he smiled that slow sexy curl of his lips with the sparkle in his icy-blue eyes, every bone in Kate's body melted into a puddle of goo.

"How long have you been standing there?" she asked.

His smile broadened. "Merry Christmas to all and to all a good night."

Her cheeks heated and she eased from beneath Jake's cheek. "You should have said something."

"What? That you and Jake looked adorable? I didn't want to interrupt a great story."

"Jake was already asleep. He wouldn't have known any better," Kate whispered, bending over the little boy's inert form. She shifted his head to the pillow and drew the covers up to his chin, tucking them in around him to keep him warm.

"You're good at that," Jake commented.

"I should be, I helped raise my little sister."

"I didn't know you had siblings. Somehow I thought you were an only child."

She shrugged. "So now you know a little more about me."

"Are your parents still alive?"

"Yes."

"You talk to them much?"

"Not enough." Again she shrugged. "They live in the Texas panhandle. My sisters and their families live close by." Kate's chest tightened at the thought of her family. She hadn't been home since her surgery. Her mother had wanted to come out to be with her in the hospital, but Kate downplayed her injuries, insisting that her mother should stay home to help her younger sister who was due to deliver a baby soon.

Her sister had a little boy. Her second baby in as many years.

"Is being here with us keeping you from going home for the holiday?" Chase asked.

Kate shook her head and crossed the room, determined to end this line of questioning that only caused her pain. "No."

"Don't you want to go home and be with your family?" Chase blocked her exit, his body filling the door frame.

Her heart beat faster at the expanse of muscles and the questions he posed. "What is this, fifty questions?" she snapped back at him. She wanted to plant her hands against his chest and shove him aside, but was afraid she wouldn't be able to push him away once she touched him.

Instead she planted her fists on her hips. "I'm not here to answer questions about myself. We should be poring through Sadie's black book and the stack of letters. The sooner we get to the bottom of the threats and attacks the sooner I can leave you all to your own Christmas celebration."

"Touchy, touchy." Chase straightened and stepped backward into the hallway, allowing her to pass through the doorway.

"And for heaven's sake, put on a shirt," she said as she breezed past him.

He chuckled and followed her down the hallway.

Kate could kick herself for mentioning the lack of shirt. It would only prove to him she was aware of him and sensitive about his naked chest.

God, she hoped he hadn't seen the hunger she had for him reflected in her eyes or in the gravelly tone of her voice.

She returned to her room, gathered the book and the letters and stepped out into the hallway.

Chase came out of his room, pulling a black T-shirt down over his chest. As tight as it fit over his muscles it did little to tone down her awareness of the man.

A moan rose up her throat and almost escaped before she could turn away and march down the stairs to the first floor and the wood-paneled office she'd seen several times in passing. The room smelled of linseed oil and leather. Three of the four walls were lined with floor-to-ceiling bookshelves. A massive mahogany desk took up the center of the room with two dark brown leather wingback chairs in front of it and a leather office chair behind.

Kate laid the book on the desk and untied the bundle of letters. When she turned, Chase stood immediately behind her. Heat radiated from low in her belly outward. Kate closed her eyes, willing it to stop, struggling for focus. "Do you want to search the computer or read the letters?" She opened her eyes and gave him a level stare, refusing to fall victim to her desires. They had too much work to do.

"I'll take the computer." Chase dropped into the office chair while Kate took several of the letters and settled into one of the wingback chairs, tucking her feet beneath her to keep them warm in the drafty room. A strangely comfortable silence stretched between them with only the tap of keys and rustling of pages to disturb the calm.

An hour passed and Kate had read twenty letters.

Chase pushed away from the desk and stood stretching.

"Find anything?" Kate asked.

"Nothing so far. I've gone through twenty-eight names and haven't had a significant hit yet. Sure, some of them have been in the news, but nothing major." He nodded toward the stack of letters. "What are the letters about?"

Kate's lips curved. "They're love letters."

"Love letters?" Chase rounded the desk. "Let me see."

She handed one to him and he skimmed the contents, flipped it over and frowned. "It's not signed."

"I know." Kate lifted the stack of letters. "I've been

through every one of them and have yet to determine who wrote them to Sadie's daughter, Melissa." Kate sighed. "I wish Sadie wasn't in a coma."

"You and me both. For her own sake as well as ours." Chase strode to the long, velvet drapes on the one wall that didn't have bookshelves on it. "We might have a better chance of identifying her attacker if she was around to answer a few questions." He drew the drapes aside and stared out at the night.

Kate stood and stretched her back, finding a few sore muscles from being knocked down by the man in Denver. "Did you hear from the Denver PD? Have they identified the man who attacked us?"

"I called while you were in the shower earlier. So far nothing. They're sending prints to a latent print expert. I asked them to send a copy of the prints to Hank as well. Hopefully we'll know something tomorrow. That's assuming the man has a police record."

"Other than a book of names, a stack of love letters and a dead man, we don't have much to go on." She crossed to the window and stood beside Chase, staring out at the mountains tinged in the deep blue light from the moon. It was so beautiful it took her breath away. "Wow. The view is stunning."

"Yeah." Chase spoke softly, reverently. "It's one of the reasons I've stayed as long as I have."

Kate tilted her head toward Chase. "You inherited the ranch from your grandfather, but you didn't plan on staying?"

He laughed, the sound a short bark. "According to the will, I only had to live here for two years, and I would own it outright and could sell it if I wanted. I counted all 730 days until the time was up."

"When was that?"

"Two weeks ago."

"And you're still here."

He nodded toward the blue snow covering the mountains in the moonlight. "I guess I knew within six weeks that my heart was captured by the place. When it came time to leave, I couldn't let go."

"Sounds like you love it." Her heart warmed to the sound of his voice as he spoke. The playboy she'd read about had found a home in a place that didn't seem to fit with his previous lifestyle.

Kate had never enjoyed living in the city. The few years she'd spent working in and around Houston and Dallas had shaved years off her life in the stress of traffic and the overwhelming number of people.

Having grown up on a big ranch, where the nearest neighbor was two miles down the road, she'd adjusted to the city, but hadn't loved it. Kate preferred the wide open spaces and fresh air of life in the country. Places like the ranch she'd grown up on or the Lucky Lady Ranch.

Yeah, she was definitely homesick for her family, the noise and bustle of a Sunday dinner at her parents' house with all her sisters, their spouses and…their kids.

An arm slipped around her waist and a big, callused hand curved around her hip, pulling her close.

Kate knew she should resist. But the sudden bout of homesickness, the happiness she's experienced reading a story to a little boy and the residual memory of all the places that hand had touched the night before worked against her.

Instead of pulling away, she leaned into Chase, resting her head against the solid expanse of his rock-hard chest, and gave in to her need for comfort and so much more.

"Ready to go to bed?" he asked.

She nodded.

Chase scooped the black book and letters up and carried them to a painting on the wall. "Kate, meet my great-great-grandmother, Lady Jones."

Kate studied the painting. "She was a beautiful woman."

"Thus her success as a madam." He grabbed the frame and swung it out like a door. Behind the painting was a wall safe. He twisted the knob one way, then the other and back again, until a loud click sounded and he opened the safe door.

"Good idea," Kate said.

"This safe is as old as this house. Lady Jones was a smart woman." He tucked the book, the letters and the list of bank accounts into the safe, closed and spun the lock. Then he covered the safe with the painting.

Chase took her hand and led her up the grand staircase to the second floor.

Kate walked past Jake's room and continued on. When they reached her room, she pushed the door open and stepped inside, still holding Chase's hand.

Chase stopped at the threshold.

Kate turned, frowning, words poised on her lips to ask what was wrong.

He smiled, released her hand and cupped her cheek with his palm. "As much as I'd like to make love to you. We both need rest. If I stay with you, I promise we won't sleep at all."

Her belly clenched as his words sank in. "Sleep can be overrated," she offered, praying he'd change his mind and fill that aching void inside her like he had in the hotel in Denver. In his arms she'd managed to forget that her body wasn't whole, that she would never have children.

"Maybe so, but you and I have a lot to think about.

I want to go into town tomorrow and find out who's been hanging around Fool's Fortune. I want to know who the dead man is and what all this has to do with Sadie's black book."

"You can't do any of that until tomorrow." *And tonight you could be with me*, she wanted to add, but bit down hard on her tongue, hoping he'd hear the words implied.

His lips curled upward. "Maybe you're right. When this is over, you'll be leaving. Why set ourselves up for disappointment?" He bent over her, his lips skimming hers in a feather-soft kiss.

Anger bubbled up with Kate's desire. She laced her fingers around his neck, pushed up on her toes and deepened the kiss, thrusting her tongue past his teeth to dance with his, teasing and tasting until she had to break it off to breathe.

When she stepped back, she forced a smile and closed the door in Chase's face. "Let him sleep on that," she muttered.

A chuckle sounded on the other side of the hardwood paneling. "I heard that. And you made your point. I didn't say sleep would come easy."

She crossed her arms, leaned her back against the door and slid to the ground, tears pooling in her eyes. Why did life have to be so damned difficult?

Chapter Ten

Chase tossed through the night, barely sleeping. Several times he rose and walked to the door of his bedroom with every intention of storming down the hallway to Kate's room to declare he'd been wrong.

Every time, he'd stopped with his hand on the doorknob, the same question halting him in his tracks. What did he want from Kate?

He'd just met the woman and made love to her. Hell, he'd had more women in his life than most men dreamed of. He'd had no trouble walking away from all of them after one, maybe two dates.

The problem was that Kate was different from any other woman he'd ever known. She was tough, gritty and beautiful. Beneath her hard shell was a vulnerable heart. One he refused to break.

What did he want from Kate?

He wanted to hold her, touch her, make love to her through the night. And after that?

Do it all over again.

Chase paced the length of his big bedroom and back. He stretched out on the bed and closed his eyes. As soon as he did, he saw Kate as she'd been in the hotel room, lying naked against the sheets, her long dark hair splayed across the pillow, the scar on her belly a jagged but beautiful reminder of her service to others.

She deserved a better man than him. A man worthy of her love. He'd spent his life traipsing around the world, hell-bent on destroying himself and careless of others' feelings.

When his grandfather died, his wayward life had come to an end. Though Chase and his grandfather didn't always get along, his grandfather, the one person who took the time to get to know him, had died and Chase hadn't been to visit him in the years before his death.

He hadn't wanted to come to the Lucky Lady Ranch, hadn't wanted to live in the place his grandfather had loved so much. It reminded him of what he'd lost. A chance to spend time with his grandfather and a chance to say goodbye.

The two years he'd been at the Lucky Lady Ranch had started as a penance, a guilt trip he had to endure to appease the conditions of the will. He'd resisted at first, drinking himself into oblivion in Leadville when Sadie had found him beaten up in a gutter and taken pity on him.

She'd been the only one to understand him.

Now she lay in a coma in the hospital. Chase hadn't found the person responsible and he was falling for the bodyguard.

Falling for Kate was wrong and wouldn't solve anything. Until he found Sadie's attacker, and until he knew what he wanted, he was no good to Kate. She'd had enough heartache to deal with as it was, having lost her partner and a dream most women hold dear. Children of her own. She didn't need someone like Chase to make her life more of a hell.

When the clock on his nightstand blinked a bright green five o'clock, Chase gave up on sleep, left his bed, dressed and tiptoed downstairs to his office. Pulling the black book from the safe, he spent the next hour searching the web for names from the book, sure he'd missed something important. He entered the name *Melissa Smith* and several different key words. He found her obituary from six months ago. She was survived by her son, Jake Smith, and her mother, Sadie Lovely.

She hadn't had many relatives, but at least she had some. If Chase were to die, there wouldn't be another family member to write his obituary. Chase Marsden would be survived by no one.

Pushing aside the morose thought, he tried several more combinations with Melissa's name including *Colorado State Capitol.*

This time, a news article popped up on the screen with a young woman and a young man at a campaign rally. The caption read, "Assistant District Attorney Benson Garner and his executive secretary, Melissa Smith, help build communities with their efforts in Houses for Heroes."

Chase leaned forward. Benson Garner was the current candidate for the US senatorial race.

Sadie's daughter wore blue jeans, a Denver Broncos sweatshirt and a hard hat. She appeared young, like a college coed. She held a hammer in her hand and smiled up at Benson Garner, who was smiling down at her.

Was there more to their smiles than just putting on a show for the newspaper reporter?

Chase searched again with *Benson Garner* and *Melissa Smith* as his keywords. Two more articles appeared. In one, Benson had his arm around Melissa, who wore a classy black cocktail dress, as they stood smiling with several others in a ribbon-cutting ceremony at a posh downtown spa in Denver. In the other, Benson and Melissa were visiting the children's hospital. Chase checked the dates on all three articles. All three were dated six years ago.

Six years.

Chase did the math.

Jake was five years old.

"Hey," a soft voice called out, jerking his attention away from the screen to glance up.

Kate stood in the doorway, dressed in blue jeans and a red sweater that complemented her dark hair and green eyes. "How long have you been up?"

Chase glanced at the clock, surprised that it was seven already. "Two hours."

Her lips quirked on the corners. "Have trouble sleeping?"

He shook his head knowing the lie would stick on his lips. "Look at this," he said, deflecting his focus back to the screen.

Kate crossed the room and stood behind him, her hands resting on the back of his chair. He could feel the heat of her body, and it had an immediate effect on his overactive libido.

Kate leaned closer until her face was inches from his. "Who are they?"

"Melissa Smith, Sadie's daughter, and Benson Garner." He turned Kate. "Benson Garner is a senatorial candidate."

"That's interesting. Have we been searching for the wrong information all along?"

"Maybe."

Kate's eyes widened even more. "The love letters." She turned to fetch them.

"Right here." He pushed them across the desk. "These articles were all from six years ago. What were the dates on the letters?"

Kate lifted the envelopes and studied the postmark. "Six years ago." Then she glanced up and met Chase's gaze. "Jake."

"We don't know that for sure. Only a DNA test could give us a definitive answer."

"Do you think Jake is Benson Garner's son?"

"I'm just guessing based on a few old photographs and newspaper articles. It's something to consider."

"He's coming to Fool's Fortune for a campaign rally, isn't he?" Kate said.

Chase nodded.

"We could get a DNA sample."

"Hold on." Chase held up a hand. "We're working off pure conjecture. We could be adding one plus one and getting five."

"Melissa died in a car crash. Maybe someone ran her off the road." Kate reached for the phone. "I can have Hank pull up the accident report and check for other marks on the car."

"The vehicle burned on impact. If there were marks, the heat from the fire would have destroyed them."

Her hand still on the phone, Kate stared at Chase. "It's a lead. I should at least let Hank know."

As her fingers curled around the handset, the phone rang and she jerked her hand away.

Chase chuckled and lifted the handset. "Marsden."

"Chase. Hank here."

"Hank." Chase winked at Kate and hit the speaker button and set the receiver down. "Got you on speaker. I'm here with Kate. We were just about to call you."

"Yeah? Have you learned anything new?"

"As a matter of fact, I found several articles on the internet about Melissa Smith and Benson Garner all dating back six years ago." He explained the connection and their initial assumption. "We could be way off base, but it's worth checking into."

"We can check with Brandon and see if he's found anything on Melissa in public records and newspaper articles. We'll also look for Jake's birth certificate. If there's something to be found, he'll find it."

"Garner is due to speak in Fool's Fortune the day after tomorrow. Any suggestions?"

"I doubt he'll hand over a DNA swab, and DNA testing can take a long time."

"We might not have that long, the way things have been going around here."

"Exactly."

"The man who attacked us in the garage was after the black book," Kate said. "He specifically went for it. Not for Melissa's letters."

"Brandon's still running searches on all the names you texted. We've had a couple hits, but nothing worth pursuing yet. There is a chance some of the names are aliases. Some men would be in a world of hurt if their affiliation with a madam were to be made public knowledge."

"How do we decode aliases?" Chase asked.

"We really need Sadie to come out of that coma. I'm certain she knows what her clients' real names were," Kate said.

"In the meantime, we go with what we have," Hank said. "Oh, and I have the name of the man who attacked you in Denver."

Chase and Kate leaned toward the speaker.

"Kyle Bradley, former army infantry soldier. Three

tours in Iraq, got out of the army and went to work for TG International, a mercenary group providing contracted security for the big contractors brought in to rebuild Iraqi infrastructure."

"Who's he working for now?"

"He's not on record as working for anyone. Brandon's digging deeper. I hope to have something to you soon."

"Check for names of others he could have been working with. Since we were attacked again after Bradley died, there is more than one mercenary after Sadie and her black book."

"On it," Hank confirmed. "Will let you know what we find." Then he rang off.

"Someone hired a mercenary," Kate whispered.

A chill slithered across Chase's skin. "More than one." Chase knew how to fire guns, but he was not a trained soldier or a member of law enforcement. How was he supposed to protect Jake, the Quaids and Sadie? He stood and stared down at the computer terminal, overwhelmed by what he'd learned.

"Hey." Kate touched his arm. "Hank only hires the best. I'm trained to handle situations like this. So are Angus and Chuck."

"You heard Hank. These men aren't thugs from the street. They're highly trained mercenaries. We don't know when they're going to strike or where."

Kate rounded to his front. "We'll be ready."

"We weren't ready in Denver."

"But we survived. Bradley didn't."

"If he'd been perched on the corner of a building with a sniper's rifle, we'd be dead." Chase gripped Kate's arms and pulled her against him. "Perhaps we should give them what they want. Sadie wouldn't want her book to be what gets any of us killed."

"Chase, what if the book isn't all they're after? What if they come after Jake?"

His hands tightened on her arms. "We can't let them get to him. He's just a kid."

"If we give them the book, assuming we even know who they are, and they take Jake. We have nothing to bargain with to get him back."

Chase leaned his forehead against Kate's. "What has Sadie gotten herself into?"

"We're going to find out."

"And who will end up in the hospital next or, worse, in the morgue?" He pulled her into his arms and held her tight against him. "Damn it, Kate, I thought I could stay away from you, but the thought of you getting hurt…"

Kate's arms circled his waist. "We're going to be okay." She leaned up on her toes and pressed a kiss to his lips. "You'll see. When this is all over, you'll look back on it as a bad dream."

"Only if you don't get hurt. Or Jake. And if Sadie pulls through."

Kate kissed him again. "*When* Sadie pulls through."

He cupped the back of her neck. "Your optimism never ceases to amaze me."

"You're pretty amazing yourself. Look at all you've done for Sadie and Jake."

He brushed his mouth across hers, loving the way her soft lips felt beneath his, and how her body molded to his as if they fit together. "I haven't done anything."

She stared up at him. "You've given them a home and hope."

Her green eyes melted his resolve from the day before and he couldn't pull away from her. "You deserve a much better man than I am, Kate. You're selfless and strong."

"That's funny, because I could describe you the same way."

"I spent so much of my life living in the moment, never caring about others, just going through the motions."

"That's not the Chase I'm getting to know. Perhaps it was you in the past. But that's not who you are now."

Chase claimed her mouth with a crushing kiss, threading his hand through her dark silky hair, holding her so close, the only way they could get closer was to be naked.

Kate leaned into him, her tongue twisting and gliding along his, hungrily devouring his mouth. Why had he thought he could walk away from her when he wanted to be with her so badly?

When he finally lifted his head to catch his breath, he held her. "Kate, darlin', I'm glad you've come into my life."

"We're going to find out who's trying to hurt the people you love and take them down."

"Uncle Chase?" Jake's voice called out in the hallway. "Uncle Chase?"

"In here." Chase let his arms fall to his sides and stepped away from Kate. "We're in here, Jake."

Jake skidded to a halt in front of the door, still wearing his pajamas, his dark hair standing up on one side. "Mrs. Quaid said we can go to town today."

"She did, did she?" Chase dropped to his haunches. "And why is that?"

Mrs. Quaid appeared behind Jake. "Haven't you heard? John Michaels challenged Benson Garner to a debate and they are conducting it here in Fool's Fortune, since Garner had to cancel his speech at the tree-lighting ceremony on Friday."

"Did he give a reason why he canceled Friday?"

"He told the media that since it was so close to Christmas, he wanted to spend time at home with his family. Namely his mother since his father passed.

"I wanted to hear what the candidates have to say. If you and Miss Kate have more pressing matters, William and I can take Jake with us."

Chase shook his head. "No, we'll be just fine. We can take Jake with us." He'd feel better knowing exactly where Jake was all the time. Especially if someone turned the attacks toward the boy.

"Good. I'm sure Jake would prefer hanging out with you two over two old people."

"You and William aren't old," Chase protested.

"Tell my bones that." Mrs. Quaid moved past Jake. "Now, if you'll excuse me I have to get breakfast started or Mr. Quaid will be old *and* grumpy."

"We're going to town." Jake threw his hands around Chase's neck and held on as he straightened, lifting the little boy off the ground. "Can we go to the hospital and visit Grandma Sadie?"

Chase exchanged a glance with Kate. "I don't know, Jake. They don't let little kids in to visit when they are as sick as your grandmother is."

His face scrunched into a frown, his happiness drooping like a sad little dog. "Is Grandma Sadie going to die?"

Chase leaned back and caught Jake's gaze with his own. "Jake, your grandma is very sick, be we're going to pray really hard that she gets better soon. We want her to come home before Christmas."

Jake cupped Chase's face with one of his little hands. "Do you think if I ask Santa, he'll bring her home to us?"

"He might." Kate brushed the boy's hair back from

his forehead. "Why don't you write a letter to him and we'll mail it when we're in town?"

Jake leaned toward Kate, forcing her to take him into her arms. "Will you help me write a letter to Santa, Miss Kate? Please?"

Kate held him close. "You bet. Go change out of your pajamas and come down to breakfast. We'll write that letter when we're done eating."

"Okay." Jake planted a kiss on her cheek and then wiggled out of her arms. He landed on the ground and took off running. He was out of the office and up the stairs before either adult could comment.

"I wish I could bottle his energy," Kate said.

"Me, too." Chase stared at her, wanting to take her back into his arms, but the mood had been broken. "I guess we're going to town."

"Looks that way. We should ask around and find out if there have been any strangers hanging around. Is there a place most locals go to gossip?"

Chase grinned. "If you want gossip, the diner and the feed store are the places to go."

"We could take Jake with us to keep an eye on him and make some subtle inquiries. From what I saw of Fool's Fortune, it's small. Strangers would stand out."

"Except during big tourist seasons. Like summertime and, unfortunately, Christmas. We get a lot of visitors from the cities who come out to enjoy a small-town Christmas. People spend their holidays here, arriving the weekend before Christmas and staying through New Year's Eve. And with the political debate scheduled for today, it will be chaotic."

Kate grimaced. "Well, it still doesn't hurt to check out the candidates while they're in Fool's Fortune. If we can get them alone, all the better. We might have the opportunity to question them about Sadie and Melissa."

"Agreed. Lunch at the diner for local gossip. We might discover if someone's been lurking around town. We need some feed, too, so we can stop by the feed store, as well." Chase pulled a set of keys out of his pocket, walked to one of the bookshelves and pulled it open like a door. Behind it was a vault-like gun safe his grandfather had installed during the Cold War. "I have my concealed carry license." He opened the safe and showed her the arsenal of weapons inside.

Kate laughed. "Are you preparing for a war?"

Chase shrugged. "My grandfather was a gun collector. He liked to hunt and enjoyed target practice. He also taught me how to shoot."

Kate's brows furrowed. "And are you any good? Because if you're not comfortable with the gun, you're in more danger carrying than if you weren't carrying at all."

"I'm very comfortable with the nine-millimeter Beretta." He lifted a handgun out of one of the racks.

"My .40-caliber HK goes with me everywhere. Hopefully we won't need it. It'll be broad daylight and there will be plenty of people around."

"Whoever is after us isn't shy of attacking in broad daylight, considering the run-in we had on the road back from Denver."

"True. This time they don't have a tracking device to follow. And we'll be more vigilant."

Chase nodded, his jaw tight. "We'll have to be. Jake's coming with us."

Chapter Eleven

Kate insisted on driving her truck to Fool's Fortune. As banged up as Chase's vehicle was, it would cause more commotion than either of them wanted, drawing too much attention to them when they wanted to blend into the crowd for their investigation.

They'd had breakfast as usual and helped Mrs. Quaid clean up. Afterward, Kate and Jake sat at the kitchen table, crafting a letter to Santa, asking him to bring Grandma Sadie home for Christmas. Jake dictated what he wanted to say, Kate wrote it and Jake signed it in big block letters.

They sealed it in an envelope, addressed it, and Jake stuck a stamp on it and carried it out to the truck, excited to mail his first letter.

His enthusiasm was contagious despite the gravity of the current situation. Kate couldn't wait to stop at the post office to let him slide his letter into the mailbox.

Chase and William spent a couple hours in the barn, taking care of the animals and breaking ice from the outside watering troughs. By the time they finished, showered and changed, half the morning had gone by.

On the curving mountain road into town, Kate's gaze bounced between the road in front of them, the rearview mirrors and any side road they passed along the way. If something were going to come at them, she'd be ready. Her years on the highway as a Texas Ranger gave her the experience to drive defensively and to be on the alert for anything.

The trip to Fool's Fortune was uneventful. Jake sat in a booster seat in the back, and Chase in the passenger seat facing her most of the time.

Her chest tightened and her eyes stung. Jake wasn't hers, but she already loved the little guy. This must be what it would feel like to have a family of her own.

Then Kate remembered she and Chase weren't married and, though the sex was great, they'd only been together for a few days. They weren't in love. They couldn't be. And she was building a fantasy around nothing. When this assignment was over, there'd be no reason for her to stay.

As she neared town, Kate's foot left the accelerator as though by slowing the vehicle she could postpone her inevitable departure from Fool's Fortune, the Lucky Lady Ranch and, most of all, Chase Marsden.

"Let's start at the Lucky Lady Saloon. I usually check in two or three times a week." Chase's lips twisted. "My manager is fully capable of running the place without my interference, but I like to let him know I care. And we can look at the guest register and see if there are any names that stand out."

"Or if any of them are from Sadie's black book." Kate drove down Main Street. It had only been a couple days since the last time she'd driven this same road, but it seemed like a lifetime. So much had happened since then.

In the daylight, the Lucky Lady Saloon had the quaint appeal of an old-fashioned saloon straight out of a Wild West movie set with real hitching posts out front. Though it had snowed, the winds had died and the sun came out, the sky was blue and the temperature was a balmy twenty-one degrees. Even the air sparkled like glitter as what little moisture was there crystallized.

Kate parked in front of a hitching post and climbed down.

Chase came around and helped Jake out of his booster seat and lifted the boy into his arms. "Is Grandma Sadie singing?"

"Not today, Jake. She's still in the hospital."

He looped his arms around Chase's neck. "I miss her. When is she coming home?"

"When she gets better," Chase assured him.

Kate's heart ached for the little boy. The people he depended on seemed to have deserted him. "You two go on in. I'm going to make a call." She mouthed the word *hospital* in a way Jake wouldn't see or hear.

Pulling the collar of her jacket up around her ears, she called Chuck at the hospital.

"Hey, Kate. I hear you and Marsden had a little trouble in Denver and on the way back."

"We did. We're fine, but I'm concerned about Sadie."

"I've been here all the time. No one has made another attempt to reach her so far."

"That's good news."

"I'm not a doctor, but I think she's showing signs of improvement," he said. "Today, when I was talking to her, I asked her if she wanted to go home for Christmas. I could swear she squeezed my hand. When I told the doctor, he mentioned he might bring her out of sedation tomorrow and see if she comes to."

"That's great news." Kate stared at the door through which Chase and Jake had passed. Jake might get his wish to have his grandma Sadie home for Christmas, if nothing else happened to her in the meantime.

"Hank's sending Agent Harding. He should be here later today, as long as the weather holds out. We need backup in case I have to leave. PJ has been having a lot of Braxton Hicks contractions. She might go into early labor."

Kate smiled. PJ was one tough lady, having delivered her first baby without Chuck by her side. This time she'd want him there. "I'm sure she wouldn't mind delivering a few days early."

"She's holding out for when I get home. God, I love that woman."

Kate gulped at the passion in Chuck's voice. What would it be like to be loved that much? She forced a chuckle past the lump in her throat. "Babies have a way of choosing their own time." The words came out and she realized they didn't hurt nearly as badly as when she'd first learned she would never have children. "I'm glad Hank's sending Harding. You really should be closer to home for PJ."

"I want to bring PJ, Charlie and the baby up here next summer to hear Sadie sing. I hear she has a great voice. And camp out. It's beautiful here, at least what I can see from the hospital window."

"Colorado is beautiful." Kate could picture herself living in the mountains. With a man like Chase— passionate about the people he loved and his heritage. And an ardent lover, as in tune with his lady's needs as his own.

Her core warmed, spreading heat throughout her body, despite the frigid temperature of the wintry mountain town.

As Kate rang off, a limousine pulled up to the curb

across the street from the Lucky Lady Saloon at the county courthouse, where both candidates would deliver their speeches later that day. Already carpenters were building stands and sound technicians laid in the wires for the microphones and speakers.

The limo was followed by several news crew vans. As soon as the vehicle came to a complete halt, the chauffeur jumped out and opened the door for a man and a woman to alight.

Kate's pulse jumped. She didn't recognize the woman, but the man could be none other than John Michaels, senatorial candidate, and one of the names in Sadie's little black book.

Kate sent a quick text to Chase: Delayed out front. Michaels just arrived.

As soon as the news crews were in place, reporters jammed microphones in Michaels's face. "Will there be a debate here in Fool's Fortune today?"

John Michaels lifted a hand and answered, "Today is about presenting our platforms, not about debating which is right or wrong."

"Mr. Michaels, what makes you the right candidate for the position of US Senator?"

The former governor smiled for the cameras. "Experience. I've held several political offices, and I understand a broad spectrum of how to maneuver through political red tape to get the job done. The position requires honesty, integrity and full commitment to the people."

"Mr. Michaels, have you ever been dishonest with your constituents?"

Kate jerked her head around to the source of the question to discover Chase had emerged from the Lucky Lady Saloon and crossed the street. He faced Michaels, his gaze direct, Jake perched in the curve of his arm.

The man looked like a concerned father. Chase would make a good daddy to any child.

John Michaels shifted on his feet. "I strive to be as open and honest to the people I represent as I am with my family."

"Mr. Michaels, have you ever lied to your family?" Chase persisted.

"No, sir. Family is the most important key to a full and healthy life, no matter what you do for a living. Family comes first." He leaned over to a man standing behind him and whispered something to him. Then Michaels smiled again for the news crew. "Any other questions before I take my beautiful wife to lunch?"

Kate made her way through the crowd to where Chase stood. When Jake spotted her, he held out his arms.

Kate dropped to one knee and took him in her arms, loving the feeling of his little body against hers. She hugged him close and stood, keeping hold of his little gloved hand. She leaned close to Chase. "Way to go putting Michaels on the spot. Wouldn't you have been better off catching him in private?"

"Probably." He winked. "But then, I've always been a little impatient."

The news crews asked a few more questions before Mr. Michaels ended the brief interview and handed his wife into his waiting limousine.

Chase turned to her. "Well, where to?"

"It's getting close to lunchtime. I'd like to head to the diner before it gets too crowded. We can stop at the feed store afterward. The political rally starts at two. We could head back to the steps of the courthouse around one thirty."

"Sounds like a good plan." Chase turned toward

his truck but his path was blocked by a man in a business suit.

"Sir, Mr. Michaels would like to invite you to have lunch with him at the Gold Rush Tavern."

Chase's gaze met Kate's. "Does that invitation include my fiancée?" He slipped his arm around Kate's waist.

"Sir, Mr. Michaels would like to have a private discussion with you." The man in the suit didn't glance at Kate, his gaze focused on Chase.

Chase turned to Kate.

Kate smiled. "Go. Jake and I will have lunch at the diner. If you get through early, join us there. I have my cell phone."

Chase touched the boy's cheek. "I'll see you later, buddy, maybe in time for dessert."

Jake grinned. "Can we have chocolate cake?"

"We can have whatever you like," Chase answered. He bent to brush his lips across Kate's. "See you soon." Then he leaned closer and whispered in her ear, "Stay safe."

The warmth of his breath on her cheek made Kate warm all over. "We will. Question is, will you be safe?"

He winked. "I can take care of myself. You have Jake now."

Chase followed the man in the suit to an SUV and climbed into the rear of the vehicle.

Kate didn't like being apart from Chase. They'd been together since she'd arrived in Fool's Fortune. Though she'd performed many of her assignments as a Texas Ranger on her own, she'd become accustomed to having Chase around these past few days and felt strangely bereft with him gone.

Shaking it off, she smiled at Jake. "Come on. I bet we can find something yummy to eat at the diner."

"Can I have a hot dog and fries?" the child asked, his enthusiasm infectious.

"If they serve them, you sure can." She crossed to her truck and helped Jake into his booster seat, buckling him in snugly.

A few minutes later, they parked in front of the diner. It was early and only a few cars filled the parking spaces.

Kate helped Jake out of the truck and entered the diner.

Her gaze swept the small restaurant. The few guests were seated at booths and tables scattered around the room.

A young woman wearing a colorful apron smiled. "You can sit wherever you like. I'll get menus. Is it just the two of you?"

"Yes." Kate chose a seat in a corner that would provide a good view of everyone coming through the door. She settled Jake across from her and took her seat.

The woman in the apron returned with a glass of water and one in a cup with a lid for Jake. "You're Jake, Sadie Lovely's grandson, aren't you?" She ruffled his hair. "I'm sorry to hear your grandmother isn't feeling well." She glanced at Kate and held out her hand. "I'm Kitty Toland, owner of Kitty's diner. I know most of the regulars, but I haven't had the pleasure. Welcome to Fool's Fortune."

Kate took Kitty's hand, immediately liking the young woman and her open, friendly demeanor. "Kate Rivers." She hesitated before adding, "I'm Chase Marsden's fiancée."

Kitty's face broke out in a grin. "I'd heard he got engaged. Well, congratulations." She gave Kate's hand a hardy handshake. "I wish all the happiness you two can stand." She handed Kate a menu and placed a kids menu in front of Jake and handed him a blue crayon. "I'll give you a few minutes to look at the menu and be right back."

The door to the diner opened and a couple entered, stamping the snow off their feet. "Hi, Kitty."

"Hello, Deb, Jasper. Find a seat, I'll be right with you."

Kate liked that warmth and welcoming atmosphere of the diner and especially the owner, Kitty. She made each guest feel like family with her bright smile and the way she knew so much about each person.

Chase was right, the diner was a good place to start for local gossip.

Kate glanced over the menu. By the time Kitty returned, she was ready with her order and Jake's. Kitty wrote the order on a pad and skipped off to fill it.

Kate and Jake talked about his favorite colors, their conversation drifting back to the ranch.

"Uncle Chase said he'd teach me to ride a horse when the weather gets warmer. I want to ride Sundance."

"Isn't he the black stallion?"

Jake nodded. "He's the biggest. I want to ride him so that I can touch the sky."

Kate chuckled. "I'm sure Uncle Chase will be a good teacher."

"Will Uncle Chase teach you, too?" Jake asked.

"I already know how to ride."

"Which horse are you going to ride?"

Kate's heart constricted. The weather wasn't going to get warmer before this case closed. Then she'd be on her way back to Texas. She wouldn't have the opportunity to ride a horse on the Lucky Lady Ranch. "I'd probably ride Penance."

"She's pretty. If I weren't going to ride Sundance, I'd ride her."

The boy was fearless. Kate hoped he wouldn't lose

that intrepid sense of wonder. Life had a way of beating the fear into people, if they let it.

And hadn't she let it? She feared her life wouldn't ever be normal. Yet, here she was having lunch with a little boy talking about horses. What could be more normal than that?

When she left Colorado, she'd leave sad that she didn't get to spend more time in the beautiful state with the incredible views of mountains and valleys. But she'd leave with hope in her heart and the knowledge that she had a future, even if it meant she wasn't going to have babies of her own.

Kitty delivered their food and conversation stopped while she dug into a juicy hamburger and Jake ate a hotdog with ketchup only. They shared a huge order of fries and washed it all down with chocolate milkshakes.

As they were polishing off the last of the fries, two men entered the diner with an older woman. The men wore suits and expensive overcoats and the woman was dressed in a tailored pantsuit and a long, faux-fur, shiny black coat.

Kate leaned forward, trying to get a better look at one of the men. If she wasn't mistaken, he was Benson Garner, the other candidate who would be speaking later at the courthouse. From the pictures Kate had seen on the internet, the woman had to be his mother, Patricia Garner.

The trio settled at a table near Kate and Jake. Patricia sat with her back to Kate and Benson took the seat facing Kate.

Her pulse pounding, Kate wondered how she'd get Benson alone. For all they knew Benson might not even know Melissa had a baby. If he were aware that Jake was his, would it be sufficient reason for him to want to hurt Sadie?

Kate wasn't sure, but if the opportunity to question him arose, she'd take it. She took her time finishing the last of the fries and the milkshake. If Benson Garner had anything to do with the attacks, Kate couldn't leave the diner without at least talking to the man.

Chapter Twelve

The man in the suit who'd asked Chase to meet with John Michaels introduced himself as Peter Barons, Michaels's campaign manager. After the introduction, the man sat silent beside Chase as they drove the few short blocks to the Gold Rush Tavern.

Once deposited at the entrance, Peter led him into the tavern and into a private dining area where John Michaels sat with his wife, Deborah.

Peter backed out of the room and closed the door.

Michaels stood and held out his hand. "You're Chase Marsden, right?"

Chase nodded. "I am."

Michaels turned to the woman beside him. "This is my wife, Deborah. We're pleased to meet you. Please have a seat."

Chase shook the man's hand and his wife's before sliding into the seat across the table from both of them.

A waiter entered the room carrying a tray with three covered dishes. He set them in front of Chase, John and Deborah. "If you need anything else, all you have to do is ring the bell." The waiter backed out of the room, leaving the three people alone.

John Michaels nodded to the plate in front of Chase.

"I hope you don't mind. I had them prepare a steak, medium rare for you."

"Thank you." Chase lifted a fork and knife, then paused. "I'm curious. Why is it you wanted a private meeting with me?"

John nodded. "Two reasons. I never miss an opportunity to seek campaign contributions from wealthy constituents. And two, I wanted to know the basis for your questions earlier."

Chase sliced into the steak and took a bite, letting the silence lengthen while he phrased his response. "First of all, I like to hear from all candidates before I commit dollars to their campaigns. Second..." Chase caught John's gaze and held it. "Are you sure you want me to open this can of worms in front of your wife?"

John and Deborah exchanged glances.

Deborah spoke. "I know about all the skeletons in John's closet. You aren't going to offend me." She reached across the table to take her husband's hand.

Chase admired the woman for standing by her man. He hated bringing up her husband's indiscretions in front of her, but Sadie's life depended on finding out more about his connection to the little black book and who might want to get his hands on it. "I suppose then you know who Sadie Lovely is?"

Deborah's hand tightened on John's. "I do."

"John, you visited her in the past." Chase raised a hand. "That's not a question."

"Let me set you straight—"

"John." Deborah shook her head. "You don't have to answer to anyone."

He patted her hand. "Please. It's bound to come up again." Michaels met Chase's gaze head-on. "I'm not proud of the fact I visited Sadie, but I'm not ashamed.

That woman might have been a madam, but she's a saint in my books."

Deborah smiled, her hand curling around her husband's.

John went on. "I went to her because Deborah and I had a rocky point in our relationship. I thought all I needed was to blow off some steam. I heard about Sadie from some men who had used her...services. They told me she was discreet." He glanced down at where his hand was entwined with Deborah's. "You might not believe me, but we didn't have sex. She let me talk and she listened. When I was done, she told me to go back to my wife and tell her everything I had just told her, and kiss her and never let her go." John raised his wife's hand to his lips and pressed a kiss there. "I did. It was the best decision I've ever made."

Deborah's eyes grew glassy. "He told me what he'd done. I was angry at first, but when I finally listened, I couldn't blame him. He'd been under a lot of pressure and our squabbles added to it. John needed someone to talk to and I wasn't listening." She smiled at her husband. "I am now."

Chase sat across the table, wondering if he should believe them. He'd never known a couple to be so open about philandering, especially to a stranger. "What would happen if the word got out that you had an affair with Sadie Lovely?"

John Michaels shrugged. "I'd be honest and tell the media it was somewhat true. No, I didn't have sex with her, but I wouldn't expect the public to believe that, and I'd tell them so. I would also tell them that my association with Sadie saved my marriage. I've never been happier or more secure in my love for Deborah."

"And the same goes for me. I have nothing but good

thoughts where Sadie Lovely is concerned. She's a woman with a good heart," Deborah added.

"Did you know someone tried to kill her several days ago?"

The surprise on their faces could not have been faked.

"Oh, dear Lord." Deborah pressed a hand to her lips.

"Is she okay?" John leaned forward. "Is there anything we can do to help?"

"I'm looking for the person or persons responsible for putting her into a coma. That person not only wants her dead, but wants something that belonged to her. Something that could link her to them."

John's lips twisted. "That's why we're having this conversation, isn't it?"

"Yes, it is," Chase confirmed.

"You think that because I'm running for Senate, I might feel the need to eliminate the skeletons in my closet?"

Deborah shook her head. "I know about Sadie. It wouldn't hurt me."

"No, but it might hurt my campaign." John nodded. "I can see why I would be a prime suspect. If it helps to clear the air, I will make an announcement at today's rally that I was involved with Sadie in the past. It will get it all out in the open. If the voters can't forgive that, I don't need to be their representative."

Chase shook his head. "That's not necessary." He found it hard to believe a politician would expose himself in such a way when it could undermine his bid for office. If John Michaels did what he claimed he would and aired his dirty laundry in public, it would raise him in Chase's estimation considerably. He'd even consider contributing to his campaign fund.

"I don't want to keep secrets from the voters," John

said. "They trust me to be honest, to tell the truth. If I can't be aboveboard about my personal life, how will they ever trust me with their needs and desires as a senator?"

Chase inhaled and let it out slowly. If John Michaels wasn't concerned about Sadie and her little black book, it left only a hundred-fifty or more names to check out.

"Mr. Michaels, you say you learned of Sadie from someone else. Would you know of anyone who would be eager to erase all evidence of a relationship with Sadie to the extent of murdering her or anyone who has her list of clients?"

John shook his head. "My connection with Sadie was over fifteen years ago. The man who told me about her died last year. I wish I could help." He glanced at his wife. "Is Sadie in the hospital here in Fool's Fortune?"

"She is."

"Does she have sufficient protection? I know of a good security firm that has the most highly trained bodyguards."

Chase's lips quirked at the image of Chuck standing guard over Sadie. He trusted the man with the life of his friend. "She has a bodyguard assigned to her already, but thanks."

"Well, if you need more help, you can call TG Securities, I think it was. They only hire former military. The company was set up to provide security to contractors working in Iraq after the American military pulled out."

Chase's brows dipped as he remembered what Hank had said about the man who'd chased them down in Denver. "Could it be TG International?"

John nodded. "That's it. I hired a bodyguard from them once when I had a stalker following me around during my time as governor. The experience had me in knots. Didn't have any trouble after the bodyguard came on board."

"Do you still have the bodyguard?"

"No. My stalker stopped following me once he saw I had protection." John picked up his fork and sliced into the steak. "I highly recommend them. They're based out of Denver."

"Thank you." Chase pushed back from the table. "If you'll excuse me, my fiancée is having lunch without me. I'd like to join her."

John stood and shook his hand. "Thank you for taking the time to talk with us. I hope you find the person who put Sadie in the hospital. My driver will take you where you need to go."

Chase left the Gold Rush Tavern and climbed into the SUV that had brought him there. Peter Barons didn't join him, giving him ample time alone to digest what he'd learned from John Michaels.

His gut told him Michaels wasn't the man responsible for the attacks, but he couldn't rule him out completely.

He texted Kate and told her he'd stop at the feed store to order feed and see what he could find out from the men who worked there. When Kate got done with what she was doing she could join him at the store with the truck so that he could load the feed he needed.

With Michaels in the back of his mind, he stepped out at the feed store, a couple blocks from the courthouse.

KATE WAS ABOUT to run out of ways to keep Jake's attention when the man with Benson Garner stood and held the chair for the woman Kate believed was Benson's mother.

Benson stood last. "I'd like to stay for a few minutes going over my speech in silence, if you two don't mind."

"By all means. Robert and I will check out the setup and we'll circle back to get you. Will thirty minutes be sufficient?" his mother asked. "That will get us to the courthouse with fifteen minutes to spare."

"Thank you, Mother." Benson kissed her cheek and waited until she and Robert exited the diner, and then he took his seat and pulled a set of index cards from his pocket.

Kate waited until the vehicle carrying Benson's mother left before she rose. "Come on, Jake. There's someone I'd like you to meet."

Jake folded the paper he'd been drawing on and tucked it into his pocket, then scooted out of his seat and stood beside Kate, holding out his hand for her to take.

With a smile teasing her lips, Kate walked over to the table where Benson Garner leaned over the cards in front of him.

Kate cleared her throat, hoping to break through Benson's concentration. When that didn't work, she said in a soft, but clear voice, "Excuse me."

Benson's head jerked up. "I'm sorry, were you talking to me?"

She nodded, pasting her friendliest smile on her face. "You're Benson Garner, aren't you?"

He nodded. "I am." He stood and held out his hand. "And you are?"

"Kate Rivers." She glanced down at the boy at her side. "This is Jake."

Benson squatted in front of Jake. "Nice to meet you, Jake."

Jake placed his hand in Benson's and gave it a firm shake. "Nice to meet you, too," he said with his best manners.

Kate's chest swelled with pride. "Do you mind if we sit with you for just a minute?" she asked.

"Not at all. I was going over my speech for the rally."

"We won't keep you long." Now that she was there, she wasn't sure how to start, especially with a very curious little boy sitting with a man who could potentially be with his biological father. Choosing a tact that Jake couldn't question as a lie, she said, "I'm a friend of Sadie Lovely's family."

She waited for a reaction, studying Benson intently, looking for any body language that she could construe as guilt or fear.

He shook his head. "I'm sorry. Should I know Ms. Lovely?"

Interesting. Sadie's daughter hadn't told her lover about her infamous mother. Then again, Sadie had given up her role as madam before Melissa and Benson met. Perhaps she saw no need. Kate dug a quarter out of her purse and handed it to Jake. "There is a gumball machine by the counter over there. Why don't you go see what prize you'll get from it?"

"Thanks, Miss Kate." Jake hurried toward the counter with his quarter in his hand.

Keeping a close eye on the boy, Kate said, "You might know Sadie's daughter, Melissa Smith?" She glanced at Benson in time to see him react.

Instantly his brows V'd toward his nose. "You knew Melissa?"

"No, I didn't have the pleasure. I know about her from her mother, Sadie."

Benson lifted an index card and tapped it against the table. "Yes, I knew Melissa." He looked up, the expression in his eyes one of loss. "She died in a car wreck six months ago."

"You and Melissa were pretty tight at one time?" Kate asked.

Benson glanced toward the window. "We worked at the state capitol six years ago." He shrugged. "We went out a few times." He glanced back at the cards. "Why do you ask? That was six years ago. I haven't seen her since then."

"Did you know her mother at all?"

"She was going to introduce me, but she broke off the relationship and quit her job before she did."

Kate frowned. "Any idea why?"

Benson shook his head. "No clue. One minute we were getting close, the next she left Denver and left a message on my voicemail that she didn't want to see me again. I went to her apartment, but she'd already moved and left no forwarding address." He dragged in a breath and let it out. "I have to admit, I was pretty upset about it."

"Upset enough to want to hurt her or her mother?"

"No." Benson scrubbed a hand through his hair. "I loved Melissa. I was going to ask her to marry me. I even took my mother shopping with me to find a ring." His voice drifted away, breaking on what could only be described as a sob. "Why do you want to know?" he asked, his voice ragged.

"Her mother was attacked recently. I'm trying to find out who might want to hurt her."

"And you think I'd hurt someone Melissa loved?" He pushed to his feet.

"You two were close. Perhaps there was a misunderstanding that caused the rift."

"I went through every conversation leading up to the last time I saw her. Nothing she or I said could be remotely misconstrued. I told her I loved her. She said she loved me, too. Unless she was lying. Why else would she leave without saying goodbye?"

"I don't know. Do you know anyone who would know Melissa's mother, Sadie Lovely? Anyone who would want to hurt her?"

"I didn't even know Melissa's mother. Sadie, you say?" He snorted. "This is the first time I'd heard her name. Sorry. I can't help you. Now if you'll excuse me, I have a speech to give."

"Miss Kate, look." Jake ran up to her with a cheap keychain, a small, fuzzy red heart dangling from the end. "Do you think Grandma Sadie could have this? It might make her feel better."

Benson stared at the little boy, his eyes narrowing. "Is this Sadie's grandson?"

Kate tensed, unsure if she should tell Benson the truth or walk away.

Jake answered for her. "Yes, I'm Grandma Sadie's grandson. She's sick in the hospital and they won't let little kids visit, or I would go and give her this." He held up the keychain with the fuzzy heart on the end. "Do you think she will like it?"

Benson's face paled. "How old are you, Jake?" he asked, his voice tight.

"I just turned five." He held up his right hand, his fingers splayed wide. He glanced up at Kate. "Can we go to the feed store now? I want to see the boots and saddles."

Kate glanced at Benson.

The man stood as still as a statue, his gaze fixed on the boy, his face drained of color. Then he looked up at Kate. "Is Jake—" His voice caught and he didn't finish his question.

Kate's brows rose. "Jake is Sadie's grandson."

Jake ran back to their table to grab his crayon.

"He's Melissa's son," Kate added.

Benson shook his head. "I didn't know."

Kate's eyes narrowed. "And you still don't know. My main concern is that someone is trying to kill his grandmother and I want to keep that from happening. She's all he has left."

"Who would want to hurt Melissa's mother?"

"I don't know, but I will find out. If you or anyone you know tries to hurt Sadie or Jake, I'll take you down," she warned him, her voice dropping low, threatening.

"I wouldn't hurt either of them. I loved Melissa." He ran a hand through his hair. "If there is any chance Jake is mine…"

"You'll have to take it up with Sadie when she comes out of the coma."

Jake ran back to Kate. She grabbed his hand and led him to the door.

Once outside, she sucked in the fresh mountain air, second-guessing her confrontation with Benson. If he or anyone he knew were after Sadie and her list, would knowing Jake could be his son put the boy in more danger than he already was?

A dark limousine pulled up in front of the diner and the man who'd accompanied Benson and his mother climbed out of the car. "Are you ready?" he called out.

At first Kate thought he was talking to her. Then she glanced over her shoulder. Benson stood in the doorway, his gaze following Kate and Jake.

Kate hurried past the open door of the limousine.

Benson's mother sat inside, her eyes narrowed.

Without slowing, Kate lifted Jake into his booster seat and climbed into the truck, locking the doors, determined to get Jake away from Benson. She needed to talk to Chase, and a call to Hank wouldn't hurt. Jake had to be protected at all costs.

Chapter Thirteen

Chase stepped out of the SUV in front of the feed store. No sooner had the vehicle left, he spotted Kate's truck headed his way. She pulled into the parking space beside him and jumped out of the truck, her eyes wide, glancing back in the direction from which she'd come.

Chase rushed toward her. "What's wrong?"

She grimaced. "I might have started something I shouldn't have." Kate shook her head. "Now that I have, I'm not sure what will happen because of it."

"Uncle Chase!" Jake called out. "I got a present for Grandma Sadie."

Chase smiled and waved at the boy. "Tell me in a minute. Let me grab Jake and we can step inside the feed store."

Kate stood by while Chase unbuckled Jake and lifted him out of the truck.

As soon as they stepped through the door, Jake took off.

Kate lunged after him.

Chase grabbed her arm. "It's okay. He's only going to sit on the saddles. We can see him from here." Chase gripped her arms and stared down into her eyes. "What happened?"

"We ran into Benson Garner at the diner," she said,

biting her lip. "When I started asking him about Melissa, he put two and two together and came up with Jake."

Chase's brows twisted. "Whoa, wait. I'm not sure I understand."

Kate let out a long, steadying breath. "He knows Jake might be his."

Chase shot a glance toward Jake, who was happily riding a horseless saddle, shouting, "Yeehaw!" like a regular cowboy.

"What did you learn from Benson? Is he the one after Sadie and her black book?"

Kate shook her head. "He didn't even know Sadie. He said he'd never met Melissa's mother."

"Do you think he was lying?"

Kate's brows puckered. "I don't think so."

"If he didn't know about Sadie, why would he want to hurt her?"

"He wouldn't." Kate's shoulders sagged and then she perked up. "What did you learn from Michaels?"

Chase's lips pressed together. "Nothing that helps us figure out who is after Sadie."

"What do you mean?"

"He admitted to being one of Sadie's clients but claimed he didn't have sex with her. She sent him home to his wife. He credits Sadie with saving his marriage."

"Does his wife agree?"

Chase grinned. "Actually, she does. She was there with us the entire time. She said their marriage has never been better because of Sadie."

"The public will never believe he didn't have sex. Wouldn't that ruin his chances at political office if it gets out?"

"We'll find out. He's going to confess at the rally."

"Holy smokes." Kate threw her hand in the air. "That

takes us back to square one. Who else in Sadie's book stands to be ruined if his name gets out in conjunction with Sadie's?"

"I don't know. But the funny thing is when I told him Sadie had been attacked, he suggested the name of a firm that provided security for contractors in Iraq, stating they hired former military only and they are based out of Denver."

Kate's brows rose. "TG International?"

"That's the one."

Pulling her phone out of her pocket, she said, "I'm calling Hank. Hopefully he has something on this security firm."

"I already called him. He said the firm is owned by a corporation, which is owned by another corporation. He's got Brandon following the trail to who might be behind the corporations."

"My bet is whoever owns it is one of the names in Sadie's little black book."

Chase glanced down at Kate. "Anyone ever tell you that you're beautiful when you're so intense?" He bent to press his lips to hers.

"No." Kate rolled her eyes. "And what a time to do it. We're in the middle of an attempted murder investigation."

"What better time to tell a woman she's beautiful?" He winked and kissed her again. "Come on, let's ask the owner if he's heard anything about strangers in town the day Sadie was attacked."

Keeping a close eye on Jake as he happily played on the saddles, Chase and Kate got into a discussion with the feed store owner and a couple of the local ranchers about strangers.

They all congratulated Chase on his engagement,

even before he introduced Kate as his fiancée, proving the grapevine was alive and well in Fool's Fortune.

By the time they left the feed store, they had tentative leads on a man that ate at the diner the night before Sadie was run down. Unfortunately, he'd driven a one-ton pickup, not a dark SUV like the one that had run over Sadie and Chase.

Every man in the store promised to keep a lookout for anyone suspicious, claiming any friend of Chase's was a friend of theirs and the people of Fool's Fortune took care of their own.

Chase left the store feeling more a part of the community than he'd felt since, well, since ever. And to think when he first got there, he had been counting the days until he could leave. Now he couldn't imagine living anywhere else. He loved Fool's Fortune and the Lucky Lady Ranch. And he'd love to find a woman strong enough and as passionate as he was about it to share the ranch with him.

He helped Jake into the booster seat and glanced toward the driver's seat where Kate was sliding in.

They'd only known each other for a few days, and already Chase knew Kate was special. She could be the one for him.

If only they could have enough time together for him to convince her.

They'd spent longer than Chase had expected at the feed store and were late getting to the rally. Kate ended up parking a block away. The streets were crowded, but the sun shone on the courthouse steps, encouraging a good turnout, despite the below freezing temperatures. The people of Fool's Fortune were used to the cold and wouldn't miss out on a community gathering as long as the wind was mild and the sun shone down on the mountain valley.

Chase took one of Jake's hands while Kate took the other. The boy swung between them as they walked toward the back of the crowd.

Not wanting to disturb the people who'd gotten there earlier, Chase stopped at the rear of the gathering and listened while the candidates each spoke, giving the basis for their platforms.

As promised, John Michaels surprised the crowd with his confession. His wife stepped forward, her show of support making the man appear even stronger. The news crews zoomed in on the couple.

"He did it," Chase said.

Kate leaned over Jake and whispered into Chase's ear, "Benson still appears pale."

Her warm breath made Chase's heartbeat kick up a notch. After sending her to bed the night before with only a kiss, he'd lain awake wishing he hadn't stopped at just a kiss, calling himself a fool for his misplaced sense of chivalry.

Tonight, he'd kiss her. If she returned the kiss with as much enthusiasm as she had the night before, he wouldn't hold back this time. He wanted to get to know her and her body better. He wanted her to know him, as well.

"Kate."

She glanced over at him. "Yes?"

His gaze met hers. "Promise me you'll stay through Christmas no matter what."

Her brows wrinkled. "What brought that on?"

He held her gaze. "Just promise."

Kate's eyes narrowed slightly. "It's only three days away."

"So you'll stay, even if we resolve the case earlier?"

"What if another case comes up?"

Not the answer Chase was looking for, he tried a different approach. "If not for me, will you stay for…" He tipped his head toward Jake.

Her lips quirked. "You'd use a little boy as blackmail?"

Chase maintained a straight face. "Whatever it takes."

Kate's cheeks reddened. "Okay." Then she turned toward the speakers, her lips curling upward.

Feeling better about life than he had in a long time, Chase let loose the smile he'd been holding back. Kate had promised to stay through Christmas. That was three more days to get to know each other and for him to convince her she should stay even longer. After all, Angus lived at the Last Chance Ranch and worked for Hank Derringer. Why couldn't Kate live in Colorado, as well?

Too soon. The logical side of his brain echoed through his head.

Chase's heart pushed the thought to the back of his mind. That's why he'd asked her to stay longer, even if they found the attacker before then. He wanted more time with her.

Standing next to Kate with Jake swinging from their hands between them, Chase wanted the moment to go on forever.

Something slammed into his shoulder, making him twist around. His grip on Jake's hand loosed and he fell forward into the back of the person in front of him and slid to the ground.

A woman screamed and then another. The noise level swelled to a roar.

Then Kate was bending over him, her voice coming to him as though it was whispered down a long tunnel. "Chase, stay with me."

He wanted to tell her he was there, but he couldn't

form words, and the tunnel was sucking him into a very dark place. Then the blue sky blinked out like someone flipped the light switch.

IT ALL HAPPENED so quickly, Kate didn't know what was going on until Chase pitched forward into the woman standing in front of him. Then he seemed to slide down her back, leaving a swath of blood down the back of her coat.

"Get down! Everyone, get down!" Kate yelled, crouching low, using her body to protect Jake from flying bullets.

Some people dropped to the ground, others screamed and ran, creating mass hysteria.

Kate held her ground, growling at anyone who dared to step close to the man on the ground. Several men formed a barrier, guiding people to the left or right of Kate, Jake and Chase.

"Chase!" Kate dropped Jake's hand and knelt beside Chase. "Chase, stay with me." She glanced around at the crowd. "Call 9-1-1! Hurry!" she shouted.

Blood oozed from a bullet-size hole in the back of Chase's jacket.

Her heart seized in her chest and she struggled to focus and not fall apart. It was happening again. She felt like history was repeating itself with the loss of her partner. "Chase, baby, I'm not going to lose you, damn it."

"What's wrong with Uncle Chase?" Jake cried.

"He's not feeling good, Jake," Kate called out, focusing all her attention on the man down in front of her as memories hit her like a tsunami.

She'd been there when her partner had been gunned down. No amount of pressure on the wound stopped the flow of blood. He'd been shot straight through the heart and died instantly.

The bullet in Chase's back had hit his right shoulder. As long as the trajectory was straight on, he had a chance.

Knowing the exit wound would be worse, she rolled Chase over. The front of his jacket was a bloody mess but not anywhere near his heart.

Grateful tears welled in her eyes and she blinked them away. Chase wasn't in the clear yet. Kate ripped his jacket open and assessed the wound. She had to stop the bleeding before he lost too much blood.

Kate shrugged out of her jacket and dragged her sweater over her head, then removed the cotton blouse from beneath. The frigid air hit her naked skin.

As quickly as she'd stripped, she pulled the jacket back on and zipped it. Her hands shaking hard, she ripped the shirt into strips, folded one into a pad and pressed it against the wound. "You will not die on me, damn it," she muttered. "You're the only man who has ever kissed me the way you do. Like I'm a desirable woman, not a cop or tomboy."

She pressed down on the wound with one hand and felt for a pulse with her other. Despite the wound and blood loss, his pulse beat strong beneath her fingertips. "I liked it and want you to kiss me again."

Chase's eyes blinked open. "You like the way I kiss?" he asked, his lips curling into a smile, though his face was pale.

Kate almost sobbed her relief, "Yeah, but don't get a big head. I might get tired of them."

"I'll try to change things up." He chuckled and coughed. "Can't have my fiancée getting bored." He glanced around at the faces staring down at him. "What happened?"

"You were shot," she said around a lump in her throat.

He turned his head. "Where's Jake?"

"Right next to…" Kate kept her hand on the wound and turned. "Jake?" she called out. When he didn't respond, her heart skipped several beats and then launched into a gallop. "Jake!"

Chase gripped her wrist. "I'll be okay. Find Jake."

Kate pointed to a man standing nearby. "Hold this down, apply pressure and don't let up," she commanded.

"I won't." The man dropped to the ground on his knees and took over.

Reluctant to remove her hand, she did so, her heart slamming against her ribs. Where was Jake?

Staggering to her feet, she pushed through the small crowd brave enough to gather around after a shooting. "Have you seen a little boy about this tall?" she asked.

The responses were shaking heads and noes.

The police that had been there for the rally parted the remaining throng to allow the ambulance closer to Chase. More law enforcement officers arrived to help search the area for the gunman. A siren blared and the ambulance appeared.

And still no Jake.

"Oh, dear Lord," Kate prayed out loud. "Please."

The cell phone in her jacket pocket vibrated. Shaking, she scrambled to answer. The caller ID registered Hank.

"Kate, we found out who the owner is of TG International."

Kate looked around, desperately searching for the little boy with hair the color of hers, barely listening to Hank.

"It's Thomas Garner. Or it was the late Thomas Garner. He assembled the security group several years before his death, but because he was a senator, he didn't want it associated with him. Apparently some of the men he hired to provide security in Iraq and Afghanistan had questionable backgrounds and ethics. A couple of them killed some kids and raped women in a small village outside Baghdad and left the country before they were caught. There was a big scandal and it took a lot of government money to pay off the local officials."

Kate doubled over, her belly hurting her eyes filling with tears. "Hank. We have a problem." A sob escaped and she fought back others.

Apparently Hank heard the distress in her voice. "What's wrong, Kate?"

"Chase was shot during the political rally and in all the confusion, Jake disappeared."

The line went silent for a second. Then Hank said, "Don't panic. It could be he got scared and is hiding. Seeing someone shot has to be pretty frightening."

"It's freezing and the sun will set soon. And worse…" She inhaled a shaky breath. "Benson Garner met Jake before the rally. He knows he's Melissa's son and thinks he might be his."

"Do you think Garner took the boy?"

"I don't know. I'm worried. Benson didn't seem to know anything about Sadie. He claimed he never met Melissa's mother and that Melissa broke things off with him right before she was going to introduce them."

"Since Thomas Garner's death a few years ago, Benson and his mother have slowly taken over Thomas's holdings. The older Garner ran things."

"Do you think Benson found out about his father's indiscretion with Sadie and sought revenge?"

"I can only guess. Why would he care that his father had an affair with a madam, when the man's been dead for a few years?"

"Benson is running for office."

"True, but he's not accountable for the sins of his father."

"Some might claim the apple doesn't fall far from the tree." Kate gasped. "He might want Sadie dead to destroy evidence of his father's shady past. But why shoot Chase? Unless, he doesn't want his own sins exposed. You don't think he took…" She couldn't go on.

"Jake," Hank concluded.

"We have to find him." Kate gripped the phone. She headed back to where the EMTs worked over Chase, loading him into an ambulance. "I'll put the word out to the police to be on the lookout for Jake, and we will set up a search for him."

"Ben Harding is on his way in the plane and should be there in an hour, or I'd send more resources immediately. The first twenty-four hours is crucial," Hank said. "I'll call Angus and have him head to Fool's Fortune to help in the effort to find the boy."

"Thanks, Hank." She rang off and hurried toward the ambulance.

The emergency medical technicians wheeled Chase over to load him in.

Kate caught up to them before they loaded him.

"Did you find him?" he asked, trying to sit up, but unsuccessful against the straps holding him down.

"Not yet. But we will. He probably got scared."

"You have to find him."

"Angus is on his way and Hank sent Ben Harding. He should be landing in Fool's Fortune within the hour." She laid her hand on his uninjured shoulder. "Let the doctors get you stitched up. Hopefully, I'll be by the hospital soon with Jake."

Chase closed his eyes. "Kate."

"Yes?"

"I know we've only known each other a short time, but in case anything happens..." He paused.

"Yes?"

"I think I love you."

Kate bit down on her bottom lip to keep it from trembling her eyes misting with tears. "Do they have you on morphine?" she quipped.

The EMT shook his head. "Not yet."

Chase stared into Kate's eyes. "I meant what I said. So be careful."

"I will. And I'll find Jake." She forced herself to sound confident, when inside she knew the odds.

To hell with the odds!

Chapter Fourteen

Chase refused any general sedatives or mind-numbing painkillers.

The doctor frowned over him in pre-op. "I won't have you punching me while I have a scalpel in my hands. The result could be worse than what the bullet did to you."

"Fine. Just get it done. I don't have time to be in the hospital."

"Sir, you'll need to remain overnight for observation," the surgical nurse argued.

"Just stop the bleeding, damn it. There's a little boy out there that could be in real trouble. A bullet hole is the least of my worries."

The doctor's jaw tightened. "Well, it's top of my list right now, so let the nurse restrain you or I'll be forced to inject you with a sedative."

Chase clamped his lips shut and allowed the nurse to tie his wrists to the table.

Thankfully, the doctor applied a local to deaden the area around the bullet's exit point, which considerably lessened the pain and allowed Chase to maintain mental clarity throughout.

When the doctor finished and laid his tools on the tray, he announced, "You're fortunate. The bullet didn't penetrate any vital organs. Your heart and lungs are intact. You'll have a scar but you'll live."

"Good. Untie me."

"Not until you promise me you'll lie still for at least one hour."

"You can't keep me here against my will." Chase pulled at the straps and winced when the stitches on his chest pinched painfully.

The doctor's brows rose. "If you're not careful, you'll rip your stitches open and start bleeding again. If you lose any more blood, you'll be of no use to anyone."

"Then untie the damned straps," Chase growled.

The doctor nodded to the nurse.

"Loosen his restraints." The doctor sighed. "We can only do as much as the patient allows us."

Chase forced himself to be calm. Acting crazy wouldn't get him out of the hospital any sooner.

The doctor left the operating room, leaving the nurse in charge.

She planted her fists on her hips and squared off with him. "I'll remove your straps, but you're not going to get up off that table and walk out of here. We'll help you onto a gurney and take you to a room."

"I don't need a room."

"You're going to a room where we can help you dress in the clothes you wore into the hospital."

He calmed down when she said that. "I guess I can't quite walk out in the cold in a hospital gown," he admitted.

"No, you can't. Unless you have a death wish."

Chase conceded to being helped off the table onto the gurney and let the nurses roll him to the elevator and down to one of the rooms he would have stayed in to recover, but he wasn't staying.

Kate and Jake needed him.

As soon as they pushed the gurney into the room, Chase attempted to sit up, the effort making him gasp when pain shot through his chest.

"If you'll wait long enough for us to set the brake we can help you up." One of the nurses clucked her tongue. "You're in no shape to help search for the boy. My husband is one of the sheriff's deputies helping in the effort. They have the entire town out, combing every inch of Fool's Fortune. A wounded man with a hole in his chest isn't going to be of much assistance to what they're already doing."

"I have to be there. I promised Sadie I'd take care of Jake."

"You couldn't know that you'd be shot." The nurse took pity on him and helped him off the gurney.

When he stood on his bare feet, he swayed, his vision blurring.

A nurse on either side of him kept him from falling flat on his face. After a moment, his head cleared and he stood on his own and stepped away from the women. "I can dress myself."

"You might be able to, but humor us. It isn't often we get to help a handsome young man into his clothes." The older nurse winked and shook out the jeans he'd worn when he'd been shot. There were dark bloodstains on the denim, but he didn't care as long as he had something covering his body when he walked out into the cold night air.

Embarrassed to have to rely on the assistance of two women to dress him, he was equally grateful for their silent help as he stepped into the jeans and they pulled them up around his hips. "I can button and zip, thank you."

A soft knock on the door caught his attention. He hoped it would be Kate with Jake.

Instead of Kate, Reggie Davis poked her head around the door. "Chase Marsden?" she queried, caught a glimpse of him and smiled. "There you are." She dangled a fresh flannel shirt. "Thought you could use a shirt. From what I heard, your last one was ruined and covered in blood." Her smile faded and she stared hard at him. "Are you doing all right?"

"I'm fine, but I need to get dressed and get out of here."

Reggie pushed into the room and handed the shirt over to the nurse, her face serious, worried. "Kate's still out there searching for Jake."

"I figured as much." Chase let the nurses slip the shirt over his arms and up onto his shoulders. The less he moved, the less it hurt. "Can you take me to her?"

"Angus sent me over to check on you. I suppose I can take you where you need to go." Her glance switched to the nurses helping him dress. "Should you be up and about after being shot?"

"If that were your kid out there, would you let a bullet keep you down?" Chase countered.

Reggie pulled the edges of her winter coat closer. "I'd be dragging myself out there if Tad were the one lost."

One of the nurses held up his coat. "We wiped as much of the blood off as we could, but it's ruined."

"It'll do." Again, he was dependent on them to help him into the coat. He moved his arm farther back and a shooting pain ripped across his chest, making him sway, the gray edges of fog closing in on his vision. He placed a hand on one nurse's shoulder.

She steadied him. "You should be in bed."

He fought his way back out of the cloud and let go of her. "I have a kid to find."

"Keep your right arm close to your side. It'll help stabilize the wounded area." The nurse zipped him into the jacket and stood back, shaking her head. "Don't bleed to death, will ya?"

"I'll try not to." He gave the nurses half a smile. "Thanks for the help."

"Come back when you find the kid."

Chase didn't respond. He was already halfway out the door, headed for the elevator.

Reggie jogged to keep up.

Inside the elevator car, Chase leaned against the wall, fighting another wave of pain as the local anesthetic wore off around his wound.

"You should let Angus, Kate and Ben take care of finding Jake."

"What if they don't?" Chase asked. "What then?"

"What more can *you* do?"

He didn't know what he could do, but he knew he couldn't lay around in a hospital bed when Jake was in grave danger.

KATE WORKED WITH the police and members of the community to organize a search party to comb the town for Jake. No matter how many places they looked, going through every yard and knocking on every door, the boy was nowhere to be found.

The sun angled toward the mountaintops and Kate was beginning to lose hope. If Jake were just lost out in the cold, hypothermia would kill him before morning.

As the gray light of dusk crept over the mountain village, snow began to fall in earnest, limiting their visibility. The police made the call to suspend the search, sending volunteers home before they ended up lost in the snowstorm.

Kate trudged through the snow back to her truck and called the hospital to check on Chase's status. She'd checked earlier when he'd been in surgery. The nurses felt confident he'd come out all right, although he'd refused sedation.

The woman at the information desk asked Kate to wait while she checked the patient database. "I'm sorry, but I can't find... Oh, wait." She looked up. "Chase Marsden checked out of the hospital fifteen minutes ago."

Kate hung up and glanced around the street, her chest tight. Where had Chase gone and was he even well enough to be up and about? Chuck was still guarding Sadie, but that left Chase exposed to the gunman.

Ben Harding had arrived an hour before and was with Angus, looking for Jake. She should gather them and come up with another game plan. Since they had not been able to find Jake, she could only hope he'd been kidnapped.

She laughed, the sound catching on the lump in her throat. The irony was not lost on her. To hope the boy had been kidnapped seemed ridiculous. But the alternative of being lost in a snowstorm was certain death. A kidnapping might have a way of negotiating a return of the boy to his home and family.

If they didn't kill him first.

Kate's heart ached for the boy. He must be scared out of his mind. Having watched his uncle Chase shot down and then himself being grabbed by a stranger from the crowd...

The one good thing was that Sadie's black book was locked in Chase's safe back at the Lucky Lady Ranch.

Thankfully, Chase had entrusted the combination to her. Since he was out of commission, it would be up to her to make the trade for Jake.

The question was, who would they call to make their demands? They'd call Chase Marsden's phone number at the ranch. The Quaids were helping with the search. No one was at the ranch to receive the call.

Kate punched in the number for Angus Ketchum. "I'm headed to the Lucky Lady Ranch. If this is a kidnapping, I need to be where they are most likely to call with their demands."

"Understood. We'll keep looking as long as we can see. Then we'll head out to the Lucky Lady Ranch."

"Thanks. I hope you find him."

"Me, too. I can't imagine how I'd feel if Tad was the kid missing. That kid might not be my own, but I couldn't love him any more than if he was flesh and blood."

Tears welled in Kate's eyes and she fought to keep them from falling in the frigid cold. "I know what you mean. Jake is a special kid, too. I can't conceive of anyone wanting to hurt him."

"Go to the ranch. Let us know what you learn. Don't try to do anything alone. CCI has your back. Let us help."

"I will." Kate ended the call and dialed Chase's phone number. It rang and rang, finally transferring over to his voice mail. "I'm headed out to the Lucky Lady Ranch in case kidnappers try to contact you there." She wanted to say *I love you*, but the words were choked off by the sob rising in her throat.

Damn it! Why did this have to happen? She should have been prepared for a sniper attack. Especially knowing the men working for TG International were trained killers.

Kate climbed into her truck and headed for the ranch. The going was slow with the snow coming faster and harder, with flakes the size of nickels. She hoped the Quaids were on their way home, or they'd be stuck in town for the night.

After creeping along the highway for what seemed to be an eon, she finally turned into the gate of the Lucky Lady Ranch and slowed to enter the code. The snow was so thick that at first she didn't realize the gate was wide open.

Perhaps the Quaids left it open when they'd gone to Fool's Fortune. They were last to leave the ranch earlier that day. Kate found it hard to believe it had only been that morning she, Jake and Chase had set off for town together, like a little family on a happy outing.

Her fingers tightened on the steering wheel.

Of the three of them, Kate was the only one returning to the ranch tonight. So much had happened during the few short hours they'd been away.

Determined to be there for any call the kidnappers might put through, she hurried up the curving drive to the mansion Lady Jones built so long ago. Jake had been so happy living there and hopeful of better weather so that he could learn to ride a horse that was far too spirited for a new rider.

She hoped his intrepid spirit proved strong enough to hold up to a scary kidnapper and that the kidnapper didn't hurt him.

The house was bathed in darkness, the illumination from her truck's headlights barely penetrating the heavy snow falling now in earnest.

Kate's headlights remained on as she left the truck

and climbed the steps to the house. Not until she reached the door did she recall she didn't have a key. She tried the door anyway and the knob turned beneath her fingertips. She made a mental note to tell the Quaids to lock up, even if they lived out in the middle of nowhere.

She reached for the light switch on the wall inside the door, her hand freezing before she touched it. Something about the silence made the hairs on her arms stand up.

Kate couldn't remember the house being as quiet as it was. Then she realized Barkley hadn't come running when the door opened. The big black-and-tan Saint Bernard usually greeted everyone who came through the door. Had the Quaids locked him in a crate somewhere in the house? She couldn't recall the dog ever being confined to a crate. He usually had free-roaming privileges of the house and grounds.

A chill slipped across the back of Kate's neck and she unzipped her jacket. Her hand went to the .40-caliber pistol nestled in her pocket.

A weak woof sounded to her left, setting her pulse racing. The sound came from the living area where the giant bear towered beside the oversize fireplace.

Kate pulled her pistol out, clicked the safety off and inched into the living room. A dark lump lay in front of the brown leather couch. As she neared, it stirred and a weak whine rose up from the furry mass.

Kate kneeled beside Barkley and smoothed her hand over the dog's fur. "Shh. I'll be back to take care of you," she whispered.

The dog whined, his tail thumping the floor, but he didn't rise to follow her. She prayed he would survive until she could get help.

Heart pounding, she worked her way back to the foyer and listened. A soft thump was followed by muttered curses coming from the office down the hall beneath the sweeping staircase.

Kate held her gun in front of her and slipped along the wall until she was outside the office. The door was closed, and she could hear movement inside.

Kate raised her hand to the knob and paused, remembering her promise to Angus. Now was not the time to go in alone. She was a trained cop. She never went into a dangerous situation without backup. She eased back from the door and reached for her cell phone.

Before she could hit a button to dial, a thick-muscled arm clamped around her, trapping her arms to her side, and the cold hard metal of a gun barrel pressed to her temple. "Move and I'll shoot," a deep, male voice said.

Kate froze. "Okay. I won't move."

"Toss the gun," he demanded.

She let go of the .40-caliber pistol but retained her hold on the cell phone, pressing what she hoped was the redial.

The man holding her banged the toe of his boot against the door to the office. "Open up. I've got Marsden's girl."

The door swung open into Chase's wood-paneled office.

Kate gasped. Another man stood behind the massive mahogany desk, a drawer in his hands. He wore a ski mask and he was dressed all in black. He dumped the contents on the desk and tossed the drawer to the side. "It's not here."

"Did you look behind the pictures on the walls?" The man holding Kate asked. "These rich people always have a safe hidden behind a picture of some old dead man."

Tossing another drawer to the side, the man behind the desk moved to the walls.

Kate scanned the room. Jake was nowhere to be seen. Her gut clenched, but she refused to think they had killed the boy.

The man searching for the safe ripped paintings off their hooks, sending them flying across the room. One by one, he eliminated the possibilities until the last one, the painting of Lady Jones. The huge portrait didn't budge when the man tried to rip it from the wall.

Kate stiffened.

"It ain't movin'," the man said.

"The safe's behind there, isn't it?" Her captor tapped the gun barrel against her temple hard enough to hurt.

"How would I know? It's not my house," Kate insisted.

"You're his fiancée. Doesn't he trust you enough to give you the combination to his safe?"

"We're not married yet." She stalled.

"You better hope you know the combination to that safe. If not for your own sake, then for the kid's," the man growled.

"Where is he?" Kate twisted in the man's viselike grip. "Where's Jake?"

"Now wouldn't you like to know?" The arm around her tightened enough to compromise her breathing.

"Please. Where's Jake?" she gasped.

"Got him as collateral in case we can't find what we're lookin' for."

"What are you looking for?" she asked, knowing exactly what it was.

"You know," the man holding her said, the gun tapping her temple. "Same thing Bradley was after."

The man across the room glared at her. "We want Sadie's black book."

"And we know you and Marsden have it," her captor said.

Kate shook her head. "It's not here."

"You better hope it is, or the kid won't live to be six."

Kate struggled to free herself. "Leave Jake out of this. He's just a boy."

"I don't give a damn if he was the queen of England. Either we get that book or I take the kid for a walk." The man's voice lowered and he moved closer until his lips brushed the back of her ear. "And I promise you, he won't come back."

Kate shivered. She had no doubt that these were some of the men Hank had mentioned. The men who'd killed innocent women and children. To Kate, they were no more than animals. Anyone who could kill children didn't deserve to live.

Her mind raced through the scenarios. If she tried to escape now, she might never learn the location where they had hidden Jake. If she played along with them until they slipped up and told her, she might be able to break free and rescue Jake.

Kate let out a heavy sigh. "There's a latch on the left side of the painting," she said. "Flip it up. The painting is on hinges. You can swing it open like a door."

The guy near the wall did as she directed, exposing the combination lock on the front of the safe. "Now we're getting somewhere."

Her captor shoved her away from him so hard she stumbled before she righted herself.

When she turned to face him, his pistol was pointed at her chest. "Open it, or I'll shoot you."

"I don't know the combination," Kate insisted.

"Then you better figure it out quick. Time and my patience are nearing an end."

She crossed to the safe and twisted the knob. "Maybe he used his birth date." Kate turned the knob one way, vaguely realizing she didn't know Chase's birth date or any of the little details a fiancée would know about her lover. "Where's Jake?"

"In a safe place."

She turned the tumbler back the other way and twisted it several times. "Why do you want the book?" She glanced at the man pointing the gun at her. He, too, wore a ski mask, his features indiscernible.

"Now, that's just about none of your business." He waved the gun. "Move."

She turned the knob back the other way going slower. "It's not his birthday."

"You really do want me to shoot you, don't you?" The gunman nodded to his partner. "Go get the kid."

Her heart skipped several beats and then slammed against her rib cage, pounding fast and furious. Jake was there. Kate sent a silent prayer of thanks to the heavens. Now all she had to do was disable two trained killers and get Jake safely out of their grasp.

The gunman's partner nodded and exited through the French doors leading out onto the back porch. Frigid air blew in through the opening and, with it, a flurry of snowflakes.

A moment later, he carried a kicking, scratching, fighting bundle of snow jacket and tennis shoes into the room and dropped Jake on his feet.

"Let me go, you...you...bad man!" Jake swung his fists and kicked his feet out.

The man who brought him in spun him around and pinned the boy in one arm, squeezing so tightly Jake's eyes widened. "I can't...breathe," he wheezed.

"Let him go!" Kate cried out.

"Open the safe or my friend will crush the boy's ribs."

"Wouldn't take much," the man holding Jake said.

Jake stared across the room at Kate and wheezed, "Miss Kate. Help me."

Her heart in her throat, Kate knew that even if she gave them the book, she and Jake would be expendable. The book was her only bargaining chip.

"Let the boy go, and I'll give you the book."

"How about you give me the book and I'll let the boy go?" the gunman said.

"Don't let them hurt you, Miss Kate. They're bad. Real bad," Jake said, his voice but a whisper, his cheeks turning a faint shade of blue.

She had to do something.

Jake kicked his legs and fought like a wildcat.

The man holding him took a little heel to the groin, cursed and clamped a hand over Jake's mouth.

The boy sank his teeth into the hand, biting down hard enough that his captor jerked his hand away and loosened his hold around the child.

Jake wiggled free and dropped to the ground.

"Run, Jake!" Kate yelled. While Jake's tormentor dove after the kid, Kate grabbed the nearest thing she could lay her hands on, a book, and sent it spinning across the room at the man holding the gun on her.

His attention temporarily diverted toward Jake, he didn't see the book until it was too late. It hit him in the face, as he pulled the trigger.

Chapter Fifteen

Reggie broke the speed limit between the hospital and the courthouse where the search had begun.

Chase grit his teeth, his right arm clenched to his side to protect his injured chest. He clutched the armrest with his left hand and held on, trying to absorb the sharp turns to keep from setting off stabbing pains from pulled stitches.

Trucks, emergency vehicles and police cars lined the street on both sides, and some parked in the middle.

Reggie eased her way through the maze trying to avoid hitting the people milling about as the snow fell, blanketing the town. Three inches had fallen in less than an hour and it didn't appear to be slowing.

"There's Angus and the new guy Hank sent up from Texas." Reggie pointed toward two men wearing cowboy hats talking to a couple of police officers.

"Where's Kate?" Chase craned his neck, praying for a sign of the sexy brunette.

Reggie frowned. "She should be here. Let me help you down from the truck."

Chase didn't have time for help. He had to find Kate. He reached across his middle and opened the truck door with his left hand. Getting out was more difficult. He slid on the ice-caked running board and bumped into the door, eliciting a stabbing pain to his chest.

For a moment, he squeezed his eyes shut, biting down on his tongue to keep from yelling. When he opened his eyes again, his vision was foggy. Chase blinked twice and it cleared.

"You okay?" Reggie stood beside him. "If you want, you can lean on me."

"Thanks, but I can make it on my own." He trudged through the snow, every step jarring his body and making his chest ache. The more it hurt the angrier he became. He wanted to rip apart anyone who messed with his family and that family included Jake, Sadie and Kate.

As he neared the group of cops and CCI agents, he demanded, "Where's Kate?"

Angus turned, a frown denting his brow. "Chase, shouldn't you be in the hospital?"

Responding to Angus's question was a waste of time. "Where's Kate?"

"She went to the ranch in case Jake was kidnapped and the kidnappers called to demand a ransom. She figured they would call there, since most cell phones are unlisted."

William and Frances Quaid rushed toward them.

"Chase, honey, I'm so glad you're okay." Frances opened her arms to hug him.

Chase held up his left hand and backed away. "I'm okay, but sore. Save the hugs for another time." He faced Angus. "We need to get to the ranch. If Kate's there and they're after Sadie's black book, she could be in trouble. I left it in a safe in my office."

"What about Jake?" Angus asked.

"If you haven't found him by now, he's been kidnapped. My bet is they'll use him as a bargaining chip to get that book."

Angus tipped his head toward the other man in the cowboy hat. "Chase, Ben Harding. Hank sent him. Let me brief the cops and we can leave."

After two of the longest minutes of Chase's life, he, Angus and Ben left in Angus's pickup, speeding down the snowy highway as fast as they could, but slower than Chase could stand.

According to Angus, Kate had left fifteen minutes before Chase showed up. That gave her a giant lead on them. If the men after the black book were already at the ranch...

The drive out to the ranch was hair-raising with the amount of snow that had fallen so fast. The road crews had yet to make it out on the highway and the sides of the roads were difficult to discern buried in snow.

When they finally turned off the road, Chase's blood ran cold. The gate, which usually remained closed, was wide open and listing as if it had been forced.

Kate knew the code and wouldn't have rammed her truck into it. Which meant someone else was on the ranch besides Kate.

"Hurry!" Chase wished he was capable of driving. He knew every curve in the road and could navigate it in a blizzard if necessary.

Angus took the curves as fast as he dared, but it didn't seem fast enough.

When they neared the last curve before the trees parted and the house would come into view on a clear day, Chase said, "Stop here!"

Angus hit the brakes a little too hard. The back end of the truck slid sideways for several yards until they came to a halt.

"Shut off the lights. We'll walk in from here. We don't want anyone to know we're here any sooner than necessary."

Angus glanced at him.

Chase grit his teeth. "I'm going in. And don't worry about me. Get to Kate before they do. I'll go through the front. You two circle around the back."

"Will do." Angus and Ben dropped down out of the truck and carefully closed the door. They each pulled out their pistols, checked the clips and moved forward, clinging to the tree line for as long as they could. Not that it mattered, the snow was coming fast and thick, masking their convergence on the house.

Chase eased out of the truck a little slower and trailed behind the other two men, holding his gun in his left hand. When he had to, he'd switch to his right.

The two CCI agents disappeared around each side of the house while Chase took the front steps to the entrance. No lights shone from the living room window or the foyer. If Kate was inside she had to be farther back in the house.

Transferring the gun to his right hand, Chase eased the door open and stepped inside and listened.

He heard a shout, muffled by walls or doors coming from the back of the house.

Kate.

Chase ran through the huge foyer, past the grand staircase to the rear of the building. As he neared the hallway leading to his office, a shot rang out, sending a cold chill down his spine.

He ran for the door of the office and eased it open, sliding into the room while pointing his pistol straight forward. Pain ripped through his chest, but he ignored it.

Kate lay on the floor beside a bookcase, stretching her arm out to reach for a book.

A man in a ski mask aimed his pistol at her, "Bitch! You had your chance."

"And she'll get another," Chase said, his voice low.

The man in the ski mask spun, leveling his gun on Chase.

Chase stepped out of the way as a book sailed across the room and hit the man in the side of the head.

A gun went off, the sound deafening in the wood-paneled room. Chase pulled the trigger on his weapon and hit the intruder. The man's eyes widened and he stared down at the hole in his chest. The gun in his hand slipped free, clattering against the floor, and then he followed it, toppling like a cut tree and landing with a crash against the polished wood.

Kate leaped to her feet. "Chase!" She ran to him and started to throw her arms around him, but stopped short. "You shouldn't be out of the hospital." Then she cupped his face, kissed his lips and turned. "They had Jake, but he escaped. I have to find him before the other guy does."

Angus and Ben burst through the French doors into the office.

"We heard gunfire," Angus said.

"One down, one on the loose," Chase said. "He's after the boy."

"I bet Jake ran for the barn." Kate dove for the gun her attacker had dropped, then pushed past the men to run out into the cold.

Angus and Ben followed, leaving Chase to bring up the rear.

Footsteps in the snow didn't leave much to guesswork. Jake had made a beeline for the barn, the attacker right behind him.

Chase prayed he'd made it there before his pursuer. Once inside he had a dozen places he could hide, if he was fast enough.

Kate reached the barn before the rest of them and charged in.

Gunfire erupted, two shots.

Chase sprinted the rest of the way, praying Kate and Jake weren't hit.

Angus and Ben entered ahead of Chase, slipping into the darkness. Chase entered, sliding to the side of the door in case he might be silhouetted against the falling snow.

Another shot rang out, hitting the wall beside Chase's ear, sending splinters flying.

He gave a silent curse and moved farther away from the door, holding his weapon out in front of him in his right hand as he reached for the light switch with his left.

For a moment everything was still. Then he flipped the switch and light filled the center of the barn.

"Move and I'll shoot her," a cold voice called out from near the entrance to the tack room. A man in a ski mask held a gun to Kate's head, fisting a free hand in her hair, tipping her at an angle. Blood dripped down her face from a scrape near her hairline.

Rage rippled through Chase. "There's three of us against one of you. Put down your weapon. Maybe we can cut a deal with the DA." Chase forced his voice to be calm, reasoning when all he wanted to do was blow the guy's head off for threatening the woman he was falling in love with.

"Chase, I'm okay," Kate said. "This guy won't hurt me."

The man snorted. "You don't know what you're talking about. All I have to do is pull the trig—"

From behind him, a cat leaped through the air, landing on the captor's back, and then dropped to the floor, scampering up the ladder into the loft.

Kate stomped her heel on his instep, jabbed her elbow into his gut and ducked away from the hand holding the gun.

Chase raised his weapon and fired off a round.

The man in the ski mask fell against the wall behind him and sank to the ground, clutching a hand to his side, and aimed his weapon at Chase.

Kate threw a kick so hard the gun flew through the air and crashed against the far wall. She jumped on him and slammed him into the ground, pinning him beneath her. "Don't ever try to shoot my fiancé," she said through gritted teeth.

Chase laughed at her fierce attack, making pain sear through his chest like a hot poker. Pressing his right arm to his side, he glanced around. "Jake?"

Kate flipped her attacker onto his face. "I saw him for a second when I entered the barn. This bastard nearly had him in his grasp so I flipped the light switch off."

Chase smiled between waves of pain. "Quick thinking."

Ben took charge of their captive, freeing Kate to stand. He yanked a zip tie from his back pocket and wrapped it around the man's wrists, pulling it tight.

Kate straightened, a frown denting her brow. "Jake? It's okay. You can come out now."

"I wasn't scared," a little voice said from inside the tack room. Jeans-clad legs dangled from a shelf near the door.

Angus hurried forward. "Here, let me help you down." He hooked the boy beneath the arms and lifted him off the shelf.

As soon as Jake was in range of Kate, he held out his arms.

She took him and hugged him so tightly Chase thought the boy might pop.

His chest ached and his body was weak from blood loss, but his heart couldn't have been fuller. Kate and Jake were all right.

Jake leaned back and stared into Kate's eyes. "Do you think the mama cat will let me pet her kittens after I threw her on the bad man?"

Kate's eyes rounded. "You threw her?"

"Well, she wouldn't go by herself. And that man was hurting you."

Kate chuckled. "You're my hero, Jake. You saved my life. You and Uncle Chase." She crossed to Chase.

He wrapped his left arm around her, pulled her against his uninjured side and pressed a kiss to the top of her head. "You saved *me*, sweetheart. If you hadn't come along, I'd still be wandering through life without a reason to live."

"Hey, that's my line." She leaned into the curve of his shoulder.

Ben grabbed the ski mask and pulled it off the man's head. "Looks like one of the pictures Hank sent just before we headed out to the ranch." He pulled his phone from his pocket and brought up the photograph with the name. "Trent Geisen. Worked for TG International."

"Question is," Kate said, "who sent him on this mission?"

"We should pay a visit to the Garners. I believe the snow kept them in town for the night at the Gold Rush Tavern."

Kate frowned. "And when we're done, we'll stop by the hospital and check you in for the night."

He smiled at her and bent to kiss her lips. "I'm not staying the night in a hospital."

"Uncle Chase, can we go by and see Grandma Sadie?" Jake clung to Kate, his eyes wide. "Please."

"She might not be awake, and she still has lots of wires and tubes hooked up to her to help her breathe." Chase ruffled Jake's hair. "Are you sure you're up to that?"

Jake nodded. "I'm not afraid. I just want to see Grandma Sadie."

"Okay." Chase smiled at the boy, though his strength was beginning to fade. "We'll do that, after we stop by the Gold Rush Tavern."

William burst into the barn, his eyes wide. "Oh, thank God, you found Jake. Mrs. Quaid will be so relieved."

"You might want to warn her there's a man down in the office."

"Oh, she found him already. He's not going anywhere." William dismissed the dead man. "She's on the phone with Doc Richards to see if he can meet us at the vet clinic." William nodded to Angus. "We could use some help getting Barkley in the back of Mrs. Quaid's SUV. The dog's hurt pretty bad."

Chase stiffened. "How bad?"

William shook his head. "Won't know until the vet takes a look at him."

Jake pointed at the man on the ground. "That bad man hit Barkley with a baseball bat. Hard. Real hard." Jake's bottom lip trembled. "Will Barkley be all right?"

"He was awake and wagging his tail when I saw him," Kate said. "The vet will take good care of him."

Angus tipped his head at Ben. "You got him?"

Lights flashed through the open barn door.

"The sheriff's here," Angus said. "I'm going to help load Barkley."

"Come on, the sooner we get this over with the better." Kate, still holding Jake in her arms, let Chase lean on her.

"I wish my chest didn't hurt so bad, I'd hug you properly. Maybe even steal a kiss."

"Hey, you're alive. That's all that matters." She squeezed his hand. "And it wouldn't be stealing if I gave kisses freely."

"You have a point." His chest tightened for an entirely different reason, filling him with warmth the chill air couldn't dissipate. Kate might just like him. But was it enough for her to stay a little longer?

Kate loaded Jake into her truck and hurried around to help Chase in. "You're staying at the hospital tonight."

"I'm not. I just need to sleep when this is all done."

"Uh-huh." She gave him a narrow-eyed stare and stood on the running board to plant a kiss on his lips, careful not to touch him anywhere else. "You look like hell, but I'll take you any way you come."

"Good thing. I kinda like having you around."

"Let's see if you still do after our conversation with the Garners."

"Think you'll scare me away?"

"If not you, I hope I put some fear into those two."

Chase leaned back in his seat and smiled. If he slept a little on the way back to Fool's Fortune, he wasn't going to admit it to Kate. She would insist on him staying the night in the hospital. No way. Not when he planned on sleeping in the same bed as one tough CCI agent who saved his life.

Chapter Sixteen

Kate drove through the snow back into Fool's Fortune, keeping a careful watch on the road in front of her, doing her best to stay between the ditches.

Despite his argument, Chase was weak from blood loss and it worried her. She wanted him to stay in the hospital in case they had to give him a blood transfusion. But short of knocking him out with a sedative, she'd have no luck convincing him to stay.

She parked in front of the Gold Rush Tavern and helped Chase down out of the truck before going around to unbuckle Jake.

Reggie stepped out of the tavern and hurried toward them. "Angus called and had me stake out the Garners to keep an eye on them. I'll take Jake. Benson and his mother are sitting in the dining room finishing their supper."

Chase touched Reggie's arm. "Thanks for coming on short notice."

"Fortunately, after the search broke up for Jake, I headed over to the diner for dinner with Kitty. I was hanging around town just in case Jake showed up." She hugged the boy. "I'm so glad you're okay. Tad's been asking about you. We'll have to set up a playdate for you two."

"Can Tad come over for Christmas?" Jake asked.

"We'll have to talk about that with your grandma." Reggie shot a glance to Kate and Chase. "I'm betting he didn't have supper."

Kate frowned. "As a matter of fact, he hasn't."

"Then we'll be over at the diner, having something to eat. Take your time."

Reggie settled Jake in her vehicle and drove off. As she left, two sheriff's SUVs pulled in beside Kate's truck.

The deputies climbed out of their vehicles and walked toward the tavern.

Kate's eyes narrowed. "Did you call the law for this meeting?"

Chase shook his head. "No. But it's dinnertime and they could be an asset to our conversation with the Garners."

Kate smiled. "Let's do this." She reached over to grab Chase's left hand and held on. Even with as much blood as he'd lost, he was game to see this case through.

Kate only hoped the Garners weren't armed. She'd had enough shooting for the day.

They stood at the entrance to the restaurant inside the Gold Rush Tavern and scanned the seated patrons.

"Back right corner," Chase said, tipping his head in that direction.

Benson Garner leaned close to his mother, his brow furrowed, speaking fast and intense. His mother's eyes narrowed and her face grew red and angry. She slammed her palm on the table, making the silverware rattle.

Benson stood abruptly.

Chase and Kate crossed the dining room and stopped short of their table, on the fringe of an argument that had started before they'd entered.

"What are *they* doing here?" Mrs. Benson sneered at Chase and Kate.

"What does it matter, Mother?" Benson said. "I'm done with your *plans* for me."

Her nostrils flared and she leaned toward him. "You're not done until I say you're done."

"Did you know Melissa had given birth to my son?" Benson asked, his face turning a blotchy red.

His mother laid her napkin over her plate. "No. And if I'd known that tramp was pregnant—"

"What, Mother? You'd have sent your mercenaries after her sooner, like you did her mother?"

"Who said I sent anyone anywhere?"

Benson shook his head. "What is wrong with you?"

"Nothing's wrong with a mother wanting to help her son make the most of his life. Or a wife standing by her husband as his political career takes off." She stood, her face getting redder. "I worked too hard for the men in my life to squander it on trash."

"Melissa Smith was not trash. I loved her and wanted to marry her."

"The girl at least had the sense to know she wasn't good for you."

"Why, Mother? Because you told her she wasn't good enough?" Benson stared at his mother, his eyes unwavering. "Is that it? Did you tell her she wasn't good enough. Is that why she left without saying goodbye?"

"Don't you see?" His mother looked at him as if he couldn't see what was obvious. "She would have ruined any chance you had for a career in Washington."

"She was pregnant with my son." Benson ran a hand through his hair. "Your grandson."

"He's no grandson of mine. And, if you've got any sense whatsoever, you won't claim him."

"I can't believe we're the same blood." Benson reached for his wallet, tossed some bills on the table and faced his mother. "You're poison. If I find out you had anything to do with Melissa's death or her mother's injuries, I'll be the first to call the police and have you hauled away."

"You're as bad as your father, chasing a pretty skirt around—you after a secretary, him after her whore of a mother. All the while I smiled and pretended I didn't know." Her lips thinned into a sneer. "*I knew.*"

Chase stepped forward and asked, "Is that why you killed your husband?"

"He deserved it," Patricia Garner shouted. "The bastard was having an affair with a madam. I knew, all along, and turned the other cheek. But when he threw it in my face, I'd had enough."

"And Melissa Smith? Why did you kill her?" Kate asked.

"She was going to tell Benson about her son. I couldn't let him fall victim to her blackmail." The woman stood, her eyes filling with angry tears. "That whore ruined my family. She, her daughter and the book with all the lies inside, ruined my life!" Patricia Garner flung her hands in the air and sank to the floor, sobs racking her body. "She ruined my life. I had to ruin hers. She deserved to die."

The patrons of the dining room stared at the woman as she lay on the floor, sobbing loudly.

The two sheriff deputies stepped around Benson. As they helped the woman to her feet, one of the deputies said, "Mrs. Garner, you are under arrest for the murders of Thomas Garner and Melissa Smith, and the attempted murder of Sadie Lovely. You have the right to remain silent..."

Benson sank into a chair, burying his face in his

hands. "Oh my God. I can't believe I didn't see it. I could have stopped her if I'd had any idea she was this crazy."

Kate laid a hand on his shoulder. "You couldn't have known."

He looked up, his face haggard, his eyes bloodshot. "I have a son who doesn't even know me. A mother who murdered my father and my sweet Melissa. How does a person move on after that? How?"

Kate shook her head. "One step at a time."

After the deputies hauled off Mrs. Garner and Benson left, Kate wrapped her arm around Chase's waist and led him toward the exit. "I'm glad we didn't have to beat a confession out of her. I'm tired, and you are in no condition for physical violence or anything else." She winked and tightened her hold around his middle. "Let's stop at the hospital and then go home."

"Home. You do realize you called the Lucky Lady Ranch home."

Her cheeks heated. "I could have been referring to your home."

"Nope. It was all you." He kissed the top of her head and wrapped his injured arm around her shoulders. "It could be your home, too."

"Are you adopting another stray to add to your collection?" she quipped, a charming pink flush staining her cheeks.

He grinned. "Not this time. I want you to stay, but I want you to stay for you, more than for me."

Kate hesitated for only a moment. "I'll stay."

When Chase's face lit up like the Fourth of July, she felt compelled to add, "I'll stay through Christmas. After that…" She paused. "We'll see. We barely know each other."

"Fair enough. I'll take anything you'll give me." A

few more days gave him time to show her how serious he was about her staying for the long haul.

She helped him into the passenger seat. "Let's go get Jake and head back to the ranch."

KATE STOOD BY the Christmas tree, wearing a bright red dress, the first one he'd seen her wear since he'd met her. The flirty hem emphasized her long sexy legs and made Chase's jeans tighten every time he glanced toward her. But damn, he was having a hard time looking away.

It had been three days since Patricia Garner had collapsed during the damning confession she'd volunteered to the people eating dinner at the Gold Rush Tavern. Two days since Sadie was taken off the ventilator and brought out of the effects of sedation.

Sadie had continued to improve, determined to be home for the holiday. The doctor signed her release on Christmas Eve and she returned to the Lucky Lady Ranch, granting Jake his most fervent Christmas wish. "Thank you for taking care of Jake while I was out of it. I can't believe I missed all the excitement." She chuckled softly, holding on to her cracked ribs. "But I'm kind of glad I did."

"We're just glad you're here and able to enjoy the holiday with us," Chase said.

William and Frances, Angus and Reggie, Kate and Chase sat around the Christmas tree in the living room watching Jake and Tad unwrap the gifts left for them under the Christmas tree by Santa Claus.

Jake tore into several presents, finding a new cowboy hat, cowboy boots and a saddle just his size.

Sadie lounged on the couch, wrapped in a warm

blanket, a smile on her face. "I had a call this morning from Benson Garner," she said, her gaze drifting to Jake.

All adult eyes shifted to her.

She sighed. "He wants a chance to get to know his son."

Kate's brows dipped. "Aren't you afraid he'll take Jake away from you?" she asked, her voice low enough Jake wouldn't overhear.

"Did you know he backed out of the race for senator?" she asked.

"That doesn't surprise me," Chase said. He glanced at Jake playing with Tad by the tree. "It might be good for Jake to get to know him."

"I was thinking the same," Sadie said. "I won't be around forever and you can never have too much family who loves you."

"We love you, Sadie," Chase said. "And, as far as I'm concerned, you're family."

Her smiled spread across her face. "Thanks, Chase."

Jake jumped up from the floor and rushed over to Kate, carrying a small box. "This one is for you. It's from Uncle Chase."

"For me?" Kate took the box and settled on the sofa beside Chase. "You weren't supposed to get me anything. I'm the hired help."

Chase shook his head. "Not anymore. The case is closed. Patricia Garner is well on her way to an insanity plea and officially off the job. And you're out of work."

"Then it wouldn't be wrong of me to kiss you?" Kate leaned close and brushed her lips across his.

"Not wrong at all, but amazingly right." His left arm circled her back and drew her closer. "Open the box."

Kate tore the wrapping off the package and opened the lid. Inside was a sapphire and diamond ring. "It's beautiful."

"It was my great-great-grandmother's ring. The gold on the band came from the Lucky Lady Mine."

Kate shook her head. "I can't accept such a gift. We barely know each other." She pushed the ring toward him.

Chase curled his hand around hers. "Maybe we haven't been together for months, going on dates and getting to know what we like to eat, favorite colors and sports teams, but I know enough about you to know you're the one for me."

Kate started to talk, but Chase wanted to finish what he had to say first. He wanted to get it right. "If you don't feel the same way about me, I hope it will come with time and that you'll stay long enough to give me a chance to show you that I could be the right man for you. Because you see, I love you, Kate Rivers, and I want to be with you for always."

Kate's eyes welled and tears slipped down her cheeks. "I can't give you children."

"There are so many children in this world who need parents. Why deprive some of them the chance to have a mother like you?"

"Or a father like you." Kate's voice caught in her throat and she swallowed before continuing. "You're an amazing man and true to the ones you love. I couldn't find a better mate."

William snorted from across the room. "Is that how the young folks are proposing nowadays? No wonder the divorce rate is so darned high. Ask her proper."

Chase chuckled and eased onto his knee in front of Kate. "He's right. I didn't do a proper proposal. Kate

Rivers, will you consider marrying this former playboy and make an honest man out of him?"

Kate cupped his cheeks in her hands and kissed his lips. "If you'll promise to take me riding at least once a month and love me every day for the rest of your life."

"I promise."

She dragged in a deep breath. "I can't believe I'm saying this after knowing you for so short a time, but here goes. Yes!"

Chase rose and pulled Kate up into his arms, wincing.

"Hey, you're not ready for a full-on hug." Kate leaned back, not allowing herself to touch his wounded chest.

"I'll risk it. On a momentous occasion such as this, a peck on the lips isn't enough."

Kate laid her cheek against him, careful not to put too much pressure on him. "Chase?"

"Yes, darlin'?"

"Can we take Jake and Sadie to my parents' house for the new year?"

"Anywhere your heart desires."

Kate had her heart's desire in her arms. But it was time to see her family and all her sister's children. Because family was everything and went beyond blood and genes. Family was the people you held in your heart.

* * * * *

"Can we talk about the rules for a minute?" he asked.

"Rules?"

He waved his hand. "Expectations. Firm expectations. We remain in visual contact at all times. That means you don't even step outside for a quick breath of fresh air without me. If you have to go to the bathroom, I'll check it first and then stand outside the door."

"I know we're supposed to be newlyweds, but won't people think that's just a little over the top?"

"I'll do it in a way that people won't even notice." She thought he perhaps underestimated that every woman's eyes in the place would follow him. He was just so darn handsome, so darn male. "Got it. Visual contact. At all times. It's just that I'm a little disappointed."

"Why?" He looked very concerned.

She lowered her lashes. "Well, Detective Hollister. That wasn't the only kind of contact I was hoping for tonight."

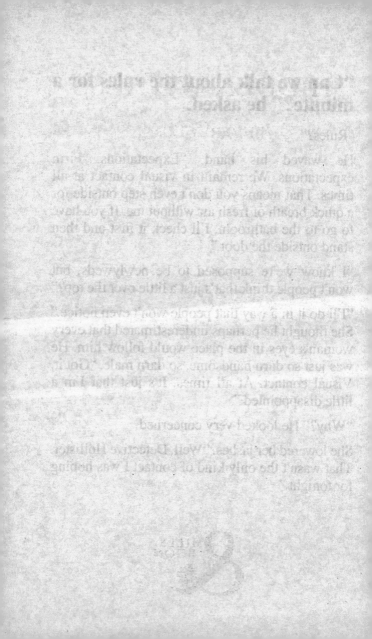

"Can we talk about my value for a minute?" he asked.

Ruthie

He waived the third. "Expectations. Firm expectations. We remain in visual contact at all times. That means you don't even step outside for a quick breath of fresh air without me. If you have to go to the bathroom, I'll check it first and then stand outside the door."

"I know you're supposed to be anonymous, but won't people thinking a girl a little over the top"

"I'll do it in a way that people won't even notice." She thought for a moment and realised that every woman's eyes in the place would follow him. He was just so damn handsome. So damn hot. "Got it." Sound counsel. At all times. It's just that I am a little disappointed."

"Why?" He looked very concerned.

She lowered her lashes. "Well, Detective Holmes. That wasn't the only kind of contact I was hoping for tonight."

HIDDEN WITNESS

BEVERLY LONG

Published in Great Britain 2015
by Mills & Boon, an imprint of Harlequin (UK) Limited,
Eton House, 18-24 Paradise Road, Richmond, Surrey, TW9 1SR

© 2015 Beverly R. Long

ISBN: 978-0-263-25324-5

46-1115

Harlequin (UK) Limited's policy is to use papers that are natural, renewable and recyclable products and made from wood grown in sustainable forests. The logging and manufacturing processes conform to the legal environmental regulations of the country of origin.

Printed and bound in Spain
by CPI, Barcelona

Beverley Long enjoys the opportunity to write her own stories. She has both a bachelor's and a master's degree in business and more than twenty years of experience as a human resources director. She considers her books to be a great success if they compel the reader to stay up way past their bedtime. Beverly loves to hear from readers. Visit www.beverlylong.com, or like her at facebook.com/beverlylong.romance.

For Kate, Nick and Lydia,
who have a wonderful new home in Missouri.

Chapter One

Chase Hollister heard his cell phone ring and used his forearm to pull the pillow that he slept half-on and half-under closer around his ears. It rang four times and clicked over to voice mail. Thirty seconds later, it started ringing again.

"Damn," he muttered, tossing off the pillow. He glanced at the number, saw that it was his brother and reached for the phone.

He pushed a button. "I have not had any sleep for twenty-eight hours," Chase said. "This better be good."

"Brick is dead," Bray said.

Chase sat up in bed. He hadn't heard the man's name in over eight years. Hadn't spoken it himself for much longer. "How?"

"Car accident. His sister was with him. They had a double funeral two days ago."

Chase had met his stepfather's older sister once, maybe twice. He recalled that even as a teenager, he'd known there was something odd about her. That family had a bad gene pool.

"Anybody else get hurt?" Chase asked.

"Nope. One car. Only Brick and Adelle in it. They were on their way to Brick's doctor's appointment."

He lay back down. He didn't care about the details. "I'm going back to bed."

"I got a call from Mom's attorney," Bray said. "The house is ours."

In one smooth movement, Chase swung his body out of bed. His bare feet hit the soft rug first, then the polished hardwood. He walked down the short hallway and into his kitchen. The blinds were up and he was naked. He didn't care. He needed coffee. "That doesn't make sense. Brick had a son. I assume the man is still alive."

"I'm not sure but it's a moot point. When Mom died eight years ago, the house was in a trust for us. Brick had been granted lifetime use. The attorney said that we should have been made aware of that upon Mom's death but it was a slipup."

The irony was not lost on Chase. They could have fought the lifetime-use thing and booted him out of there. He'd have been on the outside looking in, kind of like Chase had been whenever Brick got a wild hair and locked him out.

He dumped some coffee in a filter, poured water in the coffeepot and flipped the start button. He didn't put the pot on the burner. Instead, he held a cup directly under the streaming coffee.

"You've got to go there and see what we need to do to get rid of the place," Bray said.

Chase jiggled the cup and hot liquid burned his hand. "No way," he said. "You go, you're the oldest."

"I would if I could. I'm three weeks into a new assignment. I can't pull out now."

"Cal will have to do it. We're older, we can make him." Chase added the familiar taunt, knowing there was nothing easy or familiar about his relationship with Cal.

"He's out of the country."

Cal had spent most of the past eight years out of the country. That was what navy SEALs did. For the past six months, following his discharge, he'd been working as a contractor. That was what his business card said. Chase supposed it could be true if the new breed of contractor was trained to blow up the bad guys, disarm bombs and generally screw with the enemy. "Well, I don't care if he's on the moon. I'm busy, too, you know. I've only been back for a week."

"How is the leg?"

Functional. Still not up to full strength. "Fine," Chase said.

"I thought you were going to be out for six weeks," Bray prodded. "You went back at four."

"We're short staffed."

"Aren't we all? I was especially impressed when your name popped up on one of my search engines. Then, when I dug a little deeper, I realized you were busy being a hero on your second day back."

Chase didn't answer. He'd hated the photo, the article, the attention. Hadn't considered that it went beyond the print edition.

"'Detective Chase Hollister, one of St. Louis's finest, keeping the streets safe for the rest of us,'" Bray recited.

His brother did his own part to keep the streets safe. Working undercover for the DEA wasn't easy. He would have hated the attention, too. But now he was picking a fight in hopes that Chase, wanting to end the conversation, would agree to take care of things. It wasn't going to work.

"Listen, Bray. It's simple. I'm not going back. The house can rot for all I care," he said. Chase hung up and tossed his cell phone onto the granite countertop. The noise echoed through the quiet apartment. Then he stood in his stainless-steel kitchen and sipped his coffee, burning his tongue in the process.

Ravesville, Missouri. Two hours southwest of St. Louis. A little town in the middle of the country, undisturbed by major highways and big box stores. A place where everybody knew their neighbor, talked about them freely and dropped everything when they needed a hand. It was the kind of place where a kid got on his bike at eight o'clock on a summer morning and didn't come home until dinner. The kind of place where there were community-wide chili dinners and pancake breakfasts and people stuck around to clear the tables and wash the dirty dishes. It had been home. And he'd been a happy enough kid.

And then everything had changed the summer his dad died. Chase had been fourteen, just about to enter high school. And as bad as his dying had been, it had gotten worse two years later when his mother had remarried and Brick had become his stepfather.

There probably wasn't a meaner man in the entire state. Why he'd married a woman with three teenage boys when he didn't appear to like kids was a mystery. He was estranged from his own son, who was quite a bit older than the Hollister boys. Chase could only remember meeting him once.

When the phone rang again less than five minutes later, he picked it up, ready to give his brother an earful. At the last second, he realized it was his partner's number. The man should have been sleeping, too. He'd been awake the same twenty-eight hours.

"Yeah," Chase said.

"The boss called. He just heard from the chief," Dawson said. "Somebody used the Florida witness in the Malone case for target practice."

He and Dawson hadn't worked the Malone case but the man was suspected of murdering three Missouri women about a year ago, one of whom was the chief's godchild. Harry Malone was currently locked up in the county jail awaiting trial and everybody in the St. Louis Police Department, from the janitor up, had an interest in the case. "That doesn't make sense. That woman should have been sealed up tighter than your wallet."

"Funny."

"Was she injured?"

"No. Lorraine Taylor got lucky."

Then, it was the second time she'd gotten lucky. He wasn't sure of the details but through the grapevine he'd heard that she'd somehow managed to get away from Harry Malone. She'd told the cops about the pictures of the dead women that Harry Malone had proudly shown her and the admission Malone had made about killing the women. She'd been able to lead them back to the apartment where she'd been held. Unfortunately, by that time, Harry and his pictures were gone. But her DNA had been in several places in the apartment and she'd had injuries consistent with her story.

But Harry had been careful and there was no physical evidence linking him to the Missouri murders because there were no bodies.

Even so, based on the information that Lorraine Taylor had provided, Harry Malone had been picked up and charged with kidnapping and assorted other crimes and three counts of murder. Lorraine Taylor had likely assumed that she'd done her civic duty by leading the police to the man and that she could get on with her life.

However, she'd no doubt quickly reevaluated those plans six weeks later after almost being killed by a hit-and-run as she walked to work. Witnesses had substantiated that the attack was deliberate. That was where it got complicated. Following her escape from Malone, Lorraine Taylor's identity had been closely guarded and her name had never made the newspapers.

Unfortunately, in the information age, that didn't mean much. Cops in both Florida and St. Louis knew her name. Then there were the people in the prosecuting attorney's office and the judge's office. Harry Malone certainly knew who she was, and jail might impede communication with the outside world but it certainly didn't stop it.

The cops considered whether the attack on Taylor could have been unrelated to her potential testimony against Malone. But even if that was true, it didn't really matter. Any attack, for whatever reason, had the potential of robbing the State of Missouri of their prime witness.

They'd decided to put her in a safe house. That was the last that Chase had heard.

Now somebody had shot at her. That was going to make a lot of people nervous, people who were counting on the fact that Lorraine Taylor was going to be an excellent witness.

She was going to have to be. Harry Malone, a rich, second-generation hedge-fund trader from New York, wasn't stupid. He wasn't talking and he'd retained a very good defense attorney. He'd been deemed a flight risk and denied bail so his attorney was working expeditiously to get the trial under way.

Plus, the scuttlebutt was that Malone was confident that he was going to walk free.

Was it possible that he wasn't as confident as he wanted others to believe and he'd decided to ensure his freedom by getting rid of Lorraine Taylor?

"The chief wants her moved to St. Louis," Dawson said.

The chief was a known control freak and, given his personal interest in this case, there was probably no talking him out of it. But Chase understood. They needed Lorraine Taylor.

"He told the boss that he wants us to start working on it," Dawson said.

"Why us?" They weren't the most senior detectives on the force. He'd barely spoken ten words to the chief and he figured it was the same for Dawson. He didn't care; brown-nosing his way to the top wasn't his style. Besides, who knew how long he was going to stick around? Maybe there was a better job around the corner.

"According to the boss, the chief said that we did a hell of a job in the Brodger case."

Hamas Brodger had been a drug dealer who had executed three teenage boys who'd tried to screw him out of a couple hundred dollars.

A fourth boy had managed to get away. Chase and Dawson had babysat him, twelve-on, twelve-off, for six weeks. It hadn't been a good assignment. The kid didn't bathe regularly and had forgotten all the manners he'd learned in kindergarten. And he hadn't been able to keep his fingers away from social media and had led the bad guys to their door. Chase had taken a bullet in the leg as a result but had managed to get his own shot off.

The kid had testified and Brodger was going to call the state penitentiary home for a long time.

"I think you maybe should have let the guy shoot him," Dawson said. "The way it turned out, it's just getting us more work."

"Maybe next time," Chase said. "But listen, I may need to take a day off pretty soon. I've…uh…I've got something I need to take care of. Family business."

"Your brothers okay?" Dawson asked, his tone serious.

"Yeah. They're fine. My stepfather just died."

Dawson didn't offer the normal platitudes. He didn't know everything but he knew enough. "Can I help?" he asked.

"Nope. Just got to take care of a house. The lieutenant doesn't expect us back in, does he?"

"He said tomorrow was soon enough. Lorraine Taylor will be here then. The question is, what are we going to do with her?"

RANEY TAYLOR WAS FURIOUS. The nightmare that had started the evening Harry Malone had wandered into Next Steps and volunteered to help was never going to end.

Wasn't it enough that she was going to have to testify and relive every awful moment of the fifty-four hours that she spent with him? As horrible as that would be, she knew she had to do it. The man had to be stopped.

Once he'd been arrested, it had never occurred to her that she would still be in danger. She'd gone back to work, brushed aside the comments from coworkers that she really should take more time off and hoped that someday, she'd be able to trust again. And each day had gotten a little easier. But six weeks later, when a dark SUV had tried to run her down three blocks from her house, she'd realized that things were about to get a lot harder.

The police had promised that they could keep her safe. *Don't worry,* they'd said, handing her the keys to the two-bedroom house in the modest Miami neighborhood. *We keep witnesses here all the time. Nothing ever happens.* Now they were going to have to change their sales pitch because last night, eleven days after moving in, someone had taken a shot at her as she took the garbage to the curb.

If she hadn't bent down to chase a wayward napkin, she'd be dead right now.

She'd assumed she'd be moved to another place. She hadn't expected them to announce that she needed to pack quickly because she was getting on a plane. And going to St. Louis.

She'd known that at some point she'd have to travel to the Midwestern city. Harry Malone's trial was taking place there because his three other victims had all resided in Missouri.

She'd never met the other victims but she *knew* them. Could easily imagine the terror they'd lived through. After her escape, she hadn't been able to keep from looking up the news stories. Had wanted to see the women as people, had wanted to know they had lives and that they'd been loved. Had needed to replace the images she carried in her head with something else.

She did not want to be in the same city with Malone. She'd made a terrible mistake in trusting him. And had almost paid the ultimate price.

She rubbed her ribs. He'd cracked three of them with a well-placed kick after he'd dumped her blindfolded on the floor of his squalid apartment. The doctor had told her that the bones would knit back together quickly but it might take months for the bruising to heal. Every night when she rolled over in bed, it woke her up.

Not that she was sleeping a whole lot anyway.

Maybe that would change in St. Louis. Maybe she could sleep away the next month until she had to testify at the trial. Leaving her job pained her more than anything. She loved her work.

Her clients, most of whom came from disadvantaged circumstances, wanted to work but for one reason or another had trouble securing employment. The assistance she provided took many forms. She taught basic communication skills to some. Took others shopping so that they understood what to wear to work. She'd helped with table manners, organizational skills and conflict management.

It made her day when a client showed up with his or her first paycheck. It made her week when they were still working at that same job three months later. She was over the moon when they celebrated their first anniversary.

Now Harry Malone had taken that away from her. That and more.

She jumped when there was a light tap at the door. "Ready, Ms. Taylor?" the officer asked. Luis had been with her since day one of her *captivity* and he'd been unfailingly polite.

"I don't understand why I have to go to St. Louis," she said for the twentieth time. "This is a big city, a big state. Surely you have other safe houses."

The older man shrugged. "All I know is that you need to be on the nine-fifteen flight to St. Louis. Maybe it won't be as hot there."

In late September, Miami was still stifling hot. Not that she'd been outside much lately. It would be wonderful if they stashed her someplace where she had access to a balcony or a porch.

"Fine. Let's just get this over with," she said.

CHASE MET DAWSON in the front lobby of police headquarters and they rode the elevator in silence. "How's Mary?" Chase asked as the doors opened.

"She said her ankles have swelled to the size of cantaloupes and her back feels as if a small army of angry men with sharp knives have taken residence."

"Damn. Want to stay at my place for a few days?"

Dawson shook his head. "I'd have to stay thirty-six days, and if I did that, I don't think I'd have a happy home to return to once the little princess is born."

Chase pulled open the heavy door that led them to the interior office. "I don't like coming here," he whispered.

Dawson shrugged. "Then, quit doing crazy things that get you noticed by the top brass."

"I don't do crazy things," he denied.

"Five weeks ago, you took a bullet in your thigh and still managed to return fire. You pushed your recovery, got the doc to release you early and came back to work last week. A day later, you walked through a wall of fire. And it was all caught on a cell phone. The newspaper called you a hero and the video played on the evening news—both the six o'clock and the ten o'clock," he said. "And you hadn't even clocked in for the day," he added, sounding exasperated.

It had been early and the two young men had been drag racing on their way to work. He'd just gotten the first guy out of his car when the second car had exploded, potentially trapping the young driver. "You wouldn't have left that kid to die."

Dawson smiled at the young woman behind the desk. "Detectives Roy and Hollister here to see Chief Bates." When she picked up the phone, he turned to Chase. "I wouldn't have wanted to," he said, his tone serious. "But I'm not sure I'd have had the guts to do what you did," he added. "You had to have been concerned that your leg might not hold up."

He'd considered the possibility. Then ignored it. Those kids were going to have a future. That was what mattered.

The chief only made them wait ten minutes. When they were ushered into his office, Chase was again reminded that Chief Bates was one tough dude. While he was close to sixty, he was six-five, with a barrel chest and a handshake that could bring a man to his knees.

He extended his arm to Dawson. "Detective Roy," he said. "Good to see you." He turned toward Chase. "Detective Hollister. How's the leg?"

"Fine."

The chief nodded. "Saw you on the news the other day. Nice work."

Behind the chief, Dawson made a big deal out of rolling his eyes. Chase ignored him.

"Sit, please," the chief said, pointing to the leather chairs in front of his big cherry desk. "You know what our situation is?"

Chase nodded. "There was a second attempt on Lorraine Taylor's life."

"Yes. Malone has access to considerable resources. It's possible that he managed to organize a hit on her before the Florida police got him picked up. It's also possible that he did it from jail."

The words lingered in the air. Good cops hated that there were dirty cops but it was a fact of life. Palms got greased and instructions often made it over the prison wall. Or maybe it had been a visitor who carried messages back and forth. The possibilities really were endless.

Chase leaned forward in his chair. "Could Malone have had an accomplice? Somebody who knew Lorraine Taylor. Knew her because it wasn't an accident that she was the victim. Maybe she was cherry-picked and when things went badly for Malone and he was picked up, the accomplice slipped into action?"

"It's possible. But Taylor didn't see anybody else while she was with Malone or hear him refer to anyone."

But Malone was smart—nobody was disputing that. He'd managed to kill three women and hide their bodies.

The chief steepled his big fingers together. "It's even possible that we've got some crackpot who somehow managed to find out Taylor's identity and he or she has decided to finish what Malone started."

Chase nodded. "I guess the only thing we really know for sure is that we need to keep Lorraine Taylor alive to testify at Harry Malone's trial."

"Alive and unintimidated," the chief corrected. "I'm worried that she's not going to be a good witness if she's frightened that her life is in danger. We need her confident. Relaxed," he added, then had the wherewithal to look a little sheepish. "As much as one can be at a murder trial."

"What can we do to help, sir?" Dawson asked.

The chief looked at his watch. "Lorraine Taylor's plane should be touching down in forty-five minutes and nobody has given me an option that I'm happy with."

Chase took a sideways glance at Dawson. There were a number of safe houses that they used in the city, even a few in West County. Those were the ones he knew about. The chief probably knew of others.

"Her location was compromised in Miami," Chief Bates said. "I can't have that happen here. She's already not happy about coming to the same city where Malone is sitting in jail. I'm thinking of stashing her downstate, maybe Springfield."

Chase could see the concern on Dawson's face. He would not want to be hours away from his wife if the baby decided to come early. He waited to see if Dawson would say something. But he didn't. Chase understood. Turning down an assignment that the chief personally handed you was career suicide.

Chase leaned forward in his chair. He was going to regret this. "My brothers and I own a house in Ravesville. It's sitting empty right now. It's a mile and a half outside of town. Only a couple neighbors on the same road. Brick... uh, my stepfather just died."

The chief's eyes lit up. "Did you grow up there?"

Chase nodded.

"When did you move away?"

He'd left the day Calvin had turned eighteen, when both of them were legal to be on their own. He'd been twenty-one. "Thirteen years ago, sir. I went back once, about eight years ago."

The chief tapped his middle finger on the wood desk. He stared at it. Finally, he looked up. "I like it. We'll have your file reflect that you're on personal leave. If anybody asks," he said, looking at Dawson, "Detective Hollister is dealing with family stuff. Nobody besides the two of you and the few people that I personally involve will have any knowledge of the truth. Nobody else."

He switched his laser-sharp gaze to Chase. "Congratulations, Detective Hollister. You just got married. Lorraine Taylor can pose as your wife."

Chapter Two

By the time the plane had landed and Luis was hustling her through the airport, Raney had a headache that wouldn't quit. They exited into a wall of very warm, humid air.

"I thought the Midwest was cooler than Florida," she said.

Luis didn't respond. He was busy looking at his phone. Then he signaled for a cab.

"Where are we going?" she asked.

"I don't know," he said, sounding irritated. "I just got a text with a street address from my contact."

"That makes me feel very secure," she said drily. Sweat was gathering between her breasts and the hot sun made her feel sick to her stomach. "You'd think they'd at least spring for a car," she said grumpily.

Again Luis did not respond, which surprised her. In Florida he'd been polite, almost chatty. He'd been quiet on the plane. Now he seemed edgy. It made her feel off balance.

The cab drove for about thirty minutes before finally pulling into an empty spot behind a brown UPS truck. The driver was out of the vehicle, stacking boxes high on a cart.

It dawned on her that she was just another kind of package. She'd been wrapped up and sent halfway across the country, to be handed off into someone else's care. And they were going to cart her somewhere else and put her on a shelf for a month.

She looked at the sign in the nearest store window. It was a frozen yogurt shop. At least things were looking up. "Is this it?"

Luis didn't answer. He was watching the street closely. They got out of the cab and hadn't walked more than three feet before a big man, probably close to the age her father would have been, fell into step next to them. He had a plastic bag looped over one hand.

He nodded at her and spoke quietly to Luis. Luis extended his hand and the men shook. Luis turned to her. "This is police chief Bates. He'll take over from here."

"Great," she said.

"We're happy to have you in St. Louis," the man said. "Thank you, Officer Vincenze."

Luis nodded at the chief and looked at her. "Good luck," he said before turning quickly away. He got back into the same cab they'd arrived in. Chief Bates waited until the cab had pulled away from the curb before turning toward her.

"Rest assured that we're going to keep you perfectly safe," he said. "Right now we need to get a few things taken care of."

"What things?" she asked.

"I'll answer all your questions," he said. They walked past the frozen yogurt shop. Turned a corner. Walked another block. Turned another corner. Second store in, he stopped. "But first, let's just step inside here." He opened the door to what appeared to be a hair salon. The lights inside were dimmed and there were no customers. Just a woman standing behind the high counter.

"Morning, Marvin," the woman said.

"Ms. Taylor, this is my sister, Sandy. Work your magic, honey," the chief said to the woman.

The day was getting stranger by the minute.

An hour later, Raney's shoulder-length brown hair had been chopped off and she was a platinum blonde. Without the heavy weight, her hair had a natural wave that surprised her. She liked that she could tuck the wispy strands behind her ears. She also had to admit that the new hair color made her light blue eyes pop in a way that eye shadow had never managed. It was a startling change and she had trouble taking it all in.

"She's done," Sandy said. They were the first words she'd spoken since she explained that she was going to lighten up and trim her hair. Sandy was clearly a master of understatement.

The chief, who had looked ridiculous perched on one of the small chairs in the waiting area, stood up. "Everybody else should be here soon."

He was right if "everybody" was three men. She could see them through the glass window. One was in his midfifties with a camera around his neck, carrying what appeared to be a big bag of dry cleaning. The second was a handsome black man dressed in a nice gray suit. The third man, and the one who held her attention, was in a tux and carried a small suitcase with him. He was tall.

If Sandy planned to trim him up, she didn't have much to work with. His dark brown hair was already cut short, maybe not military short but pretty close. It showed off his chiseled good looks.

The chief opened the door and locked it behind them. The room was suddenly filled with testosterone. Raney, who was still sitting in the stylist's chair, felt at a disadvantage. She stood up quickly, tried to take a step, got the heel of her sandal caught in the lower rung of the chair and pitched forward.

Tuxedo Guy caught her before she landed on her face. His grip on her bare upper arms was secure but light. He gently pushed her upright and she passed within inches of his body.

He smelled delicious, an earthy citrus that evoked images of a tropical rainforest.

"Okay?" he asked, his voice low, sexy. His skin was very tan and his eyes were an odd shade of brown, almost amber.

"Ah, sure," she managed. She'd been off balance since leaving Florida and the past fifteen seconds hadn't helped. Who was this man?

"Ms. Taylor," Chief Bates said. "You need to get changed."

Huh?

The man with the camera extended his dry cleaning in her direction. She automatically reached out, noting the bag was heavier than it looked.

Sandy pointed to a door. Raney stood her ground. "Maybe you're thinking that someone has explained to me what's going on, but nobody has. And I don't think I'm changing my clothes or anything else until somebody does."

The black man looked at Chief Bates. Tuxedo Guy was staring at her, and she thought she caught a glimpse of appreciation in his eyes.

"Of course," the chief said. "I apologize. I'm just

anxious to get you to a safe place. This is Officer Henderson. He's a photographer for the police department. This is Detective Roy and Detective Hollister."

"Thank you," she said. "Why do I need new clothes? I have my own," she said, inclining her head toward her suitcase, which was still sitting near the front door.

"There's a wedding dress in there," the chief said. "You need to put it on and Officer Henderson is going to snap a few pictures of you and Detective Hollister as the happy bride and groom. He's assured me that he's managed to manipulate the date on his camera so if anyone digs into the pictures, they'll believe they were taken several weeks ago, on August 15. We've filed a license with the county clerk's office dated that same day in case someone bothers to check. Under a different name, of course."

She felt her face grow hot. What was this guy smoking? Wedding dress? Marriage license? Different name? "I'm not getting married," she said. She'd been married. It hadn't gone well.

Chief Bates looked as if he wasn't used to people disagreeing with his plans. Detective Roy stepped forward. "Of course not," he said. "Your cover for the next month while we await Harry Malone's trial will be as Detective Hollister's wife. You'll be living at Chase's parents' home in rural Missouri, about two hours from here."

Her head, maybe feeling light because she'd lost a lot of hair or maybe because she was in an alternate universe, swiveled on her neck. She stared at Tuxedo Guy. "We're going to be married," she repeated. "Actually, we're already married, if the wedding was August 15," she said, rather stupidly she thought, the minute the words were out of her mouth.

"I guess that's right," he said.

"And we're going to live with your parents?"

He shook his head. "They're dead. The house is empty."

She rubbed her forehead. "What's my new name?" she asked.

Chief Bates stepped forward. "In these types of situations, it's better if we can keep your first name the same. Less confusion for you. In the event of an emergency, you'll react to it better. We'll list your maiden name on the wedding certificate as Lorraine Smith. It's common enough. Then, of course, you'll be Lorraine Hollister for the duration of this assignment."

"Somewhere in Missouri," she said.

"Yes, ma'am," Chief Bates said.

She clutched her wedding dress tighter. "I swear to God, if I ever get a chance at Harry Malone, I'm going to kill him myself."

THE BLOND HAIR had set him back because it was such a dramatic difference from the picture he'd studied on the way over to the hair salon. In the photo, her brown hair had hung past her shoulders, her face had been pale and her eyes had been dark with fatigue. It had likely been taken the morning that she'd first been interviewed by the Miami police after her ordeal with Harry Malone had ended.

Today, she looked amazing. The hair was sexy, her skin was clear and fresh and her blue eyes were gorgeous. She would make a pretty bride.

Once Chief Bates had determined the plan, they'd swung into action. The chief had left to intercept Lorraine Taylor. Chase had been dispatched home to pack a suitcase and then to the mall to get a tux. He had met

Dawson back at the police station and they'd picked up
Gavin Henderson, who'd been busy in his own right.
He'd been sent home to get his daughter's recently
cleaned wedding dress. All of them, including the chief,
had been at her wedding five weeks earlier.

Dawson had managed to pull him aside before they'd
piled into the car. "I know why you offered up the house
in Ravesville," he'd said. "And I appreciate it."

"It's no problem," Chase had replied, lying. He hated
the idea.

"Newlyweds?" Dawson had needled. "You going to
be okay with that?"

Dawson was well aware that Chase wasn't interested
in marriage. Even so, because he was besotted with his
own bride, Dawson had a tendency to overencourage
Chase to commit and ragged his tail when Chase easily
dismissed the idea. It had gotten to the point that Chase
had stopped telling him about his occasional dates because the man made too damn big a deal out of them.

That, of course, had led Dawson to worry that Chase
was becoming a monk. "You're not getting any younger,"
he said. "You might want to catch one while you're still
in your prime."

He sure as hell wasn't going to admit to Dawson that
his leg now ached as though he was ninety.

The next month was going to suck but he'd make the
best of it. He was pretty confident Lorraine Taylor felt
the same way. When she'd said *Missouri*, it had sounded
an awful lot like *misery*. She hadn't slammed the door
when she'd gone to change into the wedding dress but
she'd surely looked as if she wanted to.

But as much as he hated the idea, he had to admit, it
wasn't a terrible plan. No one would question his pres-

ence at the house. After all, he and his brothers had lived there for many years and it would be common knowledge in the small community that Brick had recently died. People there would be expecting somebody from the family to come back and take care of the property.

Now, courtesy of some just-in-time photography, Dawson was going to upload the wedding photos onto a couple social media sites, publicizing that he'd recently done best-man honors for Chase and his happy bride. That way if anyone bothered to search for Chase Hollister, the cover story would hold. Chief Bates had instructed that if anyone at the department happened across the photos and asked, Dawson was to hold tight to the cover story. Once the trial was over, Chase could tell people the truth.

It had the potential to be a win-win. He'd be there to watch over Lorraine. He'd also be able to get the house ready for sale, and the State of Missouri would preserve their witness in what was likely to be one of the biggest trials of the year.

He and Lorraine simply needed to act the part of happy newlyweds. He heard the door open and in a rustle of silk and lace, Lorraine stepped out into the hallway, wearing the wedding dress. She was blushing.

"I'm going to need some help with the zipper," she said.

None of the men moved. Chase was pretty sure he'd stopped breathing.

Finally, Sandy got behind her and Chase heard the gentle rasp of a zipper. With every inch, Chase felt his mouth get drier. She was beautiful. Once the zipper was up, the dress hugged her curves and the cut showed a generous portion of her pretty breasts that, quite frankly, hadn't been all that visible in the T-shirt that she had been wearing.

Dawson looked at him, his dark eyes wide with speculation. Chase ignored him.

"Let's get this over with," Chief Bates instructed. He bent down, opened the plastic sack at his feet and proved that he hadn't wasted time while waiting for Lorraine's plane to land. He pulled out two items. The first one was flowers. They were wrapped in clear plastic and Chase recognized them as the kind you could buy for fifteen bucks at the grocery store. The chief thrust them toward Lorraine.

She didn't move, just stared at them.

"Hang on," Sandy said. She opened a drawer, pulled out a pair of scissors and efficiently cut off the plastic wrap, then trimmed off the long stems. When she finished, it was a very presentable bouquet.

The second item in Chief Bates's bag was a birthday cake. With pink and yellow balloons on it. "This was all they had," he apologized.

Chase thought he caught the glimpse of a smile on Lorraine's face.

"I can make it work," Gavin said. "Chase and Lorraine, I need you to stand in front of this wall."

Chase moved to where Gavin pointed. After a second of hesitation, Lorraine did the same. Up close, he realized that he was probably about eight inches taller than her, which gave him a truly excellent view down the front of her dress.

He felt his whole body get warm.

He jerked his head up and stared at Gavin, who had his camera out. The man looked up, irritation on his face. "I can add a church background with Photoshop but I can't make the two of you look happy. Come on. Work with me."

Chase licked his lips and sucked in a deep breath. Then he wrapped his arm around Lorraine's shoulders. He bent his head, looked into her eyes and gave her his best smile.

He thought she might tell him to go to hell. But after a long minute of staring into his eyes, she pasted on her own smile.

And for the next fifteen minutes, he and Lorraine Taylor responded like trained seals. Gavin snapped pictures of them facing one another, side by side and even feeding each other pieces of cake off plastic plates that Sandy had found in the bottom drawer of her desk. Snap, snap, snap. Finally, Gavin instructed him to move out of the frame and for Lorraine to give the camera her back. "Pretend you're just about to throw your bouquet," he said.

She did. Snap, snap, snap. Then he said, "Okay. I've got enough."

Lorraine let the flowers sail. Without thinking, Chase reached out to catch them. When she turned, her blue eyes were big.

"Congratulations, Detective," she said. "I guess a real wedding is in your future."

Chase let the flowers fall to the ground. Everyone in the room stared at them.

Gavin coughed loudly. "Let's finish up with the groom kissing the bride."

Chase felt his racing heart skip a beat. He looked at Lorraine. He no longer felt like a trained seal but rather a fish out of water.

"Ready?" he said.

"Ready," she whispered.

He walked close and bent his head, intending to merely brush her lips.

"Make it look good," Gavin said.

She opened her mouth and he felt himself settle in. She tasted like chocolate cake and her mouth was warm and wet, and it had been a long time since a kiss had made his knees weak.

But when it was over, he had to admit that this one had done just that.

But he sure as hell wasn't going to give Dawson the satisfaction of seeing it. "Is that a wrap?" he asked, making sure that his tone was nonchalant.

He ignored the soft hiss he heard from Lorraine.

"We need to hit the road," he said. "I want to get to Ravesville before dark."

DETECTIVE HOLLISTER WAS an amazing kisser. His lips had been warm, his breath sweet and his hands confident as they'd cupped her face. It was as if someone had hit a switch, kicking off an electrical charge that had started in her toes and rapidly spread through her body.

She'd felt alive.

And she'd been stupid enough to think that it had affected him the same way. Of course it hadn't. And she suspected she should be grateful that he'd been an ass about it afterward because she had been about thirty seconds away from crawling up his body.

That would have been a real photo opportunity.

There weren't going to be any more kisses. Not that Chase was probably inclined. He might have played the role of besotted groom, but she could tell that he hadn't been thrilled to be participating in the farcical marriage.

After their ceremony, he had quickly changed into jeans and a T-shirt and, if possible, had looked even hotter. But his attitude didn't match.

He was polite. Definitely. But she'd sensed his irritation when they'd had to kill thirty minutes at the salon. She'd looked through the tattered magazines spread about the various tables and he'd focused on his smart phone.

Chief Bates had been insistent that they wait while the photographer ran a quick errand. He'd come back with a driver's license for Lorraine Hollister that in every way looked real. She suspected they probably had a back room at the police station where credentials were fabricated on a routine basis.

She'd looked at her picture. Who was this woman? This blonde Raney. She'd tossed it into her purse and they'd left without further delay.

Chase had continued to be polite. Had carried her suitcase and opened the car door for her. Waited until she was buckled in before he took off. "Cool enough?" he'd asked ten minutes into the journey, nodding at the air-conditioning controls.

Other than that, he hadn't said a word.

Which maybe worked okay for him, but it wasn't helping her acclimate to her new life.

"I can't imagine that you're any happier about this than I am," she said finally.

He shrugged, never taking his eyes off the road. "It's important to keep you safe. I can do that," he added confidently.

"What's the plan once we get to Ravesville? Should I be mentally preparing myself for a big wedding reception?" she asked, trying for humor.

He turned to look at her. "Have you ever lived in a small town?"

She shook her head. "I'm a city girl."

He looked back at the road. "Here's how it works in small towns. On our way to the house, we'll stop for dinner at the local café. Not sure of the name of it any longer but for as long as I was in Ravesville, there was always a café on the corner of Main Street and Highway 20. I'm sure it's still there. I'll casually mention my name and that I'm back in town to take care of the old house and that I've brought along my new wife. By the time we get to dessert, the story will have reached half the community and by morning, the other half will have heard."

"Fascinating," she said.

"Not really, just the way it is. After that, Lorraine, I hope that you'll spend most of your time at the house, where it will be easier to provide protection."

"Raney," she said. "I go by Raney. Not Lorraine."

He seemed to consider that. "What did Harry Malone know you as?"

"He called me Lorraine. That was what was on my name tag. And because he was only at Next Steps a couple times before…well, before, he probably didn't hear anybody refer to me differently."

There was a significant pause and she could hear the tires on the rough highway. Finally, he turned to her and said, "Raney it is."

She was relieved that he hadn't pushed for more details. Even though she'd told the story several times, it still made her sick to talk about her time with Harry Malone. Pushing that image aside, she closed her eyes and focused on the way her name had sounded on his lips. *Raney.*

As if he knew her. Which of course he didn't. No more than she knew him. This was simply his job.

And given that somebody had tried twice to kill her, she sure as hell hoped he was good at it. He'd sounded confident when he'd said he could keep her safe. "So how long have you been on the job?" she asked.

He glanced her way, surprise in his eyes. "You know a lot of cops?"

She shrugged. "A few. Why?"

"Because when most people ask that question, they ask, 'How long have you been a police officer?' It's a subtle difference but one that a cop notices."

She waited. She wasn't ready yet to tell him about her work at Next Steps, about some of the people whom she'd helped, some of the people who had needed a hand. She'd virtually stooped, cupped her hands and given them a foothold. She was proud of her work, knew the impact she'd had.

"I've been a cop for thirteen years," he said. "Covered a beat for eight of those before I became a detective. I mostly work homicides."

"But you've done witness protection work before?" she asked.

"I have. I know what I'm doing," he said. She could tell that she'd offended him.

"I'm sorry," she said. "It's just that…"

"I know," he said, his tone gentler.

"So you live in St. Louis?"

"Yes."

They drove a few more miles. The silence in the SUV was oppressive. "In a house?" Lately she'd had houses on the brain.

He shook his head. "A thirty-year mortgage isn't my

style," he said. "I've got a six-month lease on an apartment in the Central West End."

"What happens after six months?"

He shrugged. "I sign another lease. Or I don't."

"How long have you lived there?"

"Five years."

That was weird. He'd been on the job for thirteen years and lived in the same apartment for five years but he was still only interested in a six-month lease. Maybe that was how things were done in the Central West End.

She had no idea where that was but assumed it was likely sort of upscale, like Chase. He wore a nice watch, good leather shoes, had nice manners and he'd looked very comfortable in a tux.

"I've been saving for a house," she admitted. "I love my apartment building and my neighbors but lately, I've been thinking that it's time for me to get a house. But now…I'm not sure. Maybe the security of having neighbors close by is what I need."

He took his eyes off the road in order to look at her again. "You've had a tough couple of months. Don't make any big decisions right now. Sit back, consider, then act when you're ready."

Others had given her the same advice, although not in those exact words. She let out the breath she'd been holding. Maybe in Ravesville, she could do that. Just relax.

She felt the ever-present knot in her stomach release just a little. Now the quiet was no longer oppressive. It felt safe. Nice. She closed her eyes and didn't open them again until she felt someone lightly shaking her shoulder.

"We're here," he said.

She was surprised to see that it was getting dark. She looked at the clock on the dash. Twenty minutes after six. Her stomach rumbled and she pressed the palm of her hand against it.

"I imagine you're hungry," he said.

She'd had toast for breakfast, nothing for lunch and a bite of cake that he'd popped into her mouth. "Yes," she said, turning her neck slowly to get the kinks out. "So this is it?"

It was a wide street, lined with freshly painted perpendicular parking spaces. The buildings were mostly old, lots of red brick, nothing over three stories. There were a few flower boxes with brightly colored mums below the windows and some more pots scattered down the sidewalk. There was an empty bike rack at the end of the block.

He'd been right about the restaurant. The Wright Here, Wright Now Café had its lights on and there were a few cars parked in front of the two-story brick building. Other than that, the only other cars were three or four gathered together at the end of the next block. "What's down there?" she asked, pointing. "Besides the edge of town?"

"A bar. Everything else closes up tight in the evenings."

She'd grown up in Manhattan and moved to Miami when she was sixteen, after her mom got a new job as the general counsel for an insurance company. Her dad had been a writer and had worked from home. They'd been killed by a drunk driver four years later. She'd stayed in Florida, hadn't really had anyplace else to go. While not Manhattan, Miami was still a large city where they didn't roll up the streets at half past six.

"I hope the food is good," she said, almost under her breath.

"Don't get your hopes up," he said. "But we need to eat. I'm not confident that there will be anything at the house."

They got out of the car. When Chase crossed in front of the hood, she thought she saw just a hint of a limp. She hadn't noticed it before. "Did you hurt your leg?" she asked.

He waved it off. "Stiff from driving," he said.

"So how did your stepfather die?" she asked as they walked down the sidewalk toward the restaurant.

"Car accident."

"I'm sorry," she said. "Was it a big funeral?"

He didn't answer. But he did hold the door open for her. She walked into the restaurant. It was brightly lit. There were three tables with customers. On the nine other available tables, there were tan paper placemats and silverware wrapped in white paper napkins.

A woman, maybe midthirties, with gorgeous long red hair to her waist pulled back into a low ponytail, walked through the swinging door at the rear of the restaurant. She carried plates in both hands. She gave them a quick smile, but when her gaze settled on Chase, it faded.

She set her plates down with a thud, startling the older couple at the table, who also turned to stare at the two of them.

"Damn you, Chase Hollister," she said. "You just cost me ten bucks. I bet that you wouldn't come back."

Chapter Three

She watched as Chase reached into his pocket, pulled out a ten-dollar bill and handed it to the woman. "Now we're even."

The woman threw her head back and laughed. "How's your good-for-nothing brother?" she asked.

"Still thinks he's the boss of me," Chase said.

She laughed again. "Nobody was ever the boss of you, that's for sure. People round here still talk about some of the stuff you pulled."

Hmm… Was it possible that there was more to Detective Hollister than his professional attitude let on?

Chase turned toward her. "This is my wife, Raney," he said smoothly, as if it were really true and he'd been introducing her for a long time as his wife. "Raney, this is Trish Wright."

"Wright-Roper," the woman corrected.

"Didn't realize you were married," Chase said.

"Widowed," she said.

"I'm sorry," Chase apologized, sounding as if he meant it.

The pretty woman shrugged but Raney could tell that the pain was still there. But she lifted her chin and extended a hand in Raney's direction.

There was a history between Chase and Trish but Raney couldn't quite put her finger on it. Not lovers. But something. She shook the woman's hand.

"Been to the old place yet?" Trish asked.

"Nope. Just got into town."

"You'll have your work cut out for you," she said. "It's gone downhill in the past few years."

Chase shrugged as if the news didn't bother him. But Raney saw him swallow hard. "Not planning on staying there long," he said.

"Well, don't be a stranger while you're here," she said. "I know Summer would like to see you. She works the day shift." Trish grabbed two menus from the counter and led them to a table in the corner of the café. Raney noticed that Chase didn't make eye contact with anyone else in the room.

They sat down. "Old friend?" Raney murmured, opening her menu.

He nodded. "I've known Trish since I was a kid. My older brother, Bray, dated Summer, Trish's sister. I always thought they might get married someday but he enlisted in the marines right out of high school and she married some other guy."

"How long since you've been in Ravesville?"

"I came back once, about eight years ago, when my mother died. Other than that, thirteen years," he said. "What are you having for dinner?" he asked, quickly changing the subject.

So he hadn't come for his stepfather's funeral. That was why he hadn't known whether it was big or small. But he clearly didn't want to talk about it. She tried to tell herself that she didn't care. She didn't need his life story. She just needed a place to stay where she'd be safe. Someplace in the middle of Missouri was as good as any.

When Trish returned, pen in hand, Raney closed her menu. "I'll take a salad with grilled…" She caught a glimpse of her reflection and almost jerked back in surprise. The change was almost too much to take in. If Sandy had been more forthcoming about the intended results, she'd have probably bolted from the chair.

But she was glad that she hadn't. She liked the new look. Had never considered going blond but now she might never go back.

One thing she could thank Harry Malone for.

"Actually," she said. "No salad. I'll take a bacon cheeseburger. With fries."

Chase ordered the meat loaf. Once Trish had walked away, he looked at her. "Salad just wasn't going to cut it?" he asked, obviously trying to think of something to say.

She was going to shrug it off but then decided that if they were going to live together for the next month as husband and wife, she needed to be honest with him. "That would have been BHM. Before Harry Malone. Now I pretty much treat myself to whatever I want, when I want it."

Come to think of it, maybe that was why she was digging the new haircut and look. It *fit* the new Raney Taylor. The Raney Taylor that she was molding.

He studied her, then spoke quietly but with conviction. "If it's any consolation, the son of a bitch is going to pay. He's going to go to prison and, trust me on this, there will be somebody there that will make his life a living hell."

She was counting on that.

When Trish delivered their food, it looked delicious.

She picked up her burger, squished the bun so that it would fit in her mouth and took a bite. A bit of sauce leaked out and she licked her lips. And then swallowed too quickly when she realized that he was watching her.

"Ouch," she said, pressing on her esophagus.

"Careful," he said.

She always used to be. And look where it had gotten her. "So what did you do to earn your reputation as the town bad boy?" she asked.

He scratched his head. "A little of this, a lot of that."

"And you became a cop to redeem yourself?"

"I became a cop because the St. Louis Police Department was hiring and I needed a way to support myself and my younger brother. Fortunately for me, it was a good fit. Maybe because of my troublemaking youth."

She took another bite, smaller this time. "There wasn't much you hadn't seen or done."

He smiled and shook his head. "Trust me on this. I might have made some people talk here in Ravesville but what I was doing was kid's play in comparison to what I saw my first six months on the street."

"So you were just naughty enough to cause your parents some angst."

His very nice amber eyes clouded over. "Something like that."

They ate in silence. Trish swung by and picked up their dirty plates and left a check. Chase pulled some bills out of his pocket and tossed them on the table.

"Ready?" he asked.

WHEN HIS WIFE nodded that she was good to go, he almost said, *Hell no, let's have some cheesecake.* Anything to delay a trip back down memory lane.

But he wasn't going to make it any better by putting it off. He led her back to the car and drove a mile and half farther on the highway before taking a right on Mahogany Lane. The road turned to gravel and he slowed his SUV. He passed the Fitzlers' house and noticed that there were lights on. Was it possible that Old Man Fitzler and his wife still lived there? Or maybe they'd moved on to one of those assisted-living centers and one of their daughters had moved in.

Damn, he'd envied those girls.

He didn't think Mr. Fitzler had ever even raised his voice, let alone his hand.

He slowed the vehicle even more and turned into the driveway. His lights picked up the details of the old house.

Over a hundred years old, the two-story white farmhouse looked sturdy enough. It had been the traditional four rooms down, kitchen, dining room, living room and bath, and four rooms up, three bedrooms and a bath, until sometime in the mid-1960s. The owner had pushed out the back wall and added to the downstairs, putting in another large bedroom and private bathroom. They'd done a nice job with the construction and the addition seemed to fit nicely with the rest of the house.

When Chase's parents had looked at the home some ten years later, it had seemed perfect to the young couple who were anxious to have a family. Chase always figured that once three boys had come along, his mother had been eternally grateful that she could ship them upstairs.

There were a few changes, Chase noted dispassionately. Brick had added green shutters at some point in the past eight years. They hadn't been there when Chase and his brothers had come home for his mother's funeral.

The wide wraparound porch looked the same, down to the hammock that was strung in the corner. He'd slept in that more than a few times. Nights when it was warm and he chose to. Nights when it was cold and Brick had banished him from the house. Those were the nights when he'd wanted to keep walking, to wake up somewhere else, but he would not do that to his mother, to Cal.

The bushes near the foundation were wildly overgrown and as he pulled closer, he could see that the paint on the house was peeling and the front steps looked as if they were rotting away in places.

He chanced a glance at Raney. Her eyes were moving, taking it in.

She was probably getting ready to bolt from the car. "Hopefully, it's better inside."

She shrugged. "It's got good bones," she said. "I love the porch and all the big windows."

Brick had pushed Calvin's hand through one of those windows one winter night. That was when Chase and the man had come to a deal of sorts.

He turned off the car and killed the lights. It made him realize how dark the yard was. "Watch your step," he said when she opened her door.

They each grabbed their own suitcase and picked their way across the patchy grass. When they reached the long sidewalk that led to the house, he stopped. Bray had sent him a text letting him know that the attorney was putting a key in the mailbox. Chase flipped down the rusted aluminum door and sure enough, it was there.

He led the way up the sidewalk and stairs and onto the porch. "Be careful," he warned again. He unlocked the door, pushed it open, listened for a minute but didn't hear anything. He reached his hand around to feel for the light switch and, he had to admit, felt better when light flooded the area.

To the right was the living room with a couch and two chairs that he didn't recognize and to the left, the dining room with his mother's big wooden table. He glanced down the hallway. In the back of the house, still in darkness, would be the big kitchen. It had a window over the sink and his mother had loved to stand there and watch the deer and the wild turkeys wander through the backyard.

At some point Brick had painted the dark brown woodwork white, but it must have been a poor grade of paint because it was peeling in multiple places. There were cracks in the plaster walls and multiple brown patches on the ceiling, suggesting that rain had leaked into the second floor all the way to the first floor. That wasn't a good sign.

He flipped on additional lights as they walked. When they entered the kitchen, the first thing he saw was the open newspaper on the table, along with a half-drank cup of tea with the bag still in it. Out of habit, he felt the cup. It was stone cold.

There was a dirty plate in the sink. Brick had had eggs for his last meal.

He opened the refrigerator. Not full by any means, but there were small packages of cheese and lunchmeat, some half-used bottles of salad dressing and ketchup, and a quart of milk. Something, he wasn't sure what, had spilled at some point on the top shelf and dripped down, leaving remains all the way to the bottom. It smelled sweet.

Brick had gotten sloppy in his old age. Or maybe he'd always been a pig and Sally Hollister had managed to cover up for him.

He turned, realizing that Raney had ventured off into the direction of the downstairs bedroom. He followed her, his chest feeling tighter with each step. He didn't want to look at Brick's bedroom, didn't to have that intimate of a connection to the man.

Raney stopped in the doorway. Chase stood behind her. There was a regular-size bed, made up with an ugly shiny green bedspread. The matching drapes were drawn tight, giving the room an eerie feel. The gold paint on the walls made the room look dirty. The door to the bathroom was open. With its dated green fixtures, it looked exactly like he remembered.

He sure as hell wasn't sleeping down here. "Let's take a look upstairs," he said.

The wooden steps creaked as they made their way upstairs. He saw Raney flick her hand over her hair and realized she'd disturbed a large cobweb. The carpet in the hallway was threadbare and all the doors were closed.

"I don't think your stepfather was up here much," Raney said.

He nodded and opened the first door. This had been Bray's room. He felt for the light switch and flipped it up. The room was completely empty.

He walked down the hall a few steps toward his old room. He turned the handle of the door, expecting it to open, but it didn't.

The door was locked. And for some crazy reason, that irritated the hell out of him. Without conscious thought, Chase lifted his good leg and kicked the damn door. It flew back, breaking the top hinge. He heard Raney's gasp but he ignored it. He felt for the light switch, flipped it and, when nothing happened, he stepped back so that light from the hallway could filter in.

The room was completely empty. He looked up at the ceiling light fixture. Even the lightbulb had been removed.

"Do you think perhaps there's an air mattress somewhere?" Raney asked, her tone light.

There was only one bedroom left to try. Cal's. The door swung open and the light worked. In the middle of the room was a queen-size mattress, still with its plastic wrapper, without any bedding or even a bed frame. The mattress and box spring sat directly on the wood floor. There was a bedside table with a lamp. There was no other furniture in the room.

Why the hell had Brick bought a new mattress and put it upstairs in Cal's old room? And never put sheets or a blanket on it? Based on the layer of dust on the plastic, the mattress had been up here for some time. It wasn't as if Brick had done it recently and just hadn't finished the project.

Well, whatever the reason, it wasn't great but it was better than sleeping on the wood floor. "You can sleep in here," he said. He pulled a pocketknife out of his jeans, sliced open the plastic and ripped it off the mattress. Dust flew into the air and she sneezed.

"Sorry," he said. "We can get some sheets tomorrow."

She sat down on the edge of the mattress. "Where will you sleep?" she asked.

"Downstairs. On the couch. There's no reason to believe that anybody knows that Lorraine Taylor is in this house. But if anything scares you, just yell. I'm a light sleeper. I'll hear you."

She looked around the room. She sighed a little dramatically. "All these years and I never ever envisioned my wedding night would go exactly like this."

For the first time since Chief Bates had announced that he and Lorraine Taylor were posing as husband and wife, he felt like smiling. She was being a good sport. Her last safe house had no doubt been better.

He wanted to promise that everything would look better in the light of day but based on what he'd seen tonight, he thought the opposite was probably true. He would not have volunteered to bring her to Ravesville if he'd known the house was in this bad of shape.

"Good night," he said.

He stuck his head into the bathroom that was across the hall. Ran the water in the faucet until it turned clear and flushed the toilet a couple times. There was toilet paper but it was covered with a layer of dust. He unrolled several sheets, ripped them off, and threw them in the small empty garbage can. There were no towels so he ran downstairs, got several clean ones from the cupboard in the downstairs bathroom and took them back upstairs.

It wasn't camping but it was close.

Finally, he went back downstairs and, still fully dressed, stretched out on the couch. It was too short for him and his feet hung over the edge. He was so damn tired. He hadn't been kidding when he'd told his brother that he'd been awake for more than a day. He had managed to grab some sleep after he'd talked to Dawson but the knowledge that the chief was counting on them had weighed heavily on his mind.

Now, even though his body craved rest, he lay awake, staring at the ceiling, his mind trying to wrap itself around the fact that he was back in Ravesville, back in the house that he'd left thirteen years ago, swearing that he'd never return.

On the drive here, he'd wondered if he'd feel Brick in the house. Or even his mother. But the house just felt empty, so empty it seemed as if there had never been life here.

But that wasn't true. There had been life and love when Jack Hollister had been alive. His father would have despised Brick, would have hated what had become of the family.

As odd as it seemed, he could feel his father in the house. He hadn't been able to do that when Brick was alive and living here. But now it felt very different. It was almost as if he could see him standing in front of the big windows, waving at him and his brothers to come in for dinner. Could see him walking through the house, a fishing pole in one hand and sack lunches in the other, yelling for his sons to hurry up, that the trout were biting.

As if he'd conjured up old spirits, he heard a noise. Something soft. Outside. He eased off the couch, used a finger to pull back the heavy drapes and watched the yard.

Nothing moved in the darkness. He waited, continuing to watch. Five minutes later, a dark shape, low to the ground, crossed the gravel.

A groundhog. He let out the breath he'd been holding. He'd been spooked by an animal.

He lay back down, rubbed his sore thigh and closed his eyes. Upstairs, he heard a door open and close, then the sound of water running through the pipes as Raney turned on the shower. She'd had a hell of a day but had seemed to handle it well. She'd been shot at yesterday, hustled out of Florida this morning, pushed into a fake marriage and had ended up here, in a house of neglect.

He'd clean up the place tomorrow, at least get the top layer of dust off. Then he would pitch everything in the refrigerator and make a quick trip to town for food. If the dinner Raney had eaten tonight was any indication, she had a good appetite. Which was surprising considering she was pretty slim.

But the curves were there. He'd seen that firsthand in the wedding dress. That image had stayed with him the entire drive from St. Louis to Ravesville. That and the memory of the feel of her mouth.

He heard the water shut off. Let himself have the guilty pleasure of imaging Raney's wet body stepping over the edge of the old tub. Of her drying off on the threadbare towel.

He heard the door open and the floor creak as she crossed the hall. He wondered if she'd brought pajamas or if she slept naked.

He let out a breath, happy to let that image rest on his brain.

WHEN HE WOKE UP, the sun was low in the sky. He checked the time. A little past seven. He sat up, stretched and went in search of coffee.

There was no coffeepot on the counter. He opened cupboards. Not even a jar of instant. It was another reason to despise Brick.

He walked up the stairs and muscle memory kicked in, making it easy for him to avoid the same squeaky boards that had been there thirteen years ago. Raney's bedroom door was closed. He considered knocking but decided against it.

She probably needed her sleep.

He opened the door and stopped. The woman knew how to take up a bed. She slept on her stomach with her head at ten o'clock and her feet at four o'clock. She wasn't naked but her sweet little body was plenty sexy in her lime green shorts and white-and-green-striped T-shirt. She was breathing deeply.

She'd tossed the clothes that she'd been wearing the night before into a pile. On top was her bra and panties, a silky pale yellow with lots of lace.

His face felt warm and when she stirred, he thought maybe he'd moaned.

Dawson was right. He needed to get more regular sex.

He took a step back, carefully closing the door. He could run into town, pick up some coffees and pastries from the bakery and be back before she ever woke up. Maybe that would make up for stashing her in this dump.

He left the house, making sure that he locked the door behind him. The drive to town took just minutes and when he walked into the bakery, the first thing he saw was the cakes in the display case.

It made him remember how the birthday/wedding cake had amused Raney. He debated buying another one just to see her reaction but instead got six doughnuts and a coffee cake along with two extralarge coffees.

He sipped his coffee on the way home. When he pulled into the yard, he did not notice anything amiss. Which was why, when he opened the door and looked down the hallway into the kitchen, he got caught short.

He saw the man. Catalogued his dirty blue jeans and dark sweatshirt and the greasy hair that hung to his shoulders.

Saw all that but what Chase focused on was the knife

that the man held. It had a shiny six-inch blade and was raised and pointed.

At Raney.

Still in her pajamas, she had her back pressed up against the sink. Her face was pale and her eyes were big.

The man leaped toward her. Chase pulled his gun but knew that he was going to be too late.

Chapter Four

Raney twisted, brought a knee up, connected with something and used every bit of strength in her arms to push the man backward.

It was enough to buy a few seconds and give Chase a chance to leap across the space that separated them. She saw the knife go flying and within moments, Chase had the man on the ground, his knee in his chest and his gun pointed at his head.

He turned to look at her. "Are you hurt?" he asked. His eyes were dark, flashing with anger.

She managed to shake her head.

Chase looked down at the man. "Who the hell are you?" he asked, his voice hard.

The man squinted his eyes. "Get off me," he said. "You're heavy."

Raney took a closer look at the man. He'd surprised the heck out of her. She'd just gotten a drink of water when she'd heard a noise behind her. She'd turned, seen the man and the still-open back door, and realized that she was in a world of trouble.

Chase had walked in just in the nick of time.

Chase used the palm of one hand to knock the man's

head back against the dirty kitchen linoleum. "Start talking."

"You need to get out of here," the man said. "You need to get out of my house right now."

Raney saw the change in Chase's eyes and realized that he'd figured something out. Good, because she didn't have a clue what was going on.

Chase let up on some of the pressure on the man's chest but he didn't let him get up. "Lloyd?" he asked.

"How do you know my name?" the man asked.

"I'm Chase. Chase Hollister."

"I know you," the man said. He smiled.

Chase looked up at Raney. "This is Lloyd Doogan. He's my stepfather's biological son."

"So you're sort of related?"

"I don't generally think of it that way." He looked back down at the man. "Lloyd, I'm going to let you get up. I'm not giving you back your knife. You need to sit, so that we can have a conversation."

Chase was speaking deliberately and didn't move until the man nodded his understanding.

Lloyd got up and sat. He looked at Raney. "Who are you?"

"Her name is Raney," Chase said, jumping in. "My wife."

Lloyd seemed to consider this. "I thought you were one of those teenagers from town. The ones who are always causing trouble."

Teenager. Granted, she wasn't dressed for success in her shorts and tank top, but she surely didn't look sixteen. Chase turned his head but not before she caught a glimpse of a smile.

"Hey!" she challenged.

"I think it's a compliment," he said, somewhat sheepishly. He turned back to Lloyd. "This house never belonged to Brick. He was just living here after my mom died. This house doesn't belong to you now. It belongs to my brothers and me."

Lloyd didn't answer. But he was frowning.

"Do you understand, Lloyd?" Chase pushed.

"He told me I could live here," Lloyd said. "A couple years ago. Said he bought me a bed and everything. But then he got mad about something, I don't even know what. All I know is that he stopped talking to me, told me I couldn't come here no more. That ain't no way to treat a son."

Chase didn't say anything.

"I hated him. I really did," Lloyd added.

"I imagine so," Chase said quietly.

Even Raney was tracking now. They might not be blood but these two men shared something.

Chase looked over his shoulder and made eye contact with her. "Lloyd," he said, his eyes still locked on her. "I need to talk to Raney. I need you to stay in your chair."

Chase pulled her to the side, keeping her back to Lloyd, which allowed him to keep his eyes on his stepbrother.

"I don't know Lloyd well," he whispered. "But I'm sure he really did think you were trespassing in his house. Now, that didn't give him a right to go at you with a knife," Chase said, his tone hard, "and if he'd managed to hurt you, we'd be having a very different conversation." He paused, looking back at Lloyd, then at her again. "We have a choice to make. We can call the police or we can pretend this never happened."

Calling the police would attract attention to them,

which was what they didn't want to do. Plus, Chase would likely be putting his stepbrother in jail. By the looks of him, she thought it might be possible that the man wouldn't have the resources to post bail.

"I'm not hurt," she said. "No harm done, right? Although we may want to make sure that we confiscate his key to the back door," she said, nodding at the silver key on the floor near Lloyd's feet. "Let him go," she added.

"You're sure?" Chase asked, his eyes searching her face.

She nodded.

"Thank you," Chase said simply.

He moved around her and sat down across from his stepbrother. "Lloyd, do you understand that I could call the police? That you would be the one in trouble because we belong here?"

Lloyd nodded.

"Do you understand that you can't come back to this house?"

Lloyd nodded again.

"I need to hear you say it," Chase prodded.

"I won't come back," Lloyd said. He shifted his gaze to Raney. "I'm sorry, ma'am, if I scared you."

Ma'am? She liked it better when he thought she was a teenager. "Raney," she corrected.

Chase picked up the key. "Lloyd, is this your only key to the house?"

"Yes. *He* never knew I had it," Lloyd said. "I sneaked into the house one day about a year ago and took it off his dresser."

She saw Chase swallow hard. "Lloyd, I'm not going to call the police. I'm going to give you back your knife and you're going to leave the property and you're not coming back. And if you happen to see Raney again, you're going to treat her nicely, right?" Chase picked up the knife and laid it on the table, near enough for Lloyd to reach. He was watching the man closely and Raney was confident that he was still conflicted about letting him go.

"Goodbye, Lloyd," she said, hoping to give the man a hint.

Lloyd stood and picked up his knife. He kept the blade down. "Bye, ma'am." He didn't say anything to Chase. Just walked out the back door.

She and Chase went to the door. Lloyd had an old motorcycle. He got on, started it and left without giving them another look. From the back of the house, they couldn't see him after he rounded the corner but they could hear the acceleration as he turned out of the lane and headed down the highway. Then the noise faded.

The kitchen was very quiet.

"Did you know him as a boy?" she asked.

"I met him once," he said, not looking at her. "He lived with his mother. Brick didn't have anything to do with him. I'm not sure whether that was his choice or maybe his ex-wife had told him to stay away. The one time he did come around, he and Brick had a big fight. I remember my mom yelling at Brick, telling him that Lloyd didn't understand whatever Brick was trying to tell him."

"Does he live nearby?"

Chase shrugged. "I don't know." He turned, walked over to the counter, grabbed a towel from a drawer and walked back down the hallway. "I'll do some research on him, figure out where he lives and if he works. He won't surprise us again."

"I'm not worried," Raney said, following him.

Chase looked over his shoulder. "Maybe I should be. You were pretty quick with that knee. And you had good aim."

She shrugged. "You weren't so bad yourself." She looked past Chase, at the floor. "Was that coffee?" she asked, trying hard not to whine.

Chase picked up the two cups that he'd dropped. All the liquid had spilled out onto the floor. Some of it had seeped toward the bakery sack. He picked it up and opened it. "The ones on top still look fine," he said, holding out the sack.

She reached for one of the doughnuts and took a big bite. "I need coffee," she said.

"Put some different clothes on," he said. "We'll have breakfast in town."

CHASE HOPED TO hell that he'd done the right thing in letting Lloyd go. The man truly seemed to think he had a right to be in the house. And he probably had no idea that he was real lucky to still be walking and talking because Chase had been this close to wringing his neck once he'd had him subdued on the floor. All he'd been able to think about was how close the man had gotten to harming Raney.

At first, he'd given him the chance to talk because he'd wanted to know if somehow, someway, Harry Malone had managed to find them and send another goon after Raney.

Then the pieces of the puzzle had started to fit together. And when Lloyd had admitted to hating Brick, his head had started to roar. No doubt Lloyd had suffered at the man's hand, too.

He recalled his mother saying something after that one time Lloyd had been in their house, that it was a shame to be a grown man with the smarts of an eighth grader. Chase had been close to finishing high school at the time and remembered that even knowing the man had some limitations, he'd been damn jealous of him because at least he wasn't still living with Brick Doogan.

He was rubbing his injured thigh muscle when he heard Raney's footsteps on the stairs. He moved his hand quickly. His leg had taken the brunt of it when he'd tackled Lloyd and it was letting him know that it didn't appreciate it.

He looked up. She was wearing a tan-and-turquoise skirt and a sleeveless turquoise shirt. It brought out the color of her eyes. She was a beautiful woman and pretty damn brave, too. He'd known that at some level—after all, she'd managed to escape from a madman. And she'd survived another attempt on her life. But this morning, seeing her in action, seeing her willingness to fight back, had made him realize it in spades.

While she'd been upstairs, he'd sent a text to Dawson, asking him to find out everything there was to know about Lloyd Doogan. He figured he'd hear something by late afternoon.

They got in his SUV and drove the short distance into town. He took the one empty parking space that was in front of the Wright Here, Wright Now Café. Today the street was bustling with activity. People walking to their cars, into shops, chatting on the corners. There were no traffic lights, just a series of four-way-stop signs at the end of each block. It would have been a traffic nightmare in a larger city but here it was manageable.

Near the café, there was a table that hadn't been there

last night. Behind it were two teenage girls in cheerleading outfits waving pom-poms. The table was covered with candy bars with a big sign indicating they were two dollars a bar. He saw that Raney was staring at it. No one walked past without stopping and buying a candy bar. She opened her purse and pulled out a five-dollar bill.

"You don't have to buy anything," he said.

"Are you crazy? That's chocolate."

When they got up to the table, he saw that it was actually chocolate with caramel inside. Which must have been even better because she pulled out another one-dollar bill so that she could buy three of them. She handed one to Chase.

"In Missouri, if you're married, everything is owned fifty-fifty," he said, just low enough that she could hear.

"Oh, please. They weren't thinking about chocolate when that law passed."

Chase was smiling when he opened the door. As they walked in, he recalled what Trish had said the night before. *Summer works the day shift.* He had absolutely no difficulty identifying the woman his brother had almost married. She was at the cash register, giving change back to a customer.

"She looks so much like Trish," Raney whispered.

"She should. They're twins." They'd looked just alike in high school and there was still a great resemblance except that Summer wore her red hair shorter than Trish, just to her shoulders. He led Raney toward a booth and took the side that gave him a clear view of the door. Raney put her candy bars off to the side. He made a point of putting his in his pocket, as if he might be afraid that she'd steal it if he put it on the table.

While they were waiting to order, an older woman

passed by their booth. She was carrying two candy bars. She stopped at the table and looked at Raney. "Good morning. I noticed you bought some chocolate outside."

Raney nodded.

The woman put the bars on the table. "Do take these, then. I can't eat it. But we do like to support the schools, isn't that right? You two have a good day."

"But…" Raney said.

The woman kept walking. Either she didn't hear Raney or she was ignoring her.

Chase reached for the candy bars.

Raney tapped his knuckles with her fork. "She was talking to me."

He rolled his eyes.

"Fine." She took one and pushed the other in his direction.

Summer had finished up at the cash register and was walking toward their booth. She smiled at Raney and leaned in to give Chase a hug. "Trish told me you were back," she said. "It's good to see you."

"You, too," he said. "This is my wife, Raney."

Summer extended her hand. "Welcome to Ravesville."

"Thank you," Raney said. "It smells wonderful in here."

"We bake all our own breads and muffins. Would you like to start with some coffee?"

"We'd both be eternally grateful," Chase said. He motioned to the full restaurant. "You and Trish have quite a business here."

"We love it."

Chase heard the door open and Summer must have, as well. She turned to look and her posture stiffened.

Chase looked a little closer. The man was in his late thirties, balding and wore a police uniform.

"He looks familiar," Chase said quietly.

"That's Gary Blake, my ex. Excuse me," she said. "I'll be back in a minute."

"Do you know him?" Raney asked, once Summer was out of hearing distance.

Chase shook his head. "I've seen him before but it's been a long time. He was a couple years older than me."

"So he's the one that Summer married after your older brother enlisted?"

"Yeah. Guess that didn't work out so well for her," he said. "Too bad. She was always a real nice person." He picked up his menu. "What are you having?"

Raney leaned across the table. "Is your brother married?"

Chase shook his head. "Bray never married."

"Maybe you should call him. You know, tell him that you ran into Summer and she's single."

Chase closed his menu. He was glad to see the sparkle back in Raney's eyes. "Don't tell me that you're the matchmaking type."

Raney waved a hand. "I'm just saying that maybe he'd want to know."

"You're just like my partner, Dawson. He's happily married and I don't think he'll be content until the rest of the world is just like that."

"You sound like a cynic," she whispered.

"A realist. What we have is about as close to married as I plan on getting," he added.

Raney didn't say anything else because Summer returned, with two big cups of steaming coffee. The woman's cheeks were flushed. Chase had been watching her conversation with her ex. It hadn't lasted more than thirty seconds.

"Everything okay?" he asked.

"As good as ever," she said cryptically. She pulled a pad from her smock pocket. "What can I bring you?" she asked, clearly not wanting to share.

Chase ordered pancakes, eggs and bacon. Raney went for the vegetarian omelet. Summer wrote it down and stepped to the next table to take their order, too.

"What's the plan for today?" Raney asked.

"We probably need to take care of the basics," Chase said, sipping his coffee. "Get some groceries, some cleaning products, new sheets for your bed, and paint."

"We can do that in Ravesville?"

"First two can probably be had from the supermarket at the edge of town. Sheets and paint, no. We'll have to drive to Hamerton, twenty miles west. It's got a downtown that looks a lot like Ravesville but it sits close enough to the highway to have a mall and a couple big-box stores. Maybe has a couple thousand people."

Raney stared off into the distance. "When I lived in New York, there'd probably be a couple thousand people within a few blocks."

"Sounds horrific," Chase said honestly.

She shrugged. "You settled for something in the middle. St. Louis isn't New York but it's certainly not Ravesville."

He nodded. "I guess I did. It's okay for now."

"Are you thinking of leaving?" she asked, as if she expected him to bolt for the door.

He smiled. "Well, not in the middle of this assignment. But I like to keep my options open."

He'd gotten a few calls as recently as last month from

headhunters who specialized in recruiting law enforcement. There had been a head of security position open for a large hotel in Chicago and his name had been recommended by someone. He'd listened to the voice mail from the recruiter but hadn't returned the call. Maybe the next one he would. Anything was possible.

She sipped her coffee. "You're lucky to have options," she said. "Many people don't. I suppose that's especially true in small towns like Ravesville."

He nodded.

She was silent for several minutes. "I guess my best hope is Ravesville is so small that whoever is behind all the crazy things that have happened doesn't know about it."

"You're safe here. I guarantee it."

At that moment, Summer delivered their food. It looked amazing and he smiled when he heard Raney's stomach growl.

Raney waited until the woman had walked away. "Well, if I have to be stranded in the sticks, I'm grateful that Summer and Trish are close by. By the way, what kind of paint are you getting?"

"Off-white."

"For?"

"Every room. Upstairs and downstairs." He could tell by the look on her face that wasn't the answer she wanted to hear. "That's what sells. Neutrals."

"But the woodwork in your house is amazing. At least it will be once that paint is stripped. And the fireplace in the living room is stunning. Off-white isn't going to work."

He rubbed his head. "What would you do?"

"Well." She leaned forward in the booth. "The dining

room, a soft sage green with the windows trimmed in tan. The living room, I'd do the wall with the fireplace and the one that butts up to it in a nice brick red with the other two walls in taupe. You know, the paint colors won't actually be called this—they'll have some much fancier name—but you get the drift."

He did. She wanted to decorate and he wanted to get it cleaned up enough that a prospective buyer wouldn't run out the door.

His mother had never been much of a decorator. Perhaps she figured with three boys there was really no sense trying. And from the looks of it, Brick hadn't spent much time watching HGTV.

He didn't care enough about the house to even have this discussion. "I'm pretty set on off-white," he said.

THE GROCERY STORE wasn't big, but it had the basics. Chase went to the coffee aisle first and bought grounds and filters. "We'll get a coffeepot when we buy your sheets," he said.

Raney took control of the cart and found the produce aisle. She loaded up, selecting several of almost every fruit and vegetable they stocked while Chase, reluctantly it appeared, added a bag of chopped lettuce. When she was finally done, Chase made a point of looking at his watch. She ignored him.

She might have lost the paint discussion but she wasn't losing the grocery store. She added whole-wheat bread, cereal and skim milk. Chase added chips and peanuts. In the meat aisle, Raney picked up chicken breasts and Chase went for the ground beef. "I'm starting to see a pattern here," Raney said.

"Yeah," Chase agreed. "You're too healthy. I had high

hopes for you when you ordered the bacon cheeseburger last night, and then again when I discovered you were a candy hoarder. But I can see that I was wrong."

"I'm not a hoarder, I'm a connoisseur."

In the condiment aisle, she got some olive oil and Chase grabbed mustard, mayonnaise and ketchup. "I'm throwing away everything in the refrigerator and cupboards," he said.

She couldn't argue with that. The kitchen was a hazard. She'd been trying to figure out what to do first when Lloyd had burst through the back door.

"Ready?" he asked, once they added bleach, ammonia and other assorted cleaning products along with gloves, sponges and a mop.

"Yes," she said. She was halfway to the front when she remembered orange juice. "I'll meet you at the cash register," she said.

She found the orange juice, remembered that she wanted peanut butter, and by the time she finally got to the front of the store, her *husband* was hugging another woman.

To be fair, he was being hugged by the woman ahead of him. She had her arms wrapped tight around his neck with her breasts pushed up against his chest. His arms were down at his sides. She watched as he stepped back, breaking contact. He couldn't go far. There was a cart behind him and the older woman steering it was grossly engaged in what was going on ahead of her.

Chase made use of what space he had and he and the woman were no longer touching.

The cashier, wearing a black T-shirt and jeans, was watching everything. She had a little smile on her well-lined face.

The woman who'd been hugging Chase wasn't smiling. She had her lower lip extended. She was pretty, Raney thought. A little too made-up, perhaps, for a morning grocery store run. Foundation, blush, eyeliner, the whole bit. Her dark hair was perfectly straight and worn in an angled cut around her face. She had on tan linen pants and a matching jacket with heels that made her tall enough to almost look Chase in the eye.

Raney felt short and oddly inadequate in her cotton skirt and casual shirt.

"Don't I at least get a hug after all this time?" the woman asked.

Chase looked over his shoulder, saw Raney and motioned for her to come. She excused herself and stepped in front of the shopper behind Chase. He wrapped an arm around her shoulders. "Sheila, this is my wife, Raney," he said. "Raney, Sheila Stanton. We went to high school together."

The woman tilted her chin down. "Wife?" she repeated. "Terri from the bakery told me you were back. She didn't say anything about a wife."

"Raney was sleeping in while I got pastries," Chase said.

"You're not wearing a ring."

"Both of ours are getting sized. We're just newly-weds," Chase answered.

Sheila finally looked Raney in the eye. "Congratu-lations."

She didn't sound as if she meant it.

"Well, I should be going," Sheila said, grabbing the plastic sack that the cashier was holding out in her direction.

She was barely out the door when the cashier started

laughing, a low chuckle that didn't show any signs of ending soon.

"What?" Chase asked. He was looking out the big front window of the store. When he turned, he looked as if he was ready to strangle someone.

"I saw her sitting in her vehicle when I came into work an hour ago. I wondered what the hell she was up to. I guess she was waiting for you because you hadn't been here three minutes when she suddenly came in."

Chase pulled out his billfold and Raney thought about what he'd told her the previous night about how news traveled in a small town. Sheila had gotten word that Chase was back, had made a logical assumption that he'd need to get groceries at some point and staked out the location.

It wasn't noon yet and she already had her fill of crazy for the week. Chase appeared to be thinking the same thing.

He didn't say another word while they were getting checked out. They had the groceries in the SUV and were belted in before he looked at her. "Sorry about that," he said.

"Somebody you knew well?"

"We dated off and on for a few years after high school. Got arrested with her one night," he added with a smile.

"Arrested? What did you do?"

"A little misunderstanding about some drag racing. Charges were dropped when the cop realized it was Sheila in the car with me. Her dad was the mayor."

She laughed. "I'm beginning to think that you had quite a reputation when you lived here," she said. "I'm married to the local bad boy."

He smiled at her. "Does that make you the new bad girl?"

The minute he said it, he seemed to realize how suggestive it sounded. "Sorry," he said.

The old Raney, with the mousy-brown hair, would have politely ignored it. Looked in the other direction. Not so with the new platinum blonde Raney. Her mind was suddenly fixated on what she might do to earn a reputation.

And almost every thought that came to mind had Chase Hollister playing a predominant role. Her face felt warm. "I guess I've always wondered what it would be like to have my reputation precede me."

He stared at her. His eyes were dark. Sexy.

But like her hair, her courage was new and obviously fleeting. She swallowed hard. "We should go home. The groceries are getting warm."

GROCERIES WEREN'T THE only things getting warm, Chase thought as he drove to the house. Sometimes his mouth was a step ahead of his brain. Certainly suggesting to Raney that he was interested in a bad girl was evidence of that.

He was supposed to be protecting her.

But who was going to protect him from the crazy connection he seemed to feel every time she was within three feet? Truth be told, it had nothing to do with physical distance. She'd been upstairs last night and he'd lain on the couch, wanting her with a vengeance. Even the ache in his leg hadn't been able to shift his focus.

He'd known her for less than twenty-four hours but when he talked to her, it was as if they'd been friends for a lifetime. He couldn't recall ever having a reaction like that to any woman.

This morning, Sheila had surprised him. When they'd dated, it had been an intensely physical relationship. Truth be told, that was about all it had been. As a nineteen-year-old boy, that had been just perfect. He'd always figured she was looking for the same thing. She hadn't made any big scene when he'd left, although after moving with Cal to St. Louis, his brother had told him a couple times that he'd seen Sheila outside of their apartment. Chase had dismissed Cal's comments, assuming he was seeing things.

But then about five years ago he'd gotten an anonymous letter, calling him every name in the book. And while there was nothing overtly connecting it to Sheila, there was something about the sentences, the disparate thoughts that ran together, that reminded him of the woman.

It hadn't been threatening and he'd basically ignored it. By that time, he was hip deep in catching bad guys and didn't have time to worry about hate mail.

But now, the cashier's chuckle ringing in his ears, he wondered if he'd missed something with Sheila.

He and Raney would just need to stay clear of her.

When they got home, he asked Raney to stay in the car while he checked the house. He didn't expect Lloyd to have come back, but he wasn't taking any chances.

The place was clear and if anything, looked even more dismal in the daylight than it had last night. They carried the groceries in but before he put them away, he made good on his promise to toss everything that was in the refrigerator. He dumped a liberal amount of ammonia into a clean bowl, added some water and wiped out the appliance. When he was done, he realized that Raney was wiping down the stove.

"You don't have to clean," he said. "I'll get it."

"Don't be ridiculous," she said. "What am I going to do, watch you?"

"It's not your mess," he said.

"Yeah, but it's my house for a while."

He ran his hands through his hair. "I'm guessing your last safe house was in better shape."

She looked at the trash-strewn counters, the table laden with papers and dirty dishes, the floor that her sandals were sticking to. "You got one thing going for you."

"Really?"

"Yeah. Nobody's shot at me yet today."

He stared at her for a long minute, then a slight smile crossed his face. "The day's early," he said.

She slapped a sponge in his hand. "Got to love an optimist."

Chapter Five

Toward evening, they drove to Hamerton. They hadn't gotten very far before Raney, her face toward the window, said, "I didn't expect it to look like this. It was dark when we came in last night and I guess I didn't fully appreciate it."

Chase glanced across the countryside. They were on a two-lane highway with cornfields on both sides. One of the farmers was more industrious than the other, evidently, because his crop was freshly picked. The trees were just starting to turn. "In a couple weeks, these trees will be really pretty. People come from all over to see the fall colors."

"When they told me I was going to Missouri, I thought Midwest, which made me think flat. And I wasn't expecting all these trees."

"We're far enough south of St. Louis that if you slip up and say you're in the South, nobody will throw green tomatoes at you. And the heavily wooded areas, all part of the Mark Twain National Forest."

"Did you camp around here?"

He had. It was another thing that had changed once his dad died. "Yeah."

"I've never been camping. It seems as if it would be fun."

He studied her. "At the risk of generalizing, the women I've known have associated camping with being wet, cold, hungry and bitten up by mosquitos. That was before we got into the discussion about the possibility of snakes."

"None of that sounds nice, so maybe I've romanticized the idea in my head. I was thinking of hiking the trails during the day. I'd have on cool boots and one of those insulated vests with lots of pockets that would make it look as if I knew what I was doing. Oh, yeah, I'd have a walking stick, too. I always wanted an excuse to use one of those. At night, I'd sit around a big campfire wrapped in a blanket and eat marshmallows. There are no snakes in my camping world."

He laughed. "Maybe when this is all over, you can come back here for a week and give it a try."

"When this is all over," she repeated, her voice more serious. "That has a nice ring."

"A month," he said.

"Seems like forever."

"It'll go faster than you think," he said, hoping it was true. Right now, a month in Ravesville sounded like a very long time. But it would take every bit of that to get the house ready to sell.

They drove another ten miles, to the outskirts of Hamerton where the big box stores were located. They wandered around the store, getting sheets, a coffeepot, more cleaning supplies, and finally ended up in the paint aisle. Chase picked up six gallons of Eggshell White and put them in the cart. Raney did not say anything.

"Don't give me that look," he said.

"What look?"

"The look as if you just lost your dog."

She shook her head. "I don't have a dog."

"Neutral walls. Ask anybody. Neutrals sell."

"Maybe in a five-year-old ranch, but not in a hundred-year-old farmhouse." She continued to walk.

He stopped the cart. "I'm not going to hear the end of this, am I?"

She turned around to look at him. "Don't be ridiculous. I'm not the one talking about it."

He whipped the cart around, unloaded the Eggshell White and waved toward the wall of paint samples. "You've got five minutes."

She skipped back to him. "To pick or to pick and have it mixed?"

"Five minutes."

It ended up being a total of seventeen minutes but he walked out with two gallons of Toasted Meringue, two of Prickly Pear Delight and two of Sunset Wonder. "These are ridiculous names for paint. Why can't they simply call it Sort of Yellow, Pale Green and Orange Red?"

"Because those are boring."

"Uh-huh." They unloaded everything into the car and got buckled in. "Are you hungry?" he asked.

"I could eat. I guess I worked up an appetite this afternoon."

She'd worked hard. They'd made good progress on the kitchen and then she'd gone upstairs to clean the bathroom while he'd walked outside. There, in the corner of the porch, had been a chain saw, which made him think that Brick had probably intended to do the bushes after he got home from his doctor's appointment.

Chase had ruthlessly gone after the big bushes that were crowding the house, not wanting to give anybody with bad intent an opportunity to get close without being seen or worse yet, a place to hide.

Now he had a hell of a pile of brush that he didn't have any idea what to do with. Maybe he should burn it. Wait for a windy day, strike a match, and maybe the house would go, too. Save everybody a whole lot of trouble.

But then he'd have to find another place for Raney and he wasn't sure how that would go. As crazy as it seemed, she was settling in at the old place.

"That looks like a steak house," he said, pointing off to his left. "Does your enjoyment of red meat extend beyond the hamburger?"

"I'm fond of medium-rare filets with sautéed mushrooms."

"Excellent." He pulled in and they got out. "Let me go in first," he said.

"Okay," she said, her tone letting him know that she thought it was kind of unnecessary. "I really doubt that somebody is inside just in the off hopes that we might stop in for dinner." She stopped in her tracks, very dramatically. "Wait, I take that back. Maybe there's another old girlfriend in there, who sat in the parking lot all afternoon, chewing off her lipstick, confident that you'd come this way."

He cocked his head. "You're funny, aren't you?" he said drily. He opened the exterior door and motioned for her to wait in the small vestibule, between the inside and outside doors. He went inside.

He did a quick scan. It was crazy but he didn't like leaving her alone for even a minute. He had always had a good sense of these things, and something was telling him that Raney was still in danger.

He stuck his head back into the vestibule. "Looks okay.

Six other tables. I didn't recognize anybody. And they have both a six- and a nine-ounce fillet on the menu."

"Do they have flavored vodka?" she asked quickly.

He pulled back. "I have no idea," he said. "Let's go." He held the door open for her. Once the hostess seated them, the waiter approached. He was early twenties and was checking Raney out. Chase could see the appreciation in his eyes. Raney smiled up at him.

The guy greeted them, still looking at Raney. "Evening," he said. "We get a lot of regulars here but I don't think I've seen you before. You live nearby?"

Chase used his foot to give her a quick nudge on the knee. Maybe he needed to buy her a ring sooner than later. "My wife and I just moved to Ravesville," he said, jumping in.

The man finally looked at Chase and he could read the message loud and clear. *Lucky son of a bitch.* "I don't live too far from there." He pulled a lighter from his pocket and lit the small candle in the middle of the table. "What can I bring you to drink?" he asked.

Raney ordered a chardonnay and Chase ordered an iced tea. No drinking for him. He was on duty.

The waiter walked away. "I thought you were interested in vodka."

"No. Not really." She laughed. "Just making sure that you don't start thinking that you're always a step ahead of me."

Not to worry. His head felt muddled whenever she was near. He was pretty sure it had something to do with her scent and the way she crossed her legs at the ankles, like a lady.

Which was a bit at odds with some of the other clues that he was getting. Muddled, for sure.

"I'm going to wash my hands," Raney said, pushing her chair back.

Chase almost said that he'd check the bathroom first but decided that really was going too far. "Okay."

While she was gone, his cell phone buzzed. He looked at the text message from Dawson. He'd done his homework. Lloyd lived on the other side of Ravesville, about three miles from their house. About six years ago, he'd been arrested several times for shoplifting and public intoxication. He'd spent some time in jail because he'd failed to show up for his court dates and a warrant had been put out for his arrest. He'd never married and there was no record of children. His work record was spotty up until a few years ago when he started working for Fitzler Roofing.

Well, that answered one question. Mr. Fitzler's company was still going strong. He'd either sold it to someone and they'd kept the name or maybe one of the daughters was running it.

When Raney got back, they ordered. And when the food was delivered, the steaks were cooked just perfect. They ate, both skipped dessert and by the time they were out of the restaurant, it was already dark.

"Tired?" he asked as they settled in for the half-hour drive home.

"A little," she admitted. "I haven't been sleeping all that well lately."

"It will all be over soon," he said, thinking of Harry Malone's upcoming trial.

"I suppose," she said.

He glanced over at her. "You don't sound convinced."

"I'm conflicted."

"Conflicted," he repeated. "Testifying against Harry Malone is the right thing to do," he said, his tone adamant.

She waved a hand. "I know that. I'm conflicted because I can't help feeling that there was a reason that I got away. I mean, three other women died at his hand. Those are the ones we know about. But I didn't. I lived to tell about it." She turned to him. "Why me?"

Her tone gripped him, making his chest feel heavy. He didn't know what to tell her. "I don't know," he said.

"Maybe I have unfinished business," she said. "Maybe I'm supposed to accomplish something significant. Something that will make a difference."

"Maybe," he said.

"Well, that doesn't make any sense," she said. "I'm not going to discover the cure for cancer or anything remotely close. I'm a career counselor. That's it."

"You probably help people all the time. With their career, right?" he added, a little lamely. "You have an important job."

"'Had,' you mean? I suspect they're going to have to fill my spot."

She didn't sound angry, more resigned if anything. "Are there other jobs for career counselors?" he asked.

"I suppose. It's just that I really loved my work at Next Steps. I worked almost exclusively with young people—many of whom dropped out of school only to discover that there are very few opportunities for someone with no credentials. They can't even qualify for entry-level positions."

"Pretty shortsighted, right?"

"Sure. But there are always lots of contributing

factors. I've seen everything from learning disabilities to teen pregnancy to homelessness to jail."

"You work with ex-cons?"

"Sure. Sometimes I work with the currently incarcerated, depending on when they are going to be released."

"And you visit them in jail? Prison?"

She chuckled, her head leaning back. "Well, they can't exactly come to me."

"That could be pretty dangerous. There are bad people in jail and prison. That's what got them there."

"I know." She turned her head to look at him. "But in my case, it's the classic example of the person you least expect being the person who is going to cause you the trouble. Harry Malone has never been incarcerated. He has a fine reputation."

"That's going to change," he said. He didn't want her focused on Malone. "Tell me more about your job. What is it that you do exactly?"

"It depends on the client. For those that are new to the program, it might be getting them enrolled in a GED program and helping them develop the confidence and the study skills to be successful. For those further along, who are looking for a job, I work on their soft skills and teach them what most of us intuitively knew when we entered the workforce."

"Like?" Did she realize how her voice lit up when she talked about her work?

"Like how to have a conversation, a real conversation. Many of the clients I work with have been talked *at*, not talked with, and they've developed a response pattern that doesn't help them much in a job interview. They need help on what to wear and help on answering questions about why there are gaps in their employment because they were in jail. That kind of thing."

"I'll bet you're good at it," he said.

"I am. I was," she added, after a few seconds.

"You will be again," he said.

She didn't answer. It made him crazy that some dirtbag had caused this. She'd been tormented for days and now the nightmare was continuing. It wasn't fair.

But life rarely was.

He'd learned that the hard way the first time Brick had taken a belt to him. And when he'd gotten strong enough that he could challenge Brick, the man had been smart enough to change tactics.

And then Chase had had the very real worry that either his mother or Cal wouldn't survive Brick's next episode. So he'd done the only thing he could.

When they pulled into the drive, nothing looked disturbed. He realized that Raney had fallen asleep. He gave her shoulder a gentle shake. "We're home," he said.

She gave him a couple slow blinks. "I'll just sleep out here," she said. "In the car." She closed her eyes again.

"I don't think so." He got out, walked around the car and opened her door. He held out his hand.

She took it. Her skin was warm and soft and so absolutely feminine. He gave her arm a gentle tug and she stood up, a little unsteady. He put his hands on her waist.

Her hair smelled like raspberries and without thought, he raised one hand and touched the very tips. "This surprised me," he admitted. "But I like it. It's cute. Sexy," he added.

She tilted her chin up. Her lips were close. So close. And he desperately wanted to kiss her.

He bent his head.

She closed her eyes.

And then he saw the reflection of lights on the road and heard a car engine. He watched. It turned into the Fitzlers' lane.

This time.

What the hell was he thinking? He'd said he would protect her, had promised that he could keep her safe.

"Chase?" she whispered, her eyes now wide-open.

"I'm tired, Raney. Let's get inside now."

RANEY WAS EXHAUSTED but still her body felt hot and needy. She'd torn open the packaging on her sheets and quickly put them on the mattress. Then she shucked her clothes and climbed in.

Chase had almost kissed her. And she had definitely wanted him to. How the hell she was going to pretend tomorrow that nothing had changed was beyond her.

She needed sleep.

Which was easier than admitting she needed sex.

As tired as she was, she tossed and turned and once when she woke up, she heard noises downstairs. Her heart started beating fast and she looked at the window. Then she heard the sounds of old pipes. Water running. As quietly as she could, she crossed the room and eased the door open.

The lights were on downstairs and Chase, wearing just blue jeans, low on his hips, was using a sponge mop to clean the living room floor. It was one of those fake wooden floors that people wanted to believe looked like wood but it never did. She watched for several minutes, enjoying the show. His biceps flexed with the effort, the strong muscles in his back rippling.

He was working hard. When he shifted, she got a glimpse of the sweat on his chest.

She could feel her own body get warm.

She supposed it was possible that he simply couldn't abide a dirty floor. But somehow she didn't think so. It was much more likely that Chase was having a little troubling sleeping, too, and he was taking it out on the unsuspecting laminate.

She stepped back, closing the door. She returned to her bed and stared into the darkness. What the hell was happening between her and Chase Hollister?

The old Raney would have been intrigued but likely too shy to do much about it. Blonde Raney? She wasn't sure.

The only thing she was confident of was that it was strangely comforting to know that Chase was losing a little sleep over her.

CHASE WAS SITTING at the kitchen table when Raney got downstairs the next morning. Like last night, still in his blue jeans. But this morning, he'd put on a shirt. He was drinking a cup of coffee and there was a bowl and a cereal box next to it.

"Morning," he said.

"Good morning."

"Sleep well?"

"Pretty good," she said. "How about you?"

He shrugged. "Good enough."

Uh-huh. She poured herself a cup of coffee and sat across from him. "The living room floor looks great," she said. "Did you mop it?"

He stared at the back of the cereal box, as if it was the most interesting thing he'd ever read. "Yeah, I got an early start."

She thought about calling him out but decided there was little to be gained. If he wanted to pretend that their *little moment* outside the prior evening had meant nothing, so be it. "I thought I might work upstairs some more today," she said.

"I really hate that you're getting sucked into cleaning this place," he said.

"Don't worry about it. It fills the time. At the last place, all I did was watch television. If I see another *Friends* rerun, it won't be pretty. What are your plans?"

"More outside work. I'll probably mow the grass first, then take a look at the roof."

"Do you know how to fix that?" He was a cop, not a carpenter.

"I'm pretty good with my hands," he said.

She let his words hang in the air. "Really?" she said. She stared at his blunt male fingers that were wrapped around his coffee cup. His nails were clipped short.

Capable hands.

Capable of what? Her imagination was running wild. She could see him cupping her breast, judging the weight, running his index finger over her nipple.

She felt hot.

She should retreat.

That would have been BHM.

Now she gathered her courage, channeled blonde Raney and looked him in the eye. "That's good to know," she said, her tone perfectly level. Then she turned on her heel and escaped upstairs.

TEN MINUTES LATER, when Chase sharply turned the wheel of the old riding lawn mower, he was still thinking about the look she'd given him. He made another pass across the ratty yard, his mind reliving every moment in the kitchen.

He was tired. Had given up all pretense of sleep around two and had started mopping the floor. He'd been quiet and Raney had slept through it. Safe in her bed. Alone.

He'd been this close to kissing her the night before. Standing beside the car, with the moonlight washing over them, the urge had been overwhelming. If the other vehicle hadn't come along, he'd have made a big mistake.

He was going to keep his distance.

They had a month. How hard could it be? It wasn't as if there wasn't anything for him to do. After he'd finished mopping the floor, he'd made a list, trying to prioritize the work. If he had to be in Ravesville, he intended to get the house ready to sell.

While the weather was good, he should work outside. There was absolutely no curb appeal. He needed to trim bushes and trees and mow the grass. The front steps needed to be fixed and the roof was a must. In fact, the roof was probably the priority. He shouldn't do anything inside until he was sure that when it rained, the water wasn't going to come flowing down upon newly painted walls.

When he'd told Raney this morning that he thought he could fix the roof, he hadn't been bragging. That was how he'd gotten to know Gordy Fitzler. His neighbor was a roofer, the only one in Ravesville. It had been a godsend for Chase when Old Man Fitzler, as the boys he hired liked to call him, had offered Chase a spot on his summer crew.

He'd taught Chase how to scramble across a roof without losing his balance, how to use a nail gun and how to keep a packet of shingles, weighing a hundred pounds, from shifting on you as you went up the ladder so that you didn't end up in the rose bush thirty feet below.

He'd put on roofs in the blazing sun, which had been painfully intensified by Missouri's high humidity, for two summers. Today, the late-September weather was about perfect for roof work. The sky was a clear blue and the morning temp was a cool sixty with an expected high of seventy-eight.

He walked to the two-car attached garage that sat fifty yards west of the house. When he opened the side door, the smell of mustiness, in sharp contrast to the clear, clean air outside, hit him hard. As expected, there was a lawn mower. Some tools, too. A few shovels and spades stacked in a corner. In addition to that, the building was full of boxes that had not been totally spared from the elements. He glanced upward and wasn't surprised when he saw spots on the ceiling that indicated the garage roof was likely leaking, the same as the house roof.

There were stacks and stacks of newspapers. He suspected they were condo living quarters for any number of rodents. There were balls of snarled-up twine, as if Brick had saved every piece he'd encountered for the past seventy years. Empty coffee cans filled with rusted, bent nails and screws and nuts and bolts. Nothing besides the lawn mower, which appeared in decent shape, looked as if it had been touched for many years.

What the hell had Brick done all day? Shaking his head, Chase grabbed a ladder that hung on the far wall. He tucked it under his arm and left the building. He'd tackle the garage another day.

Ten minutes later, he was on the roof, surveying the damage. It was no wonder that there was water damage inside the house. The shingles were old and brittle and their edges were lifted, allowing water to seep under.

In several small areas, the shingles were missing altogether, probably due to severe wind.

He realized, rather disheartened, that rather than a few quick repairs, the house really needed a new roof. He supposed he had a choice. He could nail down what was there the best he could and then pick up a couple packets of shingles at one of the big box stores for the missing sections. The new ones wouldn't match the old ones and it would look like hell, but at least the roof wouldn't leak. It would get him and Raney by for the time being. Then, when he and his brothers listed the house, they could price it lower than market, to make up for the fact that the buyer would need to install the new roof.

Or he could put a new roof on. Which was a hell of a lot of work. Working alone, it would take weeks.

He'd be on the roof; Raney would be inside.

Distance. That was what he'd told himself was the answer.

He was halfway down the ladder when he heard the sound of an approaching car. He twisted to see the road.

Chapter Six

It was an old pickup, maroon with white lettering on the door. He smiled. He remembered that truck from when it was brand-new. Had driven it a couple times with a firm warning not to get it scratched up ringing in his ears.

The truck turned into the lane. Chase waited until it came to a stop and the old man driving it slowly climbed out. Gordy Fitzler's hair was thin and completely white and he looked thinner than Chase remembered. He approached, extending his hand. "Mr. Fitzler," Chase said.

The man made a scoffing noise. "It's been a long time, Chase, but there's no need for formality. Call me Gordy or Old Man, the way you used to."

"Didn't know you knew that we called you that," Chase admitted.

"Made me laugh every time I heard it. You and your friends were forty years younger than me and I could still work circles around you. I thought I saw lights here the other night and then this morning when I was having coffee in town, I heard you were back."

"Just to get the house ready to sell," Chase corrected.

"You'll have your hands full with that, I suspect." Gordy looked at the ladder that was leaning up against the house. "Brick should have redone his roof years ago."

"Just discovered that. You're not still getting up on roofs, are you?" Chase asked.

Gordy shook his head. "Retired for many years. My old knees couldn't take it anymore. But my son-in-law took over. Jonah's doing a good job. He could get you what you need and probably drop it off this afternoon."

Chase didn't bother to ask about the price. He knew it would be fair. "How is your wife?"

Gordy shook his head. "Glenda's been gone now for almost two years."

"I'm sorry. I didn't know."

"Figured as much. Suspected that Brick didn't keep you up-to-date on the news. You know, Lloyd Doogan works for my son-in-law."

"How's he do?"

"Okay. Works hard when he's there. Has a few demons that chase him once in a while."

Hard to tell what he suffered as a child. And if there was anyone in Ravesville who knew the truth about Brick Doogan, it was Gordy. He'd been witness to the assorted bruises and other injuries that Chase had shown up with. It was probably why he'd offered him a spot on his couch whenever Chase had been desperate enough to knock on the door.

"Tell me about those demons," Chase said.

Gordy shrugged. "I don't know all the details. Just know that every once in a while, he'll get into the sauce and be too hungover to climb on top of a roof. Anyway, I heard you got a wife."

"Raney," Chase said, feeling bad that he was lying to Gordy. But Raney's safety was more important. "She's inside."

"I'd like to meet her."

"Of course." They walked up the porch, him pointing out the spots that Gordy should avoid. He opened the door. There was no sign of Raney.

"Raney," he called out. "There's a friend here who'd like to meet you."

She walked out of the kitchen, a towel over her shoulder. She'd put on old jeans that molded to her firm body and a light gray V-neck T-shirt. She looked at him, then Gordy. "Good morning," she said.

"Ma'am," Gordy said, extending his hand. "I'm Gordy Fitzler. I wanted to offer my congratulations. You got yourself a good one here."

Raney smiled. "I know," she said, playing her part perfectly. "It's a pleasure to meet you."

"I'm just the next house down the road. You ever need anything, just stop by."

"I will," she said.

"The roof is worse than I thought," Chase said. "It needs to be replaced. Gordy's son-in-law will drop some shingles by this afternoon so that I can get started on the work."

"Sounds like a big job," she said.

"He knows what he's doing. Best roofer I ever had," Gordy added. "Now, don't be a stranger," he said, turning to leave.

Chase walked the man to his truck and made sure he got off okay. Then he went back inside. Raney was standing at the window. "Sweet guy," she said.

Gordy had had high expectations, hadn't tolerated any backtalk and had restored Chase's faith that a man didn't have to yell to have himself be heard. "Yeah."

He suddenly found himself wanting to tell Raney about Brick Doogan, about the crazy things the man had done and about how he used to fantasize that his mother had married Gordy Fitzler instead.

He'd forgiven his mother. For letting it happen. For choosing to ignore it. For not being stronger. He'd forgiven her because she'd finally asked him to. She'd been on her deathbed and it was the only peace he could offer her.

But those weren't things he talked about. To anyone. Especially not someone who was just passing through his life.

"I'm going to start tearing off shingles," he said and walked out the door.

Two hours later, he was still on the roof ripping off shingles when he heard the front door open. He looked down. Raney had changed her clothes and was wearing a skirt that showed off her pretty legs and a shirt that showed off her other assets.

Distance, he reminded himself.

"Hey," she said, looking up and shading her eyes with the palm of her hand. "I thought I might make spaghetti for dinner but I forgot to buy Italian seasoning yesterday. Can I borrow your SUV to run into town?"

"I'll go with you," he said, starting to climb down.

"Do you really think that's necessary? You said yourself that no one has any reason to believe that Raney Hollister is Lorraine Taylor. Nothing is going to happen."

He stopped, halfway down. Distance. She was right. It was safe. And they should act as normally as possible. Which meant that one of them could run to the store without the other.

"Okay," he said. "Keys are on the counter."

"Want anything else?"

"Yeah. Some really good bread from the bakery."

"Got it," she said. "Try not to fall off the roof while I'm gone," she teased. She seemed more lighthearted. It made him realize that she was probably really glad to have the freedom to leave the house, to do something as mundane as grocery shopping after having been confined to the house in Miami.

A few minutes later, the SUV pulled out of the driveway. He watched it until it turned the corner, no longer in view. He checked the time on his watch and then went back to pulling up shingles.

The next time he checked his watch, it was a half hour later. Raney should be home soon. He used the back of his arm to wipe away the sweat gathering on his forehead. Damn, it was hot. He should probably get some water.

He got down and drank two big glasses, standing at the living room window, watching the road. What the hell was taking her so long?

Ten minutes later he was really worried.

He tried her cell phone but she didn't pick up. Moving quickly, he put his gun in the small of his back and slipped on a loose shirt. He rubbed his thigh, hating that his climbing up and down the ladder and crab-walking around the roof were taking a toll on his injured muscle.

Before he'd been hurt, he'd regularly jogged. The mile and a half into town would have been nothing. But he hadn't run for six weeks. When the doc had given him the release to return to active duty, he'd suggested he lay off vigorous training for another week or two.

That couldn't be helped now and he wasn't letting it hold him back. He felt an overwhelming need to get to town, fast.

He had just opened the front door when he saw his SUV sedately driving down the road. He watched, and with every damn rotation of the tires, he felt his irritation grow.

She was barely out of the car when he stalked off the front porch.

"Hi," she said, as if there was nothing wrong.

"Where the hell have you been?" he asked, his tone harsher than he intended. He took a deep breath, struggling for the control that generally came so naturally to him.

She frowned at him and held up the plastic bag in her hand. "I went to the store."

"It's a mile and a half," he said. "And the store has five aisles," he added, sarcasm in his tone. "I called you."

She pulled her cell from her purse, pushed a button. "I'm sorry. I had it on silent."

"What took you so long?"

"I met someone," she said. "The waiter from the restaurant last night."

Little red dots danced at the edge of his vision. "I didn't realize the two of you had set up a rendezvous."

"I... I..." She dropped the bag and small tins of basil and oregano rolled out onto the ground. "What the hell are you talking about?"

"In case you've forgotten, *honey*, you're married. And he knows it, too."

She walked toward him. When she got close enough, she poked him in the chest with her index finger. "You. Are. An. Idiot."

Huh?

"Before I went to the grocery store, I went to the little bookstore on the corner. I forgot to pack any books. And I like to read. Anyway, he was there, looking through a stack of used books. We recognized each other and started talking. He admitted that he was looking for business books, the kind that might help him be prepared for the job interview that he has next week."

"Oh." As responses went, it was pretty inadequate.

And she didn't appear to be inclined to let it go when she repeated, "Oh?" then added, "That's the best you can do?"

Pretty much. He felt like a fool. "I'm sorry," he said. "I was worried when you were gone so long."

Her eyes softened. "I assumed you'd be busy on the roof."

"The house is secondary. My first responsibility is to protect you."

"Don't you think I'm safe here?" she asked.

"You should be," he said. "But a good cop never assumes anything."

"We're meeting again tomorrow," she said.

He felt his emotions spike. "The hell you are."

"He's interviewed for five jobs and hasn't gotten any of them. He knows that he's doing something wrong."

"That's not your concern."

"Of course it isn't. But I have the skills to help him. God knows I have the time," she added.

In her tone, he heard frustration that might have been edging toward bitterness. He remembered hearing the pride in her voice when she'd spoken about her work.

Harry Malone had taken a great deal away from her. And now Chase was about to compound the issue.

He swallowed hard. "I want his name, his address, his previous address. Hell, I want to know his damn shoe size."

She opened her mouth, then shut it without speaking.

"And you'll meet here. Where I can watch him," he

added. Wouldn't that be fun? Standing by while the two of them huddled over the idiot's résumé.

Finally she nodded. "Ten," she said.

"Ten what?" he asked, already preparing to go outside where he could hit something. Hard.

"I think he wears a ten. I spent one summer selling shoes. I'm a pretty good judge."

He wanted to laugh. Damn her, he wanted to laugh. "Well, I wear a twelve and if he so much as steps an inch out of line, I'm going to plant it where a foot should never go."

He turned and stalked back toward his ladder.

And finally did let a smile loose when he heard her quiet laughter.

RANEY MADE SPAGHETTI, a big salad and garlic bread for dinner. She let Chase know about a half hour before it was ready so that he could come inside and shower. He'd been working outside all afternoon. The shingles and all the other assorted supplies needed to replace a roof had been delivered midafternoon along with a big Dumpster to catch all the old shingles that he dropped from the roof.

"Smells good," he said when he came in. "Really good."

Raney's stomach did a little flip. It had been a long time since she'd cooked for anyone. "You've got fifteen minutes," she said.

He took eleven. He helped her carry the bowls from the counter to the table. And then he proceeded to eat his way through two platefuls. He finally pushed his plate away. "What else can you cook?" he asked.

She shrugged. "I guess about everything. I was brought up that if you could read, you could cook."

He shook his head. "Not true. I'm a literate man. I can't cook." He pushed his chair back, picked up both their dirty plates and carried them to the sink.

Relaxed, she rested one elbow on the table and used her fingers to play with the ends of her short hair. "I suspect it's that you choose not to cook, not that you can't."

"I've had some spectacular disasters," he admitted. He turned the faucet on and added dish soap.

"Well, I detest doing dishes. So I'll cook and you'll clean up. This is a marriage that could work," she added.

He turned around, his face much more serious than her casual remark. "Why aren't you married?"

"I...I was." She answered before she considered whether she wanted to have this discussion with him.

A quick look of surprise crossed his face before he managed to shut it down. "I didn't know that."

"Probably didn't get to the fine details in my file. It was short-lived. Just two years. We've been divorced for over five years."

"Does your ex know about Harry Malone?"

"I doubt it. He lives in Hawaii. He surfs. Professionally."

"Let me guess. You didn't want to move to Hawaii?"

She shook her head. "I didn't want to share with his mistress."

Even though she'd known the marriage wasn't working, Mike's duplicity had hit her hard. His training schedule had required them to live apart for long stretches of time. Still, she'd never expected him to cheat. When she'd stumbled upon the note in his pocket, she'd been so angry.

She'd confronted him with it and he had readily admitted that it had been going on for months, leading her to believe that the accidental discovery might not have been so accidental. He'd wanted her to know, wanted to be out of a marriage that he was no longer interested in working at.

The divorce had been fast and as amicable as a divorce could probably be. The ink on the divorce paperwork hadn't been dry before Mike and Lenore were living together.

Raney had thrown herself into her work. And friends had told her not to worry, that she'd meet someone. She'd smiled, neither agreed nor disagreed, but in her lonely bed, she had spent some time wondering if this was it for her. Was she going to be alone?

It was a suddenly chilling thought to think that *this* might be as close to a real marriage as she was going to get.

"He was an idiot," Chase said, his tone hard. His gaze was intense, the set of his jaw stiff. He came back to the table and sat down. His chair was at a right angle to hers and he leaned forward, reached out a hand and touched her arm. The nail on his bare ring finger was bruised, and she suspected he'd hit it with a hammer. His skin was hot. "You know that, right?" he added.

What she knew was that Chase Hollister affected her in a way that no man, even Mike, had ever affected her. He made the nerve endings in her body come alive and almost beg to be touched, stroked, loved.

"It was a long time ago. We were both young."

"No excuse for what he did," Chase said.

And she knew for sure that while Chase might have

been the bad boy in his youth, he'd grown into the kind of man who knew right from wrong. He would do the right thing.

He would protect the witness.

He wouldn't cross the line.

Which meant it would be up to her.

But he had the advantage. While he might not know everything, he knew more about her than she did about him. He'd casually brushed off the idea of marriage when they'd discussed it at the café but that didn't mean that he wasn't in a committed relationship. If so, it didn't matter how blond her hair was—she wasn't doing anything about the attraction. Having been on the receiving end of that once, she didn't ever want to cause that kind of pain for someone else. "I know you mentioned some aversion to marriage," she said, deliberately keeping her tone light, "but are you involved with anyone right now?"

He stared at her, his amber eyes intense. His handsome face was even more tanned from his time on the roof. "I'm pretty busy at work," he said.

It was sort of an answer.

"I imagine you are," she murmured.

"I haven't dated anyone for over a year," he added.

Did that mean that he hadn't had sex in over a year? Maybe if her hair was fire-engine red she would be brave enough to ask for clarification.

What did it matter? He'd had the chance to kiss her last night and he'd pulled back. She'd been rejected once before by her ex-husband. It had hurt badly. She wasn't going to put herself in that position again.

She pushed her chair back from the table. "I'm tired," she lied. "I think I'll turn in."

CHASE WANDERED AROUND the downstairs, completely avoiding Brick's room. The only television in the house was in there, but he wasn't that desperate to watch something.

He could start taking off the paint on the woodwork, but that would involve the use of turpentine and the fumes might get bad. He could always open some windows, but that wasn't something he was willing to do at night. He wanted the house closed up tight. A locked door or window wasn't much of a deterrent, but it might buy a second or two and sometimes that was all a person needed.

He should just go to bed and get up really early in the morning to make use of the daylight. But he felt unsettled. He'd made his fourth lap around the house when his cell phone rang. He looked at the number and smiled.

"You still owe me," he answered.

"Of course I do," Bray said. "What's the house look like?"

"It's in pretty rough shape. Needs paint and new carpet most everywhere but that's cosmetic. I'm going to replace the roof. It's leaking in several spots."

"I really wish I could be there to help. But this case is just about to crack. I've been after one of these guys for two years."

"Don't worry about it. We're doing fine."

"We?"

"I'm guarding a witness while I'm here. We needed a safe place to stash her and Ravesville seemed like a good option."

"What's her name?"

"Raney. She's pretending to be my wife."

"Now I really wish I could be there. You've probably got everybody in the town talking about it."

"Speaking of town, I saw Summer Wright."

There was silence on the other end. "Summer Blake, you mean," Bray said, his voice tight.

"Nope. Summer Wright. She's divorced. Not gossip, got it straight from her."

More silence. He gave Bray a full minute more, but he still didn't say anything.

"She's got a couple kids."

"Hey, you know what, I've got another call coming in. Take care of your witness and get that house ready to sell."

Chase stared at his phone. His brother regularly dealt with the dregs of society. Nothing much ruffled him. But hearing Summer Wright's name had practically rendered him speechless.

That was interesting.

He lay down on the lumpy sofa, suddenly feeling better that he'd talked to his brother. He closed his eyes. He got up once in the middle of the night to make sure the house was still secure and to take off his jeans and pull on athletic shorts. It was hot. He did not want to run the air conditioner or even the fan because it could make it difficult to hear an intruder. When he lay down the second time, he didn't open his eyes again until he heard Raney came downstairs the next morning.

"Morning," she said, her voice husky from sleep.

He shifted to a sitting position. "What time is it?"

"A little after six," she said. "I didn't mean to disturb you."

"No problem," he said. He got up and quickly pulled at the hem of his shorts. He sure as hell didn't want

Raney to see the scar on his leg. Didn't want to answer any questions. Didn't want her to have any concerns that he might not be 100 percent.

What he had on was what he wore when he sparred with Dawson at the gym, but suddenly it felt insufficient.

He needed to wear a parka around Raney. Something that zipped, and buttoned, with a little Velcro just in case. Something that would take some time to shed. Something that would give him some time to develop a little perspective.

Right now, he had none. Because she was leaning forward from the waist, looking at the stack of books on the end table, and her little pajama top was gaping at the top, giving him a truly excellent look at her breasts.

She was not wearing a bra.

He could not look away.

But then she straightened up, looking at him. Assessing.

And he lifted his hand.

Chapter Seven

And clamped it down hard on the back of his neck. Holy hell. What was he thinking?

He practically ran to the kitchen, grabbed the empty coffeepot, filled it with water and then completed the whole coffee routine. He didn't turn around until the first drops hit the bottom with a quick sizzle.

She was sitting at the table, as if nothing had happened. Had he imagined it? Was it simply wishful thinking?

Was he losing his mind?

"What time is that guy coming?" he asked, needing something concrete to focus on.

"His name is Keith. He'll be here around eleven. I thought I'd clear off a spot on the dining room table where we could work."

Chase craned his neck to see into the other room. The old wooden table was covered with newspapers and brown sacks and milk cartons that had been emptied and then refilled with water, as if Brick was afraid the well was going out. There were stacks of bath towels at the far end. He suspected they'd been clean at one time but now they had a heavy layer of dust. In the middle, there was a pile of mail, looking as if it had been opened and then just tossed. He supposed he'd have to go through it at some point.

There was a matching china cabinet in the corner that had nothing in it. His mother's dishes, the ones she'd gotten from her mother, chipped and probably full of lead, had been packed away after his mother's death eight years ago. Bray had taken them, said he'd put them in storage. Chase didn't care as long as Brick didn't have them.

It was one of the few things that her sons had gotten from the house. They'd left the furniture, the cabinet, the table and the six wooden chairs, the same color as the table but not quite the same pattern. He could still remember how delighted his mother had been when she'd discovered them at a neighbor's sale. They'd replaced the ones that had come with the table but had fallen apart after three boys and a husband had used them hard.

She'd bought them after his dad had died and before Brick had come into the picture. The idiot had been in the house for less than a year when he'd picked up one of the chairs and thrown it at the china cabinet, cracking the front pane of glass.

The crack was still there.

"I found a couple garbage cans in the garage yesterday," he said. "I'll get them for you."

"No problem," she said. She pushed her chair back, walked over to the coffeepot, getting just close enough that her arm brushed against his bare ribs. "Sorry," she murmured.

He couldn't say anything. Had she done that intentionally?

She moved away. As if it was nothing.

He was pathetic, trying to read something off a blank page. "I'm going outside," he said.

"Did you eat?" she asked, sounding concerned.

There was no way that he could stay in the kitchen. "I'll grab something later," he said. "I want to work while the day is cool."

Outside, he walked to the garage. He'd considered leaving the extension ladder out the night before so that he didn't have to go back into the garage but had discarded that notion immediately. He didn't want to give anyone easy access to the second story of the house, to Raney's room. So he'd stashed the ladder behind some boxes, making it tough for someone to find.

He carried the ladder to the side of the house, tied his tool belt around his waist and started climbing. Fully extended, the ladder was just tall enough for him to reach the roof of the second floor.

Bray and Cal would both be appreciative of his work on the house. They would not second-guess his decision to replace the roof or anything else. They would be grateful that he had taken charge. Cal would not likely say it. Cal never said much to him anymore. Something had changed about the time of his mother's death. There hadn't been a big blow up. Nope. It was as if Cal had just shut down.

They needed to talk about that. But Cal hadn't been around much in the past eight years, and on the rare occasions the two brothers had been together, Chase hadn't wanted to dredge up old issues. He'd settled for stilted conversations and awkward silences. It was past time for that to change, and for the first time in a long time, felt as if now might be the time to press the issue. He and Bray always tried to get together on Thanksgiving. It had been their mother's favorite holiday. There were times when either or both of them had to work on the actual holiday because crime never took a break. In those cases, they had a flexible approach.

It might be on Monday or Tuesday or Wednesday, it didn't matter. It was still Thanksgiving dinner and they did the whole traditional thing. They generally found a place that cooked the turkey and all the trimmings and packed it up all nice and pretty so that the customer could take it home and eat it off real plates.

If the house wasn't sold by Thanksgiving, he could invite Bray here. And Cal, too. He wouldn't take no for an answer.

The idea was oddly appealing.

He got to the top of the ladder, stepped off onto the roof and squatted next to the area where he'd started prying off shingles with his crowbar. By Thanksgiving, the trial would be over. Raney would be home.

He jabbed the edge of the crowbar under the shingle and jerked his arm, sending the old shingle flying. It was a crazy idea to think about celebrating here. The house needed an exorcism, not a family holiday.

CHASE HAD BEEN working outside for more than three hours when he saw an old Toyota Camry drive down the road, slow well before the driveway and make the turn. It was black but filthy with road dust. When Keith got out, with the loose-limbed stride of someone in his early twenties, Chase felt a sharp pain in his thigh that had been dully aching all morning, as if damaged nerve endings had picked that exact moment to wake up.

Dawson's taunt, *You're not getting any younger*, rang in his ears as he sidestepped his way down the steep slant of the roof, caught the top rung of the ladder with his foot and climbed down.

He wasn't, that was true. But then again, at any age, taking a bullet was a kick in the butt. It hadn't helped the head games when the surgeon said that had the bullet been an inch to the right, he'd have probably bled out at the scene. It had been a postsurgery buzzkill that no amount of narcotics had busted through.

After a crappy twenty-four hours, he'd chosen to focus on the positive. It hadn't been an inch to the right and he'd lived to tell about it.

So his leg hurt a little. Big deal. Didn't mean that he was going to sit back and let some punk kid get the best of him. Not on his home territory.

Home. Territory.

Again, crazy thoughts.

It was just that since almost the moment he'd arrived, there'd been something right about being back in this house that he'd sworn he'd never return to. And that had a lot to do with Raney.

Who was about to get cozy with Keith.

Chase slammed the door on his way into the house.

RANEY TOLD HERSELF that she absolutely would not let Chase distract her from the task at hand. She had barely invited Keith into the dining room when Chase stormed into the house, scuffing his boots on the floor, banging cupboard doors and scraping chairs across the floor.

She reviewed Keith's résumé and tried to ignore the noise. Keith showed no reaction to it. After a few minutes of enduring the commotion, she looked up.

"Can I help you with something?" she asked, pitching her voice so that he could hear.

Chase stuck his head around the corner of the doorway. "Don't mind me," he said. He was chewing peanut-butter crackers. Noisily.

She narrowed her eyes at him.

He showed no response, simply pulled his head back. He did, however, quiet down a bit. He did not leave.

What did she care if he wanted to act like a fool? She turned to Keith, smiled and got started. Two hours later, they had discussed potential modifications to his résumé, reviewed his answers to common interview questions, talked about his short- and long-term goals and developed a reasonable plan to get there.

Chase had to be bored out of his mind. He was behaving, though, quietly sitting in the kitchen.

"I do so much better when you're the one asking the questions," Keith said, giving her a big smile. "I need you to be with me at the interview."

A cupboard door slammed. She ignored it.

"I really appreciate all this help," Keith added. "At least let me buy you lunch."

Something hit the floor in the kitchen. Hard. She suspected it might have been the toaster.

Keith, finally catching on, rolled his eyes. "I guess not," he said.

She shook her head, stood up and walked him to the front door. "Let me know how your interview goes," she said.

She waited until his car turned onto the road before turning to find Chase. He was standing at the stove, his back to her, spatula in hand. She was ready to blast him.

Then he turned, still holding the spatula but now also a plate. He'd cooked a grilled-cheese sandwich.

"I thought you might be hungry," he said. "You missed lunch."

Oh, good grief. "I thought you didn't cook."

"This isn't cooking. It's survival."

"Thank you," she said.

"He can't really think that 'I was underutilized' is a good answer for why he only lasted three months at the telemarketing company," Chase said.

"He's Gen Y, like me. We all think we're underutilized. You're Gen X, apples and oranges."

"Thanks for making me feel a hundred years old."

Sexiest hundred-year-old guy she'd ever met. She smiled. "Sorry. Next year I'll be in my thirties. We'll be in the same decade of our lives. If that makes you feel any better," she added.

"Stop, please. In any event, we'll probably both be working for him in ten years."

"I hope not. Didn't you hear that his long-term goal is to own his own restaurant?"

"It'll be great. You can be the short-order cook and I'll be the bouncer at the door."

"Restaurant. Not biker bar." She wiped her mouth on a paper napkin. "That doesn't seem like a great next job for you."

He shrugged. "Always got to be open to the possibilities. Ready to move on to the next opportunity."

She'd been teasing, but now he was serious. She wasn't sure what to say.

"How's the roof coming?" she asked.

"Pretty good."

"Can I take a look?"

He studied her. "I don't think that's a good idea. This is a big two-story house. I'm pretty high in the air. It doesn't bother me but I'm used to it—like Gordy said, I did it for years."

"But I've never seen a roof get put on. If I do get my own house someday, that would be a good thing for me to know. I'm not afraid of heights."

"The first summer that I worked for Gordy, about midway through the season, Brad Morgan, who was a year older than me, made a mistake. A costly one. He fell more than twenty feet. He broke his pelvis and cracked several vertebrae. He was in bad shape. I won't take that chance that you might get injured. And I certainly don't think it's what Chief Bates had in mind when I described this as a safe house."

She wasn't going to be able to budge him. "Oh, fine. Then, I'm going to open the Toasted Meringue and get started in the kitchen. It's the one room where the roof doesn't seem to be leaking."

"You know, I really appreciate everything you're doing in the house."

It was hard to be irritated with him when he was such a nice guy. "I know you do. I appreciate that I'm not opening Eggshell White."

"I'd have probably woken up one morning and you'd have painted me Eggshell White."

"Maybe." She wanted to talk to him about the house but didn't know exactly how to do it. Her friends who had remodeled their homes were always asking her opinion on things, saying that she had a good eye for color and design. But she didn't think Chase was especially interested. *Neutrals sell.* He was totally focused on that. But she felt compelled to say something.

He had a gem here. It had taken her a little bit to see it. From the minute she'd arrived, she'd loved the outside, with its wide porch and the big windows on both floors. She'd been a little disappointed with the insides, because it was dark and dismal and had so much clutter that it was hard to see past that. But now that she'd had some time to look around, she felt differently.

"Hey, I had a chance to look around this morning while I was waiting for Keith. I needed to make some space for us to work at the dining room table and while I was in there, I happened to take a look under the carpet. It's sort of coming up on that one side." If it hadn't been before, it was now because once she'd spied a small section of the floor, she'd had to see more. "Did you know that there is really lovely hardwood flooring under there? I mean, it needs to be refinished and all that, but it's nice."

"The next owner can refinish floors. For now, I'll get the carpet cleaned and tack down that corner."

She hated the idea of that carpet staying. She knew she wasn't going to be living here but really, it was just a shame to cover beautiful wood like that.

"You know what the living room is missing?" she asked.

He smiled at her. "I have no idea."

"Bookshelves. You could build them into the two corners and that room would pop."

"Pop," he repeated.

"And I'd take those curtains down and put in those shades that you can raise from either the top or the bottom, depending on the time of day and the position of the sun. And it goes without saying that flooring in there, which is intended to look like wood but doesn't, would need to go. But you could probably find something that would closely match the wood in the dining room."

"Which will be covered by carpet. No bookshelves," he added. "I will take the curtains down only because they smell, but the next owner can do his or her own windows. I'm not decorating. Refurbishing. Or gentrifying," he added.

"But you're sort of flipping. I mean, I realize you didn't buy this house with the intent of fixing it up and selling it to make a nice profit but you did inherit it, it needs to be fixed up and you *could* make a nice profit."

"I want a quick sale. That's more important to me." Chase pushed his chair back. "Speaking of which, I better get busy. I may need to run into town this afternoon. I'm almost out of nails."

She was disappointed that she hadn't been able to get him to see the possibilities in the house. But it really wasn't her worry. "I'd be happy to do the nail run. I forgot to buy oatmeal yesterday and I want to make some granola."

She could tell that he wanted to say no. But he probably felt bad about not letting her on the roof and shutting down her decorating pleas. "Okay. I guess there's no reason to think there's any risk."

A HALF HOUR LATER, Raney had her oatmeal and two bags of chips, because it did seem as if Chase went through them at an alarming rate. As she drove down the street, she saw that the big church on the corner was having a car wash to raise money to assist with the winter heating bills of the elderly. There was a line of cars that stretched around the block, waiting to be washed.

None of them looked that dirty.

Small towns were certainly interesting. A hundred feet from the Wright Here, Wright Now Café, she made the decision to stop. She wouldn't stay long but she was thirsty and an iced tea would do the trick. The weather was changing. Late morning, when she'd been working with Keith, it had been comfortably warm and sunny. But now it was hot and very humid. The wind was picking up.

She wondered if a storm was headed in their direction. She definitely shouldn't stay long at the café. Chase would need all the nails he could get in hopes of having the roof patched before the rain hit.

Raney opened the café door. Summer was behind the counter and she looked up and smiled. "Hi, Raney. Nice to see you again."

Raney took a stool at the counter. It was well past lunchtime and only two booths had customers. She eyed the pie case on the back counter. "Is that lemon meringue?" she asked.

Summer nodded. "Made fresh this morning."

"I'll take one," she said. If Chase could see this, he'd probably make some crack about her falling off the healthy-eater wagon. He liked to tease her.

That was what she'd been doing this morning. Teasing him. When she'd woken up, blonde Raney had taken over. Instead of getting dressed, she'd come downstairs in her pajamas. And then she'd gotten even bolder and deliberately leaned over to look at the books, knowing that he'd be able to see down her shirt.

He'd looked. And when he'd raised his hand and she'd thought he was going to touch her, she'd about melted.

But then he'd double-timed it to the kitchen. The image of what might have been had given her the courage to brush up against him.

His skin had been very warm. And he'd been very sexy with his bare chest and shorts.

But he'd left the kitchen quickly, as if he couldn't wait to get away from her. Blonde Raney had struck out.

Which was a silly thought because there was a distinct possibility that blonde Raney was all talk and no action. That, when push came to shove, if Chase was interested, she'd be the one running for the door. Her inexperience would catch up with her.

She'd dated Mike for three years before she'd married him three weeks after graduating from college. Two years later, at age twenty-four, she was already divorced. A divorcée.

Gun-shy. She'd made a mistake about Mike and that had caused her to question her judgment skills. And she'd chosen to play it safe for the past five years. But now, a month past her twenty-ninth birthday, that wasn't feeling right anymore.

Harry Malone had changed things. Sure. But this was even more than making good on a terrified promise in the dark that if she ever got away, she was going to live. Really live.

Even more because Chase Hollister heated her blood like nobody else had for a very long time.

The man was gorgeous, and sex appeal hung tight to his very nice rear end and broad shoulders. She ached to touch him.

The door to the café opened and Sheila Stanton walked in. She made eye contact with Raney and sat at the counter, one empty stool between them.

There was absolutely no reason to not be polite to her. Other than that she'd had her arms wrapped around Chase's neck. But Raney had been raised to be the bigger person. And Chase had left the grocery store with her, not Sheila. "Hi," Raney said.

Sheila smiled without showing any teeth. She ordered coffee but didn't touch it once Summer had poured it. Instead, she turned to look at Raney. "Where's that handsome husband of yours?"

"Home. Working on the house."

"Where was it that you two met?"

A skitter of alarm ran through her. She and Chase hadn't really practiced their story. "We met in St. Louis," she said. "Mutual friends introduced us."

"And what is it that you do there?"

She thought of Chase's comments of how information flowed in a small town. "Adult education," Raney lied. It was close enough to the truth that if Sheila happened to hear about the help she'd offered to Keith, the story should hold.

Raney opened her purse, pulled out some bills and looked for Summer. She was at the far end of the restaurant, leaning over a booth, wiping down the table. Her shirt had come untucked in the back and Raney could see a couple inches of smooth skin.

Holy hell. What was that? Summer had a bruise the size of a baseball on her lower back. Not fresh but rather the purple and green of an injury that had occurred sometime earlier.

She could feel the pie in her stomach start to roll. She'd had bruises like that after her encounter with Harry Malone. She straightened up when her ribs began their familiar ache.

Almost as if Summer could sense Raney's inspection, she stood straight, pulling her shirt down self-consciously. She turned and made eye contact with Raney.

There was a plea in Summer's eyes. For what, Raney had no idea. *Please don't tell anyone what you saw. Please don't ask me how I got it. Please help me.*

Raney quickly checked to see if Sheila had also been looking, but the woman was punching keys on her smartphone. Raney turned on her stool, just slightly, and mouthed the words, "Do you want to talk?"

Summer shook her head. Sharply. Definitively.

Okay, she wasn't asking for help. Raney had to assume it was one of the other choices. Perhaps Summer had fallen or run into something. Raney knew the possibility of that was slim. The woman had been beaten. But by who?

Her ex-husband? Was that what had sparked Summer's unfavorable response to the man that first morning that Raney and Chase had eaten breakfast at the Wright Here, Wright Now Café? But surely they'd been separated for some time if the divorce was already finalized. The bruise was old but not that old.

She understood the woman's reluctance to talk about it. After Harry Malone…well, she'd *had* to talk about it. The police had been relentless in their questioning. But every damn conversation had been painful, so painful.

When Summer was behind the counter, Raney pushed a twenty in her direction. "Thanks," she said, not waiting for change. "See you soon."

When she got back in her SUV, it was sticky hot, the black leather interior almost burning her bare legs. She turned the key, flipped on the air conditioner and put on her sunglasses.

She was halfway home and she still hadn't decided whether to tell Chase about what she'd seen. What would he say? "Mind your own business"? "We have our own problems"? She didn't think so. He would encourage

Summer to make a police report. But her ex was a cop. What a mess.

She saw a dark car approaching fast from behind. The road was narrow, and up ahead, it was double-striped, indicating a no-passing zone. She slowed, thinking she'd let it squeeze by now. She saw it move to the other lane and figured it would zip past her.

It got parallel and she caught a glimpse inside right before the driver cranked the wheel, making the vehicle swerve sharply toward her.

Raney jerked her own wheel. She felt her front right tire drop off the road, and suddenly she was rolling. She felt her head hit something and suddenly, she felt nothing at all.

Chapter Eight

Chase had sixteen nails left when he heard the rumble of an engine. He looked down and recognized Lloyd Doogan's old motorcycle. He was going very fast, and when he turned onto the lane leading up to the house, his back tire slid on the loose gravel.

What the hell? Chase was off the roof and down the ladder in seconds.

"You've got to come quick," Lloyd said. He was wringing his hands.

"What's wrong, Lloyd?" Chase asked.

"Your wife, that woman, she's hurt."

Chase felt his chest tighten up. "Raney?" he said. "Raney is hurt?"

"Yes. On the road."

Chase dropped his nail gun. In two strides he reached Lloyd's motorcycle. "We're taking this and I'm driving."

Less than five minutes later, he'd have known he was close even if Lloyd hadn't been yanking on his arm. There were three vehicles alongside the road, none of them his SUV, and all empty. He jammed on the brakes, got the bike stopped and was across the road in seconds.

It was a steep ravine and about fifteen feet down, his SUV was wheels up, resting on its driver's side. Four people, none that he recognized, were standing near the vehicle. One woman was squatting and it looked as if she was trying to talk to Raney.

Who was still inside. Slumped over the steering wheel. *Please let her be alive. Please. Please.*

He half slid down the rocky, weed-covered slope. He heard sirens coming closer but he wasn't waiting. He squatted next to the woman and knocked gently on the window. "Raney," he said.

"She's unconscious," said the woman.

"Raney, sweetheart," he said.

She opened her eyes, turned her head and gave him a weak smile.

"I guess she was just waiting for you," the woman said, awe in her voice.

Chase ignored the comment. He looked Raney in the eye. "Hang on," he said. "Just hang on. Help is coming. We're going to get this back on its wheels and get you out of there."

Her eyelids fluttered shut.

Chase pounded his hand on the frame of the SUV. "Stay with me, Raney. Stay with me."

He turned and saw four men in matching coats. Volunteer firefighters. He recognized one of them. Hank Beaumont had been their senior class president. He was pretty sure the man knew him, too, but fortunately, he wasn't interested in chatting it up. He was all business, his eyes focused on Raney.

"One person in the vehicle?"

"Yes," Chase said.

"Do we know the extent of her injuries?"

"No. Listen, we need to get this vehicle righted and get her out of there."

"Step back," Hank ordered.

Chase didn't move. "I'm a cop. St. Louis PD."

The man's eyes softened. "I know. I heard you were back in town, Chase. That was my mother-in-law who was behind you checking out at the grocery store. I'm guessing this is your wife, and I'm sorry about that, but it also means that you're not acting in any official capacity. So stand back and let us do our job."

Chase moved and shoved his hands in his pockets. Lloyd came up and stood next to him. "She's not dead," the man said.

No, she wasn't. But whoever had caused this accident was a dead man. Chase split his attention—shifting quickly from watching the four firemen right the vehicle to viewing the small crowd that had gathered.

It wasn't all that unusual for a perpetrator to hang around a scene. Whether it was in celebration or defiance that they could be in plain sight, or maybe some crazy need for closure, a good cop always watched the people at the scene. Sophisticated police departments caught it on film.

The Ravesville Police Department was neither sophisticated nor timely since they had yet to arrive.

But the SUV was upright and they were opening the driver's door. Hank had his head inside, talking to Raney.

Chase had waited long enough. He skirted around the small group and approached from the passenger side. Before anyone could stop him, he opened the door and slipped inside.

"Hey," he said softly.

She was still wearing her seat belt. It was pulled tight and he suspected she'd have some bruising. The air bag had inflated, then deflated, leaving a thick residue behind. It was on her shirt, her cheeks, her nose. He could see a red mark on her forehead, near the hairline on the left side. The skin had not broken but it looked as if she had a lump.

"Mrs. Hollister," Hank said, still at the door. "I'm going to put a neck collar around you, just as a precaution."

"Okay," Raney said. "But I didn't hurt my neck."

"You hit your head," Chase said, working hard to keep his tone neutral. He didn't want to scare her.

She lifted her fingers to her forehead. "I did?"

Hank reached in and fastened a cervical collar around Raney. It made her look even more delicate, and Chase fought down the anger that was threatening to cloud his ability to think. Focus. He needed to focus.

The firemen transferred her from the SUV to a gurney and an EMT took her vitals. Chase stood close enough that he could hear. Blood pressure, 123 over 77. That was fine. Pulse, 79. Maybe a little fast but that was to be expected. The EMT checked her eyes, her reflexes, asked about pain. Raney asked to sit up and the EMT agreed. Chase let out a breath.

Chase finally heard the sounds of an approaching siren and figured it had to be the responding officer. When the car came into view, it slowed quickly and pulled up close, blocking the road. The door opened and Gary Blake, Summer's ex, got out.

He walked up to Hank Beaumont, and Chase didn't see what he'd expected. Cops and firefighters were kindred spirits, especially in a small community. They showed up at all the same events, shared bad jokes and a general dislike for administration. But between Beaumont and Blake there was no friendly recognition, no casual camaraderie. The exchange seemed more forced, as if both men knew they had to do it and just wanted to get it over with as quickly as possible.

If Raney had a head injury, this had the potential to end badly for a number of reasons. Was she seconds away from blurting out that she was Lorraine Taylor and what had brought her to Ravesville? He hated to put pressure on her but the stakes were too high. "Remember," Chase whispered, barely moving his lips. "You're Raney Hollister."

"I know," she said, her tone almost sounding amused. "I'm not—"

Blake turned away from the fire chief and stepped toward Raney. He looked bored. "You were the driver," he said when he got in front of Raney.

Chase couldn't tell if it was a statement or a question.

"I need to see your license," Blake said.

It pissed Chase off that the man hadn't even bothered to inquire whether Raney was okay. But Chase kept his thoughts to himself. He and Raney were trying to stay under the radar. Mixing it up with the local police would only hurt those efforts.

Chase had pulled Raney's purse from the vehicle and now he handed it to her. Raney unzipped it and pulled out her billfold. Without hesitation she handed over her license, the Lorraine Hollister one she'd been given shortly after the wedding ceremony. Chase sent a silent prayer upward. At the time, he'd thought it was unnecessary to go to such extremes. He'd been irritated about waiting around for it. But now it might be what got them out of this.

Blake took it without comment and looked at it quickly.

He copied down the number onto the report he was making. He handed it back to Raney. Then he shifted his attention to Chase and narrowed his eyes. "You're that Hollister kid that everybody's been talking about."

That good-for-nothing, troublemaking Hollister kid. The man's tone said it all.

Chase rubbed his forehead where a raging headache that had started when he'd seen Lloyd's motorcycle flying down the road and intensified when he'd seen Raney with a cervical collar around her neck was simmering behind his right eyeball. He'd be ninety and the good people of Ravesville would still be talking about him.

"I've heard about your brother Bray," Gary Blake said.

"I imagine you have," Chase said.

"I'd have been better off if I'd have let him marry Summer Wright."

Neither Chase nor Raney responded. Blake didn't seem to notice.

"What happened here?" he asked.

"A car attempted to pass me. They got a little close and I moved over. My tires caught the edge of the road and my car rolled."

"How fast were you going?"

"The speed limit," she answered.

"Of course," Blake said, as if he couldn't care less. As if he'd formed an opinion and that was that. Raney had been either going too fast and paid the consequences or she was a hell of a poor driver.

Chase doubted it was either. She was simply not used to these roads and the driver had unfortunately picked the narrowest portion of the road to pass.

"Where's the other vehicle?" Blake asked.

Raney licked her lips. "I don't think it stopped. Perhaps they didn't see me lose control."

Now Blake looked at her. "That seems unlikely, doesn't it?" he asked.

"It certainly wasn't helpful," Raney said, not answering the question.

Blake looked at his watch. "Can you describe the other vehicle?"

"Black or dark blue. Some kind of SUV."

It was subtle but Gary Blake's jaw muscle jerked just a little. Most people wouldn't have seen it but Chase was a master interrogator. He always watched for the *tell*, the movement, the gesture, the nervous habit that said somebody was lying or just about to lie.

When Blake didn't offer anything up, Chase pushed. "Ring any bells?"

Blake looked bored. "There are a whole lot of black or blue SUVs that go through Ravesville on a given day."

He supposed that was true.

"Did you see the driver?" Blake asked. He'd put his pen down.

"The driver was wearing some kind of hooded sweatshirt and sunglasses. Had some scraggily facial hair."

Same small jerk of the jaw. Then Blake ran his pen down the paper. He looked up at Raney. "The fire chief said you bumped your head. Are you going to seek medical treatment?"

"No. I'm fine."

As far as Chase was concerned, the jury was still out on that one. Raney was doing well with Blake, not fumbling for answers. But head injuries were tricky. People had walked away from accidents fine and hours later, had blood clots and dropped dead.

Blake was only asking because he had to check a box on his report. He did that and then put his pen back in his pocket.

Chase couldn't decide if he was relieved that the incident wasn't going to blow their cover out of the water or really, truly pissed that Blake was such a lazy cop. He was acting as if they, as outsiders, were barely worth his time to fill out a report. Nobody was dead. He was still going to get to go home early.

Blake might not be interested in the other driver but Chase was. He intended to find him. His irresponsibility could have killed Raney.

Blake looked at Chase. "Planning on staying long in Ravesville?"

"Just long enough for me to get my mother's house ready to sell," he said.

"Brick Doogan was a son of a bitch."

He and Gary Blake were not going to bond over their common dislike. "Well, he's dead now."

Blake laughed, a deep bark of a sound. "Got that right," he said. He took a couple steps before turning back. "You two have a good day," he said. "I suggest you try going less than the speed limit, Mrs. Hollister."

"Good job," Chase murmured, as they watched Gary Blake walk away.

She'd just lied to a police officer. Deliberately withheld the truth. "Thank you," she said. She wasn't ready to say anything more.

"I know you told the paramedic that you didn't want to go to the hospital. I want you to reconsider."

She shook her head. "I'm okay. Really."

He didn't look happy. Well, he was likely to be significantly unhappier when he learned the truth. But she didn't intend to tell him here. She would do it at the house, where they could talk without being overheard.

She watched as the tow truck pulled away. It had Chase's SUV, which had a big dent in the passenger-side fender and a flat rear tire on that same side, and was taking it into Ravesville. Hank Beaumont came up and stood before them. "You two need a ride home?"

"Thank you," Chase said. He helped Raney into the backseat of the red SUV. It was a short drive home.

"Pleasure to meet you, Raney," Hank said. "Good luck with the recovery."

They were barely inside the house when Chase got on the telephone. She could only hear his side of the conversation but gathered enough to know that he was talking to someone about getting another vehicle. She closed her eyes, rested her head on the pillow and tuned the rest of the conversation out. When the call ended, he came into the living room.

She was lying on the couch, and he took the chair opposite of her. "Can I get you anything?" he asked.

She shook her head. "Isn't it going to look odd when we suddenly have a different vehicle here?"

He nodded. "We have to take that chance. It's better than not having wheels if we need to get out of here in a hurry. They're going to lay a paper trail so that the vehicle looks as if it belonged to Raney Smith who recently became Raney Hollister."

It was truly frightening how quickly resources could be marshaled to make something look different than it was. It made her wonder if anything in life was real.

And she had done her part to add to the deception. It was time for Chase to know the truth.

But before she could open her mouth, he asked, "Do you think you're up to going through it one more time?"

"Why?"

"Humor me," he said. "I'm going to find that other driver and make sure he understands what happened here."

Yeah, well, that might not be such a good idea. "Uh… Chase, the accident didn't happen exactly like I told Gary Blake."

Chapter Nine

There was a short pause, a very short one, before Chase said, "Okay."

He was probably a very good detective. She knew that she'd surprised him but he was controlling his response.

"How about we start at the beginning?" he said.

She stared at her hands, her fingers. It was funny how these things worked. While it had probably lasted less than a few seconds, she had a very vivid memory of seeing her hands wrapped tight around the steering wheel, her fingers tensed, as she saw the right front fender of the other vehicle veer toward her. "I probably should have been more forthcoming when I asked to borrow your vehicle. I do have a driver's license and I do drive, it's just that I don't very often. I don't even own a car. And so while I'm telling you this, I want you to keep that in the back of your mind. It's possible that I overreacted, that I made a mistake because I'm an inexperienced driver driving in an area that I'm not familiar with."

"Duly noted," he said. "Keep going."

She swallowed hard. "When I left here, I went to the hardware store," she said. "Damn." She looked up. "Your nails are in a sack in the backseat."

He held up a hand. "We'll worry about that later. Go on."

"It was hot and I was thirsty. And, while it may sound silly and sort of self-centered, I wasn't ready to come back yet. It's been a while since I've been able to do what I wanted. After I was moved to the safe house in Miami, my movements were very controlled. I could no longer go to events, or take long walks, or do any of the things that I wanted to do. So today it just felt good to be out on my own, without somebody watching my every move."

"Not self-centered," he said. "Not one bit."

"Anyway, I decided to go to the café to get an iced tea. Summer was working." She did not mention seeing the bruise on the woman's back. First things first. "While I was there, Sheila Stanton came in."

"Did the two of you talk?"

"She asked some questions, wanted to know how we met. I told her through mutual friends. It was a short conversation. Uncomfortable for me. I don't know how she felt. She's hard to read."

"Then what happened?"

"I left the café. I was coming back to the house. I saw the car behind me. I had my sunglasses on but I'm sure it was black or dark blue, maybe a very dark gray. It was coming up fast behind me and that did make me nervous. I slowed down a little, hoping that it would pass me. And when it did, it swerved toward me. I know I told Gary Blake that it got too close and I overreacted but that's only partially true. It's possible that the vehicle was deliberately trying to push me off the road."

She saw a quick change in his eyes before he shut it down. He'd gone into cop mode. "Tell me about the driver," he said, his voice still calm.

It made her feel sick to relive those few seconds. She held up one hand and put the other on her stomach. "You might want to keep your distance. The tea and pie I had at Wright Here, Wright Now may be making a return appearance."

Instead of stepping back, he moved forward and sat next to her on the couch. He wrapped an arm around her shoulder. "Take your time," he said.

She swallowed hard. "I told Gary Blake the truth about that. The hood was loose around his face, making it hard to see." She ran her hand through her short hair. "There is something that is nagging at me. Making me think that I missed something."

"What do you mean?"

"I can't explain any better than that. In the blink of an eye, I was taking in all these things. The driver turning the steering wheel. The front fender getting close. My tires losing traction. Too much stimuli. I'm worried that I may not have processed it right."

"You did fine. You're doing fine," he added.

She shook her head. "I should have let him hit me. That would have at least slowed him down. Maybe his vehicle would have been tangled up with mine."

"And you might have been hurt badly," he said. "You did the right thing. You tried to avoid the danger. If it was deliberate, I suspect he picked that spot carefully, because that's where the road is narrow and the drop-off steep."

She'd been thinking the same thing while she'd sat alongside the road, waiting for the Ravesville police to show up. But to hear him say it, to know that the action may have been so cold-blooded, made her blood turn to ice.

"Why didn't you tell Gary Blake the truth?"

She looked him in the eye. "When I first met Harry Malone, there was something about him that made me uneasy. I couldn't put my finger on it. He was pleasant, good with the clients and the rest of the staff at Next Steps thought he was wonderful. So I discounted my concerns. And look where that got me."

He didn't say anything but she could tell he was listening intently.

"In the dark, alone, a person has a lot of time to think. To make bargains. Promises. One of mine was to trust my instincts more. And my instincts tell me that Gary Blake isn't a good guy. I thought if I told him the truth, then our whole story might unravel and I didn't want to take that chance."

He smiled. "You've made me feel better."

"Why?"

"Because if you were thinking that clearly, I don't think that bump on your head can be all that bad. I'm going to give up trying to convince you to seek medical treatment."

She pulled away. "That's it? That's all you can say?"

He shook his head. "Of course not. But you need to know that I think you made the right decision. Blake may not be a dirty cop but he's a lazy one, and that's enough for me not to trust him, either."

"Do you think it's the people who tried to kill me before?" she asked, proud that she was keeping her voice mostly steady. "Have they found me?"

He tightened his strong arm around her shoulders and pulled her close. "I don't know," he said honestly. "If it was, I'm surprised that the driver didn't stick around to make sure he'd gotten the job done. But maybe others stopped so quickly that he got scared and got the hell out of there. But none of that matters because he isn't going to get another chance. I can guarantee you that."

"But if it is, then somebody knows that Raney Hollister is the old Lorraine Taylor. They can find out where we live. Come here."

"And if they do, I will handle it," he said calmly. "I will not let anyone hurt you. You have to believe me."

She suddenly felt very warm and she was very aware that they were alone in the house, unlikely to have any visitors anytime soon.

He was so close, his arm still wrapped around her shoulder. She turned her face. His lips were right there.

She should look away, get up, do something. But she stayed perfectly still. Waiting.

It was so still that she could hear the ticking of the kitchen clock, a whole room away. He took a breath. A deep one, making his broad chest expand.

"Chase," she said.

He let the breath out and carefully pulled his arm away. Her shoulder felt bare. Cold.

He got up. "Try to get a little rest. I won't let you sleep for long," he said. "Just as a precaution against a concussion."

Dr. Chase Hollister reporting for duty. "Chase," she said again.

He shook his head sharply. "I'll be outside."

CHASE DIDN'T HAVE any damn nails to hammer so he cranked up the chain saw and started attacking some trees. The wind had picked up and branches were whipping around, making the effort even more of a challenge. He held the chain saw above his head, slicing and dicing the unsuspecting limbs, and moving fast when they tumbled to the ground.

He was in trouble. He was getting sucked in by the unique combination that was all Raney. Trust and innocence along with a bold invitation to play.

When he'd talked to Dawson on the telephone about getting another vehicle, his partner had asked him how the assignment was going. Fine. That was what he'd said. He certainly couldn't tell his partner that he was a punch away from going down for the count.

He wanted her. In his bed. Under him, on top, hell, it didn't matter. As long as it happened. Lust was a dangerous thing. It had started small, probably about the time he'd seen her standing in the wedding dress, her sexy blond hair tousled from struggling with the gown, her breasts almost spilling out over the strapless top. It had spiked when he'd opened the door that first morning and seen her sprawled across the bed, her shorts short and her top riding up.

He'd managed to claw it back, to keep it at bay, until he'd seen Keith getting cozy with her at the dining room table. And now, after coming this close to losing her, his control was frayed.

She was injured. That should have been enough to cool his jets. But it didn't. Which was a big problem for her. If she was right, and it had been deliberate, then he needed to keep his head in the game and other parts checked at the door.

He kicked at some of the downed limbs. They might make some decent firewood. He started trimming the smaller branches off, then cutting the bigger limbs into manageable chunks. All the time his mind was racing.

A dark SUV.

Maybe Raney's inexperience had caught up with her and she'd overreacted. But that did not explain why the driver didn't stop. Unless he was uninsured or running from the law and didn't want to get involved in a police investigation. There were a thousand reasons why people chose not to get involved.

Whiz kid Keith's car had been black, too. Although not an SUV. Anyway, Raney was helping him. There was no reason for him to want to hurt her. Was there?

Was it even possible that it was one of Harry Malone's paid goons? If Malone was behind it, his people weren't going to get a second chance. He intended to stick to Raney like glue. He was going to put his libido on ice and she was never going to know that she had him in knots.

After Raney's confession, he'd sent Dawson a text. He wanted more firepower in the house, in more rooms, so that they couldn't ever be caught off guard.

He looked off to the west. The sky was still clear but the wind was picking up, blowing strong enough to toss the small branches around the yard. He picked up what he could and piled them around the corner of the porch, out of the breeze. His newly cut firewood went into a separate pile, closer to the house.

He wondered if Raney enjoyed a fire on a cold winter day. He had a gas fireplace in his apartment in St. Louis. His sterile little space had always suited him. Up until now.

He'd escaped from this house once. Why the hell was he letting it pull him back?

He threw more wood onto the pile. The house would be sold by winter. Another family would enjoy the fruits of his labor.

He put the chain saw away and locked the garage. When he returned to the house, it was quiet. No radio playing. No clatter of Raney's keyboard. He looked around downstairs.

Then he quietly walked upstairs. Knocked on her door. Waited. When she didn't answer, he didn't hesitate to turn the knob.

She was sleeping. This time on her back. Still sideways—head at ten, toes at four. One arm thrown above her head, the other close to her side. She was still wearing the clothes that she'd had on earlier.

She was beautiful. Even with a nasty bump on her forehead.

He knocked on the wall. She didn't move. Concerned, he approached the bed.

"Raney," he said softly.

No response.

"Raney." Loud this time.

She blinked, once, twice, then opened her eyes wide. She smiled at him. "You do not have to yell. I bumped my head, not my ears."

He wanted to laugh. "I knocked. You didn't wake up. I was worried."

"You told me to rest."

He sat down on the edge of the bed. "How do you feel?"

"I have a little headache. I suppose that's to be expected. My ribs that were already sore took a beating from the seat belt. But I was used to babying them so it will just be more of the same. I suspect I'll be fine by tomorrow."

"Do you want something to eat?"

She considered. "No, I don't think so."

She should eat. "I know how to heat up a mean cup of soup."

She smiled. "I suspect you do. But that can't be what you were expecting when you signed up for guard duty. You probably figured the witness could at least feed herself."

He'd expected to be bored out of his mind. Antsy to get back to the city. Irritated that Lorraine Taylor was keeping him in Ravesville. "I expected to make sure you stayed safe," he said. "Right now, I think that includes fixing dinner."

"Maybe just some tea and toast. I'll come down and get it."

He held up a hand. "Please. If I don't get to turn on the stove, at least let me bring it to you."

She nodded and he stood up. He thought about trying to convince her to eat more. But he knew that she was a grown woman—she could make decisions about what she wanted. If she got hungry in the middle of the night, she could get a snack.

He went down to the kitchen, heated the water and toasted the bread. Then he carried them upstairs. She was sitting up in bed.

He handed her the small plate with the two pieces of toast. He put the tea on the table next to the bed. He was more grateful than ever that Brick had purchased a mattress and box spring in anticipation of Lloyd's return home. Raney's bed was really coming in handy now.

"What are your plans for the night?" she asked, taking small bites.

"I'm going to tape up some of the rooms. I want to get them ready to paint." Maybe he'd even work up the courage to go into Brick's bedroom. He'd take a big garbage sack and just start pitching. While he didn't feel the man in the rest of the house, he suspected that would change when he entered the bedroom.

"I'll be ready to help by tomorrow. For sure," she added.

Just having her in the house helped. But he couldn't admit that. "You better be," he said, winking at her. "There's woodwork that needs stripping."

HE'D PUT BUTTER and peanut butter on her toast, just the way she liked it. Which meant that he'd been watching how she fixed her breakfast.

What the hell did that mean?

More than she could contemplate with a nagging headache. She ate toast and drank half of her tea. Then she pushed herself out of bed, took off her clothes and put on her pajamas. A trip across the hall accomplished all other necessary tasks, including brushing her teeth and washing her face.

On the way back to her bed, she opened her window. The room was warm, warmer than it had been the night before. The wind that rushed in was not significantly cooler, but she left the window open anyway. It would likely cool off later.

She crawled back into bed, tossing her new sheets to the end of it. It was not yet seven o'clock and she was settling in for the night. Like an old lady. All she needed was a cat and a cane.

You rolled off a road today, she reminded herself. *You're entitled to a little TLC.*

It had been the same way when she'd escaped from Harry Malone. She'd craved sleep but the police had been insistent upon talking to her. She could still remember sitting in cold rooms, with brown laminate tables and hard chairs. There were times when she'd simply laid her head down on the table and closed her eyes.

Cup of coffee, Ms. Taylor? Perhaps a sandwich? They'd pretended to be concerned about her needs and her welfare, but what they'd really wanted was her testimony. By the time they'd finished with her, she'd been just about finished, one nerve short of a full-blown meltdown.

She'd gone home and slept for three days.

Tonight, she thought another eight hours would take care of things nicely. Gary Blake certainly hadn't been interested in having a prolonged conversation with her. By the way he'd been looking at his watch, she'd gotten the impression that he had a pressing engagement and didn't want to be late.

On the opposite side of the spectrum, Chase had been wonderful. Since the moment he'd arrived at the scene, he'd been quietly capable. She'd felt bad about his SUV but she could tell that he truly wasn't concerned about the vehicle.

Tomorrow she'd hit the ground running. She closed her eyes.

And didn't open them again until she heard something hit the house. She sprang up in bed, her back hitting the plaster wall. The wind was howling and lightning was splitting the sky.

Heart racing, she reached for the lamp. She caught the shade with the back of her hand and barely managed to keep it upright. She felt for the switch, flipped it, and nothing happened. She flipped it again and again.

Something hit the house again and she saw movement

in the corner. She screamed, wrapped her hand around the base of the lamp, jerked hard, felt the cord pull from the wall and cocked her arm.

She would fight until her very last breath.

Chapter Ten

Chase woke up to a woman's screams. He grabbed his gun and was off the couch and halfway up the stairs before he realized that the light in the kitchen that he'd left on was now off. He wasn't surprised. It was storming and the damn electricity was always going out.

He charged ahead, listening for another scream. He had only heard one.

He turned the knob of Raney's room, pushed the door open with his foot and swung through the doorway. The room was absolutely dark. He couldn't see a damn thing.

He heard the roll of thunder. Counted. Got to two before a spear of lightning brightened the sky. Long enough for him to see Raney on the corner of the bed, her knees drawn up to her chest, holding the old lamp in her hand, as if she was going for the shot-put record. Her eyes were huge.

Then the room went dark again.

"Raney?" he said.

She didn't answer. He took a step toward the bed. "Honey, it's okay. Just a little Missouri storm."

Still no answer. He got close enough that he could touch her. For a minute, he thought the damn bed was shaking. Then realized it was her.

He forgot all about keeping his distance. He sat on the bed, gently disengaged the lamp from her fingers, set it back on the nightstand and pulled her into his arms. She was all bare arms and legs, and when he tucked her head into his chest, he caught a whiff of mint from her toothpaste. "There, there," he said. "Nothing to be afraid of." He wrapped both arms around her and gently rocked her.

After a long minute, her shaking subsided. But he didn't let go. Her skin was so soft. She smelled so good.

He moved one hand up to the nape of her neck and ran his fingers through the soft, sexy hair. He heard her breath catch.

Would she tell him to stop?

Not yet, he willed. He needed to hold her.

"What happened?" he whispered.

"I heard something and then I thought I saw something in the corner and I freaked out."

He strained his eyes toward the dark corner. He needed another bolt of lightning. "I don't see…"

"I think it was the curtain. The wind was whipping it around. I…should not have screamed. It reminded me of…before."

"Before what?"

She didn't answer for a long minute. He heard the rumble of thunder and waited for the lightning. At the exact moment it struck, she lifted her head and looked him in the eye. Her eyes were bright, shiny with unshed tears. He gathered her closer as the darkness settled around them again. The wind was really howling now.

"Shortly after Harry Malone abducted me, he left me in this small room. There was no bed, just an old two-drawer metal filing cabinet that was completely empty.

I slept on the floor. It was a beat-up old wooden floor. Worse than the floors in this house," she added.

He steeled himself. She was trying to lighten the mood but he had a feeling that whatever was coming, it was going to be hard to hear. Another rubble of thunder shook the house and Raney jerked. He gathered her just a little closer.

"It started to storm while he was gone. It was a horrific storm and the entire time, I kept praying that the wind would blow hard enough that the apartment or the house, whatever I was in, would come apart. And then someone would know I was there. Someone would see me."

"What happened?"

"He came back. Just as the storm seemed to hit its peak. I can still see him flinging open the door so hard that it hit the wall. He was drenched. Tonight I heard something hit the house and then I saw the movement and for a minute, I was back there."

He wanted to kill Harry Malone. "What happened when he came back?"

She sighed. "He was angry about something. I'm not sure what. All I know is that he punched and kicked me, adding to the assortment of bruises, bumps and cracked ribs that I already had."

Unconsciously, he stroked her ribs through her thin shirt. The idea of a man taking his foot and kicking her made him realize that killing Harry Malone would be too nice. He was going to break every one of his ribs first. Maybe his legs, too.

"I'm sorry," he said simply.

"He never…you know."

"I read the report," he said, which was why he knew

it was a damn miracle that this was the first flashback that he'd witnessed. She hadn't been raped but she'd been brutalized, kicked like a rabid dog.

"Really," she said, as if she were trying to reassure him, "I was one of the lucky ones. I got away. Those other poor women didn't."

"But you're making sure he pays for his sins. You're getting vindication for each of them."

"You know he took my picture?"

"I did know that," he said, keeping his tone neutral.

"The first time he did that, I didn't know what to think. He'd tossed me into this barren room and was acting like I'd come for a photo shoot. 'Stand up. Sit down. Put your arms above your head.' It was bizarre. He must have taken eight, maybe ten different shots. And with no explanation, he left. It was crazy, just crazy."

The storm was hitting its peak in intensity. Lightning cracked, briefly brightening the room. "Rain is really coming down hard now," he said, wanting to give her a chance to change the subject.

She didn't take the bait. "The next time he came back, he showed me pictures of the other women. I still didn't get it at first. Because the women looked okay. Scared, sure. But not hurt. In a crazy way, I was hopeful that maybe I wasn't all alone. That maybe the other women were down the hall. But he kept making me look at more pictures on his camera. And the women started looking worse. Bruised. Dirty. So tired. I started to get it. And then I saw the pictures where they were dead." Her voice had cracked at the end.

"All part of his psychological torture," he said.

"Yeah. He wanted me to know what my fate was going to be. It was so horrible to know that these women had been alive and then killed, and to know that the same thing was going to happen to me."

"He was pretty sure of himself," Chase said. The son of a bitch had underestimated Raney. He'd only shown her the pictures because he was so confident that she'd never get away.

"He told me that he was a storyteller. That the women in the pictures were characters in his story and that he liked me so much that he wanted me to have my own story. It became very clear that he got off on showing me what had happened to the others."

He could hear the anguish in her voice. He bent his head, brushed a kiss across her shoulder. "It's over, Raney."

She sucked in a deep breath. "All I knew is that if I didn't find a way to get away from him, it wouldn't be long before another victim was looking at pictures of me."

He put his hand under her chin and gently turned her face. If there had been light, he would have been able to look her in the eye. "But he underestimated you," he said. "You were smarter and braver than he could have ever anticipated. You got away when he was absolutely confident that you couldn't."

"Never underestimate the power of nail polish," she said, her tone solemn.

When he'd read the report, he'd been both fascinated and impressed. He wanted to hear her explanation but didn't want her to have to relive it if it was painful. "You didn't, that's what is important."

"It was all I had. When Malone grabbed me as I was walking home from Next Steps, he took my purse and my cell phone. I never saw them again. But he didn't think to check my pockets. And I had a bottle of topcoat. I'd polished my nails at home that morning but had been running late and decided I'd add the topcoat—that's the final coat that makes the nails shiny—during my dinner break. I did that and dropped it in my skirt pocket."

"And you figured out how to use that as a weapon."

"Not at first. There was nothing in the room but that damn empty filing cabinet. I tried to pick it up, thinking maybe I could throw it at him, but there was no way. I stared at it for hours until I finally figured out that it was put together with bolts and screws. And I could use the washers, the flat metal part that secures the screw."

"But you didn't have any tools."

"No. Not even a darn plastic knife. Malone wasn't stupid. I had to use my fingers. At one point, I was totally freaked out because I sliced my finger up and it was bleeding and there was blood on the screws that I couldn't get off. I was so afraid that he was somehow going to see that. And there was no way that I could get some of the screws loose to get to those particular washers. But I finally managed to get six. Then I used the topcoat to bind them together, so that they made a hard round stack. Each washer was thin and so six together didn't make much but I thought it might be enough."

"For?" he asked.

"To mess up the lock. Before he came into the room, I could hear him walk down the squeaky hallway and then flip the bolt lock on the outside of the door. When he left, same routine in reverse. My plan was to stuff my contraption into the bolt-lock hole so that when he turned the lock to throw the cylinder, the cylinder would get jammed and the lock wouldn't catch."

"Smart."

"I don't know about that. But it was the only plan I had and time was running out. He would occasionally give me some water but no food. That's what he used the filing cabinet for. He would set my water on it. Isn't that crazy? He didn't care about killing me but he didn't want to set my water on the floor?"

"The mind can be very twisted," he said.

"All I knew is that I was getting very weak, and based on the pictures that I'd seen of those other women, I thought my time was running out. My plan was full of holes. I needed to smear a fresh layer of topcoat on one end of my washers just at the right time so that when I inserted them into the hole, the polish would adhere to the back of the lock receptacle. Assuming I managed that, my washers needed to be thick enough to keep the door from locking. So many unknowns, not the least of which was that I needed to get near the door without him seeing me."

"But you knew you had to do it."

"Yes. And it helped that he was a man of patterns. I knew he would come in, set the water down on the filing cabinet and then start posing me for pictures. He always kept the door open when he was with me, which told me that there was no one else around. I'm sure he assumed that if I tried to escape that it would be relatively easy to overpower me. Anyway, he had a favorite pose. I would have to stand up, put both hands around my neck and tilt my head just so, to make it look as if I was strangling myself."

Malone was a sick bastard.

"So I did it. Just like I had before. But then I pretended

that I'd somehow choked myself. I started gagging and coughing and I was doing such a job of it, I actually thought I was going to throw up. I knew that Malone was a germ freak. At Next Steps, he would sanitize the workstation before he would use the computer or the telephone. He wouldn't eat food that somebody had left in the break room because he hadn't seen it get prepared. I was counting on the fact that it was going to gross him out and he'd move away. It did and he turned away. Long enough for me to shove the washers in the hole."

"What happened when he left?"

"I was shaking so hard I could barely move. I heard him flip the lock like always. It didn't catch. He opened the door, flipping the lock back and forth. The cylinder was working fine, of course. Then he looked into the hole. When you look into a dark hole, you can't see anything. He poked his finger in and maybe felt something, maybe didn't, but he just looked irritated, not suspicious of me. He closed the door. I heard his footsteps. I figured he was going in search of a flashlight or something. I didn't wait around to find out. I got out of that room fast. Made it to the street. Didn't know where I was but knew it was a poor urban area. It was nighttime. I just started running as fast as I could. I turned a corner and flagged down a car. I'm surprised they stopped because I was a mess. But they did. And the rest is history."

"Amazing," Chase said.

"He would have realized very quickly that I was gone. Maybe he tried to come after me and catch me. Maybe he simply decided to cut his losses and run. The police caught him in his car. They think that he was on the way to a small private airstrip. He has his own plane and perhaps was contemplating leaving the country. Of course, he denied everything. And he'd been smart. Besides kicking me, he'd never physically touched me. There was none of my DNA on him, just at the apartment."

But the jury would believe her. They would hear from her, from the old couple who picked her up on the road, from the detectives who had taken her original statement. They would hear from the forensics experts who could place her in that apartment because of the blood she'd left behind in the filing cabinet.

Lightning flashed and he hoped to see peace in her eyes. But he saw something else, something more.

Heat. Want.

"Chase," she said, her voice a mere whisper. "Stay with me."

He knew all the reasons why it was a bad idea. But none of that mattered. What did was that Raney, sweet Raney with her soft skin and sexy hair, was in his arms.

He leaned in, found her mouth and kissed her. Her mouth was warm and wet and when he settled in, it seemed as if he'd been waiting a lifetime for kisses like this.

He framed her face, running the pads of his thumbs across her cheeks, her little ears, her long, pretty neck. The kisses were long and succulent and he felt as though he could jump tall buildings.

The storm outside was moving away, leaving only the occasional quiet rumble of thunder in the distance. "Raney?" he whispered, giving her one last chance.

In answer, she put his hand on her breast.

He made love to her. And when she came apart in his arms, and he quickly followed her over the edge, he felt something shift in his soul, and knew that nothing would ever again be the same.

RANEY DOZED AND when she woke up, the room was dark and she was very warm. It dawned on her that Chase Hollister made one hell of a blanket.

He was naked and wrapped around her.

Delicious. The sex had been better than red-velvet cake with cream-cheese frosting. And that was saying something in her world. He'd been intensely focused on learning her body, understanding her needs, pleasuring her.

That could easily go to a girl's head.

She stretched a leg and he pulled her in just a little tighter. "Doing okay?" he asked, his voice husky with sleep. "Does this hurt your ribs?"

"No, it's fine," she said. "It doesn't sound as if it's raining anymore."

"Uh-huh," he said.

Would he roll over, roll away, now that she no longer needed his comfort? Sex with her husband had been like that. They'd do it and he'd no more than finish up before he'd flop on his back with his hands folded on his chest and be snoring in five minutes. Oblivious to her needs.

She waited. Counted to one hundred. Did it twice more. "Chase?" she said.

"Yes?"

"I...I don't want you to think that you have to keep holding me. I'm really okay."

He sighed. "So you're chatty after sex?"

Was she? "Uh...I don't think so."

"Good. Talking takes energy and I'm trying to conserve mine." He flexed his hips and she could feel him pressing into her. He appeared to be recovering just fine.

"For?" she asked, letting blonde Raney have full reign.

He neatly flipped her on her back. Still on his side,

he bent his head to her breast and took a nipple into his mouth. Heat arced through her core and a soft moan escaped.

He lifted his mouth, barely breaking contact. "For this."

Heat. Need. Blind want. It raced through her. She moved quickly, bringing a hand up, placing it flat on his chest, pushing hard. He went with it, falling onto his back.

This man wasn't oblivious. He was terribly sexy and wonderfully aroused. She straddled him. "I'm ready. But this time I get to drive."

Chapter Eleven

The next time Raney woke up, the room was flooded with light. Natural light. It was morning. She wondered if the electricity had come back on. The cord of the lamp lay on the floor, disconnected from the outlet.

Chase was still wrapped around her. His knees tucked behind her knees. His arm casually draped across her stomach. His chin resting on her head.

Perfect.

"Good morning," he whispered.

She wondered how long he'd been awake. She hoped she hadn't snored. "Hi," she said. "What time is it?"

"I'd say about seven. Ready for coffee?"

"Of course. 24/7."

He laughed. "My kind of girl."

Was she Chase Hollister's girl? Lover, sure. But girl? That somehow seemed more intimate, more special. She didn't have a great deal of experience with "the morning after." She'd dated one man after her divorce and they'd slept together but never spent the night together. It had been at his apartment and she'd always gotten up and left.

He moved, sitting up in bed. Blonde Raney shifted onto her back so that she could see him. He'd been pretty damn magnificent in the dark. And he was even more so in the light of day. He had his back to her. His sleek shoulders were broad and his back was all firm with muscle that narrowed down nicely to his waist.

She raised up on an elbow, wanting to get a better look. He shifted suddenly, as if just realizing that he was naked. But before he could pull up the sheet, she saw his leg. Saw the fresh scar.

"What happened?" she whispered.

He put his hand over the injury. "Pretty ugly, I know."

"Tell me," she said.

"About six weeks ago, I took a bullet in the thigh. Got lucky in that it didn't break a bone but I had a whole lot of muscle damage."

"Did you have surgery?"

"Right away. I was bleeding badly."

"And you've been crawling up and down off the roof," she said. *And doing other gymnastics in bed*, she silently added, feeling guilty.

"It's fine. The activity strengthens it."

"Why didn't you say anything?" she asked.

She was prepared for him to tell her that it wasn't any of her business. Instead, he looked her in the eye and said, "I didn't want you to be worried that I wasn't a hundred percent capable."

If she had been, that misbelief would have been well and truly debunked at this point. "I think you're one of the most capable people I know," she said.

"I don't want things to be awkward between us," he said, his voice giving no clue as to how he was feeling.

Awkward as in he was concerned that she might not ever let him leave the bed again?

Awkward as in she might be willing to pay for another night like the previous one?

Or awkward in that she might think that last night had meant something to him?

"It won't be awkward." Blonde Raney was such a liar.

"You're sure?"

"Absolutely," she said, swallowing hard.

"I'll get that coffee, then," he said. "Want some toast, too?"

She nodded. Anything that would keep him out of the room longer. She needed to get control.

She supposed what had happened last night had been inevitable. There had been a strong physical attraction between her and Chase since the moment they'd met. They weren't naive teenagers caught up in the moment. They were adults, responding to stimuli, acting in response and fully capable of taking responsibility for their own actions.

It sounded like a dull biology experiment when in reality it had been stunningly beautiful and absolutely exhilarating.

But he didn't want awkward.

She could give him that.

When he came back, he was carrying two steaming cups of coffee in one hand and a plate of toast in the other. He had pulled on a pair of gym shorts.

She reached for the cup, took too fast a sip and burned her tongue.

"Careful," he said.

Somebody should have told her that last night. Before she'd jumped his bones.

He got back into bed and set the plate of toast between them.

She chewed, swallowed and drank her coffee. He did the same. When he was finished, he set down his cup on the nightstand.

He gave her a long look, as if waiting for her questions to commence.

She smiled at him. "You better get started outside."

IT WAS JUST before lunch that he saw two vehicles coming down the road. Both SUVs, similar to what he'd been driving the day before. He put down the scraper that he'd been using to peel the old paint off the porch.

He'd switched jobs this morning after taking a quick peek at the roof to assess the damage done by the storm. Fortunately, it was minimal. Yesterday he'd finished removing all the old shingles and had tacked down the paper. Right before Raney had called him to dinner, thinking it felt like rain, he'd quickly finished covering the work with plastic that Gordy's son-in-law had thoughtfully provided.

He probably could have laid shingles this morning but oddly enough, he hadn't felt all that centered, hadn't felt as if he wanted to be thirty feet in the air.

Raney Taylor had rocked his world, to coin an overused phrase. She'd been warm and wet and when she'd straddled him the second time and said she wanted to drive, he'd thought, *You can take me anywhere. Anytime. Just don't get up.*

In the dark, with her body snuggled up against him, he'd been able to push the second thoughts away. Then this morning, when she'd seen his scar, he'd been truly afraid for just a brief moment that she was going to be repulsed or maybe even scared to be with someone touched by violence when her own life had been torn apart by the same.

But she'd recovered quickly, leaving him to fumble for the right thing to say. He'd settled for *I hope this won't make things awkward* when what he should have said was *I think I'm in over my head.*

So he'd escaped outside. But hadn't gone far. Just in case she happened to stick her head out the door wanting to talk. But she hadn't done that. And now he was going to have to face his partner and the chief of police and pretend as though nothing had happened.

He wiped the sweat out of his eyes and kept his stance relaxed. He had his gun in a holster, safely hidden from view by his long shirt. When the first SUV pulled into the lane and he saw that Dawson was driving, he relaxed for real. His partner got out, looked around and stood with his hands on his hips. "According to my GPS, this road doesn't exist."

Chase smiled. "So how did you find me?"

"Called your cell phone. Which you didn't answer. So I stopped at the café on the corner. A gorgeous redhead with hair to her waist gave me good directions. How's Raney?"

"She's...she's good." Chase had never been the type to kiss and tell and right now would be a hell of a bad time to start. The door of the second vehicle opened. It was the chief.

Under normal circumstances, the man would never have made a two-hour trip to deliver a car. But there was nothing normal about this situation. Raney's testimony was critically important. To the case. To the chief.

Chase shook the man's hand. "Thanks for the vehicle," he said.

"No problem," the chief said. "We won't stay long but I'd like to talk to Raney about the incident yesterday."

Chase almost said no, that he didn't want Raney to have to go through it again. "She's inside," he said. He wasn't sure what she was doing. Maybe she'd gone back to bed. They hadn't gotten all that much sleep the night before.

He held the door open for Dawson and Chief Bates. "Raney," he yelled as he pulled the door shut.

She came from the kitchen. She had on the same tight blue jeans as yesterday, this time with a white T-shirt. "Yes." She stopped short when she saw Dawson and the chief.

"Hello," she said.

"Hi, Raney" from Dawson.

"I was sorry to hear about your trouble yesterday, Ms. Taylor." This from the chief.

Raney nodded. "I'm sorry about the SUV and that you had to make a special trip here."

The chief waved his hand. "Can you tell me what happened?"

She didn't look surprised. She'd heard Chase give Dawson the shorthand version yesterday on the phone. Probably knew that he'd no doubt related that to the chief, but that wasn't going to be good enough. "Of course."

She told her story. The going to town, stopping for a drink at the café, leaving, driving, seeing the vehicle behind her.

The chief interrupted. "When did you notice the car?" he asked sharply.

Raney swallowed. "Not long before it tried to pass me."

The man nodded. "Go on."

"I saw it pull out and I assumed it was going to pass. When it got even with my SUV, it swerved in my direction. I believe it's possible that it was a deliberate attempt to run me off the road. Unfortunately, I didn't realize the shoulder was soft and narrow. My instinct was to avoid getting hit."

"So you saw the driver?" the chief barked.

Chase moved and stood behind Raney's chair. He saw Dawson's eyes widen but he ignored it. Bates might be the chief but he wasn't going to bully Raney.

"I did see the driver. But not in a helpful way," she said, her voice still even.

If the chief was getting to her, she wasn't showing it. She pushed her chair back, refilled her water, taking her time. She was going to make a terrific witness.

She sat back down. "I saw hands. I caught a glimpse of the driver's face and some facial hair but he was wearing a hood, maybe a hooded sweatshirt. It was all so fast. Once I felt my front tire go off the road, I knew I was in trouble and I was concentrating on that."

"You think it was deliberate?" the chief asked, drumming his index finger on the table.

"It seemed to me that he didn't just turn the wheel, he cranked it. And he surely had to know that I ran off the road, but he didn't stop."

The chief didn't say anything for a long minute. Finally, he stood. "Well, again, I'm glad you're okay. Let's head back, Detective," he said, looking at Dawson. He switched his gaze to Chase and inclined his head toward the door.

Chase got the message. The chief wanted to talk to him outside.

They were almost at the vehicles when the chief spoke. "I'm damn concerned about this," he said.

Chase waited.

"What do you think, Detective Hollister?"

"I think Raney got lucky, that we all did. But we don't have any reason to believe that Harry Malone knows that she's here, right?"

Both Dawson and the chief nodded.

"Then, I don't think we should go crazy. The police here aren't going to be helpful and I can't push the issue without raising a whole lot of suspicion. I think we need to be satisfied that our initial plan was a good one and go forward. I won't let Raney out of my sight. She won't go anywhere by herself and I won't leave her alone here."

The chief nodded. "I think you're right," he said. He shook his head. "I sure as hell hope you're right," he added. He took a step toward the car, then stopped. "Do you mind if I use your bathroom before we leave?"

Was the man intending to go back inside and badger Raney? But he couldn't say no. "Up the stairs. Second door on the right."

He started to follow the man inside when Dawson grabbed his arm, hard enough to swing him around. "What the hell?" Chase asked, shaking him off.

"Yeah, what the hell as in what the hell is going on here?" Dawson asked.

Chase said nothing. The silence dragged on.

"Oh, man. I knew it," Dawson said finally. "She is our *witness*."

Chase grit his teeth and tried to remember that Dawson was his very best friend. "I know what she is. And I know what I'm doing."

"Let me stay here with her," Dawson said. "I'll provide the protection."

"Don't be ridiculous. Isn't your wife about to have a baby?"

Dawson nodded. "But I'm worried about you. This is a woman who's been through a lot. Maybe not seeing things clearly. Maybe using…"

The door of the house slammed and the chief walked toward them.

"You," he finished under his breath.

By the time the chief reached them, Dawson had opened the trunk and was unloading the guns that Chase had requested. Rifles and handguns and all kinds of extra bullets. The three men carried everything up onto the porch.

They walked back to the SUV and the chief got behind the wheel. "Check in regularly," he said.

Chase nodded. He made eye contact with Dawson. Gave him another nod. Then he watched the vehicle drive down the lane, make the turn onto the road and finally disappear from sight.

He would protect Raney. He would not lose sight of that.

RANEY STOOD AT the window and watched Chase say goodbye to Detective Roy and Chief Bates. It was not even noon and already she was thinking about a nap.

This morning, she'd stayed in bed for a full half hour after Chase ran out. She had rolled over and, like a crazy woman, sniffed the sheets. She could smell him. Smell them.

The sex had been amazing. Beyond that.

It hadn't been blonde Raney or brunette Raney in his

arms. It had just been Raney. She'd lost the ability to plot or plan a response. It had just happened.

And happened again.

Holy moly.

And then he'd brought her coffee, which made him a bit of a prince. And then it had gotten awkward, just exactly what he'd said he'd hoped they could avoid.

When she'd finally gotten out of bed and showered, she'd gone downstairs and heard him on the porch. She'd peeked out the living room window but hadn't had the courage to open the door.

She wanted him to know that she didn't have any expectations that it was going to happen again. That she wasn't waiting for a marriage proposal. That she understood they were in unusual circumstances and that no precedent had been set.

She wanted him to know that he was off the hook.

She wanted him to know that it had been pretty damn terrific.

When she'd heard him yelling her name, she'd hurried from the back, thinking, *Great, he's ready to talk.* She had been surprised to see his partner and the chief of police. She hadn't heard the vehicles pull in. The chief had been a little intense but she supposed that was a job-related characteristic. On the other end of the spectrum was Gary Blake, who acted as though he couldn't care less.

If she had to choose, she'd take intensity any day. And having Chase there had made a difference. When he'd stood behind her, strength had radiated from his core and she'd suddenly felt as if there wasn't anything the chief could throw her way that was going to knock her off her stride.

Too bad she couldn't put Chase Hollister in her pocket when she was on the witness stand. She was going to be all on her own.

The only time she'd been a little nervous was when the chief had walked out with Chase and his partner, clearly interested in having a conversation that didn't include her. She knew they were discussing their plan and whether her staying in Ravesville was still a good idea.

When she'd heard the chief come back inside, she'd prepared herself for bad news. It was hard to believe that just days ago, she'd been complaining to Officer Vincenze about coming here, and now she couldn't quite imagine leaving.

The house needed them. She could feel it.

She'd relaxed when she'd realized that the man was simply using the bathroom. She was staying.

She heard the front door and turned. Chase walked in. "Doing okay?" he asked.

She nodded. "I like your partner. He's got a quiet competence about him."

It was Chase's turn to nod. "He's worried about me."

That surprised her. "Why?"

"Because he sensed the dynamic has changed between the two of us."

Well, she suspected that wasn't exactly what Detective Roy had said. At Next Steps, she frequently overheard young men talk to other young men about their women. Granted, Chase and his partner were older and the vocabulary might have improved but he didn't have to draw her a picture.

"I'm sorry," she said simply.

He shook his head sharply. "I am not sorry. Let's be clear on that."

She felt her insides melt. "We were both consenting adults," she offered.

"You were in a vulnerable position," he said, trying to give her a reason.

She thought about what blonde Raney would say and realized it was exactly what brunette Raney would have. She and Mike hadn't had an honest relationship. She was never going to do that again, regardless of what color her hair was. "I wanted you," she said.

She saw the muscle in his jaw jerk. "Wanted. As in past tense?"

She looked him in the eye. "Want. As in present tense."

He grabbed her hand and pulled her toward the stairs. "Like I told you, I'm a literate man. I understand the difference."

Chapter Twelve

They spent the afternoon making love and dozing. It was less frenzied than the night before and when she let him drive, he felt as if he had a chance of keeping things under control. When she took over the wheel and took him in her mouth, he thought his head was going to pop off his neck.

"I like it when you hold me like this," she said.

He was spooned around her, keeping her tucked close. "Self-preservation," he said. "Left to your own devices, you take up the whole bed."

"I do not," she protested.

"Yes, you do," he said drily. "Head at ten o'clock, feet at four. This way I keep you at twelve and six and we're all much happier."

She was quiet for a long time. He thought maybe she'd fallen back to sleep. But then she shifted. "I need you to know. I am happier than I have been in a long time. Even though, as recently as yesterday, someone may have deliberately tried to harm me, maybe even kill me, I'm still happier."

"Me, too," he admitted. Although he certainly wasn't settled when he let his mind drift back to the feelings he'd had when he'd approached her overturned SUV.

Over the years, he'd investigated accident scenes. Every cop had. And some of them had been gruesome. And as family members and loved ones had arrived, he'd seen the tears, the anguish. He'd thought he'd understood. Now he wasn't so sure.

Bone-deep fear was an interesting emotion.

He kissed the back of her neck. "I asked Dawson to quietly investigate blue, black or gray SUVs registered to male drivers within a 30-mile radius of Ravesville. I didn't figure that Gary Blake was going to do that."

"Thank you," she said. "Now I'm going to get up and make some dinner."

He cupped her breast, ran the pad of his thumb across her nipple. With his other hand, he pulled her tight up against his erection. "How hungry are you?"

She turned in his arms and kissed him, her tongue in his mouth. "Very," she murmured.

He flipped her on her back and entered her with one sharp thrust. She let out a sigh of pleasure. "Dinner can wait," she whispered and he began to move.

THE NEXT DAY, Chase went back up on the roof and started shingling in earnest. Around three in the afternoon, he saw Gordy Fitzler's truck turn into the driveway. He got off the roof and met the man as he got out of his truck.

"I heard about your wife's accident in town. I hope she's okay."

"She's good. Thanks for asking."

"Lucky girl," Gordy said.

It reminded him of what he'd said when he and Dawson had first discussed Lorraine Taylor. She'd been lucky a couple times now. When was that luck going to run out?

"You're making good progress," Gordy said.

"Good product," he said, trying to focus on the pallets of shingles that were still on the ground. It was his job to make sure that Raney's luck didn't run out.

"My son-in-law and daughter are doing a good job," Gordy agreed. "Speaking of them, that's why I'm here. I turn seventy-five tomorrow and tonight my kids are set on having a big party for me at the Wright Here, Wright Now Café. When I mentioned to them that I'd seen you, they told me that there's still room for a couple more before we start to have trouble with the fire marshal for overcrowding the place. I know it's very late notice but I'd be pleased to have you and your wife attend."

This man had made a difference in his life. He wanted to go. The possibility that someone had deliberately tried to harm Raney hung over his head. But he would be by her side. And she loved getting out, having the freedom to go somewhere. "We'd be honored," he said.

Gordy's face broke out into a big smile. He took off his ball cap and wiped the sweat off his forehead with the back of his hand. "Six o'clock. Come hungry. I hear the Wright sisters are going to make it something special. And no gifts. I've got my children and grandchildren, everything a man could ever want."

THERE WAS SOMETHING very comforting about being in the big old house and listening to Chase and his nail gun on the roof. *Tap, tap, tap. Tap, tap, tap.*

She was tackling her own project with vigor, very grateful for the big garbage cans that Chase had provided. While it felt odd to go through someone else's things, she hadn't found it as difficult to do as she'd anticipated. If it was something that she thought someone else could get some use out of, she put it in the keep-and-give-away pile. Otherwise, it was garbage. There were only a few exceptions that made her pause.

She heard the front door open and quickly walked into the kitchen. She was standing at the stove making a cup of tea by the time Chase took off his work boots and walked in.

"How's it going?" he asked.

"Good. How's the roof?"

"Big and steep. Other than that, fabulous." He reached for the cookies that she'd pulled from the oven just ten minutes earlier. "These look better than fabulous."

"They may be hot still."

He opened the refrigerator and poured a big glass of milk. He ate the first cookie in three bites. "Oh, these are good."

She smiled. So far Chase had eaten everything she'd made with gusto. She could probably mix straw with honey and bake it and he'd proclaim it the best yet.

"Gordy Fitzler just stopped by."

"To check on your progress?"

"I'm sure. Plus he wanted to invite us to his birthday party tonight at the Wright Here, Wright Now Café. His kids are throwing it for him."

She looked at him. "That's sweet."

"I thought we might go. If you didn't have other plans."

She wasn't exactly in the position to be making plans. But she didn't dismiss the comment. For the first time, it seemed as if Chase was tentative, not completely sure. Was it because this was almost like a date?

"No other plans," she said. "Will it be safe?"

"I wouldn't go if I didn't think so."

"We don't have a gift."

"He said no gifts."

She considered this. "Maybe we could make a charitable donation in his name to something that he supports."

Chase didn't even have to think about it. "He's always supported the local park district. When I was in high school, he donated over half the funds needed to put in the first swimming pool so that kids would have someplace to go in the summer. He's still wearing his Ravesville Park District ball cap."

"Sounds perfect."

"Can we talk about the rules for a minute?" he asked.

"Rules?"

He waved his hand. "Expectations. Firm expectations. We remain in visual contact at all times. That means you don't even step outside for a quick breath of fresh air without me. If you have to go to the bathroom, I'll check it first and then stand outside the door."

"I know we're supposed to be newlyweds but won't people think that's just a little over the top?"

"I'll do it in a way that people won't even notice."

She thought he perhaps underestimated how closely every woman's eyes in the place would follow him. He was just so darn handsome, so darn male. "Got it. Visual contact. At all times. It's just that I'm a little disappointed."

"Why?" He looked very concerned.

She lowered her lashes. "Well, Detective Hollister, that wasn't the only kind of contact I was hoping for tonight."

Shaking his head, he got up and pushed his chair

back. He leaned close, his breath warm on her neck.
"Don't you worry," he muttered. "As soon as the cake
is served, you better be ready."

FIVE HOURS LATER, Chase stood in the living room, waiting for Raney. She was excited about the birthday party.
He could tell. It made him realize that she'd steeled herself to several more weeks of house arrest and this was
a welcome respite.

When he'd come in a half hour ago, she'd been finishing up her painting in the kitchen. She was, he thought,
about the slowest painter he'd ever seen. He could whip
through a room in a couple hours and she'd been working for two days on one wall. But it gave her something
to do and he was happy enough to let her plod along.

He'd grabbed clean clothes and gone upstairs to
shower. Even though he was sleeping in her bed, it
seemed too big a jump to move his clothes into her space.
It would require a discussion and right now, that was
the one thing that neither one of them wanted to have.

He understood his own reasons. He was conflicted
as hell. He liked Raney. A lot. But he suspected that she
was looking for what most women were looking for—a
husband, someone who was willing to sign on for the
long term. That wasn't him. He was ultimately going
to disappoint her.

Why she didn't seem to want to talk about the future
was a mystery to him. She'd been married. That had to
mean that she believed in marriage. She didn't seem
terribly angry or bitter about her divorce. And so like
a good detective he watched and listened for clues, but
so far she wasn't showing her cards.

When she came downstairs, he almost showed his

whole hand. She looked incredible. While she wasn't overly tall, she had nice long legs that were looking really good in her black skirt. She had on a white silky-looking tank that he was itching to touch and put his hands under. "You're beautiful," he said.

"You're looking pretty good yourself."

He wore khakis and a loose tan shirt that would make it easy for him to carry his gun undetected.

"What time do we need to leave?" she asked.

He looked at his watch. "We have a few minutes."

"Good. I…uh…need to tell you something."

As quick as that, he saw his world changing. She was going to tell him that she'd thought it over and it had been one big mistake. A rush of disappointment filled him.

"Okay," he said.

He sat down on the couch and motioned for her to take the chair. He'd been disappointed before and survived it.

"I saw something the other day and it's weighing heavily on my mind."

She couldn't be talking about his injury. They'd had that discussion.

"I should have said something but I'm fairly confident that the person involved doesn't want that."

He was lost. But he did know that she was truly worried that she was doing the right thing. He didn't say anything. She needed to work through this.

"When I was in the café the other day, before the accident, Summer was clearing a table and her shirt rode up. I saw her back and she had a big bruise on it. An old bruise, maybe a couple weeks old." She waved her hand.

"I...I've become sort of an expert on the various iterations of bruised flesh."

That made his stomach hurt. "Did you ask her about it?"

"No. Sheila was there and I certainly didn't want her hearing the conversation, and I got the feeling that Summer was very sorry that I caught a glimpse. She didn't want to talk about it."

"There could be a thousand ways that somebody gets a bruise on their back."

"I know," she said. "That's what I kept thinking about. It's why I didn't say anything to begin with. But...it looked a great deal like the bruises I had from Harry Malone's shoe when he kicked me. I just can't get it out of my head that someone kicked her. Hard."

The picture he'd seen of Raney in her file, drawn, drained, beaten down, flashed in his head. She hadn't deserved that. No other woman deserved that and he felt a special affinity toward Summer. His brother had almost married her. What would Bray want him to do?

That answer was pretty clear. Bray fought the war on drugs because he hated the fact that the big-money punks were living large at the expense of the masses hooked on bad product. He risked his life every day to save the unknown thirteen-year-old from dying of a heroin overdose.

"I'll talk to her," he said. "Tonight."

Raney shook her head. "No. I want to do that. But I wanted you to know, because if she is in trouble, we may need your help."

BOTH OF THE Wright sisters were working. Trish, wearing a chef's hat and holding a big knife, was carving meat.

She was smiling and laughing and delightfully entertaining people as they went through the line.

Summer was greeting guests. A young man of about fourteen who looked bored to death and a girl, maybe five, who was so excited she could barely stand still, were next to her. It wasn't a leap to assume they were her children. Same skin tone, same shape of the eyes. The boy had dark hair and the little girl's hair was a beautiful strawberry blonde.

It made sense that her children were there. She was a single mom who normally didn't work nights. She probably hadn't wanted to leave her kids at home alone.

They'd placed a sign on the door that said Closed for Special Event but Raney thought it probably didn't matter. Based on the crowd, she suspected all their regular customers were on the guest list.

The café looked very different. Small twinkling lights had been hung from the ceiling and strung across the room. The regular lights had been turned down. Every table had a cream-colored tablecloth with a vase of fall flowers as well as candles.

There was music playing and they'd left space for a small dance floor.

It wasn't New York fancy but rather, small-town nice. She loved it.

They'd set the food on the counter and there was so much of it, it covered the entire length. Extra tables had been added, making it a challenge to circulate around the space. Not that that bothered Raney. She knew only a handful of people.

Mr. Fitzler, accompanied by two women she assumed were his daughters, probably in their late thirties or early forties, approached. They greeted Chase warmly and when he introduced her, they seemed delighted that she was there. "Thank you for inviting us," she said.

Reneta, the oldest one, waved a hand. "Chase is practically family. The son my father never had," she added good-naturedly. "We've got some empty chairs at our table, please join us."

It wasn't until she sat down that she saw Gary Blake in the far corner. He was out of uniform and had a beer in his hand. There were two other men with him and while they were talking animatedly and loudly, Gary was mostly staring in the direction of the far wall. At first, Raney thought he might be looking at his ex-wife and children. But that wasn't it. No, it was definitely the door. She leaned toward Chase. "Did you see Gary Blake?"

"Yep. Want a glass of wine?"

"Sure." Of course Chase had seen him. He'd probably already checked out everybody in the room.

He brought her back a glass of white wine in a little plastic glass and a bottle of water for himself. Then they started through the long line and filled their plates with roast beef, ham, mashed potatoes, roasted vegetables, all kinds of salads and finally homemade rolls.

Raney was almost done eating when the door opened and Sheila Stanton came in. She was alone. Raney saw Gordy's daughters exchange a look, and it wasn't one of pleasure.

Reneta leaned toward Chase. "You remember Sheila, Chase?"

"I do."

He wasn't giving anything away.

"She's a very good customer," Reneta explained. "Owns over half the commercial properties in Ravesville and uses us exclusively for roof work. My husband thought it was important that we invite her."

The underlying message was clear. If it had been up to the daughters, they'd have done something very different. Raney watched as Summer handed Sheila a plastic glass of wine. Sheila took a sip and made a face. Summer ignored it.

That was what Raney should do, too. Ignore Sheila Stanton. She turned the other way and struck up a conversation with Reneta's husband, who had assumed the roofing business. Within ten minutes, she had convinced Jonah to interview Keith for the entry-level office administrator position that was available at the company.

When Chase overheard the conversation, he leaned in. "I thought Keith wanted his own restaurant. Unless Fitzler's is putting a roof on the building, I'm not seeing the connection."

"Keith is a wonderful waiter and there's no doubt that he understands the customer service component. But to be a successful entrepreneur, he needs more general knowledge of how a business works. That knowledge can come from lots of places, including an office administrator job for a large roofing contractor. He wants to stay in the area. There aren't a lot of jobs that will put him on the right path. This one looks like a win-win. He wants to work for several years to save money to qualify for a loan. This would allow him to do that. And Fitzler's gets a good employee who is willing to work hard and learn."

"You're pretty damn smart," he said. She felt warm inside.

"Not so…" She caught a glimpse of Sheila Stanton, who was seated at a table across the room. She'd pushed one side of her hair behind her ear and Raney could see her chin. "Oh, my God," she said.

"What?" Chase asked.

She could tell that he was about to reach for his gun. She put her hand on his arm. "Smart. Not so smart. Chase, I think it might have been Sheila driving the SUV that pushed me off the road."

He blinked. "You said it was a man."

"I know, I did. And I thought it was. I saw facial hair. A glimpse but I was sure I'd seen it. But it's her chin. I know it is."

Chapter Thirteen

Chase was grateful he hadn't been drinking. Otherwise, the whirling in his head might have made him vomit on his shoes. What was Raney saying? Was it even possible?

When Sheila had left the grocery store that morning, he'd caught a glimpse of her car pulling out of the parking lot. She drove a black Lexus SUV.

Would Sheila have done something like this? It was crazy. They hadn't dated for more than ten years. She'd been married and divorced. He was *currently* married. Or at least she thought so. Surely she couldn't still be thinking there was a chance of a reconciliation.

But then he thought about the times that Cal had claimed to have seen her. He thought about the crazy letter. He thought about her staking out the grocery store in anticipation that he'd be shopping.

"Stay here," he said.

Sheila was getting a drink when she saw him approaching. "Chase," she said. "Lovely to see you."

"May I talk to you?" he asked. He was surprised at how level his voice was. He wanted to wring her neck if she was the one. But if Raney was right, and she'd taken the time to don a disguise, including facial hair, the crime had been premeditated and Sheila might be very dangerous indeed.

"Of course. Shall we step outside? It's such a beautiful night."

Visual contact at all times. He wasn't going to be the one to break the rules. "Over here should be fine," he said, leading her to the far corner of the room. He stood so that he could see Raney over Sheila's shoulder.

"My wife had an accident the other day," he said.

"I heard that. How is she?"

"Fine."

"A black SUV forced her off the road."

"Really?"

She was good. She didn't even look nervous.

"You drive a black SUV."

She nodded. "A lovely one." She took a delicate sip of her wine. "Are you having this same conversation with everyone who drives an SUV or specifically with me?"

Her tone was suggestive, as if she liked that she'd perhaps been singled out. It took him one step closer to losing his dinner.

"Listen to me, Sheila. Whatever you and I had is long over. We both went our separate ways. I'm married. And I love my wife. I…" He faltered. *I love my wife.* He did. He really did. He took a breath. Steadied himself. "I don't want to see anything happen to her. If she so much as breaks a fingernail, I'll be upset. And I'll hunt down the person responsible. I will make sure they pay." He paused. "Do you understand, Sheila?"

"You're a fool, Chase Hollister," she said, her facade finally cracking. "I am twice the woman that she could even hope to be."

He was not going to defend Raney. She did not need

to be defended. "I'm going to ask this question, just once. Were you driving the SUV that forced Raney off the road?"

"Of course I wasn't," she said.

He really couldn't tell if she was lying or not.

"You've been warned, Sheila. Don't forget it."

As Chase walked away, he could feel her eyes on his back. When he got back to the table, Raney's eyes were full of questions.

"I don't know how I ever thought she was desirable. Or sexy."

"You were nineteen. A jackrabbit in a dress might have done it for you."

He laughed so hard that the other people at the table started giving him odd looks. He looked at her plate. She'd cut her ham into teeny-tiny pieces, so small that it would fall through the tines of the fork if she tried to eat it. "Mad at the ham?"

"When I'm nervous, I need something to do with my hands."

He'd give her something to do with her hands. "Let's go home."

"I need to talk to Summer." She got up.

Chase let her go. He watched her walk across the room.

SUMMER WAS STILL BARTENDING, handing out little plastic glasses of red or white wine and twisting tops off bottles of beer. She smiled at Raney. "How was your dinner?"

"Wonderful," Raney said. "I'll have the chardonnay, please."

Summer poured it and handed it to her. Raney took

it. There was nobody behind her in line. "Would you have just a minute that we could talk?"

She could tell that Summer was about to say no.

"Please," Raney added.

Summer stepped out from behind the table that had been set up as a makeshift bar. She glanced around the room. It was full of people. "Follow me to the kitchen," she said.

Chase had told her not to go outside alone. He hadn't said anything about the kitchen. As she crossed the room, she made eye contact with him and nodded toward the kitchen.

He gave her a sharp nod in response. She suspected he'd be waiting outside the door when she and Summer finished their conversation.

At the far end of the kitchen, a young man, maybe sixteen, was washing dishes using a big stainless-steel commercial dishwasher. He had earbuds in, listening to something.

"We can talk here," Summer said quietly. "Jess won't pay any attention to us."

Raney decided not to waste any time. "The other day, when your shirt pulled up, I saw what appeared to be a big bruise on your back. It didn't seem to be the kind of bruise that somebody would easily get. Unless...unless somebody had deliberately tried to hurt them. I was... am concerned about you."

Summer chewed on her upper lip. "I know that you mean well. I do. But I'm begging you, don't say anything to anybody about it. It could be very bad for me. For my children." Her eyes filled with tears. "Please."

She could feel the woman's desperation. "Can your sister help you?"

"No. She can't know. You cannot tell her."

"There are people who would help you. People like Chase."

Summer shook her head. "Please," she said again. "Things are better. I can't rock the boat now."

Raney reached for the cell phone that was in Summer's shirt pocket. She tapped on the keypad and entered her name and phone number. "Promise me that you'll call me if you need help. Anytime." She knew that she was just going to be in Ravesville for another three weeks but even after she left, she would do what she could.

"I promise," Summer said.

Raney didn't know if she meant it or if she was simply trying to end the conversation. Raney turned and left the kitchen. Summer didn't follow. As she had suspected, Chase was near the kitchen door. She realized that he'd been able to see into the kitchen through the small window in the door. He'd made good to keep her in his sights the whole night.

"Well?" he asked.

"She begged me to forget that I saw it."

"And what do you intend to do?"

"I have to do that. She's a grown woman. I gave her a chance to reach out for help. Either she's got the situation under control or she's not ready. Either way, I can't force it."

Chase nodded. "You're probably right. You know, you never cease to impress me. That took some guts to have that conversation with her. It could have gotten ugly real quick, but you were willing to take the chance."

"Channeling blonde Raney," she said, not thinking.

He pulled back. "What's that mean?"

She was embarrassed. But she knew Chase well enough to know that he wasn't going to let it go. "My new haircut and color was a little surprising. It made me look different. Feel different. Blonde Raney was adventuresome. Brave. Not afraid of the dark. Whole. I liked her. And when situations came up and I had to make a choice about how I was going to respond, I could either be blonde Raney or real Raney."

He studied her. "I like your hair. I already told you that. But you don't get your chutzpah from your hair, honey. It's part of you. You weren't blonde when you were traipsing down to the prison to help inmates polish their job-seeking skills. You weren't blonde when you outsmarted a madman and figured out a way to use washers from a filing cabinet to escape. You weren't blonde when you agreed to testify."

"It was blonde Raney who slept with you," she whispered.

He didn't say anything for a long minute. "Raney, you're an amazing person. You went through something really awful, something that no one should have to endure. But you survived. And I know you feel bad because Malone fooled you. And that destroyed your confidence, in others and in yourself."

He reached for her hand. "You know what the blond hair is. It's a crutch. Not in a bad way. Everybody needs a crutch once in a while. If you'd broken your leg, you'd have used a crutch without any thought. This isn't that different. Maybe it wasn't a physical break but you got shook, Raney. Understandably so. And you made some bargains with God. And now that you're free, it's scary because now you have the chance to keep those bargains.

So it's easier to tell yourself that it's blonde Raney. But it's you, darling. All you."

She thought her heart might burst it was so full of love.

He leaned forward. "And you'd have slept with me, regardless. I know it and you know it. We were meant to be together."

At that moment, Gordy Fitzler approached. "Chase, may I dance with your wife?"

"You have to ask her."

He extended an age-spotted hand in her direction. How could she refuse? "I'd love to," she said.

The music was a country hit from a few years earlier, just right for a slow dance with a dear man. "Thank you for letting us come to your party," she said. She meant it. It had been a wonderful night.

"I can tell that you're good for Chase."

It dimmed the glow of the night to know that she was deceiving this good man, all these people. "Thank you," she managed. She heard a disturbance near the door and looked over Gordy's shoulder.

Lloyd Doogan had come in. He was staggering and talking loudly. Fortunately the crowd had thinned considerably. Sheila had left shortly after Chase had talked to her. She looked around for Gary Blake. She did not want Lloyd arrested again. She didn't see the man and assumed he'd left while she was in the kitchen.

She saw Chase turn away from Hank Beaumont, the fireman who'd assisted her at the scene. Gordy stopped dancing and took a step toward Lloyd. Chase passed him before he could make much progress. "Enjoy your dance. I'll deal with this."

"Hey, Lloyd," Chase said, wrapping an arm around his shoulder. "How about you call it a night?"

"Got to wish Gordy a slappy birthday," he said, slurring his words as he tried to get away from Chase.

"Maybe tomorrow," Chase said.

Lloyd turned his head, so that he could look Chase in the eye. "He's a good man."

Chase nodded slowly. "Yes, yes he is. Okay, I'll go with you."

Together, the men crossed the room. One smart, confident and able. The other, less so, but determined to pay his respects to Gordy.

Gordy was gracious and shook Lloyd's hand. Then he leaned close to his son-in-law's ear. The man nodded and pulled his car keys from his pocket. Chase saw what was happening and handed Lloyd off to the man. They walked out the door and Raney assumed that Lloyd would be safely driven back to his apartment to sleep it off.

What could have gone very badly had ended up fine. Due in large part to how Chase had reacted. He took care of things. Took care of people.

It was one of the reasons she loved him.

Yes. Loved. She went back to dancing with Gordy and thought about what that could possibly mean. He hadn't said a word about what would become of them after the trial, when she'd be free to return to her old life in Miami.

He'd said that he'd never marry. Could she accept that?

No. While her first marriage hadn't gone so well, it hadn't soured her on the institution. She had learned a few things. She and Mike had wanted very different things. She wouldn't make that mistake again.

She wanted… She looked around the room. She wanted this. A town where people knew each other. They came out to celebrate significant events, they bought candy they didn't want so that the pom-pom girls could go to camp, they got clean cars washed again so that their elderly neighbors could afford heat in the winter.

She'd lost her parents at a young age. She wanted family.

Chase didn't want that kind of permanency. He was the guy who was only willing to sign a six-month lease, in the event that he wanted to move on.

It was so terribly sad.

The song ended and Chase came back over. He shook Gordy's hand and Raney leaned in and kissed the older man's cheek. Once Gordy had walked away, Chase pulled her close. "Are you ready to go?" he asked.

His intent was clear. And in her heart, she accepted that it would not be forever. But she had now. Right now. "I don't know," she said. "I was thinking about another piece of cake."

"No. I have been a patient man but I want to get my hands under that shirt. Let's go home."

She nodded. It might only be her home for three more weeks but she was going to make the best of it. And that included being in Chase Hollister's bed.

Chapter Fourteen

It was four days later when Chase's cell phone rang. They were both downstairs, getting ready to make breakfast.

He looked at the number. "Dawson," he told her and pushed a button. "Hey," he answered, his posture relaxed.

Within seconds that changed. He stood up and walked over to the back door of the kitchen. He wasn't saying much, just listening intently.

But Raney knew. Something bad had happened.

The call ended. He turned. His eyes were hard.

"What?" she said.

"Luis Vincenze was found dead this morning. His throat had been cut. He's been dead for a while. Probably for longer than a week."

So maybe shortly after he'd accompanied her to Missouri. The possibilities of what this might mean settled on her heart, making her chest feel heavy. "Someone killed him to get information on me," she said.

"We don't know that for sure," Chase corrected.

"But it's a possibility."

"Of course it's a possibility," he said, sounding angry. She knew it wasn't directed at her. It was the whole terrible situation. Poor Luis. He had just been doing his job.

"But it's also possible that it was some other jerk who had a beef with him. He was a cop. Had been one for more than twenty years. You make a lot of enemies in that amount of time."

That was true. But she knew, just knew, that it was related to her. "How is it that he could have been missing for more than a week and nobody reported it?"

"The afternoon he left you in St. Louis, he left a voice mail on his wife's cell phone, telling her not to worry, that he was being pulled to do some undercover work on a case and that he'd be out of contact for several days. He also left a message on his boss's office phone, telling him that he'd decided to use some of his vacation time now that he'd safely handed you off. Nobody got suspicious until the wife got nervous after trying his cell phone multiple times. She called his boss. It took them another day to tie it to a report of a dead body found in a vacation rental in the Ozarks."

"Oh." She was glad they had not yet eaten. "I'm guessing he left those messages under duress."

Chase swallowed. "They didn't just cut his throat. They tortured him. For some time. I think we have to assume that he broke. Maybe just to end the misery if nothing else."

Outside, a barn swallow swooped down, coming near the kitchen window, causing Raney to jump. She told herself to calm down, to breathe deep, to think.

"So we don't know what he told them. Whoever did this."

"No."

"What do they want us to do?" she asked.

"To hunker down here. They're sending two officers

to provide 24/7 protection. We aren't in this alone. *You* aren't in this alone."

No, Chase was in it deep, too. She glanced at his leg, his poor injured leg that he still favored at times after a hard day's work outside. He could be injured again. Much worse. She stood up suddenly. "No. I should go. Somewhere else. And tell no one."

Chase stared at her, his face getting red. But when he spoke, his voice was still calm. "Sit down, Raney. Nobody is going anywhere. Not you. Not me."

She didn't sit. She couldn't. Deep in her bones, she knew that Luis Vincenze's death was because of her. "Is it possible that he'd been bought by Malone?" she heard herself ask. She felt terrible even voicing the speculation but her mind kept going back to the change in his attitude when he'd had to deliver her to Missouri.

"Why would you say that?" Chase asked, smoothly moving into investigator, fact-finder mode.

"When I was at the safe house in Miami, he was kind and helpful and even somewhat conciliatory. That is not a characteristic that I normally associated with the cops that I worked with at Next Steps."

He gave her a half smile. "Keep going."

"Everything changed on the plane. Once we landed, he became distant and preoccupied. He should have been overjoyed to get out of babysitting duty. He was going to be able to go home and be with his family. I should have realized the disconnect earlier, but I'd been so steeped in my own misery over coming to Missouri that I maybe didn't see the forest for the trees."

"Tell me everything you remember."

She thought back. "I know that he didn't know our

final destination. Once he received a text, we got in the cab and met Chief Bates."

"So he and the chief talked?"

"For less than a minute. Luis got back in the cab that we'd arrived in."

"Would he have seen that the two of you entered the hair salon?"

"I don't think so. We walked for at least a couple minutes, turning two corners."

Chase considered that. "I suppose there are two possibilities. That Vincenze was a dirty cop and he was supposed to make sure that you never safely arrived in Missouri. The opportunity to kill you never presented itself, at least not in any way that wouldn't make him the immediate suspect. So once he handed you off to Chief Bates, he was essentially a dead man. Probably knew that. Hence, the agitation."

Raney shook her head and pretended to be picking petals off a daisy. "Should I kill her? Should I not? Should I kill her? Should I not?"

He reached out to still her hands. "What was the word you used that one day? I know. *Conflicted.* I suspect he was conflicted. The two of you had been close for almost two weeks. I suspect he probably liked you, thought you were a nice person. And maybe he couldn't see himself following orders."

"So he got killed because he didn't do his job?"

"Yeah. The other possibility is that he was a clean cop and Malone's people tortured him to get information on where you might be in St. Louis."

"And all he'd have been able to tell them is where he handed me off to Chief Bates. That wouldn't have been terribly helpful."

"No," he agreed.

A terrifying thought dawned on her. "You have to call Chief Bates. Right now. He's the linchpin that ties this all together. They'll go after him next."

"It's possible, but don't worry. The chief can take care of himself. But I think you're on the right path. Even if Vincenze was dirty, he never saw me, never heard my name. There's still no way for them to connect Lorraine Taylor to Raney Hollister."

For the first time since the telephone had rung, she could feel her breath coming easier. He was right. There was no need to panic. "What happens next?"

"We're going to have company. They should arrive in about an hour."

She thought about what that would mean. "We're not going to be able to…be together. Not while they're here." Of course not. It could ruin Chase's career if it got back to the chief that he'd slept with the witness. That was not what the chief had likely been thinking when he'd set up this fictional marriage.

Chase shook his head, looking miserable. "No. You'll stay inside, away from any windows. I'll work with the other two officers and between the three of us, we'll keep one at the front and one at the rear of the house, 24/7. We'll rotate shifts so that we can grab some sleep."

Raney looked at her watch. "We will, however, be able to eat while they're here."

Chase's sexy amber eyes softened. "Of course."

"Maybe we should do the things now that we won't be able to do later?"

"Are you propositioning me, Mrs. Hollister?"

"I am merely asking if you can rearrange your schedule. Perhaps you could wait till later to eat? Say mid-morning."

He took her hand and pulled her out of the chair. "I've always been fond of brunch."

CHASE LAY ON the bed, Raney lazily stroking his injured leg. It tickled but not enough to tell her to stop. He loved having her hands on him, loved the feel of her heat seeping into his body.

She moved her hands up the side of his body. To his ribs. Suddenly, her fingers stopped. She lifted her head. He tensed.

"Is this another bullet hole?" she asked, her tone a mixture of what he perceived to be disbelief and horror.

He shook his head and tried to pull her hand away.

She was stronger than she looked.

"What happened here?" she demanded.

And Chase considered lying. The scar was faint enough after all these years that no one had ever asked about it, but had they, he'd have had no compunction about telling them it was a birthmark or something else equally vanilla. But this was Raney.

"It's a cigarette burn," he said.

He felt her stiffen in his arm. "How did that happen?" she asked finally, her voice soft.

"My stepfather, Brick Doogan."

She raised up on one elbow, so that she could look at him. "How old were you?"

He thought a minute. "Seventeen."

She frowned and didn't say anything. He could practically see the wheels churning in her head. She was a fighter; she'd proved that time and time again.

Chase cleared his throat. "I suspect that you're wondering why a healthy seventeen-year-old boy would let someone do that to him."

"Maybe," she admitted.

"Because he told me if I didn't sit still and take it like a man, he was going to go get Cal."

Now she sat up in bed and pulled the sheet up to cover herself. She'd obviously decided this was not the kind of conversation one had naked.

"That makes no sense," she said.

He shrugged. "Shortly after Brick Doogan married my mother and moved in, I realized he was a bad guy. I was a dumb sixteen-year-old and I got busted for skipping school. I was making all As and Bs so it shouldn't have been a big deal, but he beat the hell out of me. I didn't have anybody I felt that I could turn to. Bray, who is four years older, had already enlisted and was halfway around the world. Cal was just thirteen."

"What did your mother say?"

"I didn't tell her. She had been so sad when my dad died. And for two years, I would hear her crying in her bed. Once she met Brick, she stopped crying. I'll never know what she saw in the man but she was happy. At least at first. I didn't want to ruin it."

"That's a big burden for a sixteen-year-old."

"Yeah. I got over the beating and almost forgot about it. But then it happened again. We'd let a couple goats loose in the high school. It got people pretty excited."

She smiled.

"That was the cigarette burn." It had been seventeen years, but he could still feel the startling pain of having his flesh burned.

She reached out her arm, lightly rubbed her fingers over the scarred skin. "I'm sorry," she whispered.

He drew in a breath. "It was a third-degree burn. It got infected and I started running a raging fever. I had to tell my mother."

"What did she say?"

Now came the hard part. "She told me to tell the doctor in the emergency room that I'd been smoking and fallen asleep on my cigarette."

Raney was silent for a long minute. "Did you?"

He nodded. "Not for him. For her."

"I'm sorry your mother is dead, and I know that you're never supposed to talk badly about the dead, but that just seems awful. Yet you don't talk about your mother as if she was awful."

"She wasn't awful. She was weak and needy and when my father died, I think overwhelmed with the idea of raising three boys on her own."

"Did Brick mistreat her?"

"No. Not to my knowledge. It was always me. Until it was Calvin. And that's when I knew things had to change."

"I don't understand."

"My senior year of high school, our football team went to the state championship. I was a starting running back and it was pretty cool. My mother, Cal and Brick were all at the game. And we won. Everybody was pretty happy. What I didn't realize was that all the parents went out drinking afterward, celebrating their kids' achievement. The players were all invited back to the quarterback's house. His parents had a bunch of money and they had an indoor pool and a game room. We stayed the whole weekend. There was no way to say no to the invitation and besides, I wanted to go."

"You were a kid."

"Yeah. But I was worried about being away from home. And I warned Cal to watch out for Brick. If I'd known that he was going drinking, I'd have never stayed away. He was always meaner when he was drinking."

"What happened?"

"He pushed Cal's hand through a window. The one in the living room. It was cut up enough that my mother had to take him to the emergency room for stitches."

"And even then, no one found out."

"Nope. Cal told them he tripped."

"Why?" she whispered.

"Because Brick told him that if he told the truth, that it would be worse the next time."

He watched her. She understood. Malone had also played the game of psychological warfare with her.

"Cal had just turned fifteen years old and he was small for his age. He was scared of Brick." He paused. "You should see him now. Former navy SEAL, six feet tall, all muscle."

"What happened when you got home?"

"I saw Cal's hand all bandaged up and went crazy. Went at Brick like a madman. He was a big, strong guy and outweighed me by forty pounds but I was winning when my mother tried to break up the fight. I didn't want her to get hurt so I stopped. And I thought, too, that this will be the end of it. She'll leave the bastard now."

"But she didn't?"

"No. And when I told her I was taking Cal, she said that I couldn't, that she would fight me."

"He was a minor. She was his mother," she said. "It would have been a battle, but surely the hospital records would have helped you. Couldn't you have confided in a teacher, a counselor, anybody?" she asked, sadness in her tone.

"Probably. But I didn't. I was ashamed. I thought this was the kind of thing that happened in poor, uneducated families. I wanted to be something. I didn't want this hanging over my head. Anyway, I wasn't leaving Cal alone with Brick. So I stayed. I worked like a dog and went to school at the same time to save enough money so that the two of us would have a place to live. We left the morning of Cal's eighteenth birthday. I got hired on by the St. Louis PD and, well, you pretty much know the rest."

He could tell she was puzzled about something. *Let it go*, he prayed. *Just let it go.*

"So after the incident with Cal, Brick reformed?" she asked.

She was so smart. She would have made a good cop. Knew just where the weak points of the story were.

"I told him that if he ever touched Cal or my mother, I would kill him. I think he believed me. And, every once in a while, I let him go at me."

"What?"

"I had figured him out. He was an unhappy man. Mad that he was working in a factory, hated his bosses, thought they were all lazy. He wanted somebody to pay for his lot in life. And about every six months, he just couldn't hold the anger in. That's when I knew he'd be dangerous. When he'd start drinking and miss a couple days of work, I'd do something that I knew would make him angry and then he'd feel justified when he handed me my lunch."

She got out of bed, taking the sheet with her. "You made yourself a target?"

"I did. I never let him take another cigarette to me.

I'd let him land a punch or two and then he'd kick me out of the house for a couple days."

"Where did you go?"

"Never far. If it was warm enough, I'd sleep in the hammock on the porch. If it was winter, I'd have to go to Fitzler's. I didn't like being that far away from Cal, although I knew that Brick wasn't going to touch him."

"How could you be sure?"

"Because even though he might land a punch, I think he knew by this time that I was strong enough and fast enough that if I decided to fight back, I would win."

She sat back down on the bed. Reached out her arm. "You protected everyone else but not yourself."

"In a way. But you have to understand, I didn't want to kill him. I would have but I didn't want to because he wasn't worth it. I thought I would go to jail and by that time, I'd decided that I wanted to be a cop. My life would have never turned out the way it has."

"And you never saw him after you left at age twenty-one?"

"I saw him when my mother was dying. She asked her hospice nurse to call us. Bray, Cal and I came home. We were at her bedside for a little over two days. He was around but didn't interact with us in any way."

"I imagine Cal feels a great deal of gratitude toward you. For protecting him."

He held up a finger. "This is important. Cal doesn't know. As far as he's concerned, Brick never laid another hand on either one of us."

"And your older brother?"

"The only thing he knows about is the time Cal's hand went through the window. That was enough for him to hate Brick Doogan forever. I never told him the rest. He'd have killed Doogan for sure and then I'd have lost a brother to the prison system."

She stared at him. "You're amazingly well adjusted. Considering."

"I had to let it go. On her deathbed, my mother asked to speak to me privately. She asked for my forgiveness. And I gave it to her."

He looked at his watch. "We need to get up. They'll be here soon."

She didn't argue. Just dropped her sheet and hurriedly stepped into her clothes. But when she turned her head, he thought he caught the sheen of tears in her eyes.

Chapter Fifteen

Chase might have forgiven his mother, which she thought was pretty damn amazing given the circumstances, but he hadn't escaped unscathed. There were more scars than the one he bore on his chest.

So many things made sense now. His ability to stay calm, no matter what. He would not have let Brick know that he was getting to him.

His reluctance to sign more than a six-month lease and his comments that people needed to be ready to change jobs at a moment's notice, even though he'd been at the same job for thirteen years. Chase had not been free to go before and now he told himself he was ready to leave at any time.

His unwillingness to marry. He'd been taking care of his family for years, making sacrifices beyond any a young man should have to make. He was done.

It was heartbreaking, it really was.

A lesser man would not have endured it and come out whole.

RANEY WAS PAINTING the kitchen when their two new bodyguards arrived. Chase knew both men and made the introductions. Leo was in his early fifties with a face that had been pockmarked by teenage acne. He wore a white shirt with frayed cuffs that looked as if it had been washed too many times. His voice was gruff and he had a pack of cigarettes in his pocket.

Toby was twenty years younger, thin and wearing a lovely green sweater that was way too warm for the day. He pointed to the fresh paint on the wall. "Oh, that's nice. It picks up the natural light from the window. I'm in the middle of a big remodeling project myself." He walked over to look at the can. "Toasted Meringue. Excellent choice."

Raney lifted her nose in the air—just slightly. Not enough that the two new arrivals would think she was odd but enough that Chase would understand that others recognized good taste.

Chase rolled his eyes.

"Come see what I got for the living room," she said. Toby started to obediently follow.

"We're not filming an episode of HGTV here," Chase said, rolling his eyes.

Toby blushed and sat down. Leo looked around, probably in hopes of seeing an ashtray. When he didn't, he started nervously rubbing the edge of his thumb on the corner of the table. Raney took pity on both men and pushed some warm coffee cake in their direction.

Within minutes, Chase was briefing them on the assignment, showing them entrances, exits and going over their daily schedule.

They decided that Chase and Toby would take the first watch, leaving Leo inside to rest until it was his turn. At first Raney felt self-conscious about having the man in the other room but soon got busy painting and forgot about him.

Midafternoon, Chase came in to get a drink. Leo got off the couch and went outside to take his place.

Chase looked at the walls in the kitchen and smiled. "It does look nice," he said.

She knew he was thinking that she'd made pitiful little progress and that she must be the slowest painter on earth. But she wasn't. She was actually pretty fast and had been making good progress—just not in the kitchen.

Now that he'd told her the story, she was even more pleased that she'd followed her instinct and decided to tackle Brick Doogan's bedroom. Initially, she'd done it because she thought it was crazy that Chase was sleeping on a couch with his legs hanging off the end when there was a perfectly good bed, albeit with a hideous bedspread.

Now she understood why Chase couldn't bring himself to handle the man's things. Now he wouldn't have to.

"How's it going?" she asked him, as he drank a big glass of water.

"Fine. I think it may be a good thing that I got the roof done. There's another storm coming." He put his glass on the counter. "Will you be okay upstairs by yourself?" he asked softly.

"Yes. I'll just make sure my window is closed so there are no fluttering curtains."

He swallowed hard. "I want you to know something. I'm really glad your curtains fluttered the last time."

It wasn't an expression of love or eternal commitment but it was something. "Me, too," she said.

They were both silent, too aware that strangers were outside. "It smells really good in here," he said finally.

"I made a lasagna for dinner."

"They would have eaten a sandwich."

"I know."

He smiled at her. "You like taking care of people."

Maybe they weren't so different in that way. "Are you going back out?"

"Yep. I'm on until six." He opened the door.

They both heard the noise at the same time. It was the chugging rumble of Lloyd's motorcycle. Chase grabbed the walkie-talkie off his belt. "Approaching motorcycle. Not a threat. Stand by."

They had not seen Lloyd for four days, not since Gordy Fitzler's birthday party. They went to the front door and opened it. Lloyd parked his motorcycle and came in, none the wiser that eyes watched him from the heavy tree line.

"Hi, Lloyd," Raney said.

"Hello." He was wearing a backpack and shrugged to lower a strap. He did not look at Chase but Chase was watching him like a hawk.

Lloyd opened the zipper and pulled out something that was wrapped in yellowed tissue paper. He started unwrapping and Raney could see that it was not one thing but three things—three identical pictures, in three identical frames.

"When I took the key off his dresser," he said, "I took these. They were in his bottom drawer."

The picture was of three young boys and a woman. She immediately recognized a much younger Chase. One boy would have been Bray and the younger, Cal. It was the woman who held Raney's attention. This was Chase's mother. Widowed young, raising three boys on her own, she'd been a pretty woman. It was easy to see where the boys had gotten their height.

She might not have been a bad woman but she had made terrible choices. She'd married a bad person.

Raney understood that on some level. After all, she'd

chosen poorly, too. Not that Mike had been abusive, but
they'd been too different. He wanted notoriety, even if it
was only in the small community that followed professional surfing. He craved the next big wave, the thing
that would set him apart.

She'd weighed him down because she was most
happy living quietly. She didn't need or want public ad-
oration. She liked permanence and he loved the adven-
ture of a new beach.

But she'd owned up to her poor choice. They'd divorced and gone on with their lives.

She looked at the picture again. This woman had chosen to let her son pay the price for her flawed decision.

She watched Chase's reaction to the photo. Shock,
then awe, before he pulled on his "you can't shake me"
face.

What would make him smile again like the young
man in this picture?

Certainly not staying in Ravesville. He'd left it and
everyone in it behind thirteen years ago.

She turned the frame over. For Brayden. The other
two were similarly inscribed: For Chase and For Calvin.
"Your brothers are going to like this," she said.

Lloyd shifted from foot to foot. "I shouldn't have
taken them."

"It's okay, Lloyd. No harm done," Chase said. "I
appreciate you bringing them back."

"You don't think I stole them?" he asked.

Chase shook his head. "You borrowed them. It's different."

"I didn't remember that I had them until I heard Blake
talking about you and your brothers."

Chase frowned. "Gary Blake? The police officer?"

Lloyd nodded. "After the party the other night. It was hot inside my place and I don't got no air-conditioning. I walked outside. And I overhead them talking."

"Overheard who?"

"Blake and that dark-haired bitch. She's so rich, treats everybody bad."

Raney looked at Chase. She was pretty sure she knew who Lloyd was talking about.

"Sheila Stanton?" Chase asked.

Lloyd nodded. "Those two were arguing, practically yelling."

Lloyd had been really drunk that night. How reliable was this information? She remembered what Chase had told her about small towns and how information flowed.

"What did they say?" she asked. She couldn't help it. Even if it was just gossip, she wanted to hear it. Sheila Stanton had been on her mind. And she didn't exactly know why. Of course it was true that her two encounters with the woman, first at the grocery store and then at the café, hadn't exactly been comfortable. But it was more than that.

The woman had been Chase's lover. For a long time. And now, especially after sharing his bed, perhaps Raney had sunk to a new low and was *comparing*. Her blond, somewhat unruly curls to Sheila's thick, glossy, perfectly shaped hair. Her medium height to Sheila's sleek, almost Amazonian stature. Her rather benign oval face to Sheila's high cheekbones and sculpted chin.

With a quick jerk, she put the picture down. There was always going to be someone prettier, more successful, richer, smarter. Chasing that was a small person's game and a waste of time. Even BHM, she hadn't been inclined to spend much time doing it. After Harry Malone, she simply wouldn't bother.

"Never mind," she said.

Chase held up a hand. "No. Go on, Lloyd."

"He was pointing his finger in her face. Said that he'd been married to one woman who'd loved a Hollister and that he didn't intend to waste time with somebody else who had the same problem."

Gary Blake and Sheila Stanton. Raney's head was whirling.

"Did you hear anything else?" Chase asked.

"She said something but I couldn't hear it. Then he told her that he didn't intend to let her take him down." Lloyd picked up the yellowed tissue paper and crumpled it in his big hands. "You better be careful around Blake. He can make things bad for you if he wants."

Chase nodded. "Thanks for letting me know, Lloyd. And if Blake starts to bother you, you come tell me, okay?"

Lloyd nodded, got his backpack situated again and opened the front door. Neither Raney nor Chase said anything until the sound of his motorcycle had completely faded away.

"Well, that's interesting," Chase said.

"He was drunk that night."

"Well lubed for sure. Sloppy, yeah. But incoherent, no. I suspect he heard it more or less accurately."

"What does it mean?" she asked.

"I think it means that Gary Blake and Sheila Stanton are involved in some way. But not publicly."

Raney put her hand up to her mouth. "I saw him staring at the door. I thought it was weird. I bet he was watching for her. Waiting."

Chase nodded. "Something else makes sense. And it actually makes me sort of happy."

Raney shook her head. "Okay, you lost me."

"When you had your accident, you told Blake that it was a black or blue SUV that got too close. He reacted to that."

"He did?"

"Yeah. Subtly but definitely a reaction. He knows that Sheila drives a black Lexus SUV. It wasn't until you said that it was a man that he relaxed."

"And that makes you happy because…?"

"Because it probably was Sheila. That means it wasn't Malone's hired guns. That's good."

"True. But don't you think it's bad that the police are letting her get away with it?"

Chase shrugged. "We don't know that for sure. Maybe Blake initially suspected Sheila, based on the fact that he has some knowledge of the fact that she's still… *infatuated* with me." He ran his fingers through his hair. "I can't believe I just said that word. But once you said it was a man, he went down another path."

"In that case, he's not a dirty cop."

"Right. Stupid. But not necessarily dirty. What likely happened is that he saw me talking to Sheila. Probably got jealous, demanded to know what it was about. Maybe she told him. Then it could have gone one of two ways. Either she continued to deny it and he believed her or, more likely, she continued to deny it and he didn't believe her. Which maybe means he's not so stupid."

"Or she admitted it and he's continuing to stick by her," Raney said.

"Okay. We're back to stupid."

Raney smiled. "I like Lloyd. He's a nice guy. And it was good of him to return these photos."

Chase picked one up. "I think I was about twelve in this. My dad was still alive. He took the picture. We'd gone to some park for a picnic and my mother had said that we couldn't play until she got a picture." He paused. "That was a good day."

She stood on her tiptoes and kissed his forehead. "Keep those thoughts here. Push the other ones away. Far away."

He reached for her. "I wish to hell we were alone."

She let him hold her. In his arms, she felt safe. And it was wonderful.

But her gut told her that it was temporary, that things were about to change.

DUE TO THE need to have two people outside at all times and the way the shifts worked out, Chase stood outside in the dark while Raney was inside, eating lasagna with Toby.

He'd been crazy enough to get close to the windows once to look inside. They'd been sitting at the dining room table, paint samples in hand, staring at the far wall, likely in deep discussion about exactly how Sunset Wonder was going to look on the wall.

He was glad to be outside, alone with his thoughts. He could have stayed dry on the porch and had a place to sit but he'd chosen to walk the property, getting wet in the steady rain that had been falling for the past half hour.

Seeing that photo of his mother and brothers had been a surprise. He distinctly remembered posing for the picture but didn't think he'd ever seen the finished product. As a twelve-year-old boy, he wouldn't have thought to ask about it.

But his mother had saved it, had put away three copies, one for each of her sons. Had she done it right away? Or had that happened years later, after Brick Doogan had entered their lives? Had she perhaps found the pictures, decided they were a reflection of happier times and wanted her boys to have that memory?

He made another pass across the yard. Looked down the road, but it was raining too hard to see any lights at Fitzler's. Turning, he started back and realized there was a light in his own house where there should not have been.

Someone was in Brick's room. And for one crazy moment, he thought the man had come back. Then he grabbed hold of his senses and carefully approached. The heavy curtains hid most everything, but there was a sliver of light showing where the two panels came together. But it wasn't enough to see anything.

Had someone gotten into the house?

Someone who wanted to harm Raney?

He moved quickly but quietly. He eased open the front door, listened for Raney or Toby, didn't hear anything. The house was warm and smelled good, and when he saw that Toby and Raney had put a big strip of Sunset Wonder on the wall to test it out, his step faltered.

He pulled his gun. Got to the kitchen. Now he heard voices. Raney. Toby. Couldn't make out the words, but they didn't appear distressed.

Got to Brick's door. Listened. They were across the room, near the attached bath.

He swung around the corner, ready to shoot whoever he found there.

Chapter Sixteen

Chase almost dropped his damn gun.

Raney let out a squeak and Toby dropped the paint can he was holding. Fortunately, the lid was on.

The room had been completely emptied of its contents. The bed had been stripped down to the mattress. The closet doors were open, showing a clean space.

The walls had been painted. The ghastly gold had been replaced with the Prickly Pear Delight that he'd thought they were buying for the dining room. It looked totally different.

"How?" he managed.

Raney smiled. "I wanted to surprise you."

He walked farther into the room. She'd surprised him, all right. He struggled to maintain his composure, keenly aware that a fellow officer was standing in the room.

"Where did you put everything?" he asked.

She smiled. "It was tricky but I would wait until I heard you on the other side of the roof and then I'd run a few bags out to the garage. You have a couple of very full garbage bins out there. Things I thought could be donated are in a bag, in the bathroom. I just…just didn't think you wanted to deal with this—" she glanced at

Toby, who was clearly interested in the conversation "—this mess."

It was the nicest thing that anybody had ever done for him. When he'd talked to Raney, had finally opened up to someone about those years of living with Brick, the ever-present pressure in his chest had finally started to release. He would never have trusted anyone else with that secret. But he knew that he could trust her, knew that she wouldn't judge.

Knew that she would offer unconditional love.

Like this.

The hell with what information got back to anybody in the department or even the chief. "Toby, can we have a minute here?" he said.

The young man started to leave the room. But before he could get to the doorway, Chase's phone buzzed. He pulled it out, recognized the number and knew that it had to be bad.

"Hollister," he answered.

"This is Chief Bates. We've got a problem. We now have very good reason to believe that your location has been compromised. You need to bring Lorraine Taylor back in."

Chase walked to the window, lifted the edge of the heavy curtain with a finger. "Tell me what happened."

"There have been a string of robberies near Patch Street."

That was the street where he'd first met Raney, where she'd gotten her hair cut.

"Reports got taken by a couple different officers and we didn't piece things together as quickly as we should have."

He could hear the anger in the chief's voice.

"It wasn't until the yogurt shop got hit that the pattern was established," Chief Bates said. "Somebody had stolen security-camera footage from several of the mom-and-pop stores on that block."

Chase tried to tamp down the ringing in his ears. Vincenze had given up the drop location, maybe voluntarily, maybe under duress. Didn't matter. Once they had that, it was a simple matter of trying to identify where Raney had gone after that. And with who.

"You think they got enough to know that she went into the hair salon and then a couple hours later left with me?"

"We do. Based on the angles of the cameras."

"I didn't have a name tag on," he said, fighting for reason. "Even if they saw me, how would they know my name? How would they know that I was coming home to Ravesville?"

The chief paused. "Gavin Henderson is dead. Shot at close range after he'd taken a beating that produced very similar injuries to those found on Luis Vincenze."

Gavin Henderson. Chase felt sick. He was a good officer. A husband. A father. But it made sense. Gavin had arrived with his camera around his neck. While there were lots of police officers on the St. Louis PD, there were only a few police photographers. And only a few of them were male. It would not have taken someone very long to work through the list.

"I want you in your car in five minutes. If necessary, I'll put Lorraine in a cell if that's what it takes to keep her safe."

Let her stay here. He would keep her safe. But the chief's logic made more sense. Sure, they could send more officers to Ravesville, but that probably wasn't practical or cost-efficient. They certainly couldn't count on the local police department to be helpful. And no matter what argument Chase made, the chief was going to shoot it down. He wanted his witness where he could see her and to know that she was safe.

"All right. Expect us in two hours." Chase hung up and turned toward Raney.

"What's wrong?"

There was no time to cushion the blow, to soften the words. "That was Chief Bates. We're moving you. Now. This location has been compromised." He could spare her the details about Gavin Henderson. "You've got two minutes to throw some things in a suitcase."

"But—"

"Raney, please," he said.

She nodded and ran out of the room, past Toby, who still stood in the doorway.

Chase quietly told the officer about Henderson. "Raney and I will take one vehicle, you and Leo follow us." He used his cell phone to call Leo and quickly filled him in.

Then he set about gathering every one of the extra weapons that Dawson had brought. He separated the arsenal between himself and the other two officers.

By the time he was done, Raney was downstairs, her small suitcase with her. She'd put on a coat.

They walked out the door and the four of them got into the two vehicles.

Chase stuck his head out the window and spoke to the other men. "Let's go. Keep close to me. Under no circumstances do we get separated."

CHASE HAD TURNED on the heat but still, Raney was shivering. She'd gotten soaked just running to the SUV. But it wasn't the rain that had her blood running cold.

The wind was blowing hard, rocking the SUV. When they turned left out of the lane, rather than right, which would have taken them into Ravesville, Raney had to resist pulling on Chase's arm.

She wanted to go to the Wright Here, Wright Now Café. She wanted to sit in the booth and order a hot chocolate and a piece of cherry pie with vanilla ice cream. *I'll be safe there.*

But she wouldn't be. And she'd be putting others in danger. The way she was putting Chase in danger right now.

"I'm sorry," she said.

He turned to look at her. "What are you talking about?"

"For all this. For getting you into this mess. I'm sorry they chose you."

He took one hand off the wheel and reached over to grab her hand. He brought it up to his lips, kissed it gently. "The Sunset Wonder is a perfect match for the fireplace. Just like you said."

She tried to jerk her hand back but he wouldn't let go. "You want to talk about paint colors now?" she asked, hardly believing it.

He smiled against her hand. Then he kissed it again. "I want to talk about paint colors and carpet samples and whether bronze or silver faucets would be better in the bathroom. I want to talk about the flowers that you'll plant and the rose bushes that I'll have to drag home from the store. I want to talk about our children and the noise they'll make running up and down the stairs."

"But your job?"

"I'll find another one," he said. "We belong together, Raney. We belong in Ravesville. Marry me, Raney."

She thought her heart might burst. She turned in her

seat, to tell him that she loved him, and out of the corner of her eye saw something move.

"Watch out!" she yelled.

Chase floored it and got past the vehicle that was coming at them like a bat out of hell from the side road, its lights off.

They heard the crash and knew that Leo and Toby had not been as fortunate. Even the howling wind could not dull the horrific crunch of metal on metal.

"We have to go back!" she yelled.

"No. That was no accident." Chase took his cell phone out and tossed it in her lap. "Call 911. Tell them that there's a multivehicle accident with serious injuries at the intersection of Hawk and Billow."

Her fingers were shaking so badly that she could barely press the keys. But she managed it. She told the person on the other end exactly what Chase had told her to say. Then the 911 operator asked for her name.

"Raney. Raney Hollister," she whispered and ended the call.

Chase turned and looked at her. "Hang on, Raney. We're going to get out of this."

But that didn't seem too likely when up ahead, on the narrow dark road, their headlights picked up the shape of a vehicle parked horizontally across the road. They would have to go through it.

There was no place to go.

Chase whipped the vehicle to the right. They left the paved road, dipped down into the ditch then up again and they came out on the other side. They were in a field of corn that had been recently picked. They pounded over the roughness of the remaining short stalks, their SUV rocking. "We're going back the other way," Chase yelled.

He was making a big circle. They might make it. They just might.

And then they hit a low spot in the field and their tires sunk into the rain-soaked ground and they were stuck.

Chase flipped off his lights and threw open the door. It was still raining but there was some light coming from the full moon that was hidden by the clouds. He reached for Raney and hauled her out. "Run!" he yelled.

She thought he would go for the road but instead he pulled her farther into the field. She stumbled but he kept her upright and moving.

She risked a look behind her. The road was no longer dark. She saw lights and men and knew that they weren't going to make it.

She almost ran into the first tree before she realized that the field had given way to the woods. She could smell the wet foliage, got slapped in the face with a dripping branch.

They went maybe thirty more steps when Chase jerked her to a stop. "Get up into this tree," he said. "Don't make a sound. No matter what. And don't come down until I come back. Do you understand?"

He was leaving her. He was going to leave her and draw their attention away from her. "No," she said. "We stay together."

He put both hands on her face and kissed her hard. It was desperate with need. "It's too dangerous. Listen to me. Do exactly what I say. They won't expect me to leave you." She felt movement and thought it might be him pulling something from his pocket. He pressed a gun into her hand. "Take this. It's ready to go. Just squeeze the trigger hard. If they see you, start shooting. Don't hesitate. Do you understand?"

She was crying. "Yes."

He kissed her again. "Give me your foot," he said, bending down.

He boosted her up into the tree. She felt for the branches and climbed. She'd told Chase that she wasn't afraid of heights, but with each foothold she became more and more terrified, knowing that she was truly alone. She got as high as she could go and tried to find a spot to rest her weight so that she could remain motionless.

She was wet and cold and her hands stung. She suspected they were bleeding. After a few minutes in the dark, she heard noise off to the left, deeper into the woods, and knew Chase was deliberately trying to lead their attackers away from her.

To her right, she heard crashing through the trees, saw big lights as their pursuers hunted them down.

Felt them stop under her tree.

CHASE RAN FAST, not even attempting to be quiet. *Go. Go. Go.* The words pumped through him as he wrestled to stay upright when he skidded across rain-slicked tree roots and soft muddy patches. His injured leg felt the stress and cramped up in response. He pushed through the pain.

He prayed he wouldn't ram into a tree and knock himself out before he could get far enough away from Raney. He knew he couldn't outrun them. But that wasn't his intent. He just needed to get to a place where he had decent cover. He hadn't been able to get an accurate count but he thought there were at least two, maybe three. Not great odds but not horrific, either. If they split up, he could take a couple out at a time.

Of course, if they managed to neutralize him and

discovered Raney wasn't with him, she would be in terrible danger.

He took a step, felt the ground give way and half slid, half stumbled down a sharp embankment. He landed in water that came up over his calves. Some kind of stream. He couldn't see a damn thing now. He plunged forward, hoping that it was narrow, hoping that he hadn't gotten disoriented and he was truly crossing the stream rather than walking the length of it.

He hit the opposite bank, let himself feel a moment of relief that he was out of the water and scrambled up the side. Once up on solid ground, he found a big tree and sank down behind it. He gulped in air as quietly as he could.

Now he needed the element of surprise.

He saw the bobbing and weaving of their light. He risked a look around the tree. He would have a good angle as they crested the bank. His only chance was if they put their high-powered flashlights on the ground while they pulled themselves up over the edge. If they didn't, their light would blind him and he wouldn't get his shot off.

He held his gun with both hands, willing his aim to be steady, sure. He heard them hit the water. Two separate splashes.

Heard one of them grunt and swear and then he didn't hear them in the water anymore. He counted to three. Moved from around the tree. Raised his gun.

Target One had put his flashlight down, exactly like Chase had hoped. The light was still on but at that level it wasn't blinding to Chase. He saw the man's head. Then his torso. Waited still.

Saw the second target come over the edge. No flashlight. Maybe he'd dropped his when he'd stumbled in the stream. He was big, and having difficulty pulling himself up over the bank.

Chase waited. One second. Two. The first target was reaching for his light. Chase fired. Saw the target fall backward.

Swung his gun fifteen degrees to the right. Fired again. Target Two took a step forward. Chase hit him with a second round. He went down.

Chase counted to ten, didn't sense any movement and cautiously moved away from his cover. The light at ground level was still shining. He hurried forward. There had been three, he was sure of it. He had to find him before the man found Raney.

When he approached the bodies, he picked up the flashlight and used his foot to flip the second target over. Looked at his face. Didn't recognize him. Checked his carotid pulse, made sure he was dead.

He shined his light down into the stream. Saw the first man. He'd landed on his back. Chase didn't bother checking his pulse. He could tell he was dead. His head was underwater.

Chase crossed the stream, flashlight in one hand, gun in the other. He kept the flashlight pointed down, with his fingers spread over the lens, partially obscuring the light. He needed some help to see the way, to avoid making a misstep that would call attention to his location, and also to see the broken-off branches and other damage he'd caused as he'd charged through the forest. It was the only way he was going to find Raney's tree. He didn't know how far behind he'd left her. He'd thought he'd been running hard for at least five minutes before he'd slipped into the stream, but the terrain had been challenging so maybe a half mile at the most.

He couldn't go as quickly now. *Ten minutes, Raney. Ten minutes. Hang on.*

Chapter Seventeen

Chase had been walking for seven minutes when he heard a noise behind him. He threw himself sideways, managing to avoid the bullet that whizzed past him and hit a tree. He rolled and tried to get his own shot off but his gun was kicked out of his hand by a damn giant.

"Get up," the man said, his voice thick with an accent that Chase didn't recognize. The man picked up the flashlight that Chase had dropped and shone it in Chase's eyes. "Where is she?" the man asked.

"Who?" Chase asked.

The giant backhanded him. Chase hit the ground hard.

"Get up," the man snarled.

Chase did. Slowly.

"Where is she?"

"I have no idea."

The man swung his gun, catching Chase on the side of his head. Chase went down to his knees.

"I will ask one more time. Then I will start shooting. Your elbows first. Those are very painful. Then your knees. And you will be helpless when the coyotes come and get you. Where is the woman?"

Chase tried to make it look as though he was considering the question. He was really trying to give his ears time to stop ringing. "I told her to run in the direction of the cabin."

"What cabin?"

"It's at the edge of the forest."

"I did not see any cabin."

"You have to know what you're looking for. I grew up in this area," Chase said, hoping the man knew that to be true. "I showed it to her earlier this week. Just in case. Listen, this is just an assignment for me. I've only got seven years until I can retire with twenty years. Just leave me here and go find her. Shoot me in the arm or something if you want to slow me down."

"Take me to the cabin. Then I will shoot you like you asked."

The giant would kill him. That was for sure. But he needed to lead him away from Raney and find an opportunity to disarm him. "I'll need the flashlight," Chase said. "To get my bearings."

The giant tossed it to him. Chase started walking.

"So Malone must be paying you pretty well for this," Chase said, looking over his shoulder.

The giant didn't answer.

"You guys old friends?"

"Shut up."

"You killed a cop. That doesn't go over well here."

The man pushed him from behind. Chase stumbled but managed to stay upright.

"If the price was right, I would kill a hundred of you," the man said. "And Malone has a great deal of money. But my work here is done. After I provide proof that the woman is dead, I will leave your country and no one will ever find me."

Chase had taken forty-three more steps, with the giant close behind him, when he heard the shot. He hit the ground rolling, thinking the man had changed his mind about killing him.

He flipped over just in time to see Raney, her feet planted, her arms extended at shoulder height, fire five more rounds into the giant.

The man fell like a big tree, facedown in the mud.

RANEY HAD NEVER shot a man before. Had never fired a gun. And when it was over, she sank to the ground. Shaking badly.

Chase, sweet Chase, gathered her in his arms. "I've got you. I've got you, Raney," he repeated.

"He hit you," she said. "Your poor head."

"I'm fine. I'm not hurt, honey." He pulled back a little. "I've got to tell you, that scared about five years off my life."

"I know you told me not to get out of the tree."

He laughed. "I don't think I'm going to give you much grief about not following orders."

"I just couldn't wait any longer. I heard the first shot, then two more, and…I thought you'd been shot. And that you might be lying there, bleeding, needing me. I thought about you, the man who always takes care of everybody else. You, the man who never assumes that somebody might care enough to take care of him."

"Raney," he said, his voice sounded strangled.

"I could not stand back and do nothing," she said. "And when I saw him hit you and then do it again, I knew I was going to kill him if I got the chance."

He brushed her hair behind her ears. "Blonde Raney

in action. I love you so much. Whether your hair is blond or brown or Sunset Wonder. I love you. Just you."

She kissed him. "I will love you forever. Now take me home."

* * * * *

Don't miss AGENT BRIDE,
the second book in Beverly Long's miniseries
RETURN TO RAVESVILLE

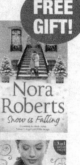